KYE BAY

KYE BAY

A novel by Brian F Turner

iUniverse, Inc.
New York Lincoln Shanghai

KYE BAY

iUniverse books may be ordered through booksellers or by contacting:

iUniverse
2021 Pine Lake Road, Suite 100
Lincoln, NE 68512
www.iuniverse.com
1-800-Authors (1-800-288-4677)

ISBN-13: 978-0-595-35909-7 (pbk)
ISBN-13: 978-0-595-80365-1 (ebk)
ISBN-10: 0-595-35909-4 (pbk)
ISBN-10: 0-595-80365-2 (ebk)

Printed in the United States of America

For Rita—my babe now and forever.

And

For all you former FighterCOps—men and women—perhaps this story will take you back to those days, good and bad.
It's just a little work of fiction and, unlike you and I, the hero is somewhat larger than life. But that's storytelling isn't it?

Finally, naked from the waist down, wearing only her sweater and light jacket she struggled to her feet and started limping along the road, still trembling violently.

When she reached a paved road, she stopped and looked around in a daze, unsure of the direction back to the station. She chose a way and staggered on. Two cars passed, both coming toward her. At sight of the approaching headlights she lurched off the road and hid; the first time in wet shrubs, the second in a muddy roadside ditch. She feared he was coming back to hurt her some more.

She didn't see the next lights when they came.

FOREWORD

The landmarks in this story do or did exist.

There is a beach called Kye Bay and there is a mountain called the Forbidden Plateau. The towns, streets, and most of the structures, existed in the fifties. (A few, such as the "Ocean View Auto Court" and the "Star Cafe," are my inventions.)

There was a C.P.R. train called *The Canadian*, which went into service in May of 1955. For the sake of my story I employed literary license to put it into service a couple of months early. I was also inventive with its schedule—I have no idea what exact time of the day that train would have departed Montreal or arrived in Vancouver. (I do remember that I used to have to catch it early in the morning.)

Otherwise, I took very few liberties, and I hope the reader will forgive those he discovers.

There were Canadian Air Force Stations at the places mentioned, and there still is one at Comox, British Columbia.

There actually was a radar unit called 51 AC&W Squadron at Comox, which ceased operations in 1958. In penning this story, I leaned heavily on my own memory—for I was there from 1955 to 1957, serving as a Fighter Control Operator.

Some of the scenes, those involving Air Defense operations, are loosely based on actual events I witnessed or had knowledge of, as well as on archival history. Certain actual persons are mentioned for historical reference (e.g. Malenkov, Lemay). Otherwise, the story and characters portrayed are pure fiction.

My heartfelt thanks to the following people, without whose assistance, input and encouragement these pages would not exist:

Rita Turner, for her patient reading, suggestion, and spell checking through-out the process—she was my wall to bounce ideas, sentences, passages, and entire chapters off. Her sacrifice must be recognized, even though she would never con-sider it as such.

Irene McRae, for never letting me lose sight of the end of the tunnel—all by long-distance.

Two old FtrCOps, Harold Hopkins and Gerry Dempsey, for keeping me honest.

Karen Turner, Ron Turner, Joey Houle, Chris and Greg Lamothe, Hazel and Earl Sutton, Sandra Lynne Engblom, Marg Sutton; all for valued criticism and encouragement.

Ren L'Ecuyer's Pinetreeline website (www.pinetreeline.org), and its many contributors, for valuable historical information (and wonderful memories).

Wayne at Grassland Graphics, for his advice on the graphics and help with the cursed writing machine.

Janet Noddings and Rifka Keilson at iUniverse Publishing, for their assistance and patience.

Finally, I acknowledge all the R.C.A.F. Fighter Control Operators from the fifties and sixties, who toiled twenty-four seven in Ops sites all across the coun-try—some at unheard of, unimaginable locales. The lowly "Scope-Dopes" who were the reason for being, yet so often the door mats, wherever they served. They were misunderstood by the other trades (with not a clue what FtrCOps actually did on the job); derided by the techs; and served up by their superiors for every "joe-job" on every station—sometimes despite having worked their regular shift. (They trudged through knee-deep snow on fire picket duty while the Firefighters sat warm watching the Three Stooges; they pulled guard duty during exercises while the S.P.s played Old Maid; or stood Honor Guard for self-important V.I.P.s on "official" golf or fishing visits.)

The FtrCOps, who through it all retained their esprit de corps, professional-ism, and sense of fun

They are the characters of my story, and I knew them.

PROLOGUE

▼

NORTH BAY, ONTARIO—OCTOBER, 1978

"Damn! I gotta get the hell out of here right now! This place is making me frigging crazy."

These are the thoughts of Master Warrant Officer (Clerk Admin) Olivia Conti of the Canadian Armed Forces.

Ten minutes earlier she sits at her desk with nothing to do, or at least nothing she wishes to do on this day. MWO Conti is in charge of the Orderly Room in the underground NORAD Command Complex at Canadian Forces Base North Bay. The complex is a huge man-made cavern carved into the Pre-Cambrian rock four miles from the city of North Bay.

She is trying with great effort to appear attentive as her second in charge, Corporal Smith, explains to a junior clerk a directive from Command about some-procedure-or-other for processing some-form-or-other, relating to personnel-something-or-other. She sighs hugely and in her mind says, *Damn!* She has lost track of—and interest in—whatever is going on around her. In her twenty-six years of service Olivia has seen and heard it all. *Damn!* She is suffering the effects of late afternoon induced, fluorescent light compounded, ennui. Conversations in the room become an unintelligible drone, competing with the hum of ventilating fans and buzz of office machines. She has attempted to shake off the mind-numbing lassitude but now allows herself to surrender to its comfort. Her gaze focuses somewhere beyond the room's reality in the direction of the clock on the wall, but her mind only subconsciously registers the time—it is 1420 hours of an early autumn day. Her eyes shift from the clock to a service counter that opens to an outside corridor near the office door.

Noticing someone passing in the corridor, she abruptly stiffens and rises half out of her chair. She mutters, "That's…I'll be damned!"

Bolting from her desk, she runs to the door.

Corporal Smith, seeing the sudden animation, calls after her, "Hey, Warrant, what's up?" Then she says to the room, "Did anybody hear what she said?"

Over her shoulder, Olivia says, "Just carry on, Smitty. I think I just saw…a friggin' ghost!"

Smith gets to her feet, "Wait up. I gotta see this." She too heads for the door, followed by the office staff of five.

In the corridor Olivia marches rapidly after her "ghost," a tall man in civilian clothes, walking twenty feet ahead of her.

Her, "HEY, HOLD IT, TANNER!" startles her quarry and he turns to see who shouted.

In an unmistakably British accent, the man asks, "Are you speaking to me?"

Oh shit, it's not him! She manages lamely, "I'm sorry! I-I thought you were someone…friend of mine…very sorry." She turns away red-faced, just in time to see half her staff ducking back into the office.

Back at her desk, "Shit-all-to-hell, Smitty, talk about embarrassing."

"Who'd you think it is?" asks the Corporal.

"Hell, I could have sworn it was a friend of mine. From way back when he was an L.A.C. and I an L.A.W., not like any of you kids know what those were. It was the Air Force, before our uniforms looked like friggin' spinach or broccoli. His name's Dan and he married my best friend. He left the service a few years ago. He used to come here in his civilian job, but he's retired from that now, too. Weird—I really thought it was him—guess I was daydreaming. Stupid of me; I should know he would call me to say he was coming."

"Happens to everyone. I've had it happen to me on the street, you just *know* it's someone so you run after them and then you feel really stupid."

"Yeah," Olivia sighs, "I think I've been working down in this hole too long, it's starting to get to me." She grins, blows her cheeks out, and adds, "Listen, Smitty, cover for me will you? I just have to get out of here today. Let's see…I have to go up to Headquarters, then to Supply…for something. And you *know* I just lied like hell, don't you!" She gathers her purse and coat from a hook behind her desk.

"No sweat, Warrant. See you tomorrow?"

"Oh yeah. Be back in the morning." To the room she calls, "Ta ta, children."

As she leaves, she hears Smith say, "Okay, any calls for the Warrant, you guys give the phone to me!"

Walking down the corridor, she checks her watch. *Five minutes till the next vehicle going topside. At least it'll still be daylight up there.*

She comes to a small group of people and joins them, waiting for the shuttle. A couple of them greet her.

She asks, "Anybody know what the weather's like up top?" No one can answer her. They have all been in "The Hole" since early morning.

After a short wait a green Econoline van pulls up, three passengers get out and Olivia and the others all pile in. They are quiet as the van takes them through the long tunnel to the surface.

When they arrive in daylight everyone gets out at a guardpost, where they turn in their security badges. Olivia takes in a deep breath of air and looks around at a bright, crisp afternoon. She can see the brilliant fall colors on the few hardwood trees still standing around the site as she crosses the parking lot and unlocks her silver-gray Audi.

She considers dropping in to the Senior N.C.O.s' Mess on the main base before going home, but she thinks, *What's the point? Same old place, same old people—same old, same old.* She smiles, remembering when she first heard that expression, over twenty years ago. She drives on past the base and through the city's center. She starts to pull into the parking lot at her West Ferris apartment building, but changes her mind, drives back onto Lakeshore Drive, and follows it to the Frontier Lounge and Restaurant, a few blocks down the road. She'll have a drink there—maybe two—before heading home to make her supper.

At this time of day the Frontier isn't busy, she sees only four other customers sitting quietly. She knows the bartender, a Sergeant Air Defense Tech, moonlighting to make ends meet.

The bartender greets her, "Hey, Ollie, escaped from The Hole early, eh? What'll it be?"

"Yeah, Ed—a fugitive from the chain gang." She normally drinks rye but today she needs a change. *No more same old, same old.* "Start me with a beer, Ed, got Heineken?"

She sits at a table by a window overlooking Lake Nippissing. It is just beginning to darken outside; the lake's surface is slate gray with small whitecaps stirred up by a westerly wind. A waitress, wife of a Com Tech whose name she can't remember, brings her a beer and a glass.

As she tastes the first sip of her Heineken, Olivia thinks about the civilian she accosted in the corridor and she chuckles. She had mistaken the man for Danny Tanner, an old and dear friend. *Damn it,* she says to herself, *I must be losing it. I think I'll phone Tanner and tell him what happened. He'll get a kick out of it.*

It takes her twenty minutes to finish the beer. The waitress comes to the table, "Another beer…?"

"No, I'll have a rye now, please, Canadian Club with ice, club soda on the side."

She nurses two more drinks over the next hour, before deciding it's time to get home.

At home in her apartment she makes a salad, pours a glass of Piat D'or, and takes supper and wine into the living room. She tunes the television to the news—no big breaking stories this day. *God!* She thinks, *talk about same old, same old. What I need is a change—a big change.* She is starting to realize her feeling of inertia might be more than autumnal blahs. She picks at her salad till she has eaten half of it, then pushes it aside.

Gulping the last of her wine, she makes a decision. She goes to the hall, picks up the phone, and gives the operator a familiar number.

A male voice answers, "Hello."

"Tanner, you big shit! How are all you guys? Not a word from you since Easter, and that just a card."

"Ollie! Good to hear your voice. We're all fine. How about you, everything okay?"

Olivia is not one to make long distance calls without good reason, but she realizes just the act of making this call has lifted her spirits.

"I'm sitting here feeling stupid…and thinking about you. You won't believe what happened today." She tells him about the mistaken identity. "The poor man jumped a foot when I yelled at him—just about had a friggin' baby! Talk about embarrassed, I could have crawled into a hole."

He kids, "That's funny, but it's nice to know you still can't keep your mind off me, Ollie."

"Yeah, right Tanner—dream on. Actually, I *have* been thinking about you…about you guys. I'm thinking of taking some leave and going out to see you. Could you put up with me for a week or so?"

"You know damn well we could, make it for a month if you want. Hell, as long as you can stay! Be great to have you here. We've fixed up the place at Kye Bay. Are you sure everything's okay with you?"

"Well, I definitely need a change. Kind of in a rut…you know."

"Get your butt out here. It'll be good for you."

"Okay, Big Guy. I'll call with the details. Hey, how about for Christmas?"

"Excellent idea! The kids will be out of school. Do it."

"I shouldn't have any trouble getting leave then. I'll call you."

"Great. Don't change your mind, Ollie!"

"I won't. Bye for now, Dan." She stands staring at the phone for five minutes after she hangs up. Aloud, she mutters, "Yeah, I'm gonna do it. No more same old, same old for Ollie."

As it turns out, taking a week's leave is not what she has in mind.

She pours another glass of wine, takes it to the living room, and sits in her favorite chair. Her thoughts focus on the man she just spoke to across three thousand miles. She lays her head back, closes her eyes, and reminisces, picturing him in her mind's eye, as he was when she first met him.

Danny had always been a good-looking man—some called him downright handsome. She remembers hearing it said about him that all the girls wanted him, and a lot of them got him. *Shit, Tanner, when I first laid eyes on you, I flipped over your looks myself.*

He wasn't large as men go, but was often thought of as being so. He stood a little taller than average in height, but didn't reach six feet. He had a square face; still boyish when she saw him last, softened by dark brown eyes and unusually long lashes. His unruly blond hair, if left to grow, had a life of its own. Women were often tempted to reach out and brush an untamed lock from his brow. No one could forget his winning smile, a smile he used so effectively. She remembers too, the sometimes-disconcerting way he maintained eye contact; declaring it was "So I can see what you're all about."

She had always seen his large, blunt hands as somehow symbolic of his toughness—for tough he was. He had proven so against men, and against circumstances. She had watched him earn a reputation as a man slow to anger, but formidable when pushed.

Those days he was often thought of as a wild one, too ready to raise hell. Olivia knew better—a free spirit and certainly not one to follow all the rules, but also not one who ever forgot his duty. *Danny Tanner, I don't know how your haywire sense of humor never got you in more trouble than it did. You were so much like me. Kindred spirits.* She remembers how they used to make up "dumb officer" jokes, and how he said the 'dumb' wasn't necessary, it was assumed! *You were no angel, Big Guy. You would tell us, quite proudly, the Air Force kept your service record on a roller.*

What Olivia remembers and treasures most about him, however, is his fierce loyalty. It was taken as fact that within the circle of those he called his friends, if you had a problem Danny would be there for you, sometimes at risk to himself and with nothing expected in return. He possessed a unique ability to see through a problem and come up with a solution, however unconventional. *You often shocked us, man, but most of us were glad to have you and your scams close by. I know I was.*

Smiling, she thinks about things they had done and places they had been; gags they had played on each other. *There are not many of us left, Dan, The Wild Dogs, and the Fearsome Foursome. You have been and are still, a cherished and special friend. The times we had! You used to say we had the world by the short and curlies and weren't letting go. In our utter ignorance, we thought we were bulletproof...*

$$*\qquad*\qquad*\qquad*$$

At the other end of the line, in Courtenay, British Columbia, Danny Tanner smiles as he hangs up the phone.

Ollie, he muses, *It'll be good to see you, be good for us to spend some time together. It's been too long. I recall the first time we met. We got along from the get go and I gave you a new name.*

He pictures Olivia Conti, with her dark beauty hinting at a Mediterranean heritage. The only slight imperfection on her strikingly pretty face a tiny turn to her slender nose. Taller than the norm at five feet seven, she possesses what is described as a willowy figure. Her classic beauty has always drawn second looks. She has an effortless grace about the way she carries herself, unconsciously presented without a hint of haughtiness.

Everyone who knew Ollie remembered her for her humor. Hers was a humor that could elevate the lowly, baffle the humorless, and devastate the pompous. It was spontaneous, original, and often irreverent. Danny chuckles as he remembers how she could break up a room full of people with a one-line crack, or turn real events into hilarious sagas. A good joke aimed at her was always received with a hearty laugh and acknowledgement, but a bad or mean-spirited one met with the derision it deserved. Her biting irony knew no limits of rank or station, and was not always "got" by its intended targets. When faced with stupidity from any source, she would often declare, "Why don't you tell that to someone who gives a shit!"

However, to those close to her, as Danny is, her selfless commitment to a friendship has always been what defines her most. Thinking back, he realizes he has seldom heard from her any declaration of friendship, but has often witnessed *confirmation* of it.

Her call tonight reminds him of the things they had been through, and of the people they knew. Talking over the miles to Olivia brings him a memory of a dif-

ferent kind, and not for the first time by far, his thoughts go to another person—
and another long-ago meeting...

C H A P T E R   1

▼

Babe—I'll remember forever the morning when we first met, twenty-three years ago. We were in a train station in Montreal, and it was only by pure chance I was catching that train on that day. There you were, standing before me so beautiful you scared me. I know now I was the luckiest man in the universe when I discovered we were there to catch the same train to the coast. To think the unthinkable—that I so easily might never have known you—never laughed with you or lay beside you or looked upon you in our bed. Never have been so blessed...

MONTREAL—MARCH 5th, 1955

A bitterly cold breeze blew down Dorchester Street outside Montreal's Windsor Station. Wind-blown grains of dry snow skittered along the pavement, pristine whiteness turning to gray city snow, grimy and icy-hard where it gathered low along curbs and at the base of buildings. Danny shivered at the sight from inside the overheated taxi as it stopped in front of the station.

Leading Aircraftman Danny Tanner was catching a train on that morning only because he couldn't get tickets to a hockey game. Had the Canadiens' game at the Forum against Detroit not been sold out, he would have stayed over one more night. He wasn't due in Vancouver for six days, leaving him two to spare, but he felt pressed now to get away from the cold Quebec winter, to the warmer clime of the Pacific Coast.

He climbed from the cab, paid the fare, and waited while the driver retrieved his luggage from the trunk; a nylon flight bag and small leather Gladstone. Before he headed for the entrance, he set his bags down on the sidewalk to grope through his uniform pockets for his ticket; he knew he had brought it but couldn't remember where he put it. After much searching and some mild frustration he felt the chill through his light Air Force raincoat, so he picked up the bags and made his way through the early morning crowd into the station. Inside, he searched again and found the ticket in a side pocket of the flight bag. He headed for the reservation desk.

Halfway across the huge waiting room he looked up at a clock on the far wall. The only wristwatch he ever owned had been left in a pawnshop in Moncton, New Brunswick, having helped to finance a return trip from Halifax to Moisie by way of Rimouskie and Quebecair. The big clock said twenty to eight—0740 hours Air Force, meaning he had fifty minutes before his train to Vancouver was scheduled to depart. He stopped, made a decision and, lugging his two bags, headed toward the washrooms at one end of the station.

In the washroom he used the urinal, then set his bags down next to an unused basin. Stuffing his service cap in the front of his uniform tunic, he splashed cold water over his face and head, then carefully combed his blond hair, taking three tries to get it just right. He wore his hair slightly longer than regulation, about as long as he could get away with. As he pondered his reflection, he muttered, "You look like hell, Danny-boy." He looked like hell this morning for the same reason he felt like hell—he was nursing a truly nasty hangover. Danny had just completed a two-week training course at nearby St. Hubert and on their last night in Montreal he and some classmates tried to drink their way from one end of Ste. Catherines Street to the other, all the way to St. Laurent Boulevard. They didn't complete the mission, but it was the second best attempt Danny had ever participated in.

Finished at the wash basin, he set his "yankee-ized" wedge cap firmly on his head, just above the brow line. He left the washroom and was strolling in no great haste toward the ticket windows when he saw her for the first time.

The Air Force "dress blue" uniform caught his eye. She walked at an angle away from him, thirty feet distant. He managed only a three-quarter-rear view, but he could see she sported a nice figure and good legs, slim ankles evident even through the Air Force issue "bullet-proof" nylons. Before he could get a closer look she disappeared around a corner in the direction of the ladies' washrooms and his interest passed to other things.

He continued on to the ticket windows where he spent five minutes successfully convincing a woman behind the counter to change his sleeping car berth, from the upper his travel warrant allowed, to a lower. His charm was such that the woman declined his offer of five dollars for the favor. From there he went to the baggage counter to check the larger flight bag through to Vancouver, keeping the Gladstone with him for the trip.

As he turned from the counter he got a second look at her. She stood fifteen feet away reading a schedule board. A small girl, no taller than five-two or three, but well distributed. Even in her uniform she showed a remarkably narrow waist and shapely bust. Her face, however, was what caught and held Danny's attention. He was sure he had never seen a prettier girl. As he stared, she turned and directed a rather formal smile at him, and in return, he flashed the always captivating Number-One-Tanner-Smile and approached her.

He said, "Hello, there…"

She hesitated for a second, then turned without a word and walked away toward the washrooms again.

What's this? As an Alpha Male of the species, he was not accustomed to such a reaction! His best effort had never before been received with such haughty indifference. The usual reaction to the pit-lamp brilliance of The-Tanner-Smile was for the intended prey to freeze in place, his for the taking; and he had just flashed the Number-*One*. He handled the unfamiliar setback bravely, *Okay, little doll, there's plenty more in this wide world. But—won't it be interesting if we're both catching the same train! Could you be heading west!* He went to find a seat at the benches near the track stairs.

When he found an unoccupied seat, he put his bag on the bench beside him, fished out a copy of *Time* and was soon submerged in yet another crisis in the Middle East.

He had been sitting for ten minutes when he heard a small voice say, "L.A.C.?"

He looked up and there she stood, right in front of his seat. Risking sending her running for the washrooms again, he mustered up The-Tanner-Smile and said, "Well, hello!"

She stayed put this time. Close up, her beauty was confirmed—short blonde hair, lighter than his, oval face featuring a small turned-up nose, big gray eyes slanting slightly upward, long lashes, and lips that looked impossibly soft.

As he gaped, he somehow managed to keep The-Number-One-Tanner-Smile from turning into The-Number-One-Tanner-Stupid-Grin. She smiled, too, and he knew it was the loveliest thing he would ever see. Then her smile faded and a troubled look took its place.

She said, "L.A.C., I am sorry to bother you…but I'm 'oping you could 'elp me?"

She's French, he thought, *and she's worried or scared about something.*

"I'll sure give it a try," he said. "You look awful serious—what can I do to help?"

She seemed encouraged. "L.A.C., there are two, um, Army guys…they are giving me a 'ard time…since I came 'ere this morning. You know, saying bad things, swearing and…"

"I understand. Where are these guys now?"

She pointed to an archway leading to an exit door. "That's them, those two by the door. They keep following me around." Danny thought he saw the shine of beginning tears.

He said, "Listen, you sit down here and watch my bag. I'll see what I can do."

She grabbed his sleeve. "You won't 'ave trouble? I wouldn't want you…"

"No. It's no sweat. Stay here, I'll be right back." As he started toward the two men in khaki, he thought, *Man! This couldn't be better. As long as I don't end up taking a shit-kicking. Oh, baby, please be on my train!*

As he neared the two men, they started to stroll away.

He shouted, "HOLD IT RIGHT THERE, SOLDIERS! I WANT A WORD WITH YOU!"

They turned. The taller of the two said, "You talkin' to us?"

"I sure as hell am, Private!" said Danny. He could see by their uniforms and demeanor that they were green recruits. He figured they would be afraid of any authority and not familiar with Air Force ranks and insignia. The hard part might be convincing them he wasn't a bus driver or something. He ran his bluff. "That's an Air Force Nursing Sister over there." He gestured toward his seat and the little Airwoman, "In case you didn't know it, a nurse is an officer! She tells me you two have been disrespectful. Now you listen up! If you so much as go near her again…"

The tall soldier interrupted him, "We weren't doing…"

Danny cut him off. He was in the man's face now—and into his role. "*I* AM DOING THE TALKING HERE, SOLDIER! *YOU* ARE *LISTENING!* IS THAT CLEAR?"

The same man sneered. "Who the hell are you, the King of England?" he asked.

"AS FAR AS YOU'RE CONCERNED, PRIVATE SMART MOUTH, I AM JUST THAT!" He lowered his voice for emphasis. "Now, unless you want to spend a month or two polishing garbage cans in some Detention Barracks, you'll listen and listen good." He raised his voice again; "I WANT YOU TWO OUT OF MY SIGHT AND NOWHERE NEAR THE NURSE! NOW—HAVE YOU GOT IT?"

Smart-mouth started to speak again, then suddenly both soldiers snapped to attention and the shorter one saluted smartly. Danny didn't notice his "nurse" arrive behind him. She had approached to see what was taking place, fearing there might be trouble. When he realized she was there, he stepped in front of her and spoke quickly, before she could blow the operation.

He used the Air Force term for addressing a Nursing Sister; "Everything's under control, Sister, these men are moving-along now." He turned back to the soldiers, "Carry-on, Privates. Quickly now!" While they hurried away, he took her by the arm and led her back to his seat.

"But, L.A.C., I am not a nurse." she exclaimed.

"Of course you're not. Jesus Chr…I thought you were supposed to be watching my bag?" When they got back to the seat he was relieved to see his Gladstone still there.

"Oh," she said, "I think you were tricking those guys!"

"No kidding," he said dryly.

She said, "I was, um, afraid you might 'ave trouble…"

"Not a chance. They're just punks, typical Army. As long as I'm around, they won't give you any more trouble." *Just me, now, sweetheart,* he didn't say. He flashed The Smile again, "Why don't you sit here until your train time."

She sat beside him, saying, "Thank you, L.A.C."

"My name's Danny—you don't call an L.A.C. by his rank."

"I want to thank you for your 'elp, L.A.C., um, I mean…Danny? Me, I'm Josie. Connor. My name I mean. It's Josie Connor." She paused. "At training we 'ad to call an L.A.C. by his rank. I am sorry I forgot about your suitcase, Danny."

"Aw, don't worry about it. It's just that you gotta watch your stuff in these places."

"I guess there is so much to remember when you travel. Have you traveled a lot? You've been a long time in the Air Force I think. Me, I'm just new from training, at Aylmer, in Ontario. I 'ad one week of leave after my course finished, so I came to my father's. It's 'ere in Quebec, at Sherbrooke. I left two days early…to make sure I…you know…" She blushed at the admission of travelers' anxiety.

He would let her believe he was an old veteran. "So, where're you headed now?"

"I'm posted to Comox. It's in British Columbia. I'm not sure what part. At Vancouver, I think."

He grinned and shook his head. "Not quite, Josie. Comox is nowhere near Vancouver."

"But they said it's at Vancouver Island, so it's Vancouver...no...?" She finished lamely when she saw him still shaking his head.

He chuckled. "It's a real big island. You'll be taking a ferry—a boat—across part of the ocean." He paused. "Josie, eh? You have a nice name, it's different."

Showing her lovely smile, she said, "Thank you. It's French..." The giggle that followed was music. "I think you could tell I'm French by the way I...by my accent." Then she frowned. "But, Danny, will my ticket get me to that big island?"

"Let me have a look at it." She took the ticket from her purse and handed it to him. He looked it over and said, "Looks okay. It's to Courtenay...about five miles from Comox. I guess you'll get a taxi from there, or phone the base for transport."

"Oh. Good." She sighed.

"Y'know what? We're going west on the same train. I'm on my way back to Jericho. It's a base, by the way, which *is* in Vancouver. So we can...have company. At least somebody to talk to. It's four days to the coast, and three nights." He started to return her ticket, then pulled it back and looked again. "Whoa. Gotta see what we can do about this, though. Come with me." He picked up his bag and led her by the hand toward the ticket windows. Ten feet from the windows, he stopped her and said, "Wait right here, Josie. Don't move and don't say a word!" He went up to a man at the window.

Danny said, "I'd like to speak to that lady over there, please." He pointed to the woman who changed his berth earlier. She looked up and came over to the counter. He gave her The Smile.

"How may I help y...oh, it's you again. Don't tell me—you want to ride with the Engineer now, right?"

He said, "Good one. You're really funny!" The Smile turned up, then down. "Seriously, though, as much as I hate to bother you—it seems the Air Force has made a mistake..." It had worked once. "That nurse over there." He pointed to Josie. "Well, I'm officially escorting her. Nurses are officers and I know they're entitled to a lower berth and they gave her an upper." As he pushed Josie's ticket to her, he said, "By the way, I like the way you do your hair, it reminds me of my mom. Anyway...if you have any lowers left...?"

The woman laughed. "You never give up, eh? Give me a minute, flyboy." She turned away, sighed, whispered, "His mom, yet." She took a list from a slot and looked it over for a few seconds. "Well, it looks like your nurse is in luck. Give me the ticket." She made the change and handed him the new ticket. "She's not in the same car as you, but I kind of think that won't slow you down."

You better believe it won't! "Thanks, ma'am. I love ya." As he turned, he didn't hear her mutter something about his loving anything in a skirt.

When he got back to Josie, he gave her the ticket, saying, "There. You're all fixed up."

She asked, "What were you doing there?"

He replied, "Oh, just getting you a lower berth for the trip. Those uppers are a real pain in the…"

She interrupted. "Oh, oh. I think maybe I'm a nurse again?"

"Hey, you're pretty sharp. You don't have to thank me. I'd do the same for any good-looking babe. By the way, don't you have any luggage?"

"I sent most of my things ahead. I 'ave just one case for the train. I put it in one of those lockers." She looked at him sternly. "Danny, I don't think I like to be called 'babe'—the same as you don't like L.A.C., I guess."

"Fair enough. It's just a figure of speech." Not exactly an apology. "We'd better get your bag—we'll be boarding soon."

She led the way to a row of gray metal lockers, found the key in her purse, located her locker and took a suitcase out.

When they got back to the seats they heard their train announced by the impersonal, metallic voice of the public address:

"Passengers for Canadian Pacific Train Number One…Vistadome Service…for Ottawa…Sudbury…Winnipeg…Regina…Calgary…and Vancouver! Now boarding…on track three."

"That's us," said Danny.

Hundreds of people were instantly on their feet, all headed for the wide stairway leading down to track level. Danny and Josie joined the throng. As they moved along with the other passengers, she nervously checked to see if she left anything behind, mentally ticking-off items. *Suitcase in hand. Purse on shoulder strap. Ticket…in purse.* She even unconsciously touched her cap, as if to verify its presence on her head.

Watching her, he couldn't suppress a grin. "Got everything? How about your shoes? You didn't check them yet."

With an embarrassed smile, she said, "Shut up, you. You're mean. We're going so far, it's best to check before…"

"Don't sweat it. If you forgot anything I'll just tell the engineer he has to back up to Montreal I'm sure he won't mind for you!"

She looked at him askance. "Not even you, I think."

At the bottom of the stairs they paused. In the comparative gloom under the station, she took in the sounds and sights. To her right the huge diesel engine that would pull their train wheezed, grunted and hissed—as if impatient to be on the move.

Danny wanted to stand aside and wait for the crush of humanity on the platform to thin out but Josie was far too anxious to wait. After a minute she said, "See? People are getting on now. Shouldn't we 'urry?"

"Okay, Nervous Nelly. Stick close to me. Check your ticket and see what car you're on."

He led her through the crowd toward the sleeper cars. At her car they waited in line to board, getting bumped from behind by other anxious passengers.

"Perhaps you were right, Danny. We should have waited," she said. She had to half-shout to be heard.

He answered with an I-told-you-so shrug.

They came to an elderly black Porter standing by the portable step to Josie's car. Taking her arm, the Porter helped her up into the car.

She said, "Thank you. I'm in number fourteen…" Then with a sly grin over her shoulder at Danny, "That is fourteen *lower*, please."

Danny hopped up beside her.

She said, "Are you in this car too, Danny?"

"No. I think I'm a couple of cars behind. Can you spot your berth?"

She looked past other passengers. "There it is. Number fourteen; right…here. Shouldn't you get on at your own car?"

"I'll go through the train. Before I go…I wanted to ask you…could we get together for lunch? You have to go through my car to get to the diner—it's back that way." He nodded at the rear of the car. "Come and get me when they call for lunch. I'll watch for you."

"I would like that, Danny."

"Okay! I'll see you later, then." On his way to the end of the car, he stopped and spoke to the Porter who was now inside. He waved to her before he went through the door to the next car.

Josie sat down in the forward facing of the two seats. The other seat in number fourteen wasn't occupied. As she watched the bustle on the platform outside her car and her fellow passengers settling in, the Porter came with a pillow for her.

"The young gen'man says I got to look after you real good 'cause this is y'first trip. Anything y'need, just give me a shout."

She said, "Thank you, you are so kind." Then, with a sharp intake of breath, "Oh, I feel so stupid! I forgot to give you a tip when I got on…" she reached for her purse.

Holding up a hand to stop her, he whispered, "No, Ma'am. You're most kind, but it's customary to give a little something at the end of my trip in Win'peg, Ma'am."

Her face reddened. "Oh. I see. I'll make sure I do that. I 'ave not traveled much…yet."

"That's quite all right. Don't forget—anything y'be needin' you just give ol' Will a shout." He fingered Danny's five dollar bill in his pocket as he walked away.

It was ten minutes before the train started to slowly move out of the station. Like most of the passengers, Josie was looking out the window. As they rolled through Montreal's West End the view was of sooty industrial buildings and grimy tenement backyards. She relaxed and sighed. She was at last leaving Quebec; her training completed, and on her way to her first field posting.

She looked forward to the future with excitement—and anxiety.

CHAPTER 2

▼

DANNY TANNER

Danny grew up in a rundown clapboard house in the rough James Bay district of Victoria, the fourth child of an often out of work shipyard worker and an always overworked waitress and chambermaid. His father, Vic Tanner, was a surly, unkempt man, feared by his wife, disdained by his neighbors and grudgingly suffered by his cronies at the Halfway and Gorge beer parlors. His mother, Betty, the consistent provider, was pretty in the Irish way but too thin and older than her years. She worked hard, sometimes at two jobs, to provide steady food for the table and booze and cigarette money for her husband. Danny arrived in this world six years after his sister Beth, the next youngest.

Beth began to distance herself from the family in her teens, when she quit school to work and took her own apartment. She completed the separation by marrying young and moving to the mainland with her husband. She gave her address to her mother and Danny only after they promised to never give it to Vic or the other boys. She soon found herself in an abusive marriage that failed after three forlorn years, leaving her with two small children to raise on her own.

Two older brothers, Ed and Jimmy, like Vic Tanner, were pretty much worthless. They had the ill fortune of inheriting the father's looks. They were all short and scrawny in stature, all had pigeon chests, skinny necks and large, thin noses. From the time they were teenagers both boys were "known" to the five police departments in greater Victoria. Ed served two-less-a-day in Okalla for break and enter, Jimmy twice got probation for petty thefts. One or the other seemed to always be working on schemes with fringe-criminal pals. Ed married at eighteen and spawned three children by age twenty-one. He and his wife soon took on marital roles similar to those of Vic and Betty. For his part, Jimmy had somehow attracted a girl from the neighborhood whom he eventually abandoned and left with child.

As a baby and toddler Danny was a bright, sweet child—his mother's pride and joy. From his pre-school years till he grew big enough to handle himself, his brothers teased him at every opportunity. They would continue the torment till they had the boy in tears. Vic Tanner often derived drunken amusement from his youngest boy's torment, which the older sons took to be encouragement; so the boy's crying just brought on more and meaner teasing. Betty's attempts to shelter him, besides turning the abuse onto her, just made his tormenters more determined and inventive. Little Danny learned he could often counter the abuse through some outrageous act of defiance or inventiveness of his own. He kicked, spat, bit, or cursed with words he should never have known, and often turned his father's amusement and scorn onto the brothers.

Before he finished grade school, Danny was headed unerringly toward delinquency, trying to be the worst of a bad lot. Betty Tanner was horrified. She feared the boy would be deeply and habitually in trouble without realizing the potential she knew was in him. In her attempt to straighten him out, she turned at first to the worst possible source of discipline—Vic Tanner. Vic would either beat the boy or try to turn her concerns back onto her. "Jesus Christ, Betty, just spend more time keepin' an eye on him, instead of babyin' him! He's just a kid—he's gotta get this stuff out of his system." He proudly regaled his mates at the Halfway and Gorge with exaggerated stories of his son's exploits, "The kid's gonna be a helluva pitcher. He hit those school windows from half a goddam block away." Or, "He beat the crap out of Pete Wesley's kid, must be three years older. Then he told Pete's old lady to go fuck herself. I had to drag the little bastard over there to apologize—my old lady wouldn't have anything but!" Or, "Kids are gettin' bolder every year. That Danno of mine—seems he got into Wendy Smith's pants. The girl's mother was goin' ape-shit about it, so we had to go an' make her happy. The cryin' an' shit—you never saw nothing like it! Likely it wasn't her first time anyway."

So his mother, intent on saving him, needed to find some incentive for change. The boy's repugnance and mistrust of his father and brothers proved to be just the thing. She never said, "don't be like them," she never had to—the examples were there daily for him to see. In her inarticulate way, she tried to teach him to respect those around him—that respect bestowed would result in respect returned. "Just try to think about how people feel is all I ask."

When he turned twelve, he tried this new cloak on for size. At first he found the fit restricting, but he more and more came to like it. He liked *being* liked! He discovered there were rewards for being respectful of others. Here was something worth working at! As he approached puberty, Danny grew closer to Betty Tanner's ideal and further from Vic's.

While it was obvious he would never reach a state of perfect grace, three elements contributed to at least a partial salvation of Danny Tanner. (Leaving aside Mom's efforts.):

First, at a young age he discovered a talent and love for athletics. He excelled at any sport he tried, his favorites being boxing, lacrosse and baseball. He boxed his way to the Golden Glove competitions, played competitive lacrosse, baseball and softball. The sports injected into his persona a need for teamwork and fairness he carried with him all his life.

His skill at sports brought to him the second saving element—girls—more to the point, how to be liked by girls! His status as a neighborhood sports hero, along with his good looks and winning smile, gained him a certain amount of popularity with the girls; but he soon figured out those girls with the most going for them were not at all interested in guys that were always getting into or making trouble. So he worked hard at the problem, and, by his early teen years had had more than his share of sexual encounters.

The third and most important grace-saving element was his innate good nature! He was, simply put, a bright, gregarious, fun-loving kid. He just wanted to enjoy life—and to surround himself with others to enjoy it with him. "Good times" became synonymous with his name.

Through all that, he remained both a tough and wily kid. His physical and psychological makeup, along with his family and neighborhood environments, all demanded hardness and cunning and he possessed both in spades. Danny's reputation as a ferocious scrapper spread, first in his neighborhood, and later wherever he went. In time, it followed that his very reputation meant he was rarely forced to fight. Only a few of his peers were willing to test his prowess once—very few twice. His courage in a confrontation was legendary. He never backed down and he never quit—and he rarely took a beating worse than his opponent did. His strategy, the moment he sensed a fight was inevitable, was "Hit first, hit hard, and keep hitting!" Nonetheless, if he saw that combat wasn't necessary, he preferred to talk or joke his way out of a situation.

At the age of fourteen, Danny avenged and ended years of torment and beatings from his brother Jimmy, by beating him to a pulp in front of friends on a downtown street. At sixteen, he earned his mother's gratitude by promising Vic Tanner he would "beat you till you're a cripple," if he ever again laid a hand on her in anger. She never again endured physical abuse from her husband.

With only the marriages of his parents and siblings as examples, he understandably formed a low opinion of the institution. He knew his mother and sister were trapped in situations they would have been better out of.

In grade school, his free spirit often got him in trouble with teachers, but he found the schoolwork easy and his marks were good. In high school, however, he placed his studies somewhere below the sports, girls and good times. His obvious native intelligence frustrated many teachers, but they soon realized he just didn't have the interest. Part way through his third high school year his off-hand attitude, combined with frequent truancies, brought an end to his formal schooling.

Now sixteen and finished with school, he joined the work force. Although he changed jobs occasionally, he was never unemployed for more than a couple of days. He got along well with co-workers and bosses at the construction sites and mills where he found work, and displayed an industry that would have surprised his high school teachers. The reason for the newly found diligence could be explained quite simply—he was only happy when he had cash in his tailored-at-the-chinks pockets! With cash, one could dress well, date well and party well. He began hanging out with Victoria's downtown crowd. Unlike in the old neighborhood, this was a more disparate group, coming from all parts of the city.

The Victoria crowd wasn't a closely-knit "gang" as, say, the Alma Dukes in Vancouver. They were a group of young people with differing backgrounds but a common desire to have a good time while thumbing noses at parents' mores. It was a time of wild parties, in someone's house or at a beach or lake. It was—"It's Saturday night, where's the party? No party? Let's make one!" Liquor played a big part—the price of admission to house parties consisted of a bottle of hard stuff or a case of beer. Dope, exclusively marijuana, was evident but rare. (The kids could normally get in enough trouble on liquor and beer.) The parties sometimes got so wild disturbed neighbors called the police.

Their dance was the jive; their music, swing, bop and popular songs. Country and western music was a bad joke, put down as "cowboy singing."

Some of the girls, employed at the provincial government offices, were able to provide false birth certificates, thus opening doors of liquor stores and beer parlors for underage boyfriends. So, when the legal drinking age was twenty-one, it wasn't uncommon to see fifteen and sixteen-year-olds drinking in the area's beer joints.

They were known as "zoot-suiters"—a name none of them ever used. To them, the term described nothing more than a style of dress. Wide pant legs draped in drastically at the cuffs, called "drapes" or "strides," with suit or sports jackets long and loose fitting. Narrow knit ties and suede or leather loafers or pointed-toed "bankers" for footwear completed the outfits. These made up the rebellion uniforms of the early fifties on Canada's West Coast. Chinatown tailors supplied the look at reasonable prices. When not wearing suits, the guys were usually seen in Levi jeans or chinos, collarless T-shirts and "bomber" jackets.

Sex came easy and casual for Danny. From his early teen years there was a continuous series of lovers. He never looked upon his sexual affairs as "conquests," so he always protected a girl's reputation by never boasting about or even admitting to "getting laid." It was a policy that, when it became known to the girls in town, eased their consciences so they more readily made themselves available to him. He enjoyed sex and couldn't see why a girl should be put down for liking it as much as he did.

For two years Danny, always popular, lived at the center of the action.

After he turned eighteen, something started to change in him. Victoria progressively became a village in his mind; the hangouts, the parties, even the girls, all started to seem too routine. His downtown friends would have been surprised to learn he had become a prolific reader, subscribing to *National Geographic* and *Time,* and joining the Book of the Month club. At first he read everything and everybody—whatever fell into his hands. Welles' *Outline of History* arrived and it became a jumping-off place for him. He gobbled-up Catton's *Stillness At Appomattox,* Shirer's *Rise And Fall Of The Third Reich* and Churchill's *Second World War.* Hemingway and Faulkner were favorites for style, Ferber, Shulman and Mitchener for story. Callaghan, McLennan and Mowat stirred his curiosity about his own country and continent—and were largely responsible for infecting him with a serious travel virus.

When a friend in the Air Force came home on leave Danny grilled him about life in the service. Six months later he enlisted. *What the hell, three years—can't kill me! It'll at least get me away from here for a while. See some country while I'm at it.* His last civilian job was in the shipping department at a roofing and paper plant where he was well paid for the time, earning a dollar and sixty cents an hour.

When the required medical examination, I.Q. test, and swearing-in were all completed he was issued a travel warrant to St. Jean, Quebec, where he would undergo R.C.A.F. Basic Training. His going-away party, the night before his departure, turned out to be one of the wildest affairs in memory. Danny never got free till three-thirty in the morning, to hurry home and pack for his trip. He almost changed his mind about leaving town when six girls, all of whom he had "known," showed up at the C.P.R. ferry dock to see him off—at seven thirty in the morning!

All his reading hadn't prepared him for the train trip across the country. He had been able till then to only imagine the great distances involved in crossing Canada. He left a few days early, to allow stopovers at major cities, where he stayed in downtown hotels and wandered the streets taking in the sights. He experienced his first real delicatessen in Winnipeg (He munched on a huge dill pickle as he strolled along Main), his first Murray's cafeteria in Toronto, and his first all-night bar in Montreal.

At the R.C.A.F. Manning Depot, in St. Jean, the street-wise kid from the West Coast found he liked the structure, the neatness, of military life. He became a "good soldier" while at Basic Training, seriously applying himself to the drilling, weapons training, and military lectures. He looked great in the uniform and happily spent time shining brass and polishing boots. He was selected as a member of the precision drill team, and, like sports back home, that brought him the adoration of the best looking Airwomen on the base. He paid attention to his instructors and was on his way to becoming a worthy member of the service.

All of which is not to say he didn't have a go at the many Air Force regulations. For example a hard and fast rule at Basic was that recruits were confined to the base for the first five weeks of training. Like hell! There were no fences high enough to hold the Alpha Male of Course 178. Not when there were all night bars and French Canadian girls just a few short blocks from camp. When asked—by a sentencing officer—how he managed to spend so much time illegally outside the fence, he replied smilingly, "Over, under or through, Sir." This escapist behavior and other similar offences against the military code were our Danny's first disciplinary problems. His high spirits and confidence didn't fly well with Air Force NCOs, who thought of him as cocky.

Although his net income went from over seventy-five dollars a week to seventy-seven a month upon joining up, he was never short of cash during basic or trade training. At the advice of his friend, he brought four hundred dollars with him from Victoria; money he had been saving toward buying a car. The young recruits at St. Jean were always short of money, often flat broke just a couple of days after pay parade, a situation Danny was happy to help. He "loan-sharked," lending out five dollars for seven or ten for twelve. In that endeavor he competed with some of the instructors on the base, but there were new courses starting every week, so there was business enough for all. So each payday became profitable. He continued the practice during his subsequent trade training. Even after subtracting what he spent on good times, he had over eight hundred dollars stashed in his barrack box when he arrived at his first field posting.

From St. Jean, AC2 (Aircraftman Second Class) Tanner was sent to Clinton, Ontario, for his trade training as a Fighter Control Operator—"FighterCOp." He had joined up hoping to become a Munitions and Weapons Technician, because he was told the "armorers" always got postings to Europe. But the Air Force in its wisdom found him to have an aptitude for the FighterCOp trade. (Coincidentally, because of the recent opening of several new radar bases demanding personnel, Air Force wisdom found almost *all* its new recruits blessed with the same aptitude!) So he and hundreds of other young men and women became "Scope-Dopes," manning radar units at Air Control and Warning (AC&W) Squadrons all across the country.

From Clinton he was posted to the Ground Control Intercept (G.C.I.) unit at St. Margarets, New Brunswick for a year and a half. Then, as an L.A.C. (Leading Aircraftman), he went on to his second field posting, an isolated G.C.I. at Moisie, Quebec, where he spent fourteen months.

At St. Margarets and Moisie Danny ran afoul of Air Force regulations on a couple more occasions; always while in pursuit of a good time. When on leave or days off, he traveled much of Eastern Canada with his friends, sometimes catching Air Force "skid flights," but usually riding his thumb from place to place.

It was also during this period, however, that he became proficient at his trade, easily attaining the level of Trade Group 3. He wanted to be the best in his trade, and spent much of his time, on and off duty, with veteran FighterCOps, always asking questions, listening, and learning the finer points that were not taught at Clinton—the tricks of the trade. He breezed through trade group exams on his first tries. When he left Moisie he was known as a "good FighterCOp." At this same time, he started feeling the pangs of ambition. During his tour at Moisie he started a Canadian Legion sponsored correspondence course, with the aim of improving his chances for advancement. When the time came he re-enlisted for a further two years. By the time he was transferred to Vancouver in December of '54, L.A.C. Tanner had found a home in the Air Force.

In early March, 1955, the abbreviations and numbers in his R.C.A.F. Unclassified Personnel File read:

06/3/55 UNCLASS PERS FILE
L.A.C. TANNER, Daniel Albert. R.C.A.F. #202864
FighterCOp, Gp. 3 Born 24/4/34. Enl. 14/5/52
Male Cauc. Ht. 5'11/Wt. 180/Hr. Blnd./Eyes Blu.
Scars—L. Brow, R. Shldr.
Eff. 22/8/54 5 Air Div HQ, R.C.A.F. Stn. Vancouver, B.C.

And now, after some Temporary Duty in Montreal, he was on his way back to the coast, looking forward to the milder weather there.

C H A P T E R   3

▼

06/3/55 UNCLASS PERS FILE
AW2 Connor, Josée Marie Jeanne. R.C.A.F. #281176W
ClkAdmin. Gp.1 Born 14/8/36 Enl. 03/10/54.
Female Cauc. Ht. 5'2 ½/Wt. 105/Hr. Blnd./Eyes Gray.
Enroute R.C.A.F. Stn. Comox, B.C. Eff. 11/3/55

JOSIE CONNOR

She was born Josée Connor, in Cowansville, Quebec, the only child of middle class French-Canadian parents. Her surname came from her paternal great-grandfather, an Irish lumberjack who eloped with the prettiest French-Canadian girl in the village of Ste. Martine.

When she was seven years old the family moved to nearby Cornwall, Ontario, where her father was a supervisor at a textile mill. Then, at eleven, she and her parents moved back to Quebec when her father accepted a position as manager at a new mill in Sherbrooke.

Paul Connor could not altogether conceal his disappointment when his marriage failed to produce more children after Josée. He had expected to have sons and his disappointment caused in him a degree of indifference toward the girl. He was never cruel, nor even insensitive, but he tacitly allowed that the responsibility of raising the child would fall to Mme. Connor. As compensation for her husband's lack of interest, Mme. Connor showered attention on her daughter. Josée wasn't pampered, so much as sheltered by her mother.

Jeanne Connor, nee Lambeau, was fully bilingual and better educated than most Quebec women of her time were, having graduated the Liberal Arts and Education programs at McGill University—that school for the English-speaking. She secretly resented the expectation that she be the correct catholic wife and mother. It was an expectation all too common in the Quebec of the fifties, of Duplessis and the Union Nationale. Her husband's four childless sisters pressured her in that direction. The spinster sisters, one a nun, were one and all devoted to the Roman church, unquestioning of all its doctrine. With regard to

Josie, they were determined to have the greatest possible influence on the rearing of "notre petite Josée Marie" as a chaste Christian child, ever loyal to church and family. The aunts did not have confidence in their sister-in-law's commitment to that admirable end.

That lack of confidence was justified, for Jeanne Connor had plans of her own for the girl.

Jeanne knew her bright, pretty little daughter must be protected from such conventional thinking—and the way to protect her was through enlightenment. From Josie's earliest years, she tried to instill in her a spirit of self-reliance and independence along with an interest and curiosity about life outside the family and community. While encouraging her to study and do well in her formal schooling, she also tutored her secretly at home. With each new birthday, the childhood sessions in her room with Mama grew progressively liberal. The lessons were designed by Mme. Connor to expand her daughter's appreciation of those things in the world beyond the confines of her Quebec education. The aunts, as well as the parish priest would have been appalled at the topics covered in those sessions. The central theme of the lessons was simple—think for yourself! When put into practice, this sometimes brought the child into conflict with teachers, priests, her father, and the aunts, but Josée counted with surety on Mama's protection.

Her fondest memories growing up were of the years they lived in Ontario. There, she was removed from the strictures of the church and the scrutiny of relatives. At first her grade two classmates teased the little newcomer—"Frenchy, Frenchy, Fren-chee!" But soon her good nature and brightness overcame and she was accepted. Her mother had taught her to speak English well, so even at age seven, she spoke it with only a slight accent. (When she became excited or stressed, she often had trouble with words starting with H.) It was at Cornwall that she picked up the less formal English of Ontario's middle and working classes. Free to behave as a normal child, Josée developed a playful, gregarious nature and a sly, mildly teasing sense of humor. Away from the aunts and the nuns of Cowansville, the liberal lessons from Mama continued. (They now included attempts to correct some of the grammar she brought home from the streets and playgrounds of Cornwall.)

Josée would always remember the freedom and the wonderful friendships with her English-speaking playmates in Ontario.

Those happiest of times came to an end a month before her twelfth birthday when the family moved back to Quebec. Sherbrooke, a city south of Montreal, was just a few short miles from Cowansville and the aunts. As time passed, she could not help but compare her life there to the carefree years in Cornwall and wished fervently to be back there. Now, as a pre-adolescent, all the forced piety, the overly proper mores and the interference by family, caused her to resent the church, the Province of Quebec, even her father, and especially her aunts. She made it a practice, however, to never express her resentment and was thought of in the school and at home as a model child. She studied dutifully and breezed through all her school subjects, including catechism. As a secret show of rebellion, she took to spelling her name as the Anglicized "Josie," a practice she continued for the rest of her life. She tried to see all the English language movies, listened only to popular music sung in English and read only literature written in English—all with Mama's approval and encouragement.

When Josie was thirteen, her mother was suddenly taken from her. Death from acute leukemia came quickly, only a month and a week from the discovery of the disease. She saw her beloved Mama go from a beautiful, vital woman to a pale, helpless hospital patient and finally, to a cold, over-rouged corpse in a silk-lined casket on display at a Sherbrooke funeral parlor. During the last day of her life, as she lay in a drug-induced coma, one of the aunts placed a small picture of the Virgin on her breast, saying it was to provide "guidance on her journey to God's side." Josie flung the thing to the floor. When the aunt replaced it on her mother's bed, she tore it in half and threw it to the floor again.

"My Mama doesn't need your church bubble gum cards! She needs our love. She needs all you people to be gone—so she can get well—or *die*, if that's what is to happen!" At an appropriate time she was severely admonished by her father and aunts for her act of heresy.

Josie had no time to prepare emotionally for her mother's death. Mama was just suddenly and irrevocably lost! Her best friend and confidante, the only truly warm and loving adult she knew, the one person who ever tried to answer a young girl's difficult questions, share her thoughts, her ideas and fears, was gone. With grief over her mother's illness and death, came disenchantment with the faith. She simply could not comprehend a God, a Jesus or a Mary, capable of allowing such a thing to occur.

At sixteen and the prettiest girl at the Académie, she graduated second in her class. She learned then her dream of a continued education died with Jeanne Connor. Her father, influenced by the aunts, declared it would be an unnecessary expense for a young lady to attend university. There was talk in the family that she should enter a convent to study for the sisterhood, but the independence instilled by her mother came to the fore and she put the notion to rest with an emphatic "Never!" Without a word to anyone, she determined she must leave

Sherbrooke and Quebec at her first opportunity. She took a job at the local Rexall drug store and quietly plotted her escape.

The owner of the store, Mr. Abe Cashman, was pleased with his young employee and soon trusted her to handle all aspects of the business except the pharmacy. Cashman's son, Melvin, two years her senior, began hanging about at every opportunity. He made no effort to hide his infatuation with the lovely Josie. At first she fended off his advances and did her best to discourage him. After several months of persistence, she accepted an invitation to the drive-in movie. He was a clean, polite boy, and she felt a need for the company of someone close to her own age. She had no feeling for Mel, beyond her need for companionship, but he was always considerate; helping her at the store, giving her rides on cold days, dropping by her home to see if there were anything he could do for her. He always insisted on paying for the movies and meals on dates. She offered once to pay her share, but he wouldn't hear of it. This was fine with Josie; she could save every extra cent for her escape. It was not till their fourth date that she allowed him to kiss her. Allowing the first kiss was a condescending act on her part—her reward to him for his kindnesses. The kissing became part of all the dates and led to more serious "necking." It dismayed her at first, to discover Mel would get an erection when they petted. The first few times she noticed it, she ended the petting session at once. The nuns at the Académie had taught the girls, in brief but explicit detail, the anatomy of sex, stressing of course, that it was for married couples only. Her mother had expanded her knowledge to include love and fulfillment, had even given her books on the subject. So Josie knew what was happening, but her own arousal confused and frightened her. Mama had always linked sex to love. She didn't love this boy, so why did she have these feelings? She was torn between her curiosity about sex and her fear of the consequences. As time passed, Mel became more insistent, first begging, then demanding that she have sex with him. He was convinced they would one day be married and repeatedly professed his love.

When she decided to allow him to have her, it was partly curiosity on her part and partly to thumb her nose at convention. Their first attempt to couple, in the back seat of his car, was a dismal failure; poor Mel had anticipated the event for so long, he went soft before he managed penetration. The second attempt was in a hotel bed and only a little better. He managed to stay firm long enough to break her hymen, jolting her with the sharp stab of pain. Afterward he expressed surprise and dismay that she had still been a virgin, apologized ad nauseam, and for the first time became anxious to get her home. Josie's reaction was, *Merde—that was so awkward—and messy!* She broke off the relationship after that second attempt. She worried about becoming pregnant, until with great relief, her next period arrived. Mel Cashman left for the university soon after they broke up. Despite those unsatisfactory efforts, she knew a time would come, with the right man and love, when sex would be fulfilling for her.

When she reached the age of eighteen Josie enlisted in the R.C.A.F. She recognized the Air Force as a practical way to effect her escape from Quebec. After her basic training at Manning Depot, R.C.A.F. Station St. Jean (disappointingly close to Cowansville), she went to Aylmer, Ontario, to be trained as a Clerk Admin. She loved the comradeship of her courses at the training bases. Because of her near-flawless English, she was spared the School of English language course many French-Canadian recruits had to attend, and instead joined hundreds of English-speaking Canadians from all parts of the country. She was surprised to find she was popular at both bases. The girls she met liked her for her good nature and sense of humor, and the men, including some of her instructors, were drawn to her beauty. She proved to be one of the best dancers at both bases, especially when doing the jive. There were some dates, always within a group, but she avoided petting or even goodnight kisses. Any further involvement with men could wait, while she concentrated on enjoying her new life.

Upon graduating from Aylmer, she was posted to Comox, British Columbia, to report there on the tenth of March, 1955. Now, proudly, if somewhat fearfully—Airwoman Second Class (AW2) Connor, Clerk Admin, was on her way to a place, and a life, as far from Cowansville, Quebec as she could ever have imagined.

CHAPTER 4

▼

So, I would have great looking company on a train for four days and three nights. We couldn't know it would someday be much more...

ABOARD THE C.P.R. *CANADIAN*—DAY ONE

Danny located his berth two cars back of Josie's. He exchanged the expected pleasantries with a middle-aged man in the berth opposite: "Yes, the Air Force is great...No, I'm not a pilot...Yes, I've made the trip before...I come from Victoria...It does rain there some...There are a few English people living there...I'm going all the way to Vancouver..."

Yappa, yappa, yappa—bullshit!

After too many minutes of this blather, with a "Hope you don't mind," he stretched out, shoes off and feet on the opposite seat. He tipped his cap down over his face to discourage further conversation, closed his eyes, and was asleep before the train cleared the station.

*   *   *   *

After the train left Montreal behind, Josie spent the rest of the morning between scenery gazing and reading. The scene passing by was pastoral Quebec with an occasional village or town and infrequent glimpses of the Ottawa River. It was all the Quebec so familiar to her, cultivated areas interspersed with stands of hardwoods, and low, rolling hills stretching northward from the tracks. (She had puzzled out that her berth was on the north side of the train.) Where the train crossed roads and highways, she looked down at waiting cars and trucks, and could make out the faint sound of the train's warning whistle and the bells of the crossing gates. She was twice jolted abruptly out of her reverie by the sudden sight and clatter of passing trains traveling eastbound on parallel tracks. Now and then, as they rounded a curve, she could press her cheek to the window and see both the front and rear of the train.

She couldn't concentrate on her book. She would pick it up for a few minutes only to realize she wasn't getting any of the words, and would find herself looking back to the window. She pictured in her mind a journey of four days and three nights. The voice of the public address announcer echoed in her mind. *"Ottawa…Sudbury…Winnipeg…Regina…Calgary…Vancouver."* She mentally filled in what she knew of Canada's geography: *The Great Lakes, Prairies, Mountains, Pacific Ocean…and ferryboats to an island!*

Her thoughts turned to the day's events. She had risen early to catch a bus to the city after spending her leave with her father in Sherbrooke. That she went there at all was only because of a lingering sense of propriety, for she more and more thought of the house as her father's home, no longer hers.

In Montreal, she took a taxi to Windsor Station, arriving there far too early, at six thirty. She thought about her problem with the soldiers, and the thoughts brought her to the L.A.C. who had come to her aid. *But such a way to do it!* Remembering, she had to smile. *Danny Tanner…nice enough. He's a bit stuck on himself and far too cocky. Probably a girl-chaser—but, tres beau.* She patted the seat of her lower berth. *No matter—I'm for sure glad he was around this morning!*

At eleven thirty, about three hours out of Montreal, Josie realized she was hungry. There had been no time for breakfast before the bus, and when she tried to eat at the station's coffee shop the soldiers had first appeared. When the first call for lunch was announced, she set out for the Dining Car and Danny's berth, looking forward to his company. When she found him, he was sleeping soundly. His cap had fallen to the floor, so she picked it up and put it on the seat.

She said, "Danny?…Danny, are you awake?" *Stupid question.* She tried again a little louder, "Danny." No life. "Danny! It's time for lunch…" Still no response. She felt a little foolish standing there. She looked around the car. *Merde. They're all looking at me.* She gave up and returned to her own car, deciding she would try again at second call.

At the next lunch call, she tried again to wake him; "Danny. Wake up. It's time for lunch." She attempted to shake him awake, but he grumbled something that could have been an obscenity and rolled over with his back to her. "Danny— I'm going to lunch—you asked me to get you." *Merde!*

She decided to go on to the diner alone.

On her way back through his car after lunch, she tried again to rouse him, with again no response. She returned to her seat with a vague feeling of disappointment.

Later, at two thirty, the train was pulling out of the Ottawa station. She was looking out on the same scenery as in Montreal when she felt the weight of someone on the seat next to her. She turned to find Danny, looking fresh and alert.

A bit surprised at how pleased she was to see him, she said, "Hello, my very sleepy L.A.C. I came for you at lunchtime. You looked as if you 'ad…passed on?…passed away."

"Yeah," he said, "believe me, I felt like I 'passed away.' I had a long and rough night in Montreal. So—you got some lunch, then?"

She smiled. "I did for sure. I could starve, waiting for you to wake up. I 'ad a nice lunch with two nice old ladies from New Brunswick." *Don't apologize, Mister L.A.C.*, she didn't say.

"Good! Right now, I gotta have coffee. There's a coffee shop up ahead. Why don't you join me." It wasn't a question and he didn't look back as he got up.

As she got up to follow, she thought, *You are so sure of yourself.* She said to his back, "That would be nice." She was forced to hurry to catch up. "Will you be able to stay awake?" *One for Josie, eh?*

He smiled over his shoulder. "Yeah. Fresh as a daisy now." He slowed down now to let her catch up and allowed her to take the lead. "It's three or four cars up."

*   *   *   *

Danny had finished two doughnuts and was half way through a third coffee, when he said, "Would you like more tea, Josie?"

She shook her head.

He asked, "So, where are you from in Quebec?"

"I was born at Cowansville. It's small. Later I lived at Sherbrooke. I lived in Ontario when I was little; at Cornwall. And you, where are you from?".

"Huh? I'm sorry…what did you…" He hadn't heard her question. He was looking at her gray eyes.

Flustered by the way he stared, she managed, "I-I just asked where you are from."

"Oh. Yeah. I'm from B.C.—Victoria." He smiled. "It's on Vancouver Island, just like Comox."

He realized his stare bothered her and looked away for a moment.

"You're going to be close to your home, eh?"

"Yeah, I guess so. Not that it's a big deal. Where did you get that name Connor? I mean you're French…French-Canadian, right? Connor sounds like it's Irish."

She laughed. "Well, my great-grandpapa was Irish. In my family they say he was a very 'andsome and very wild lumberjack. He ran away with my great-grandmama. She was supposed to be the prettiest girl in town." Unaccustomed to long discourses with strangers, she took a big breath, "And that's 'ow I am a Connor."

He had made direct eye contact again. "Really? You must take after that great-grandma of yours. You're kind of pretty too, Josie Connor."

She blushed, not knowing how to handle his directness. She changed the subject. "Where are you coming from now? Today, I mean. You said you were on the way to Vancouver, you said…Jericho?"

"I was on T.D. at St. Hubert, outside of Montreal. It's Air Defense Headquarters. I've been stationed at Jericho for about five months."

"I forget, what is 'T.D.' Danny?"

He said with a grin, "Girl, you're as green as a pea! It means Temporary Duty. I was on a course there for two weeks."

"How many stations have you been at? I mean, since training." She wanted to hear more; here was someone who had been in the service long enough to know what it was all about—what she had to look forward to.

"Let me see, I trained at Clinton…my trade is FighterCOp. I work mostly at radar units. Then I was at St. Margarets, New Brunswick and Moisie—it's up north in Quebec, near Seven Islands, Sept Iles. Jericho's my third field posting." He grinned and said, "And you, you're on your way to your first station! I think you'll like Comox and the Island, it's great country. Comox is where I wanted to be posted after Moisie."

"I 'ope I'll like it. It's all a big adventure for me, do you know?" She giggled. "That sounded silly, I think."

He shook his head. "It's not silly at all. It's why you—why *we* joined up, isn't it? To have some adventure."

"I am glad you said so. Okay, I'm *not* silly…and I had better stop thinking I am!"

"That's the way, Josie Connor," he said, smiling warmly at her. "Hey—have you been up to the Vista Dome? It's a great way to see Canada. We'll be coming to some beautiful country, any time now."

Her eyes lit with anticipation. She said, "Will you go there with me?"

"Sure will. We're sitting right under it." He put a bill and a couple of fifty-cent pieces on the counter for the doughnuts and beverages. "C'mon, let's see if we can get a seat!"

*   *   *   *

They stayed in the dome car for the rest of the afternoon, until the first supper call. He was making his fifth rail trip across the country and carried on a running travelogue, pointing out landmarks as the train rolled through the Ottawa Valley.

Danny, who was always relaxed with new acquaintances, spoke so freely and naturally that Josie, too, loosened up, overcoming her usual shyness. They talked about everything—anything—hometowns, likes and dislikes, music, books, movies, food, actors, sports and more. Danny held forth on sports and history and told her about what he called "the real Air Force," meaning operational bases. She displayed a broad, comprehensive knowledge, especially of music, literature and cinema. By the time they went for supper together, they knew a lot about each other. She couldn't believe the easy way she had opened up to him, or how she felt a need to learn everything about him.

*   *   *   *

The Dining Car was busy. They had to wait fifteen minutes to get a table.

Danny said, "Jesus—oops, sorree—I mean, *darn!* I wish somebody in there would hurry up. I'm starved."

"Me too. You know, since I joined the Air Force, I'm hungry a lot. You're always waiting to get in the mess hall so you don't miss out. You eat so regularly. The same time every day for every meal." She knew she was babbling. "I think I didn't say that well. You must think I'm a-a pig or something, going on about food like this. But, do you know what I mean…?"

He said, "Yeah. I do know what you mean. If you miss a mealtime on the base you go hungry till the next one, so you're always watching the clock. It's a wonder we don't all get fat as hell. I envy the married guys—just open the fridge and make a snack anytime."

"Yes, exactly. It's as if it's a bad…habit, and we all 'ave it." She giggled. "That sounded like a poem. Habit, have it." She blushed after she said it. *Must you sound so stupid, Josie?*

When they were shown to a table for four, there were two men at the table finishing dessert and coffees. The car was filled with the sounds of conversation and the busy clink and tinkle of silverware and china. Two menus had been set on the table at precise angles in each of their places. They were quiet until a Steward came to take their orders.

She asked the Steward, "Would you tell me what I can get with this?" She showed a meal ticket she had been issued with her travel warrant. The tickets were supposed to be restricted to the lower priced menu items.

Danny smiled at the Steward. "We don't have to worry about it, do we?"

"No, sir. Just choose anything you like on the menu." He took a ticket from each of them and gave them pencils and cards to write the orders on. After he moved on, the two men finished their coffees and left.

Danny explained, "You get to know when you make these trips a few times, the Dining Car guys are usually pretty good to servicemen—especially the crews out of Montreal. Mostly, they give us a break."

She said, "Danny, how do you always know…to get things like you do? I could never ask like that. But I'm not complaining, it's been good for me today." She giggled, leaned close and whispered, "You didn't even 'ave to tell this guy I'm a nurse! That was so funny at the station. And me, I must 'ave looked so dumb to you!"

"Oh yeah. This is you…" He parodied her in a falsetto, "But, L.A.C.! I'm not a nurse!" He grinned and aped her again "Then when you got on the train, 'Mr. Porter, my berth is number fourteen. Fourteen lower, I'll have you know!'"

She went into a fit of giggling, tried to stifle it with a hand over her mouth. "Oh, shut up, you! I didn't sound like that." She whispered, "Don't you make me pee!" realizing what she said, she blushed anew.

His eyes widened in mock alarm. "Jeez, don't do that!"

"Okay, I'll hold on so I don't embarrass you." *Am I truly talking like this?*

"Good, thank you," said Danny, then he went on, "And to answer your question though…it's like anything, Josie, if you don't ask, you don't get. It's about looking out for your self. Nobody else is going to do it for you, right? Hell, we have to get all the enjoyment we can—we could all be incinerated by the bomb soon anyway; look at the clowns that're running this world. Life's too short." He grinned and lightened the tone. "Besides, maybe this guy heard about your bad eating habit."

The Steward returned and picked up the cards. They were quiet again as they waited for the orders to be filled.

Within a few minutes the Steward brought the food. Josie had roast chicken, Danny a T-bone steak. She was surprised when the vegetables came in separate little dishes. She thought it *tres chic.*

Danny dug in like a starving man. He finished his entire plate before she had half finished.

She said, "You truly are hungry, Danny." She didn't point out he had eaten her dinner roll as well as his.

"I sure am. I'm just a growing boy." Indicating the remains on his plate, he said, "I think I'll pick up the bone and chew it. It looks tempting…"

She hissed, "Danny! Don't you dare chew a bone!" She looked around, hoping no one else heard him. She blushed again, while he grinned.

"Okay, okay, no bone! But I do want some dessert. They have great apple pie. You should try it."

"I don't know if I 'ave enough space for pie. But I'll get some. If I can't eat it all, I'm sure you can." She grinned and whispered, "Better than chewing bones, anyway!"

He ordered for both of them. The pie came just as she was finishing her entrée. When she saw it, she was aghast.

"Look! There's cheese on it!"

He laughed. "They always serve it with cheese. It's good. Try some."

"I never 'eard of such a thing!" She giggled. "I think you can 'ave all my cheese, if you wish."

*   *   *   *

There were no seats open for them in the dome car after supper. Danny suggested they check out the bar in the Observation Car.

"I could use a drink. How about you?" he said.

"I would love to join you. I don't drink much, though."

Danny ordered a rye with ginger ale at the bar. "Will you try something?"

She wasn't enthusiastic. She spoke to the bar steward, who suggested a cocktail. "Maybe something…not too strong, please?" She tried a pink lady.

She nursed the drink while Danny knocked down a couple of ryes. When she finished it, she said, "This drink is okay. What's in it, do you know?"

"I'm not sure, I think it's gin. Do you want another one?"

"No, thank you. Just one's enough for me. I have never done…any drinking."

They stayed in the Observation Car for forty-five minutes, making small talk.

Josie asked, "What was it like when you went to your first posting? I mean the first after training. Where was it? You told me but I forgot…"

"St. Margarets; in New Brunswick. I got there totally green, sort of like you are now." He grinned, not unkindly. "I only knew a couple of people there and I knew just about nothing about my trade; the training I got at Clinton had nothing to do with reality…" He went on for twenty minutes, describing his time at St. Margarets. As he spoke she watched his face, her eyes shifting from one feature to another; from his eyes to his mouth; from hairline to chin; nose to ears. It was as if she wanted to memorize every detail of him.

Before he finished his description she suddenly interrupted him, "How old are you?" She spoke low, almost in a whisper.

"Huh? Oh, I'm…I'm twenty-one. Almost twenty-two…"

"Twenty-one."

"Yes."

"You grew up in…Victoriaville?"

"Just Victoria. You're thinking of the place in Quebec."

"Oh yes. Victoria." She put a hand to her mouth, "Oh, I'm sorry, Danny…I-I interrupted you." She moved the hand from her mouth to touch his, then jerked it away in embarrassment.

He wasn't sure what was happening. "It's okay, Josie." His narrative forgotten, they sat in silence as he finished his drink.

When Danny suggested they give the dome car another try she was relieved. She wanted to be away from the observation car, to forget her spontaneous words and actions, the craziness of the thoughts she had just had. For his part, he knew the dome would be darkened at night and he wanted to be alone with her.

To his suggestion she replied, "Okay, but just for a little while. I have 'ad a long day, Danny. I'm already a bit sleepy."

They found a seat open this time. By now they were both pretty much talked-out. They were quiet as they looked out upon the darkening landscape. Danny put an arm around her shoulders.

"Do you mind?" he asked.

She said, "No…it's okay." *Okay? It's wonderful!* she didn't say. She shifted in the seat to accommodate his arm. "It's kind of nice, really." She leaned her head on his shoulder. "Don't get mad if I fall asleep. You may 'ave to carry me back to my seat." Josie couldn't believe how quickly this familiarity had developed—and how it was approaching intimacy!

They sat that way for another hour, until the darkness outside was total.

At eight thirty Josie sat up straight and said, "I'm sorry, Danny, but I am sleepy now, and I just have to get to bed. It's been good sitting with you. You've been so nice…and it's been fun. Thank you for keeping me company." She shrugged and added ruefully, "But I must get some sleep."

He walked her back to her car. The Porter was just finishing making up her berth for the night.

She took Danny's hand, gently squeezed. "You don't 'ave to wait. Good night, and…will I see you for breakfast tomorrow?" She reached up and pushed the wayward forelock from his brow, and then she jerked her hand away, so surprised was she by the intimate act.

Danny touched her arm. "I promise, I'll be wide awake when you come for me this time." He hesitated. "Okay then…well, good night, Josie Connor."

She gave him a tired smile and he left. When her berth was ready, she opened the curtain and climbed in. She fell asleep almost instantly.

*   *   *   *

ABOARD THE *CANADIAN*—DAY TWO

It was the second day I knew you. You later told me it was the day you fell in love…

At seven in the morning, Danny had been awake for two hours. He remembered waking during the night, as cars shunted around in the dark. He knew that had been Sudbury, Ontario, where the cars of the train were joined with another from Toronto, to make up the full *Canadian.* Now the complete train and its passengers would be hauled the balance of the three thousand mile journey to the Pacific.

When he arose, the car swayed and bucked, as a boat in a storm. He washed and shaved at a gyrating basin in the washroom. He dressed in civilian clothes; faded Levi's, gray V-neck pullover and suede loafers. He waited for an hour in the smoker adjoining the washroom for the Porter to make down his berth for the day. The little room smelled of tobacco smoke and stale urine.

He was back at his berth reading a Toronto paper when Josie arrived. She was wearing her dress blues again.

"Good morning!" said Danny.

"'Ello, Danny. You don't have your uniform on."

He shrugged. "This is way more comfortable. Ready for breakfast?"

"Yes!" she said, "And I am hungry…again."

On their way through the cars to the diner she said, "The train is rough today. It's 'ard to walk! We're supposed to wear our uniform when we travel, aren't we?"

He shrugged again. "The heck with that. I never do after the first day. It gets all wrinkled and you look like a bum by the time you get off the train."

With a sly smile, she said, "So, I'm going to be a bum, Danny?"

Grinning, he said "Never! Not you! You'd look good in anything. Hell, I bet you look *real* good in nothing at all!"

Her face turned a deep red. She raised a hand as if to strike him. "Shut *up*, you. You're awful!"

He ducked the imaginary blow and danced away in a boxer's crouch, hands guarding his face, "Couldn't resist, Josie."

She couldn't help but smile. "You 'ad *better* duck!" She walked on with her arms folded. Her face was hot.

"I'll remember that, Killer Connor," he said as he caught up.

As they struggled along the bucking train, she looked puzzled. "It seems longer today. It's as if there's more cars, to the diner I mean."

He explained, "Yeah. They added more cars from Toronto, in Sudbury. We went through there sometime after midnight. It didn't wake you up?"

They were in the narrow passageway near the end of a car, where the compartments were located.

"No. I think nothing could last night. I slept right through—till nearly eight o'clock."

At that moment, the train's wild movement threw her hard against him. He had to catch her in his arms and she felt the strength of him. He held her a little longer than necessary. As he steadied her on her feet she grew flustered at the closeness.

She managed to utter, "I'm sorry. Thank you." She pulled from his arms and searched for something—anything—to say. "You see? It is harder to walk. Are they going too fast?"

"They must have put the square wheels on." He was repeating some nonsense he had heard from veteran train travelers. "You'd better hold my hand—if you want."

She wanted.

＊   ＊   ＊   ＊

Except when taking meals, they spent the entire day and evening together in the dome car, shamelessly monopolizing their seats. Josie, who had never been west of Cornwall, was entranced as they watched Canada roll by.

As they traveled northwest from Sudbury the country became less and less inhabited, the landscape mile after mile of forbidding Boreal forests of mostly jackpine and birch. There seemed to be an endless number of black-green lakes, many still rimmed with ice. There were swift-running streams contrasting with fetid, reed-grown wetlands. The Pre-Cambrian rock, silver-gray, streaked with ferrous orange and pink, pushed up everywhere in confused jumbles. Worn by time and weather and deeply creviced, the rocks embraced the lakes with a protective presence, but freed the streams to dance and tumble around them.

This land seemed to cry out from pre-history, "White man, enter here only if you dare!" An observer could imagine Ojibwa or Cree war canoes appearing suddenly from behind any of the pine-studded islands. Occasionally signs of industrial man's encroachment broke the wildness, when mining communities, diamond-drill camps, and other small habitations flashed by—like scabs.

Josie avidly followed Danny's almost continuous travelogue and encouraged him with her eyes when she pulled them from the scenery. She was most comfortable with his arm around her and her head resting on his shoulder.

She was becoming aware of an important difference between this day and the one before. Feelings she for so long had kept under control were betraying her. She was falling in love with this boy, whom she had started to think of as "my Danny."

Late in the evening, a Conductor came up the stairs to announce the dome car was closing for the night. Josie, Danny and six other remaining passengers, now all couples, protested to no avail before they all reluctantly got up to leave.

As they made the way down the steep stairs, Josie stumbled and fell backward into Danny. He reached out and caught her under the arms to steady her.

"Hey, careful. Are you okay?"

She replied, "Yes, I just slipped a bit. Thank you, I'm okay now." She allowed the awkward embrace to continue by not pulling free from his arms at once. When she did, he took her by the hand for the final three stairs, and they walked hand-in-hand to her car.

All the berths in her car were made up, the curtains closed. There were just two small lights at the ends of the silent car.

"Do you want to come in for awhile?" she whispered. She put a finger to her lips and pulled the curtain open.

He whispered, "Sure, if you want me to." He held the curtain open while she climbed in and sat on the bed, then followed her. They sat one at each end of the bed. Josie surveyed the scene in the dim light. She kicked off her shoes and put them aside, then removed her tunic and hung it on a coat-hook. Danny took off his loafers and she placed both pairs at the foot of the bed.

"There." she whispered. Then, coquettishly, "I'm so glad you decided to make me into a nurse, now I 'ave a nice lower berth. I won't have to climb way to the top of the train to go to bed. I thank you my Da...my L.A.C."

Feigning bashfulness, he said, "Aw, anything fer a purty gal like you. See, I didn't call you 'babe,' even if I am still 'L.A.C.' to you."

They were quiet for a few minutes. She wondered about her decision to invite him into her berth, belatedly realizing it was, after all, her bed. But she was happy just to be there with him; she wasn't ready for sleep and he had been so good to be with throughout the day. *Was it only one day?* She wanted to make her time with him last a little longer.

Danny was struck by a crazy thought, remembering the time a friend was caught by a Conductor, having sex in an upper berth. He had been dragged into the aisle with his trousers at "half-mast" and thrown from the train at the next stop. He hoped no one had seen them getting in. There was no doubt in his mind as to his intention. How could he turn down such an opportunity? A good-looking girl had invited him to share her bed. He moved to her end of the berth and sat beside her.

"This is much better," she said. She leaned her head on his shoulder. "Mmm, Mister L.A.C. Danny, your sweater is soft...and you smell so nice."

He turned and took her in his arms. "I want to kiss you, Josie. I want to see if those lips are as soft as they look." *Jesus, Tanner, how corny can you get?* He put a hand on the nape of her neck, gently pulled her to him and kissed her mouth. The kiss was long and tender, her response immediate and eager.

When it ended, he murmured, "They are."

"Hmm? Pardon?"

"Nothing, just..."

They lay down beside each other.

Somewhat breathlessly, she said, "That's very nice..." He was kissing her again before she could finish, this time more passionately. He parted her lips with his tongue and brushed it softly along her teeth. She had never kissed like this and she stiffened just a little in surprise. She heard him go "Mmm," with a trace of annoyance. He started to pull away, but she pulled him back. Now, she, too, opened her mouth. She tasted his tongue and felt thrilled by the sensation.

When they parted again, she whispered, "That is...oh that's so good!" He kissed her softly on each eyelid, kissed the tip of her nose, her chin, and each ear-lobe. He moved his mouth down to her throat. She felt a wonderful tingle over her body, as if her skin had shrunk and tightened. She guided his mouth back to hers and they kissed again. He unintentionally brushed her breast and was surprised when she thrust her body at him, arching her back. He cupped a breast with his free hand. He gently kneaded and she moved with his hand. He undid the top three buttons of her blouse and slid a hand under her brassiere.

She abruptly started to sit up, saying, "No. Wait!"

He thought, *Shit! I'm moving too fast.*

She half sat up. She removed her tie and tugged the blouse from the waistband of her skirt. She undid the remaining buttons and reached back to unfasten her brassiere. She pulled the cups up, freeing her breasts.

A little hoarsely, she whispered, "Your sweater, Danny."

He pulled the sweater off over his head, removed his dog tags to a pocket. She placed his hands onto her breasts and again pulled his mouth down to hers.

Danny found her skin to be incredibly soft. He broke off the kiss and let his mouth travel, first to her throat, then to her breasts. He kissed her breasts and bit gently. She moaned with pleasure. She could feel his erection against her thigh. His hands moved provocatively over her upper body. He realized she was breathing heavily. As he trailed one hand down her body, her skirt had hiked up, exposing her thighs. He placed a hand on the inside of her leg, and started to move it slowly upward.

Her body stiffened. In a harsh whisper, she said, "No! Don't!" One hand pushed at his to stop him but he continued his exploration.

"I said, no! Don't!" She abruptly pulled back from him, tugging at her skirt hem. When he reached for her, she pushed his hands away and moved farther back.

"What's wrong?" he asked, puzzled.

"Nothing is *wrong*, Danny. I do not want you doing that!" She moved farther away, straightening her clothes.

He pleaded, "I thought you were enjoying it. Weren't you?" He reached over to kiss her, but she pushed him away.

"Come *on*, Josie…"

"I think you should go back to your own car, now." She sounded resolute.

"Look, can't we…"

"I *said* I think you should go now. Please!"

This whole scene confused him. According to all his past experience, her reaction didn't make sense.

"Okay, okay," he said. He found his sweater in the dark. He groped unsuccessfully for his shoes. "Could you turn the light on for a second?" She found the switch. There was a frown on his face as he picked up the loafers. He took a minute getting his things on. He had the curtain open and was half out, when he felt her touch his arm.

She said, "Danny—could you kiss me again before you go?" She was half sitting, lovely in the light from the small lamp. He sighed. He took her in his arms and they kissed. When he released her, she lay back on the pillows with her eyes closed.

"Do I still have to go?" He knew the answer before he asked.

"Yes, Danny. Please…go now."

*   *   *   *

Danny made his way through the darkened cars to his berth where he sat on the made-up bed, fully clothed. It was difficult to convince himself in his aroused state that he had done the right thing. His thoughts were jumbled. *Cock-teaser! I've got to be crazy! But hell, short of raping her, I wouldn't have got anywhere—and I was never gonna do that. She sure as hell knew what she wanted; more like what she didn't want. Damn! Lover's nuts tonight, Danny-boy. Oh, man, is she the sweetest thing I've ever met, or what! Just couldn't do anything to hurt her. You're starting to slip, Tanner.*

Knowing he would not get to sleep, he went to the observation car to see if the bar would be open. He had better luck there; a sympathetic steward served him after-hours drinks. They shared the bottom-end of a quart of whiskey and Danny was feeling mellow when he made his way uncertainly to his berth.

He could barely wait for morning, when he would see Josie—hoping upon hope he hadn't killed his chances with her.

*   *   *   *

After Danny left, Josie lay for a half an hour on top of the bed covers, not thinking, feeling empty. She closed the curtain, undressed, and got under the covers in only her panties. She thought hard about what had just transpired. Her mind leapt all over the emotional map. She had no doubt now—she was in love with this boy, her Danny! All common sense told her she was insane to think of him as hers, but common sense had nothing to do with the way she felt. *He is so beautiful. Why didn't I let him do it? I wanted it so bad!* She was torn. If she had let him have her, might it have somehow made her less than she wished to be in his eyes, or had her refusal caused him to forever lose interest? She touched her breasts, lightly pinching the nipples as he had done. She could still feel every place where he touched her body, could still feel his bare chest against hers. She felt the wetness between her legs. *I'm glad he didn't find that, at least.*

She was sure she had had at least one orgasm. *Without him even inside me!*

Josie Connor, you're a silly schoolgirl. This train will get to Vancouver in two more days and you will never see him again. He surely has a girl waiting for him out there. Her eyes flew open. She shook her head vehemently. *No! I mustn't believe that!*

After a long time passed, she fell into a fitful sleep.

$$* \qquad * \qquad * \qquad *$$

ABOARD THE *CANADIAN*—DAYS THREE AND FOUR

At sunrise on the third day, the train rolled through Western Manitoba, approaching the Saskatchewan border.

Josie had been awake since before dawn. She looked out her window on the prairie morning. Undulating grassland shimmered orange-gold in the early morning sunlight, and dust cast up by a distant farm machine became a suspended russet plume hanging motionless above the horizon. In passing towns, ugly grain elevators attained moments of elegance as the rising sun flashed golden on corrugated metal walls. Elongated shadows of trackside telegraph poles raced past her window. She recalled that Danny dismissed the prairie scenery as monotonous, but for her the utter vastness of the land and sky was captivating. She smiled, thinking she wouldn't tell him, for he was after all, a mountain and ocean boy from British Columbia.

The thought of him dragged her mind back to the previous evening and compelled her to face what she saw as this morning's problem.

She decided her action in her berth had been the correct one. She admitted she loved this boy and wanted nothing more than to have him. She daydreamed of spending a night in bed with him. She knew, somehow with certainty, they would someday make love, but they had met only two days ago and it would have to wait till she knew he returned her love. She resolved to spend as much as she could of these last two days with him, but after last night she knew she couldn't trust herself to spend even another minute with him in her berth.

These decisions brought this morning's immediate problem to the forefront of her thoughts. She must find out just how he felt about her now. The problem was a practical one, caused by the chance make-up of the train—unless he showed up at her berth, she would have to go through his car and past his berth to get to the dining car. She couldn't just breeze by without even a "hello," which might tell him she wanted no more to do with him, and that was not the message she wanted to convey. It was definitely not an option. She must engineer a situation wherein he, not she, would initiate their next encounter.

By the final call for breakfast, after nine o'clock, he hadn't come to her car. Doubt overwhelmed her and her resolve weakened. She decided to chance a meeting in his car. Taking a deep breath, she donned her tunic and set out for the diner.

To her relief, he wasn't at his berth when she passed. She spotted him in the dining car, at a table with three other passengers and no empty chairs. He didn't notice her arrival so she found a seat facing his way, where he would have to pass on his way out. She could see he had finished eating and was drinking an after-breakfast coffee. Now the first move must be his; she would just sit till he left the diner and see what happened.

She managed not to look up when he rose from his table to leave. Her insides were jelly. *Will he see me? Will he speak to me?*

He stopped at her table. She looked up at him, tried to smile, but could not.

"Good morning, Josie." He was smiling, but a little subdued.

"Oh...Good morning." she managed.

He said, "I watched for you to come by my car. I figured maybe you decided to skip breakfast...so I came on my own." She could see that he, too, was uncomfortable.

"No. I-I got up late."

"Did you have a good sleep?" he asked.

What did that mean? She felt heat on her face. "Yes, I did. I slept late. I almost missed breakfast" *Just a tiny lie.*

"I see," he said pensively. "I missed sitting with you. I-I wanted to say I'm sorry, Josie...about last night. It will never happen again. Could I come and get you later? Maybe we can find a seat up in the dome."

Thank you dear lord! "That sounds nice. It-it's okay about last night, Danny." *Help me find the right words, please.* "I'll be waiting at my bed...I mean my berth!" *Merde!*

"I'll see you there in a while then." He sounded pleased.

Josie returned to her car to find she now had company in number fourteen. An elderly woman sat in the rear-facing seat, knitting what appeared to be a large sweater. She greeted Josie with a smile and introduced herself as Mrs. Renate Kurtz, from Yorkton, on her way to visit a son and his family at a place called Chilliwack, in B.C. In their conversation, Josie learned Mrs. Kurtz was a light sleeper.

"In fact," the lady warned, "I just can *never* get to sleep on a train, no matter how hard I try! And I know I'll be dead tired by the time I get to Chilliwack. I hope I don't disturb you or keep *you* awake the whole night!"

Disturb me? Thought Josie, *You have just saved me from myself.* With Mrs. Kurtz and her insomnia in fourteen upper, any further nocturnal activities in fourteen lower must cease, so her problem was solved. As soon as they were alone she would make Danny aware of this new situation.

*   *   *   *

It came as a surprise to Danny that he realized a sense of deliverance when Josie told him about Mrs. Kurtz. His attitude toward her had changed after he had time to think about the night before. It was no longer a matter of just getting laid. He liked Josie, cherished their friendship, and wished to do nothing to harm the last two days on the train for them.

So they would spend the final night alone in their own berths. But he would be with her in the daylight hours.

*   *   *   *

For the rest of the trip they did everything, went everywhere, together. They again claimed and monopolized a seat in the dome car, where he took up his cross-Canada travelogue and she continued as his willing audience.

One moment they were in serious conversation, another giggling at some outrage or other, usually of his making. When they thought they were alone, they relaxed all pretense of adulthood. Josie's happiest times were when they were in the Vista Dome, together but alone in the crowded car, with his arm around her and her head resting on his strong shoulder. She knew there were hundreds of other travelers on the train, but she and Danny were the only two that mattered. Several times she fell asleep while they sat, to awaken later feeling the warmth of him and wondering at his patience and strength. Sometimes she would see him eye her with a look almost of puzzlement and then quickly look away.

At some of the longer stops, they left the train to explore the stations and surroundings, Josie carrying her Kodak Brownie camera with her. On one of the excursions, they lost track of time while she purchased souvenirs in the station. They had to run after the train as it started to move slowly away from the platform, with Danny urging, "Come on! Hurry up! Shit, Josie, you run like a girl!" Safely aboard after a close thing, they giggled breathlessly in the vestibule between cars, with Josie clutching tightly to him, her feet swinging free of the deck-plates.

On the third day, almost as soon as the train pulled out of Calgary the serrate outline of the Rockies came into view. The mountains, at first low on the horizon, rose in higher and higher tiers as they approached, until in no time at all, they could make out individual peaks. Two hours out of Calgary, massive snow-capped pinnacles were all around them. They were mostly quiet as they watched one majestic peak succeeding another in a passing parade. As so many before her, Josie expressed her awe, whispering, "It makes me feel like I'm so...tiny!" Followed by Danny's, "You never get used to it." Sadly, she had used up all her film and forgotten to buy more in Calgary. He bought her a new roll and a little package of black and white C.P.R. postcards when they stopped at Banff.

Later, as she slept on the seat beside him, head on his shoulder, the train entered a long tunnel. In the dark car he obeyed a sudden impulse and kissed her brow.

She stirred, sighed sleepily and raised her head, "Mmm, what a nice way to wake up."

Grinning broadly, he asked, "Pardon me? What was nice?"

"The kiss. It was nice. I love it when you kiss me."

At just that moment, they emerged from the tunnel. Danny looked around the car, feigning suspicion.

He said, "Hmm, let's see—I didn't kiss anyone." Then, to the other passengers, he shouted, "Okay, who kissed this poor girl when we were in the tunnel?" This brought a gasp from her and a laugh from the others.

She said, "You are bad, Danny!" Then louder, for the car, "He's terrible—isn't he?" She lay her head on his shoulder again and murmured, "It was nice anyway."

Josie had not read of any mountains in the west other than the Rockies, so she expected the tracks to abruptly leave the mountains and return to lower country as they traveled deeper into British Columbia. Instead, it seemed the province was all mountains, one range after another! Danny knew the names of all the ranges—after the Rockies came the Purcells, then the Selkirks, the Monashees and the Cascades. The tracks seemed to always run beside a rushing river, with stately peaks visible on both sides.

At one point, west of Kamloops, she saw a highway and railroad track on the other side of a river, both running parallel to their route. Danny told her the river was the Thompson. She spotted a long train on the other tracks, winding its way west with them. Danny said it was a Canadian National freight train. It came in sight, on and off, for three hours before they left it behind—a fellow traveler they would never meet again.

The next morning, the *Canadian* rolled alongside the wild, mighty Fraser River, following its relentless course to the ocean. They were seated in Danny's berth after breakfast when Josie realized, with mixed emotions, that day four was upon them. Before this day ended they would arrive at the end of the tracks in Vancouver. She grew more and more anxious with every westward mile; an angst brought on when she realized she and her Danny would soon be parting. She was certain in her heart they would not be apart for long, for since the night in her berth he had shown her respect and, more importantly, affection. Her hopes were up. She refused to acknowledge she might see him for the last time at the Vancouver train station.

By mid-afternoon they were still beside the Fraser, but now the terrain became as flat as a prairie and the river slow, silty and meandering. They were in the Fraser Valley. Here, for all of time, the great river had gathered alluvium from the length of its course and its many tributaries, depositing it on this broad valley to create the rich farmlands they were now passing. Spotted along with produce farms were large pastures with dairy and beef cattle. Snowcapped peaks of the Cascade Range were visible to the north and south. Danny pointed out Mount Baker, explaining it was way down in the U.S.A.

Mrs. Kurtz left the train at Chilliwack; one of the many small agricultural centers strung along the valley. The little farm towns became more frequent and closer together as they neared the coast.

*   *   *   *

VANCOUVER—MARCH 9TH, 1955

Arrival! It was the end of the line. We parted there—I from a beautiful girl I enjoyed traveling with—and you from the boy you loved.

The train rolled through the Fraser delta land and at last crossed a bridge over the big river. They swung by a body of water with houseboats and fishing craft, into the city's core, before slowing as they approached the station near the city's harbor on Burrard Inlet.

When the *Canadian* made its final stop at the Vancouver terminal Danny and Josie collected their belongings, tipped the Porter who had served them since Winnipeg, and detrained. They found themselves amid a mob of people—fellow passengers from the train and hundreds of greeters looking for friends and relatives. As they fought the way through the crush Josie was reminded of their boarding in Montreal—had it been four days ago? She waited while he retrieved his checked bag. Outside the station they found an overcast sky was sending down a warm drizzle. They stood silent in raincoats by the line of taxis outside the station. He helped her put her bag into a cab.

Josie said, absently, "Well, here you are, back in your Vancouver."

"Yeah." He looked up at the drizzle. "What the hell, back in the rain, and back to the old grind for me. But now you start your big adventure! In a few hours you'll arrive at your first real Air Force station."

"Yes! I can't wait! I'll 'ave to take a taxi, at…Courtenay?"

"Yeah. Don't forget to get receipts. You'll be fine, Josie."

"Yes, I will. I can't wait…but I said that, didn't I?"

"Okay then, we both better get moving. Maybe I'll see you around." He started to pick up his bag.

Her mind screamed. *See you around?*

In a reflex action, she put out a hand to stop him. Misunderstanding, he put down his bag and reached to shake her hand. She quickly dropped hers to her side, so he gripped her lightly on the arm instead.

He smiled and said, "See you then, Josie."

She couldn't speak. She could barely breathe. *See you Josie?* She took an involuntary step back from him. *What have I done? What will I do? See you around! Josie Connor, you are a fool! Oh, Danny—my Danny.*

In a strangled voice, she managed, "Okay, then. Thank you…for your help."

"Nothing."

You are for sure right about that, Danny Tanner. Nothing.

She turned quickly and got into the taxi. She didn't look back. She was having trouble seeing through her tears.

He waved as the taxi drove away.

She didn't see him.

✱   ✱   ✱   ✱

When the ferry left the dock half an hour after she boarded, Josie walked the decks. She barely noticed stately Lion's Gate Bridge as the ferry passed beneath it and out of Burrard Inlet into the Strait of Georgia. Her thoughts were still outside the Vancouver station. They were bitter, hurting thoughts. She went inside and sat in the ship's lounge for the rest of the trip. Ashore in Nanaimo, waiting for the E&N train to Courtenay, she determined she must try with all her being to forget "her Danny."

She knew it was not going to be easy.

CHAPTER 5

▼

You went on to your big adventure, and I was back to the old grind…

COMBAT OPERATIONS CENTER (C.O.C.) 5 AIR DIVISION, VANCOUVER

When Danny reported back to duty at Jericho, he was assigned to work with the Sector Liaison Officer. The new duty entailed communicating, principally with the U.S. Air Force's 25th Air Division, as well as some Strategic Air Command (S.A.C.) units below the border. The task was to be an attempt to coordinate air defense functions between Canadian and American forces that to date had had only token interaction. They would set up lines of communications with key U.S.A.F. personnel in the Northwest and compile a comprehensive, cross-referenced list of contacts.

The assignment was a Monday-to-Friday job, meaning he worked only day shifts and was off duty on weekends. His working relationship with the Liaison Officer, Flight Lieutenant Ian "Moe" Morrisey, was a good one. Morrisey had specifically requested Danny for the job after seeing him at work in the C.O.C. In the office, the usual protocols of rank were relaxed in favor of a whatever-gets-the-job-done attitude. His new boss took an interest in Danny's career and encouraged him in his efforts at self-improvement. During slack times in the office, he was allowed to study and work on his correspondence course and managed to put a large dent in his eleventh grade. The relaxation extended to their after hours social life, with Danny often visiting Moe and his wife, Irene, and they often went out together to downtown clubs and restaurants, ending the evening at the Morrisey house. He sometimes brought one of the girls he dated in Vancouver; a civilian clerk on the base named Evelyn Pollard.

Evelyn—Ev—was a good-looking secretarial school graduate who lived in nearby Ladner with her parents. They had been seeing each other for four months. Moe and Irene took a liking to Ev and the four of them had enjoyed some good times over supper and drinks. He didn't mention to Moe and Irene that of late the relationship with Ev was wearing. She had become far too serious, showing signs of jealousy whenever she didn't see him for a day or two. She had even started to hint at marriage, a concept of no interest to Danny.

At the same time, he had also been dating another girl, a FighterCOp named Christine Manson. Theirs was a strictly casual affair; "Chrissy" was a vivacious blonde from Alberta who wore her libido on her sleeve. She loved to dance and make love with Danny Tanner—in that order. She was an accomplished dancer and Danny was the best partner around. They competed in jive contests at Vancouver nightclubs, winning as often as not. Chrissy had no interest in being tied to any one man and, with his similar attitude, Danny proved to be the perfect companion for her. She could have any man at Jericho but, except for occasional one-night stands with others, she was happiest when with him.

Neither Evelyn nor Christine knew anything about his relationship with the other.

*   *   *   *

In the weeks following his return from St. Hubert, he immersed himself in his work and studies. He found the work interesting enough and was thankful for the Monday to Friday schedule after three years of working shifts. But he missed the immediacy of a G.C.I. Ops Room.

The ball season would soon begin and practices had started. Beginning in mid-April, he would be playing league fastball two nights a week on a team from the Air Transport Command station at Sea Island.

He didn't see much of either Ev or Chrissy after his return from St. Hubert. He had called Ev two days after his return and received a cool "Well, hello, stranger." They got together a couple of times, once at the Morriseys', on an invitation from Irene that included them both.

He of course saw Chrissy around the base, on one occasion ending up in the back seat of his car with her, parked at Wreck Beach near the U.B.C. campus.

Now and then he had thoughts about the cute little blonde, Josie, he had met on the train. He would smile as he remembered some of the events of the trip. He told himself if he were ever in Comox he would look her up—but another entanglement was one more than he needed at the moment. He must work at extricating himself from at least one here in Vancouver, a task proving to be challenging enough, thanks.

Word came he was being sent to Comox on Temporary Duty. He would be instructing FighterCOps from various bases in the Sector, preparing them for upcoming Trade Group exams. It would be his second time instructing the course, scheduled this year for the last two weeks of April.

*   *   *   *

R.C.A.F. STATION COMOX

When Josie reported for duty at Comox, she was assigned to work in the Station Orderly Room in the Headquarters Building. The Orderly Room was essentially the administrative and personnel office for the Station. She worked with one other Airwoman, two Airmen and three civilian clerks. All were in the charge of a forty-something female Sergeant named Wilson.

She was grateful for the warm reception she received from her new work mates. She soon found, just as Danny predicted, most of what she had been taught at Aylmer was outdated. She now began a whole new on-the-job training process. The pretty Leading Airwoman, whose name was Olivia Conti, appointed herself as Josie's personal tutor, and set about to teach the young AW2 all the forms, procedures and shortcuts used in the office. She also introduced her to life at an operational Air Force station.

Josie took an instant liking to Olivia and the two girls became close friends. At first, Olivia's outrageous ways jarred Josie's sensitivities, but she soon got over her shock when she realized there were intelligence, humor and warmth behind the tough facade. They spent all their off-duty time together, with Olivia showing her around the base and the surrounding area. When her roommate was transferred out Olivia invited Josie to move in and she jumped at the opportunity.

Olivia enjoyed a good time and occasionally drank more than socially. For her part Josie learned to nurse a drink to be part of the crowd. They frequented the Ordinary Ranks Club, called the "Wets" (for wet canteen), usually on Friday or Saturday evenings. At their table on the "ladies' side" they and other Airwomen were frequently surrounded by men. The table companions were often Fighter-COps from the radar unit attached to the base. This was because Olivia claimed, "The Scope-Dopes are more fun, they know how to cut through all the crap and have a good time! Even with that stupid language they use—'Roger' and 'Wilco' and 'I hear you five-by-five,' and whatever alien crap they talk."

For Cokes, burgers and other fast food, there was the Dry Canteen, popularly called the Snack Bar, situated upstairs in the Recreation Center; it had a jukebox, a small dance floor and several tables. One could buy personal care items there, too.

Their FighterCOp friends introduced them to a lounge in the newly opened Arbutus Hotel in nearby Courtenay and it became their meeting place when in town. The two girls regularly took the inexpensive taxi ride into town for some shopping or a movie, followed by a stop at the Arbutus for drinks.

Olivia drew her fair share of second looks and was more accustomed than Josie was to men being attracted to her. She had had experience with sex and now, at age twenty-two, she was selective about the men she would be intimate with. She described it to Josie in her usual offhand way, as "Waiting for Mr. Right—and hoping his first name isn't 'Always.' If some guy's going to sweat over me in the sack he damn well better be at least a good friend!" She had no rule, however, against men sitting with her at a table—and buying her drinks.

For her part, Josie was always gregarious. She joined in the group fun, often taking up offers to dance—always friendly but indifferent to the men who pursued her. She simply could not forget the boy from the train. She knew, convinced at last, there could be nothing to look forward to where he was concerned. She still seethed whenever she relived that horrible moment at the Vancouver terminal, blaming no one but herself for falling so hard in just a couple of days. Someday, the real thing would come along. A man would return her affection and she would know it when it happened, but for now, despite all her efforts, she could not get over him. Whenever she allowed her mind to return to those days on the train, she saw his handsome face, talked and laughed with him, felt his touch.

She had told Olivia only about a "beautiful guy I met on the train."

So, the two best looking and most popular Airwomen at Comox remained politely, amicably aloof from the many male admirers. Their attitude toward men resulted in some off-target conjecture, originated by disappointed Lotharios. One story asserted they were lesbian lovers, another said they "put out" for officers only; the girls got a great laugh out of the former and were angered by the latter. They were both well liked by their peers in the Airwomen's barracks for their good nature, helpfulness, and refusal to gossip.

The two friends set out to explore the Comox Valley. Sometimes one of the guys with a car drove them and sometimes Olivia, who held a driver's license, could borrow a car.

The commercial hub of the area was the town of Courtenay. Courtenay is situated a hundred and forty miles from Victoria halfway up Vancouver Island, at the north end of Comox Bay, which separates the main island from the Comox Peninsula. The peninsula juts into the Strait of Georgia in a southeasterly direction for five miles, ending at Cape Lazo. The Courtenay River, a short stream formed by the junction of the Puntledge and Tsolum rivers near the edge of town, empties into the bay's north end. In 1955 the river was crossed by a bridge that was a continuation of Courtenay's main street, Fifth Street. East of the bridge, the road became the Island Highway and continued north thirty-five or so miles to the town of Campbell River.

To get to the R.C.A.F. Station, one turned off the highway a few hundred yards past the bridge, onto Comox Road, called by all but the mapmakers "Dike Road" because it was built on a dike that kept the high tides of the bay from flooding adjacent farmland. At this point the traveler was headed southeast, following first the river and then the shore of the bay. At the north edge of the village of Comox, just past "Hospital Hill," Anderton Road turned off and headed north in a straight line for three miles, to where it met Ryan Road, which took one another mile east, to the Station's main gate.

Josie was impressed with the scenery in the area, the forests, the streams, the seashore, and the mountains of the Vancouver Island Range. *Another mountain range!* The most dominant feature in the Comox valley is the misnamed peak and glacier called Forbidden Plateau. When not obscured by clouds, the oddly flattened, ice-and-snow capped mountain can be seen from just about any place in the valley. There is snow at the summit even in mid-summer. Josie thought it resembled a colossal vanilla ice cream cone licked flat by a giant child. A road wound up the mountain from Courtenay as far as a ski lodge. The snowline in the spring of 1955 was still hundreds of feet below the lodge.

What Josie loved most about the area was the seashore—the fine white sand, the smells of the sea, tidal pools, sandbars, the plants and animals. The beaches were wonderful places to explore; her first sand dollar turned her into a three-year old! With Olivia, she spent as many of those spring days as she could there, walking the shoreline, wading the shallows or just sitting on one of the many driftwood logs that littered the high-tide line. There were several beaches near the base. One was a strand, just yards from the 51 AC&W site, where the Fighter-COp crews often held nocturnal beach parties. The always brash FighterCOps called it "51 Beach." However, in daytime Josie and Olivia preferred a beach farther along the shore at Kye Bay, because anyone they encountered there would be unfamiliar to them and they wouldn't have to handle unwanted attention. Josie would sit for hours, reading a book or gazing out across the Strait of Georgia at the B.C. mainland and the Coast Mountains, while her thoughts retreated into the far places of her mind.

She carried her little Kodak Brownie everywhere, snapping amateurish pictures of each new sight. She sometimes asked strangers to take shots of her and Olivia together. She got annoyed at Olivia for making faces or striking clownish poses but then joined in the silliness, sometimes outdoing her friend's antics. They giggled hysterically at the developed prints.

Their home on the base was the Airwomen's Barracks, a World War II vintage "H-hut," so-called because of its shape. Its two-story wings, the long sides of the H, were sectioned off into rooms, each accommodating two Airwomen. There were a bed, dresser and closet for each occupant. The center of the H held the washrooms, showers and a laundry area. There was a room for entertaining guests on the ground floor with a small kitchenette for heating beverages and snacks. Male guests were limited to specified hours and of course prohibited beyond the door leading to the girls' living quarters.

The mild weather on the coast came as a pleasant surprise to Josie. The sight of people, already outside in shirtsleeves, strolling, jogging, throwing baseballs or playing golf, delighted her. The D.R.O.s (Daily Routine Orders) at Comox called for the wearing of summer khakis, shirtsleeves allowed, starting on April fifteenth. She and her fellow Easterners would still be wearing parkas and galoshes back home!

Her new home was an operational flying base; Danny's "real Air Force." In 1955 the Station was home to three flying units of three separate Commands. 409 Air Defense Squadron flew CF-100 Canuck interceptors in defense of Canada's West Coast. 407 Squadron of Maritime Air Command flew converted World War Two Lancaster bombers, their bomb bays now housing huge fuel tanks, enabling aircrews to fly twelve-hour patrols out over the Pacific. Air Transport Command was represented by a small unit called 104K Flight, which handled transport, medical mercy flights, and search and rescue missions, using a variety of aircraft. Also lodged at the Station, but in its own off-base compound, was an Air Defense Command ground radar unit called 51 AC&W Squadron, with its huge, long-range search antennae hidden under protective domes. 51 Squadron was where Josie and Ollie's FighterCOp friends worked.

At full strength, the base was home to over 1800 personnel.

All the flying activity was a new experience for Josie. The sounds of aircraft aloft always pulled her eyes skyward. It could be a pair of CF-100s climbing straight up till they were out of sight. It could be the rapid wush-wush of a hovering Sikorski helicopter. Or it might be a Lancaster on takeoff, lumbering under its fuel load, dipping slightly at the end of the runway over Kye Bay before making its labored way out to sea. At first the sounds were disconcerting, even frightening—a three A.M. takeoff of jets rattling the barrack windows—or the prolonged, deafening roar of a Lancaster's big Merlin engines on run-up at the service area, loud enough to bring a halt to conversations all over the base. After a couple of months, however, she was able to take it all in stride, hardly noticing.

It was a fascinating and wonderful new world! Comox was the "Air" in Air Force. She was only an office clerk, but she felt considerable pride at being part of it all.

CHAPTER 6

▼

UNCLASS PERS FILE: d. 09/3/55
L.A.W. Conti, Olivia Maria. #216004W R.C.A.F. ClkAdmin., Gp. 3
Born 21/11/33. Enl. 16/06/52 Cauc. Ht. 5' 7"/Wt. 110/Hr. Brn/Eyes Brn.
Eff. 22/4/54 R.C.A.F. Stn. Comox, B.C.

OLIVIA CONTI

Olivia was the older of two daughters in a family of seven. She was born in Hamilton, Ontario, but lived from age five in Sault Ste. Marie, Ontario—"The Soo."

Guiseppe "Joe" Conti and two of his brothers, with their three families, moved to The Soo in 1938 to work in the mill at Algoma Steel. By 1955, over thirty Contis—fathers, sons, even some wives and daughters—had toiled there.

The Contis created a huge extended family. When they all got together it was like a convention of the Sons of Italy. Olivia described the family as "a cast of thousands." Every member of the family, with any trace of Conti blood or marital connection, was treated as brother or sister, son or daughter, at the riotous gatherings. She remembered them as a hundred people all shouting hugging and kissing, while music played here, someone sang there, dozens of kids ran amok and arguments over bocce or soccer games went on everywhere. The kitchen was a crowded madhouse, full of screaming women who somehow always managed to over feed the multitude. Wine flowed like the nearby Saint Mary's River and each new arrival at the door—uncle, aunt or distant cousin—was Garibaldi arriving in Naples!

When she went home for visits, Olivia always lied about the length of her leave, never staying more than a week. As it was, it became an exhausting week long festival every time. She tried but failed to convince her parents to just let her enjoy a quiet time at home with them.

But there was love! Growing up, Olivia, the oldest and prettiest girl, received a large share of the family's love. She knew Joe as a rough, dark, hairy man, always the knee to sit on, shoulders to ride and ready source for a dime or quarter. Her mother was a warm hug, a kiss on the forehead and a soft hand to wipe away a tear or apply a bandage. Her brothers were protection from all manner of harm, sometimes, to her vexation, even from potential boyfriends.

In spite of the love and protection her family provided, Olivia, like many children of immigrant parents, was sensitive about her background and its traditions, sometimes embarrassed by the old country ways of family members.

Until her sixteenth year, she was so thin her parents worried about her health, in spite of her abundance of energy. This, with her pretty face and big, dark eyes, made her even more the object of the family's love. Then, in that sixteenth year, she blossomed with the willowy beauty she carried into adulthood. Overnight, she became a popular date at her high school. She briefly studied modern dance, more to please the aunt that taught the class than anything. She felt it was mostly a lot of posing, but it did help to instill in her a certain grace of movement.

As she approached maturity she developed a skill at observation, the ability to see into the heart of matters. From this developed one of her defining traits—a wit that could absolutely break up a crowd, and entertain friends for hours on end.

The atmosphere of fanatical loyalty within her family taught her a strong sense of allegiance to friends. If you were her friend she was there for you, selflessly and without reservation.

The Soo she grew up in was a sport-loving town, and good-looking, personable girls were courted by hockey, football and baseball players. Her lifelong interest and understanding of sports resulted from dating these athletes in her teens.

Unlike Josie Connor, Olivia was accustomed to and comfortable with the attention she received from men. As a teen and as a young lady, she was discerning about whom she dated and, most particularly, about whom she shared intimacy with. By the time she joined the Air Force she was no longer a virgin but was far from promiscuous. A boy had to be presentable, respectful and above all, discreet, to be allowed anything beyond innocent petting. Only a few—those of her careful choosing—ever did so.

When she reached age nineteen and graduated from high school, Ollie was finding life in Sault Ste. Marie less than stimulating, and wished to try living in a larger city. Although she knew it saddened her parents, she moved to Toronto, where she lived in a small apartment and worked in an upscale ladies apparel shop. A year later, as a way to further expand her horizons, she enlisted in the R.C.A.F.

She made dozens of friends at her postings in the Air Force. Writing letters and cards to them all was a labor of love. They became to her as members of an extended family.

Josie Connor became her little sister.

CHAPTER 7

▼

COMOX—APRIL, 1955

On a sunny, all but windless afternoon, three weeks after Josie's arrival at Comox, she and Olivia were lounging on a blanket at 51 Beach. Olivia lay on her stomach reading while Josie sat with her thoughts, gazing out over the water, arms clasping her knees. The water of Georgia Strait shimmered blinding in the afternoon sun. Josie opened her purse to find her sunglasses, and the little package of postcards Danny had bought in Banff fell onto the blanket.

Olivia, hearing the sound of a zipper and a gasp, looked up to see Josie staring intently at the postcards with tears glistening in her eyes. Josie quickly put them back into her purse when she realized Olivia had seen her, sat for another minute, and then stood up and walked toward the water's edge, thirty feet away.

When Olivia got up to follow, Josie quickly said, "Stay there, okay?" Her voice was strained.

"What's wrong, Jo?"

"Nothing." She walked twenty yards down the beach and stood looking out at the water. When she came back to the blanket, she sat down for just a moment before she said, "Let's go back to the barracks now, okay?"

Olivia could see the tears in Josie's eyes. She sat up beside her. "Do you want to tell me about whatever's wrong?"

Turning away, Josie replied, "What do you mean? I just want to go back to the base."

With a hand on her chin, Olivia firmly turned her head so they were face to face. She said, "Look—you were crying about something. This isn't the first time in the past week I've seen you so down. If you don't want to talk about it, it's okay, but you'd better realize I'm the best friend you have—at least around here.

And damn it, Jo, when you hurt, I hurt." She put a hand over Josie's. "Look, if some turd has done something…"

"No. It's nothing like…nothing around 'ere. It's just…nothing." She hung her head.

"Bullshit! It's not '*nothing.*' Please don't fucking lie to me. It's insulting."

Josie had never heard Olivia use the word. She had to smile before saying, "It's not here. Somewhere else…"

"Is it your family? Your father…those spooky aunts you told me about?"

Josie had never referred to the aunts as spooky, but the description fit them perfectly. She decided such insight deserved an answer. Besides, it might be good to get it off her chest.

She sighed and said, "Okay. But it's a sad, stupid story about a so stupid me." She took Olivia's hand between her two. "Olivia, I am hurting so! I can't make it stop." She sniffed back tears as she told her friend all about the train trip from Montreal, her infatuation with Danny, and the way they parted. "Until now I was sure I was forgetting him; coming 'ere and meeting everybody…maybe all that just took it from my mind for a time. But, now its all back. I just want to get over 'im…maybe meet a good guy." She struck the blanket with a small fist.

Olivia took a moment to reply. "Hell, I have no idea what to say to you, Jo. You're doing the right thing in trying to get over the guy, but don't rush to some other guy just to get over this one. Sounds like you've been eating yourself up over him." She sighed before continuing. "Does this sonofabitch know how you feel…"

"No! 'E's *not* that—this is my fault, not his. There was no way for him to know we weren't just friends."

"He's still in Vancouver, I suppose. Want to go there?"

"No. God no! I just want to be able to forget about it!"

"It's going to take time, you know. But we'll work on it. Together."

Josie smiled through tears. "I'm glad I told you, Olivia." She felt she was a small step closer to accepting. She realized she couldn't tie her hopes to someone who found her so easy to dismiss. *See you around!* She decided she would be more receptive to the attentions she received from men on the base—she just could never allow herself to get too involved with any one of them.

*   *   *   *

One night in the snack bar a young Airman asked Josie to dance. She declined twice but he was persistent and she ended up dancing with him to two slow numbers. His name was Dave Timchuk. He was small in stature, about five-seven, had boyish good looks and was fun and talkative in a group. On their third encounter, he timidly asked her for a date and she accepted. He confessed it was the first time in his life he had ever been out with a girl, and she told him she hadn't dated very much either. Olivia said they were a fine looking couple.

They went to a movie in town. He spoke hardly a word the entire evening. When the taxi dropped them off he said, "Well, Goodnight, Josie. Thanks..." and fled toward the mens' barracks. The date led to another when he called five days later. His excruciating shyness when they were alone made it impossible for her to be comfortable with him. They spent much of the time in total silence. She was unwittingly comparing him to Danny, and he came off worse than second best. She broke it off after the second date without them ever having kissed.

A week later, Olivia asked, "You're not seeing Dave anymore?"

She said, "He isn't someone I want to get involved with. He's a nice guy, but so shy. I can't imagine having much fun with him. I wasn't *seeing* him, Olivia; it was only two dates."

"You mean he's not the guy from the train," said Olivia.

More to prove Olivia's not so subtle suggestion wrong than for any other reason, she dated a couple more times. She and Olivia double-dated at an Easter dance at the Rec Center with two Instrument Techs from 407 Squadron. When Josie's date confessed he was engaged to a girl back home in Nova Scotia, she left the dance and went home to the barracks.

Next, she went out with a FighterCOp from 51 Squadron. His name was Hank Couture. He wasn't an especially good-looking man, but he had a good sense of humor and was more outgoing than Dave. Much more outgoing it turned out—Hank was a groper. What started with some touching at the movie, intensified in the taxi and became downright alarming after they arrived on the base. As she grappled with him at the rear door of her barracks, she thought, *Dieu! Maybe he expects me to do it right here on the steps!* When she was able to break free, she arrived in the room out of breath and disheveled. After Olivia's initial outrage they laughed for an hour.

"It's as if he 'ad four hands! I stopped 'im here and then the hands would be here and here and here." She demonstrated with her own hands. "I was scared the taxi driver could see. I think I lost ten pounds, fighting 'im off!" She giggled. "And all I could look at were his ears. Did you see them? Like a-a jug with big handles sticking out. So funny!"

Olivia couldn't decide whether to name him "The Octopus" or "Hank the Hands." Josie was thankful when he never called her for another date.

She decided dating just for the sake of dating was not a good idea. The right man for her would someday show up. She would wait for him.

*   *   *   *

Then, in mid April, she met Gord.

She was in the snack bar with Olivia, nursing a Pepsi. Gord Schaefer introduced himself by asking, "Hey, cute little thing, do you jive?" Glenn Miller's *In the Mood* was playing on the jukebox.

She hesitated before answering, not pleased at the way he addressed her. *Cute little thing?*

He said, "Well? Cat got your tongue?"

"Yes, I do jive." *After all,* she thought, *Danny called me "babe" the first day I met him.*

"Shall we give it a try?" he asked.

"Maybe a little later. The song is almost over."

He smiled broadly. "I might not ask you later. And that'd be your loss."

She smiled. "Oh it would, would it?"

He did ask later and they did dance. He kept her on the floor for three jive numbers in a row. He was an accomplished dancer and she enjoyed herself.

After the third dance, he said, "You're Jody, right? I'm Gord…Gord Schaefer. You're a good dancer!"

"Thank you. My name's Josie Connor…not Jody. You're good, too, Gord."

They danced again later and when the song ended he invited himself to her table and she introduced him to Olivia.

Gord pursued her doggedly. After a week of "chance" meetings and phone calls she agreed to go out with him. He owned a two-year-old Pontiac, one of only a few cars afforded by Airmen on the base. On their first date they went to a Friday night dance in nearby Union Bay, with a mixed group that included Olivia. Back on the base at the end of the evening, Josie, Olivia and two other girls all piled out of his car and went straight into the barracks. The next Wednesday he called for another date. He asked her to a movie in Courtenay and she accepted, without telling him she had already seen the picture with Olivia the night before. Afterward, they stopped at Bud's for hamburgers and sat on a bench to eat them, across the street in Lewis Park.

Back at the base, she said, "Thank you, Gord, for the movie…and the hamburger. I 'ad better get in now." She opened the door.

"Hold on, Josie. Don't I get a kiss?" He was smiling.

She, too, smiled. Then she teased, "Do you think we should? It's just our second date."

He answered by taking her into his arms and kissing her. "Hmm," he said, "I could get to like this." He pulled her against him again. The second kiss was more passionate. It was Josie who broke it off and pulled away.

He said, "I bet you could, too."

"What? I could what?"

"You could get to like it—kissing me."

"Oh, that. It's a possibility," she said impishly. "We could try it again sometime so I can better judge. Right now, though, I 'ave to go in. Thank you again, Gord."

In her room, preparing for bed, she admitted she was attracted to him. He reminded her a little of Danny Tanner. It wasn't his appearance so much as his bearing. She saw in him self-confidence and roughness-around-the-edges much as she did in Danny. Taller than Danny at six-one, strikingly handsome, with curly black hair, brown eyes and features she described to Olivia as chiseled.

So much like Danny, she thought, *cocky and so handsome. I think I like him. But Danny kisses a bit better."*

They dated almost nightly for the next two weeks. After the dates, he would park the car in the lot behind the men's barracks and they would sit, pet some, and talk, mostly about him. She learned he was from Calgary and his family was wealthy. His father owned an established and lucrative oil-patch supply firm and Gord had a good future waiting when his Air Force tour ended, in eleven months.

One lunch hour, he asked her to meet him in the snack bar and specifically to not bring Olivia.

They sat alone at a table. He told her he had something to say to her.

She smiled. "Okay. I hope it's not too serious."

He hesitated before saying, "Well, it is kind of serious, but I have to ask. Are you going out with anybody else besides me?"

She thought, *When have you given me time?* She answered him, "No, Gordon, I'm not."

"A friend of mine told me you were going with a guy from the radar squadron."

"I did go out with a guy from there, just once. It was before I met you. And, in case you want to know, before him I dated one other guy...not steady." She sighed. "And there's my love-life at Comox, right up to date."

"Do you mind my asking you?"

"I'm not sure. It depends why you asked." In truth, she wondered what right he had.

He looked down at the tabletop, drew a finger absently through the wet rings from his Pepsi bottle. He appeared to be searching for words.

Oh, my, she thought, *I've never seen him shy before.*

In a low voice, he said what was on his mind; "Do you intend…will you be going out with anyone else?"

It caught her by surprise. "I don't know. I mean…it's not likely. When I met you I 'ad quit dating. And then you…we…" She sighed again. "I just don't know how to answer that, Gordon. Why do you ask it?"

"I guess I was too sudden. I'm rushing you and I'm sorry." He put a hand on her arm. "The problem is I really like you. I think I'm falling for you."

Falling for me? Dieu! She didn't say anything.

He went on, "Josie, I know it's…it's too soon, but you're just the girl…the kind of girl I would want to marry…"

Her eyes widened. She blurted, "Marry?" She looked around, afraid she had been overheard. She lowered her voice, "Marry?"

"You heard me. So, don't be surprised—if and when I ask you."

"I-I am, um, pleased…and surprised, of course, for you to think of me that way. But you are right, Gordon, it *is* too soon. I don't think I'm even close to being ready for…" Her voice trailed off.

"Fair enough. But now you're warned."

"I-I 'ave to get back. Call me later?" Bemused, she went back to work.

They went to the Arbutus that night with some of his friends from 409 Squadron and their dates. All the men, including Gord, drank a lot.

At one point in the evening, somebody said, "Josie, you haven't said two words all night. Cat got your tongue?"

Before she could answer, Gord said, "The only two words I wanna hear from her are 'I do!'"

"You two gonna tie the knot?" asked one of the friends.

Gord answered, "We sure are!" He saw the consternation on her face and quickly added, "Well, she hasn't said yes, yet…but she also hasn't said no."

Josie didn't say anything. She was disturbed by his declaration and twenty minutes later asked him to take her home. She sat silent on her side of the seat all the way to the base.

He parked the car. "You're awful quiet," he said.

She took a deep breath. "Gordon...you shouldn't 'ave told people we're getting married. I told you I'm not nearly ready for that. It embarrassed me. I hope you understand."

"Yeah, I do understand, Josie. It was stupid. It's the drinks, I guess. I'm sorry. It's just...well, you know how I feel about you...I'm in love with you."

Now it's in love. *Not just falling.*

"Okay. You're forgiven."

Back in her room, she thought about marriage—about making a home, say in Calgary, with this man. Going to bed and waking up with him. The thoughts were not altogether unpleasant, but did she want it? What of the things she cherished—her "adventure" in the Air Force, her friendships? She was torn.

She discussed the situation with Olivia.

"He says he is in love with me...he talks about *marrying* me. I like him a lot and he's good-looking but I'm not sure I'm ready to be so...serious. We 'ave known each other barely three weeks.

Olivia asked, "Did you tell him how you feel?"

"Yes, he says it's okay, he won't rush me." She thought for a moment. "He's nice to me, most of the time. Sometimes, with 'is friends and drinking, he doesn't think about my feelings. But usually he's nice."

"Has he asked you to sleep with him?"

"Not...asked. But we neck and he gets hot. We both do. I'm sure he wants it. I can't do that though."

Olivia took in a deep breath. "Jo, there are guys who use the old 'I love you and I want to marry you' stuff, to get girls into the sack. I know from experience. I'm not saying he's doing that, but you should be careful. See if he gives you a ring, maybe."

Josie stared long and hard at her friend. Then she gave a slight nod and said, "Okay. Thank you."

She called Gord and said she wasn't feeling well and couldn't see him that night. For the first time since meeting him, she took the time to think critically. She was certainly not ready to marry and there was no way she was going to have sex with him. Had she just been flattered by the attention? They had gone out together almost every night since they met, and she had had no time to think.

There was something she hadn't told Olivia. No matter how she tried to dislodge him, Danny Tanner still dwelled in a little place in her mind and her heart. She knew she didn't love Gord Schaefer—for she didn't ache for him as she did for Danny. She fell asleep wondering what the point was in continuing the affair.

She had all but decided to end her relationship with Gord when a chance encounter made the decision for her.

*   *   *   *

COMOX—APRIL 26th, 1955

We were two lives going separate ways until our brief encounter at Comox. Then you crossed a room to say hello to me and something shined there. How had I not noticed before that even the air around you was brighter!

At 1750 hours Danny was in the Wets at Comox after a day of instructing. He was with two of his FighterCOp students and one of the other instructors. The next afternoon, Friday, his two-week T.D. at Comox was finished.

"Listen, guys, it's been a gas, but I haven't eaten and I'm a growing boy. I've got to get to the Mess Hall before it closes." He drained his glass as he stood to leave. "See you all in the morning."

Josie had lost track of time and almost missed supper. She hurried to the mess hall without Olivia, who was doing laundry in the barracks and expecting Josie to bring her something to eat.

She was in the line at the steam tables when she spotted him. He was sitting at the rear of the hall, where the FighterCOps from 51 Squadron always sat. She started to take her tray to the farthest table from him she could find, but then, even thinking better of it, she doubled back.

She stood across from him. He was talking to someone beside him and didn't notice her presence.

"'Ello, Danny."

His head snapped up. "Josie Connor…good to see you! How are you?" He smiled his wonderful smile.

"I'm fine, Danny. How about you?"

She thought, *This is a mistake—but he remembers my name, at least.* "Are you just visiting here or, you know, transferred in?"

"Nah. Just on T.D. At 51 AC&W…"

"Ah, I see." she said pensively. "Well I 'ad better go and sit down." She gestured sideways with her tray.

"Do you want to join us?" He started to move a chair for her.

"No—no, I 'ave friends; I'm sitting with them." She started to walk away.

"Okay. It's real good to see you again, Josie," he said to her back.

See you around, Danny. She looked around, spotted some people she knew and sat with them. She forced herself not to look across the room at him as she ate her supper. She had almost finished when he sat on the empty chair across from her.

"Mind if I join you?" he said.

She looked to her tablemates, but they were non-committal. She said, "I guess...yes, go ahead..."

"Thanks. So, Josie Connor, how are you liking the real Air Force?" Pointing at her tray, he added, "And what the heck is this—no cheese with your pie! Didn't I teach you anything in four days and three nights?" He was grinning.

You remember that! She couldn't help but smile with him. "Well, I saw a bone over there on the floor, L.A.C. Tanner. You might want to chew it?" He laughed, rocking back in his chair. She thought, *It's just like on the train.*

"Ya got me!" he admitted, "Anyway, how do you like it here? By the way, you look as great as ever, Josie."

She blushed at the compliment. The Smile distracted her so she had to think about his question.

"How do I...Oh! I love it! It's everything I 'hoped for. This is such a great place. It's just as you told me, the beaches and everything. I just love it!" *Dieu! He has me talking like old friends again. I must stop this—but he is so beautiful!*

He didn't turn off The Smile. "I knew you'd like it." He put a hand over hers. The touch was electric.

"I do. When I think of all the postings...you know? I think this is the best. Everyone 'ere is so friendly, too."

He didn't move his hand, so she gently pulled hers from under it. He looked puzzled for a moment, then smiled again.

"Where have they got you working?"

"I'm in the Orderly Room, at the 'eadquarters building. Do you come to Comox much?" *Please don't hear that. I didn't want to say it. I don't want to know. Yes, I do!*

"No. I've only been here twice. Did I tell you, this was my preference posting, when I left Moisie?"

"Yes. You told me." *There is nothing you told me I don't remember.*

"But I got Vancouver. Close, but no cigar."

Josie had a lot of feelings she was trying to sort out. She could not believe this wasn't some crazy dream. She picked up her tray and stood up. She hadn't touched her dessert.

"I-I 'ave to get going, it's my laundry night." *Is that all I can think of to say?* "It was nice to see you." *See you!* Her legs felt weak as she walked away toward the tray rack. She deposited her tray and dishes, and then belatedly remembered Olivia. She went to the side table to make a sandwich. She didn't look back as she left the building.

Danny stared after her. He said to himself, *Jesus—she's beautiful!*

*   *   *   *

5TH AIR DIVISION, VANCOUVER

When Danny got back to Jericho early Friday evening he called Moe to see if anything new had come up at work. Moe told him Ev had been calling them at home while he was away.

He called Ev on Saturday morning. She was angry because he hadn't once called her from Comox and she was angry because he didn't call when he got back the night before. He sensed she was prepared to pick at anything he said. The call turned into a painful argument and she was sobbing when he hung up.

At the Liaison Office on Monday, Moe mentioned Irene and he were concerned about his treatment of Evelyn. She had apparently been phoning Irene, airing her and Danny's troubles. They were invited to the Morriseys' for supper the coming Friday, but Danny didn't commit, saying he would let Moe know the next day. He intended to call Ev that night, but couldn't face another scene, so he put it off for yet another day.

He phoned her on Tuesday. She told him her parents were out of town and asked if he could come to her house in Ladner. At the house she was at first sullen and argumentative, but later mellowed. In the past when her parents were away he often spent the night, and this time, in the closeness and familiarity of her room, he did make love to her. Then they argued again, and he felt manipulated. She was in tears when he left before midnight and he regretted sleeping with her. He told Moe the next morning he couldn't make it for the Friday supper and he and Ev were having problems.

On Wednesday, Chrissy Manson joined him for coffee at the Ops Center. She asked if there was another girl. He said yes—a girl he liked a lot. She gave him a big hug and said she was happy for him, and he'd better treat his new girl right! She asked if it was anyone she knew and seemed pleased when he said no. They met for drinks in the Wets after work and he was grateful she didn't seem interested in sex. They danced, she wished him happiness, and he left her at eight-thirty.

At work on Thursday, Moe noticed his preoccupation. "Dan, if you don't mind me saying it, you look down. Got a problem?"

Danny didn't know his thoughts were so obvious. He said, "Yeah, Moe, a problem. No, it's not a problem! Well, it might be...I don't know yet."

Moe chuckled. "I always admired that crisp decisiveness of yours."

"Yeah, yeah...get off my case, boss. It's just something I have to work out."

"Girl trouble?"

"Yes. Well, it's about a girl, but I hope it's not trouble. It's no one you know...not Ev. I've never even really dated this one, but damn, I sure want to."

Danny Tanner had never been in love. He had liked many girls, had bedded many girls; but he had never ached to be with any girl as he now ached to be with Josie Connor. She had been constantly on his mind since that ten-minute encounter at Comox. She was there with him at work now—had been in his thoughts even when he was with Evelyn and Chrissy, and he knew she would be everywhere he went. He felt an overwhelming urgency to see her again, to be with her in body as well as in thought. This was something he had never experienced.

The very suddenness of his feeling, his longing, confused him.

Shit, not me...please! I should just forget her. Does she even like me? She was pretty cool when she saw me on Thursday. She did warm up a little, but then she was in a big hurry to get away from me. I have to make *her be interested. Oh Christ, she's going to find someone else if she hasn't already—every son of a bitch at Comox must be after her. I have to see her. I have to try!*

He pictured in his mind the way her gray eyes crinkled when she laughed or smiled, the way her breasts thrust against the fabric of her blouse, the feel of her little hand when he touched it, and he smiled as he heard again the infectious music of her giggle.

C H A P T E R   8

▼

I had never before been so nervous talking to a girl…

COMOX—MAY 4TH

It was Friday afternoon when Josie was called to the phone in the Orderly Room by one of the other clerks. A glance at the clock told her it was 1430 hours.

She answered in the required manner, "AW1 Connor 'ere." Her Sergeant sat only fifteen feet away.

"Hello. Is this Josie Connor?"

She knew the voice; it was Danny. She answered simply, "Yes." She wondered why he would be calling her and she was nervous about taking the call in the office.

He said, "It's Danny here. Danny Tanner…from the train? I'm on the land-line, can you talk?"

"Yes." she said. "I 'ear you okay. I can't talk for long." She could *feel* Sergeant Wilson staring at her back.

"Right, I get it. It's good to hear your voice, Josie. I'm thinking of coming over there for the weekend, tonight actually. I would like to see you; are you going to be around?"

"Um…yes." *Tonight!* She was stunned. "Tonight? What time will you be here?"

"I'll try to get a ferry that'll get me there about eight-thirty or nine. Are you sure you'll be there? It's *you* I want to see. It's the reason I'm coming, if I come." He was prattling nervously, "No, hell, I don't mean *if!* I am coming for sure…if you want me to."

To see me! Or he's not coming? She felt the pain of the past month melting away. As quietly as possible, she said, "Yes. Yes, it will be nice to see you." Quick glance at the Sergeant.

"Okay!" He sounded relieved. "Where can I meet you?"

"I don't know…" She couldn't think.

"How about we meet at the Wets? Eight-thirty or nine. Do you go there?"

"Okay Da…I will be there." *Tonight. Dieu!*

"Good bye now. Can't wait to see you."

"Um, okay, good bye. I…good bye."

"See you later, Josie

When he disconnected, Danny sat and thought, *Jesus! It's happening.*

At Comox, Josie hung up the phone and returned to her desk. *Tonight!* She picked up a folder from the top of a stack and sat, unmoving, with the file in her hand, looking as if she had no idea what to do with it.

Seeing her confusion, Olivia went to her. "Got a problem?"

"No…no…" She still just sat there.

Olivia whispered, "Was it the phone call?" Josie nodded. Olivia looked up at the clock. She called, "Sarge, can Connor and I take our break a few minutes early?"

"More like half an hour early, isn't it?" said the Sergeant.

Olivia rolled her eyes and nodded in Josie's direction. Wilson got the message. "Okay, go…go!" she said with resignation.

In the lunchroom, Olivia asked, "Was the call bad news, Jo?"

Josie looked surprised. "No. Why do you ask that?"

"Well, you were sitting there like a friggin' zombie. I thought you were going to faint or something."

Josie said, "I did almost faint. It was Danny—the guy from the train. He's coming here to see me. He's coming tonight! I'm meeting him in the Wets."

"So, what do you think, is that good or bad? Do you want to see him?"

"I don't know. Yes! I do!" She took a breath. "I didn't tell you, I saw him last Thursday, here in the Mess. He was here on T.D. We had fun…just talking."

"Are you setting yourself up for more pain, Jo?"

"Olivia, I could not possibly hurt more than I 'ave. Yes, maybe I will get hurt, but I saw him and I know I have to try again. I saw him for only about five minutes, and for those five minutes, I was…it was like back on the train!"

Olivia blew her cheeks out. "Hell, kid, I wonder. Who knows, maybe you're right." She smiled.

With resolve, Josie said, "I think I'm smarter now about things…and stronger." Then, suddenly, she became panicky. "Olivia! My clothes!"

"Your clothes. What about your clothes?"

"Do I 'ave anything nice to wear? It's tonight!"

Olivia sagged visibly. "Jesus, Jo, it's only the Wets. I'm sure we can find something suitable. I'll help, okay?" With a wicked grin she said, "Shit-all-to-hell, he's probably some ugly little twerp, anyway."

Josie giggled. "Shut up, you. He's beautiful. You'll see!"

She could not concentrate on her work for the rest of the afternoon. She watched the clock turn slowly toward the 1630 quitting time.

✱   ✱   ✱   ✱

In the Mess Hall after work, Josie sat alone with Gord and told him she didn't wish to see him anymore. She was a bit mystified but not crushed when, for all his professed love, he simply said, "If that's the way you want it."

After supper, she and Olivia spent two hours in the barracks, selecting, laundering and ironing clothes. They decided on a dark gray skirt, mid-calf length, white peasant blouse and low-heeled sandals.

After the final selection, Olivia commented, "Just the outfit for the Wets. It's all washable, in case this guy spills his beer on you, or slobbers all over you."

"Shut up, you. Don't tease me!" said Josie. She grinned as she fiddled with the blouse in front of the mirror.

"Don't be afraid to show a little shoulder, Jo. Hey, you look fabulous. Honest!"

"I 'ope so. All he's ever seen is my uniform." *And my boobs too,* she didn't add. "What time is it?"

Olivia was enjoying the bout of nerves. She said, "It's just after six-thirty. If you hurry, you can get good and smashed before he gets here."

Josie didn't think her joke was funny. "Oh, no, please make sure I don't—or act stupid, okay?" She was pensive for a moment. "Merde! Should I even be doing this, Olivia?"

"Y'know what? I honestly think you should. I had my doubts, after what you've been going through over this guy, but hell, kid, a new start—you never know. And he did call you. Give it a chance, you can always pull out later."

"Maybe the way he talked that last day, maybe it was something he couldn't help."

She had often wondered if Danny had had to end something before he could start something new. He must have had a girlfriend in Vancouver; he was too good-looking not to. She had a sudden thought, "What if he gets 'ere early? I want to be there when he arrives. We should go at…eight, okay? You will come with me?"

"Oh, yeah. I'm not gonna miss this. Calm down, will you? That's my blouse you're getting all sweaty."

*   *   *   *

The Wets was divided into two large rooms: one for men only, the other for Airwomen and guests. The "ladies' side" always had more men than women, contravening the rules. It was Friday and there was the usual large crowd. Josie and Olivia sat at a table for four with Stanley Pawlsky, an Airframe Tech from 407 Squadron. Stan was much taken with Olivia but, like so many others, had to be content just being seen with her, and spending his money for her drinks. Eventually, as many others had, he would realize there were better uses for his time and his money.

Josie had made sure she sat facing the entrance door while she zealously guarded the one empty chair at the table. Stan bought beers for them but she had only taken a couple of sips.

At five to nine, Danny came through the door. He looked around uncertainly.

Josie whispered, "There 'e is! That's him." She stood up and waved a hand over her head. When he spotted her he sent her a smile and waved back before he worked his way around tables to join them.

"Hello, Josie…thanks for being here." Still smiling, he nodded at Olivia and Stan. "Can you guys give me a minute? I'll be right back. I badly need a beer." He patted Josie's shoulder and headed for the bar.

Olivia's eyes were wide as she watched him walk away. "Jo, he's *gorgeous!* I could come in my panties."

Josie hissed, "Olivia! Shh. You see, I told you." She was blushing and trying not to look at Stan Pawlsky.

Danny returned, awkwardly carrying four beers without a tray. Nodding at the empty chair, he asked, "For me?"

Josie said, "We've been saving it for you."

She did the introductions. "Okay…Danny Tanner, this is my friend Olivia, and this is Stan."

He nodded as he distributed the beers. Josie's obvious pleasure at his arrival told him they were going to be okay together and his anxiety dissolved.

"Stan and Ollie, eh?" He grinned. "I used to love your movies."

Olivia laughed, then imitated Oliver Hardy, "A fine mess you've got us into this time, Stanley!" She jabbed Pawlsky with an elbow.

Josie looked puzzled. "Do you already know…?"

Olivia answered for him, "No, Jo. Your friend just made a kinda corny joke." Offering her hand, she said, "Glad to meet you, Tanner—I think."

From that night, Olivia Conti was Ollie.

Danny turned to Stan. "What unit are you with, Stan?"

Stan replied, "407 Squadron. I'm airframe."

"Oh, yeah. The old Lancasters." Turning to Josie, he said, "And *you,* do you know how good, how *great* you look, Josie? Y'know, Ollie, until now, I've only seen her in uniform? She looked great then, but now…what a doll!"

Josie was blushing. She murmured, "Thank you, Danny."

He smiled The Smile. "So you've been here what, over a month? How many boyfriends do I have to beat up to get you all to myself?"

He was relieved to hear Ollie say, "Shit, she's had no time for boyfriends. She's been pining away for some geek she met on a train."

With mock injury, he said, "Hey, watch it! I'd like to be your friend." Then he turned his full attention to Josie.

For ten minutes, Ollie watched them closely as they spoke together softly, progressively excluding her and Stan without noticing or caring. She saw how Josie was at ease, confident, in this boy's company. She thought. *Hey good-lookin,' you'd better treat her right or you'll have Olivia to deal with!*

Snatches of their quiet conversation invaded her thoughts: "…I 'ave been looking forward to seeing you, I was hoping so much to hear from you."

"I've been pretty busy with a new job…and stuff."

"Yes. And 'ow fast the time went by. It's been almost two months already. But it seems like I just *got* here!"

He put an arm around her and pulled her close. He kissed the top of her head. "I'm glad I came."

She leaned her head on his shoulder. In a small voice, she said, "I am, too."

"Lord, look at you two," said Ollie, "when do we book the friggin' church?"

"Whoa!" said Danny. "No more crazy talk!"

Stan finished his beer and got up from the table. "I gotta go, I'm working tomorrow. Good night, girls, nice to meet you, uh…Donny." He headed for the door.

Ollie muttered, "Good." Then she said, "Listen, guys, I see my Scope-Dope friends over there." She looked toward a corner of the room where an upright piano stood, as usual the sole property of the FighterCOps and others from 51 Squadron. She got up with her half beer. "I think I'll leave you guys alone here and go join them." Then she had a thought, "Jo, how about giving me some company in the can?"

"Okay. Excuse me, Danny?"

He made a little "go ahead" gesture.

When they were gone Danny looked over at the group by the piano. He thought, *Looks like a normal G.C.I. Friday night—everybody getting pissed as newts.* A tall guy who he knew was named Zachary, one of his students from the week before, gave a "come on over" wave. Danny smiled and described a female figure in the air with his hands, then pointed to himself and the empty chair beside him. Zachary returned an exaggerated nod and "okay" sign, a circle with thumb and forefinger.

In the washroom, Ollie said, "Well? Are you gonna survive on your own?" She put an arm around Josie's shoulder. "Seriously. You be careful. He seems like a nice enough guy and you sure pick 'em for looks! I can understand why you were so messed up. I'll be here, you know, if you need me?"

"Thank you. You are a best friend. Should I call you Ollie? I think you just got a new name. I like it...Ollie! And you're the one who likes to give names." She smiled. "But you know, I'm so happy he came. When he touched me I just about turned to jelly! But I will be careful. He will 'ave to prove himself to me this time."

"Good attitude. Have fun, kid. But remember, Jell-O's something people eat for dessert."

✳   ✳   ✳   ✳

When Ollie joined the crowd at the piano, it was obvious she was popular. The already half-drunk FighterCOps greeted her warmly and loudly. She shouted, "Okay, all you Misters—and Mistresses! Brethrens and Cisterns!" she waited for the laugh that came with some boos and hisses from the girls. "Let's get down to some serious Friday night drinking and carousing and other good stuff!"

There followed a chorus of, "Roger! Right on! Let's get *smashed!*"

She continued in her best Bette Davis voice, "As Queen Elizabeth would say, '*We* are pleased.' That would be Lizzie the wunth, not our present Liz, she's I guess, hmm…the *tooth?* Yes, Elizabeth the Tooth! Anyhow, *We* are so pleased *we* are going to buy a round for you peasants!"

At this, a couple of people pretended to faint, and others expressed disbelief. One was heard to say, "Ollie must have won the Irish," another added, "Or she stole a beer truck!"

"Jake my man, here is some money—be good and do the honors at the bar, would you? A beer for each and all." She chuckled. "Shit-all-to-hell, if I were to go there, even *if* I knew the way, I may not even be recognized!"

A loud cheer and some deep bows followed. She sat regally in Jake's former chair.

After they were all sitting again, enjoying the fruits of Ollie's rare magnanimity, somebody inquired, "Where's Josie?"

"She's tied up for awhile." Ollie glanced back at the table. Josie and Danny were sitting head-to-head in conversation. Josie was laughing at something he said.

Following her glance, one of the girls said, "Oh, shit. She's with that Danny Tanner—Lover-boy. I was stationed with him at St. Maggies. He's wild as hell, but a *doll,* eh?"

Ollie said, "Lover-boy?"

"Hell, yes. Everybody wanted him, and lots of them *got* him. You know what I mean."

Another girl spoke up, "I don't agree. I know him, too. He and his friends used to come to Lac St. Denis from Moisie. He's not so bad!"

"Well, I've sure heard otherwise…"

"Bull! He always…well, I've *heard* he always treats girls well. I think he's a nice guy, and a lot of fun."

"You've got your opinion, I've got mine."

Ollie wondered at these varying opinions.

A little later, Josie came over. "We're going for a drive. He has a car, it's at the gate."

"Will I see you anytime soon? Like before lunch tomorrow?"

Josie answered with a broad grin, a blush, and an exaggerated shrug.

Ollie saw Danny was waiting by the door with Josie's coat. "Have fun but please, please—do *not* tell me about it."

Josie was already hurrying to the door.

As they walked to the main gate, Danny said, "I like your friend. She seems to be a fun type. Not so sure about her friend Stanley, though."

"Olivia is fun, but she's crazy sometimes! She 'as been a wonderful friend ever since I came here. I love her so! She's beautiful, eh? She doesn't like Stan, Danny. He just hangs around. A lot of the guys do—they all want to be with her." She looked up at him. "I didn't tell you yet, you look 'andsome tonight, my L.A.C." He was wearing slacks, a polo shirt, and a red windbreaker with knitted cuffs and waistband.

"Why, thank you, my AW2."

"I'm AW1 now." She said it with mock pride. "You look like James Dean, with that jacket."

He laughed. "I wish! Any idea where we can get something to eat? I left Jericho right after work."

"The best would be in Courtenay. Or we could just go to the snack bar at the Rec Center. It's open late Fridays."

"Nah...no snack bar. We'll go to Courtenay." He pulled her close and grinned down at her. "I'm hoping to find a tunnel where we can park."

It took her a moment to catch on. "A tunnel?" Then it dawned. "Oh! I don't know if there are any of those around 'ere—but do we need a tunnel? There are woods and stuff to park in." *You are shameless, Josie Connor.* She then said, seriously, "Danny...we're just joking...about that stuff?"

He stopped walking and turned her to him. "Of course we are. We'll never do anything you don't want. That's a promise, Josie. If I have my way, we're gonna be together for a long time, so there's no rush. Okay?"

Together a long time! "Yes, okay! Thank you. The night on the train, in my berth...I-I'm just not ready. Do you understand?" *I'm getting closer, though!*

He smiled down at her. "Yes, I do understand. Don't worry, and please don't let anything like...you know...come between us."

In the small parking lot outside the gate, he stopped by a forty-nine Ford. "Here's the old bomb. I don't have a pass to get it onto the base." He held the passenger door for her.

*   *   *   *

Olivia—Ollie—stayed in the Wets till closing time. She had drunk enough beer to affect her more than she liked. When she got to the barracks at one o'clock, she had no trouble falling into a deep sleep.

Later, Josie woke her up coming in the door. Ollie groaned and looked up.

"Sorry, I tried to be quiet," said Josie. She wore Danny's jacket over her coat. "It got cold out there."

Ollie turned a lamp on. "S'okay. What time is it?" She groped for her watch. "I feel like a friggin' den mother or something." She looked at the watch. "Jesus! Five o'clock!" She sat up. "Shit-all-to-hell! Where have you...what have you been *doing* all night..."

"Oh, just sitting and talking. Is it truly so late?" She looked tired but contented.

Wide-eyed, Ollie shrieked, "Sitting and frigging *talking?*" She flopped back onto the bed. "Hell, Jo!"

"Some necking, too, some great necking, by the way. It was wonderful, Olivia. He is wonderful. I am wonderful! I love 'im!" She did a waltz around the room, holding his jacket like a dance partner. She sang, "I love 'im I love 'im I lo-ove him..."

Ollie rolled over, her back to the room, pillow over her head. "I get the message. Go to friggin' bed!"

At eleven o'clock Josie was called to the phone in the hallway.

"Hello. It's Danny, eh?" Who else would phone her today? "How are you, my L.A.C.? Do you know how late we were?" She was sitting on the hall floor, one hand holding the receiver, the other hugging her drawn up knees.

"Oh, yeah, when I went to get a room the Orderly Corporal told me all about the time—and he wasn't exactly polite about it! I woke the poor guy up at five A.M. It's okay though, I told him some phony story. How are you feeling, Jo?"

"I am fine. *Really* fine! I think I'm old enough to stay up late. What story did you tell him? You didn't say you were out with a nurse, did you?" She giggled at her fine joke.

"Hey, I should have thought of that! I think I told him I was on a special mission or something. Don't know if he bought any of it, but I got a room, anyway."

She doubled over, giggling. "Danny! I think I believe you—special mission! Only you!"

"A guy does what a guy has to do, Jo."

"And you always find some funny way! I have your jacket."

"Good. It's the only one I brought. Are you ready to eat?"

"Yes! I'm hungry. My bad habit from the train. Could we go to the snack bar? They make good fries. Can Olivia come with us? She might not want to eat, though. I think she got drunk." More giggles. "She was all worried about me—out with a big, bad FighterCOp L.A.C. I'll bring your jacket. Could you give us fifteen minutes?"

They went to the snack bar. Ollie went too, but she couldn't eat a thing.

Danny stayed for the weekend. The girls showed him around the area, with Josie proudly pointing out landmarks, reminding them of how he had been the tour guide on the train trip. Ollie looked on, amused, correcting her when necessary. Josie was pleased when he took her hand whenever he could. He seemed not the least self-conscious when doing so.

They walked the streets of Courtenay, hiked a trail by the Puntledge River, ran over sandbars at Kye Bay, strolled among the fishing boats and yachts at the Government Dock. They skipped stones at Miracle Beach, waged a snowball fight at Forbidden Plateau and watched eagles soar at Cape Lazo. They ate almond chicken from Jan's, Combo-Burgers from Bud's and fried oysters from the old hotel at Fanny Bay. They drank beer at the Lorne Hotel, sipped whiskey sours at the Arbutus and chatted with a myna bird at the Elk.

Later, they dropped Ollie off at the barracks and spent time together sitting in his car.

*   *   *   *

Sunday afternoon at Miracle Beach, Josie was wading barefoot along a rocky bit of shore when she spotted a starfish among some deeper rocks. She hiked up her cotton print skirt and waded out to get a closer look. Ollie and Danny were higher up on the dry sand, watching her. He was carrying Josie's shoes.

Ollie said, "Tanner, walk with me a bit." She led him by the arm a few steps along the beach. She looked out at the water as she said, "Danny, I don't know you well yet—but I have to say something. Okay?"

"Shoot, Ollie."

They stopped walking. "You seem like a nice guy, Danny. I can't help kind of liking you."

"The feeling's mutual, I think you're okay, too. I'm glad Josie has you for a friend."

She looked him squarely in the eye. "Good. I hope we can be real friends. I've thought a lot about what I have to say now..." She paused. "Tanner, do you have any idea how much that girl likes you? No, that's bullshit—how much she *loves* you!"

He hesitated before he said; "She's never said." He was pensive as he went on, "I believe I do know, Ollie. I'm not sure what to do about it..." He looked out at Josie. She was thigh deep and studying the water intently, having some trouble balancing on the slippery rocks while she held her bunched-up skirt in one hand.

Ollie was watching her, too, as she said, "Just try not to hurt her. She's such a great kid. Just don't ever hurt her, Danny Tanner." She was remembering the opinions of him she had heard in the Wets.

Just then they heard the subject of their discussion.

"Eeek! You should come *see*! 'E's *moving!*" Her face was an inch from the water. Her skirt, forgotten, was floating around her thighs, sodden.

Ollie looked at Danny, then back at Josie. "Jesus! Isn't she something?" she whispered.

He shook his head. "She sure is." He said to himself, *And you think she's in love. I'll have to tell her how I feel! Never done it before...*

Ollie called to her, "Get the hell up here, before you drown, you silly bitch!"

Later, alone in the car, when he held her in his arms and told her of his love, Josie's eyes filled with tears of joy. "Oh, Danny...you 'ave made me so happy. I...I loved you since the second day on the train." She clung to him.

"You didn't tell me."

"No...I should 'ave. But you're here now. I will love you always, my Danny Tanner! I wish you didn't 'ave to go back to Jericho. I wish you could stay forever."

*   *   *   *

He came to Comox again the next two weekends.

The evenings were warming, so the FighterCops had started the almost nightly parties at 51 Beach. They would end the days partying with whatever crew of FighterCOps decided there was an excuse to celebrate. Danny and Josie sometimes slipped away, after making sure Ollie could get a ride home. They would sit in the car for hours, talking, touching, holding—content in their love.

*   *   *   *

On Friday of the third week, he called her at the barracks. It was five-thirty.

Josie was a little breathless when she got to the phone. "Hello, my Danny. Are you coming tonight?"

"No, not this week, Honey. I've got a fastball tournament on the base at Sea Island. It's all weekend. I don't want to let the guys down. I am sorry and I'm going to miss you."

She was quiet for a moment. She hadn't considered he still had a life that didn't involve her. She tried not to show her disappointment. "It's okay, Darling. I'll miss you, too. Will I see you next week?"

"You sure will! I'll be there with bells on. I hope you understand, Jo, about the tournament."

"Yes, I do. I'll miss you terribly, though." They talked for another ten minutes.

Back in the room, Ollie could see she was down. "What's up, Buddy?" she asked.

When Josie explained, she suggested, "Why don't you and I go over to Van tomorrow. Do you think he would mind? Hell, I'd like a change…get away from here for a couple of days."

Josie pounced on the idea.

They hitchhiked to Nanaimo and caught a ferry that got them to Vancouver at one-thirty, then took a streetcar the length of Granville Street to Marpole. A bus over an old swing bridge and past some dairy farms got them to the base at Sea Island by four o'clock. They got a ride to the ball field in a Service Police vehicle, after some light flirting by Ollie.

*   *   *   *

VANCOUVER

There was a game in progress on the field. They spotted him playing third base. Nervously, Josie said, "Do you think 'e will mind us coming?"

"Why should he? We'll say hi, and if he doesn't want us here, we'll say goodbye. Then we can go shopping downtown."

They took seats in the small wooden bleacher on the third base side.

Ollie commented, "Man, they won't be bunting much on him; he plays close to the batter. Do you know much about the game?"

"Not much…will you show me?" If Danny played it, she wanted to know about it.

"This is called softball, but the ball is not soft, just bigger."

"Oh." She was trying to understand such logic.

Danny's team got the third out to end the inning. Their first batter came to the plate. He struck and missed at the first two pitches.

Josie said, "Does 'e ever pitch it fast. Dieu!"

When the batter popped up to the first baseman, Ollie muttered, "Swinging way too hard. Trying to kill it."

Danny came to bat next. As he approached the batters' box, Josie shouted, "Danny! Hello!" He looked up in surprise, then grinned and waved at her. He took his place at the plate.

It was a quiet moment till Josie yelled, "Don't kill it, Danny!" It came out as "Dannee."

He stepped back from the plate. *Don't kill it? Is she kidding me?* He stepped up again and took a couple of practice swings. The pitch came in low and inside. Ball one.

"It's okay, Danny. Try 'arder!" shouted Josie. She was half standing.

Ollie pulled her down and started to explain. "Jo, he doesn't have to swing if the pitch isn't…"

The next pitch was high and out. He let it go.

Josie whispered, "I don't think he's much good at this, Ollie."

"But, I'm trying to tell you…"

The third pitch was on the inside corner. He screamed a line drive over third base. It curved foul by three feet and rolled to the outfield fence.

Josie was awestruck. "Did you see 'ow hard he *hit* it? It goes so far!" She stood up and yelled, "Okay, Danny—*kill it!* Make a 'ome run, Danny. You can do it!" Ollie was terribly embarrassed.

His teammates picked up on what was taking place. They started ragging him. "Come on, Dannee. You can do it, Dannee. Hit a home run, Dannee!"

He stepped out. *Shit, this is all I need.* He tried not to start laughing. The umpire said, "Come on, batter, let's play ball."

Now from the opponents' bench, "Dannee! Dannee! Dannee!"

Shit!

He squared around as the next pitch left the windmiller's hand. He laid down a bunt and beat the throw to first base.

Josie yelled, "Good one, Danny, 'ow to *trick* those guys!" She was jumping up and down. Ollie hid her face in her hands.

From the benches came, "Good one, Dannee! Good trick, Dannee!"

In his final two at bats, he grounded to short and lined a single between center and right field. He made a couple of tough plays in the field, impressing Ollie. His team won by two runs.

After the game, he waved the girls down to the bench, where he was changing his shoes. He stood to give Josie a hug.

"Hey, babe. This is a great surprise. How did you get here?" A teammate came by and patted him on the rump.

"Good game, Wrigley," he said.

"Thanks, Norm, you too." He noticed a lot of the players were lingering on the field longer than they usually did. The pitcher from the team they just played came by.

"Bring your own cheerleaders, Dan?"

Then his own second baseman, "How to go, Wrigley. Or should I say 'Dannee'?"

He blushed as he led the girls away from the crowd. "C'mon, my car's over here." At the car he put an arm around each of them. "Hey, this is great! How'd you get here, anyway?" He kissed both girls on the cheek. From the field behind them they heard, "Way to go, Dannee!"

Josie said, "We 'itchhiked. We got to Nanaimo just in time to catch a ferry. Then we got a streetcar, a bus, and then Ollie got us a ride with the S.P.s. It was fun."

Ollie asked, "Wrigley? Where does that come from?"

"Aw, it's just a thing they call me on the team. This was our last game tonight. We planned to go to Jericho for a beer in the Wets. Would that be okay?"

At Jericho, he dropped the girls off at the Wets and went to the barracks to shower and change.

They were sitting, drawing stares from other tables as strangers do, when they saw him come through the door. He stopped at a table and spoke to a girl there, then at another, where he spoke to a group. His path took him past where some of his teammates were seated, and he was treated to a chorus of, "Oh, DannEE. Look, Dannee got all dressed up!" He sent them a middle finger.

At the girls' table, he said, "Do you want to go and sit with the team?"

Josie looked at Ollie. "Let's," she said.

The players had pushed three tables together, and had covered them with beers. Danny pulled another table to the end of the row and made introductions all around as he held chairs for Josie and Ollie.

Pulling bills from his wallet, he asked, "How much do I owe?"

Someone replied, "We're starting with two bucks each, Wrigley." He added a five and a one to the pile on the center table. "I've got the girls' too."

With the camaraderie of a close knit team, they set about quenching their thirst and unwinding. The team's games of the day, and some from seasons past, were replayed again and again as the evening wore on. Whenever the beer on the tables got down to what was considered a dangerously low level, it was quickly replenished with a new round. The decibel level increased as the players shouted to be heard over one another. Ollie observed, "If you guys stay here bullshitting long enough, your two-run squeaker today'll turn into a ten-run slaughter!" Her remark drew cries of outrage. When Josie inquired into the name "Wrigley" she was informed it was because of Danny's habit of adding sticks of Spearmint to his wad, till, by the end of a game, he would have four or five in his mouth.

At seven-thirty the girls went to find a room in the barracks. When they returned they found the tables had lost some ball players, but gained some other partygoers. One of the newcomers was a good-looking blonde girl, the one Danny spoke to when he first came in, and whom Ollie noticed was paying a lot of attention to Josie and Danny. She introduced herself while they were up jiving to Bill Haley and *Shake Rattle and Roll*.

"Hi, we weren't introduced; I'm Olivia. My friend is Josie. Are you in the Air Force here?"

The girl smiled. "I'm Christine…just call me Chrissy. Yes, I'm Air Force, a FighterCOp. It's nice to meet you. Your friend is real pretty. So are you, Olivia."

"Thank you. And you, too, Chrissy. We're stationed at Comox—just here for the weekend to watch the ball tournament."

"Oh. Are you friends of Danny's?"

"We are."

The girl looked thoughtful and said, "But, Josie, she's more than just a friend, right?"

"That's right."

Chrissy gave a little nod, smiled again, and turned back to the right fielder.

Ollie thought, *Interesting.*

As the evening wore on more girls arrived, and soon the table was mostly couples. Second base, whose name was Doug, was still without a girl, and showing a lot of interest in Ollie. When Danny returned to the table after a dance, she slipped him a note. It read: *2B—M?—AF?*

Danny read it under the edge of the table. He said, "Let's dance, Ollie." He led her to the dance floor. The jukebox was playing Doris Day's *Secret Love.*

As they waltzed Danny said, "Your answers are yes and no. His name's Doug Carpenter, he's married with a couple of kids, and he's a civvy firefighter from the airport."

She nodded and said, "Shit, all the good-looking ones."

When the dance was finished, she exchanged seats with Danny, moving her away from second base, who got the message and moved off to sit beside a redhead he had danced with earlier.

*   *   *   *

At ten-thirty the party was breaking up. Danny informed the girls the team's next game, a quarterfinal, was at eight o'clock in the morning, so he would have to leave for Sea Island at six-thirty. The girls groaned, but he offered a solution. "Does either of you drive? I can ride with one of the guys and leave you the car. Then you can come out later."

Josie looked to Ollie, who said, "Yeah, I drive, but I don't know the way, though."

Chrissy spoke up. "I do!" She offered to ride with them and show the way. It was settled. The girls did *not* promise to be there for the first inning.

The team won the quarterfinal game. Josie, Ollie and Chrissy arrived at the field in time to see the last three innings. Even with Chrissy navigating they had made a wrong turn and ended up at the civilian terminal, located on the far side of the airport. Chrissy was terribly embarrassed, but as she so often did, Ollie jumped to the rescue.

"It's not her fault," she said, "it's mine. Somebody must have moved a cow on me. I just know I had them all memorized from yesterday!"

In the next game, the semi final, the team was beaten by five runs and eliminated from the tournament. The three girls had a great day, rooting for "our guys." Josie and Chrissy especially took to each other. Before she left with her right fielder, Chrissy whispered to Ollie, "Dan's a lucky guy. She's wonderful!"

He later took the two girls to a Chinese restaurant near the Burrard bridge before dropping them off at the ferry terminal. Danny and Josie kissed goodbye at the top of the passenger stairs, and as she and Ollie boarded the ferry, Josie said, "I think Chrissy used to be Danny's girl."

*   *   *   *

The next Friday Danny arrived at Comox with news that his close friend, a FighterCOp he had known since Clinton, was transferred to Comox from Foymont, Ontario. He was to arrive at Comox in a week.

"His name's Russ. You'll both love him. He's a great guy, and a great friend. We're real close."

"Is he ugly and stupid like you, Tanner?" said Ollie.

"You'd better like him. He's gonna be around a lot," said Danny, with finality.

*   *   *   *

VANCOUVER

Danny's friend, Russ, managed a couple of extra days off and arrived on the coast two days early. Danny met his train and they did the rounds of Vancouver's nightspots. They were both feeling the liquor as they sat eating chow mein in Mei Ling's. Danny was trying to set up a double date for the next Friday at Comox.

"No damn way!" said Russ. "No blind dates. No way, no way! Am I making it clear enough?" He could not forget the two hundred-pound cousin of one of Danny's girls, a blind date set up by his buddy as a gag. He also figured Danny had had ample time to think up revenge for some stunt or other he pulled over the years.

"Tanner, you bastard, you're trying to *get* me again! I can feel it."

"I'm not, Q…honest I'm not."

"You say this babe of yours is real good looking, right?"

"She is. But so is Ollie…"

"Bullshit! You know and I know the good-looking women always hang around with ugly ones. No way—period! End of discussion, stupid. What kind of a name is 'Ollie,' anyway? Sounds like a real winner, Champ."

Danny sighed. "Tell you what, shit-for-brains; she probably won't like you anyway, you're not exactly Tony Curtis you know. But here's what we'll do—I'll have the girls meet me in the Wets and you can stay at a distance and scope her out. If she looks okay then you join us. If she's a dog, you can just take off—deal?"

"Okay. But I think I'll bring a leash along, and some Dr. Ballards in case she shows up hungry. Christ, is she at least paper-trained?"

"You won't be sorry, Russ."

"Tanner, you bastard, I still think you're getting me again. Besides, it depends what shift they put me on. I might be working Friday night. Probably should hope I am!"

"Another drink, Q?"

"Yeah, a double. Maybe I can stay drunk till Friday."

"You'll see."

"I'll see…shit!"

CHAPTER 9

▼

UNCLASS PERS FILE—d. 10/6/55
L.A.C. KNIGHT, Russell Charles. R.C.A.F. #213046, FCO, Gp. 3.
Born 18/10/35. Enl. 02/11/52 Male Cauc. Ht. 5' 8 ½"/Wt. 155/
Hr. Brn/Eyes Brn
Eff. 10/6/55 51 AC&W Sqn., R.C.A.F. Stn. Comox, B.C.

RUSS KNIGHT

Russ could not claim any place as his "home town." Born in the Toronto suburb of Scarborough, he was the second oldest in his family, the oldest boy. His father died in a German P.O.W. camp in 1943 after bailing out of a Halifax bomber over Holland. The next year, when he was nine, his mother abandoned the family and later died of an overdose of pills. The orphaned boy, then barely nine years old, spent the next eight years of his life in orphanages and foster homes in various towns in southwestern Ontario, separated from his sisters and brother.

Russ learned to take care of himself in the school grounds and alleys of the many towns he was sent to live in, taking some beatings and dishing some out. With little adult male guidance as he grew up, he worked out his own code for living and surviving. As a teen he was, of necessity, old beyond his years. While other kids were being young, he was usually working at one or more after-school jobs.

His slim good looks made him attractive to women but he had little time to indulge them. He did have some infrequent sexual encounters, usually with older, more experienced women he met at his jobs. His first partner was an office clerk at a G.M. dealership where he worked as a lot boy, the second the wife of a traveling salesman, who seduced him when he delivered her groceries. (For months, she phoned in almost daily orders to the I.G.A. store and they would have quick, furtive sex with his delivery bicycle parked in the driveway. Russ was forced to change jobs to escape her passion and allow the scratches on his back to heal.)

With the blessing and required approval of his last social worker, he enlisted in the R.C.A.F. two weeks after reaching the eligible age of seventeen. He could barely remember his father, but Russ figured it would be right for him to follow in his footsteps and so joined the Air Force.

Russ met Danny Tanner on a sidewalk outside a hotel beer parlor in Stratford, Ontario. It was on a Saturday afternoon and he had hitchhiked the forty miles from Clinton, to have a couple of beers and see the sights. He walked out of the hotel in time to see Danny doing battle with four locals. He was holding his own, but it was inevitable he would end up taking a beating. Recognizing Danny from around the base, Russ joined in with all his hundred and fifty five pounds. He tapped one of the locals on the shoulder. When the man turned to him, Russ promptly kicked him in the knee, instantly making it a three on two contest. When the remaining locals turned to see their companion crawling away in pain, Danny took advantage, flattening one with a clubbing right, and then throwing another to the ground.

Before they could get up, Russ was back-to-back with Danny. "I got your back, man!" He kicked out viciously just missing one of the downed combatants who was getting to his feet. "The other guys are on the way—any second now!" he shouted.

"I'm with ya!" said Danny. Then, to the enemy, he said, "You guys want some more? Come and get it, you pricks!"

Now the locals, hands more than full with the two crazy out-of-towners, decided to depart the scene before "the other guys" arrived. They fled running down the street. Russ, who felt barely warmed-up, started after them. After a few steps he was brought up short by Danny's grip on his jacket.

"Hey, *whoa*, pal—I think they got the message," said Danny.

"Fuck you. Let go of me!" He twisted from the grasp and stepped back from Danny. He grinned a lop-sided grin, "I wasn't really goin' far, anyway."

Danny asked, "Just what *other guys* are on the way?"

"You're kidding aren't you? There are no other guys, stupid."

"Yeah, I get it. Hey, thanks for the help—I got in a little deep there. It started with me and just one of those guys."

"It's okay. I didn't like the four-on-one shit. I just hope you were the good guy. I've seen you around, haven't I, Champ? You're at Clinton, in the Air Force?"

"Yeah, I'm on the FCO...FighterCOp course. I've seen you, too, around the base."

"I'm FighterCOp, too, I got here two weeks ago. You're that Tanner everybody says is real tough, aren't you?"

"I don't know about the tough bullshit, but I am Dan Tanner, and you...?"

"Russ. Russell Q. Knight." He offered a hand. "Jesus, Champ—*In a little deep?* Shit, I'm surprised you were still on your feet!" He displayed his lopsided grin again. "What the hell did you do, screw one of their sisters?"

"Never saw those guys before, but the sister's a definite possibility," said Danny with a grin of his own. "I'd like to buy you a beer, Mr. Knight. Let's go back in. What the hell does the 'Q' stand for?"

"Sounds like a plan, Champ, but there may be more than four goofs in this town—they could come back with reinforcements. We'd better find another hotel. And listen, no more fights, okay? I'm not a tough guy like you. There is no Q, stupid."

Still grinning, Danny said, "Hey! Easy with the 'stupid,' man. I've still got some left, you know."

Russ grinned back. "Yeah, you could kick the shit outta me...but you still wouldn't be any smarter."

Danny looked over the irreverent Mr. Knight. He saw a wiry-built boy with wavy, almost-black hair; dark eyes below thick black brows—and a mouth always poised for an ironic crack, a cocky comeback or a winning grin. "Fair enough, Russel Q. Knight."

They started down the street in search of another hotel.

"I drink Red Cap Ale, Champ."

"Fair enough, Russ."

"If they don't have Red Cap, Molson Ex will be okay."

"Okay, Russ."

"You got a smoke on ya?"

"Don't use them, Russ."

"Shit!"

So a friendship was born.

A couple of months after they met, Danny and Russ found themselves serving as rookie FighterCOps on the same crew in the AC&W squadron at St. Margarets, New Brunswick. Both were next transferred to an isolated G.C.I. at Moisie, in Northern Quebec, where they maneuvered their way onto the same crew again. During their two years as crew and barracks-mates, in Russ' eloquent words, they "fucked, fought and faked" their way all over the Maritime Provinces and Quebec. (In mixed company, it was "screwed, scrapped, and scammed.") Their trips to Montreal, to spend accumulated days off or parts of annual leave, were especially legend. After two or three nights raising hell in the city's all-night bars, they were broke and would hitchhike the few miles north, to Lac St. Denis, a radar station in the heart of the Laurentian resort area. St. Denis had a disproportionate number of Airwomen—outnumbering the men four-to-one. As well, at the nearby ski resorts they had their choice of the many pretty bunnies. The place was a natural destination for two born pack leaders.

Danny had ample opportunity to repay Russ for his timely rescue on that Stratford sidewalk.

Early one January morning at Moisie he probably saved Russ from freezing by pulling him from a snow bank where he had passed-out—with the air temperature at minus thirty-five. When he thawed-out and quit shivering in their shared barracks room, Russ looked up at a worried Danny at his bunk side and said, "Fuck you, Tanner."

Danny soon discovered his friend's willingness somewhat outstripped his fighting skill. On more than one occasion, when Russ took on a foe larger either in size or number, he jumped into the fray to even things up. Every so often, just to keep his buddy from becoming too cocky, and if the odds were more or less even, he stood by and let him win or lose on his own.

One such incident occurred in Halifax, and became part of the Tanner-Knight legend. Russ tried to steal the girlfriend of a sailor at a dance out at Bedford. They fought, and soon he was on his back with the sailor on top about to do some serious damage. At that point Russ shouted, "Hold it, willya—there's a big rock under my back!" The sailor loosened his grip, whereupon Russ jumped to his feet and kicked him in the groin, ending the fight. He walked away with Danny and their group, stating, "Y'know, guys, we got a real stupid Navy!" The girl was nowhere to be found afterward, having left the premises with another sailor during the fight.

There developed between Danny and Russ a sometimes eerie reciprocity of thought and action they both knew existed but could not explain in words. The two boys cherished and held close the bond that held the friendship together as they moved haltingly toward manhood.

CHAPTER 10

▼

And the fun and games began. Didn't we let the good times roll...

R.C.A.F. STATION COMOX—JUNE 5TH

Russ Knight stood at the service window at the Orderly Room. It was a Wednesday morning and he was checking in to his new station. An Airman came to the window and Russ pushed his transfer orders across the counter.

"L.A.C. Knight. I'm transferred in—to 51 AC & W Squadron," said Russ.

The Airman said, "Just a sec..." He looked back to the room. He pointed to Russ and called, "Josie, I think this is the L.A.C. Knight you're expecting."

Russ saw a pretty blonde Airwoman approach the counter. She said, "Thank you, Carl, let me look after this guy, okay?" She smiled up at Russ.

"Hey, things are looking up!" said he.

Josie smiled again. "You're Russ, aren't you. Danny Tanner's friend?"

"Yeah, that's me. Oh, I get it, you must be Josie. Dan said you worked at the headquarters building and you're real good-looking, and he's so right. I'm happy to meet you!

As always in the face of a compliment, Josie blushed. She became businesslike. "Here is your signing-in sheet. I see you don't 'ave to report to 51 Squadron till Friday, so you will 'ave lots of time to do your signing-in. For a room in the barracks, you go to the Station Warrant Officer's office." She pointed to her left. "It's just down the hall, that way. Wait here just one minute, Russ." She took his orders, went to a cabinet, and got a large ledger-like book. She marked something down, went to a file cabinet and took out some forms. Before returning to the counter, he saw her go to a desk and speak to a dark-haired L.A.W. They both looked at him for a moment.

Back at the counter, she said, "Here's a map, and some information about the station. This is your signing-in form; I marked all the sections you 'ave to go to. I already told you where to go for a room so that's everything, I think. Bring this form back 'ere after it's all signed." She smiled at him again. "Did you come on the train, Russ?"

"Yeah, I did. It's my first time west of Ontario. Heck of a trip."

"Isn't it wonderful? It was my first time, too—when I came out from Aylmer. Danny was with me. 'Ow did you like it at...Foymont? It's in Ontario, isn't it?"

"You know, it's just another G.C.I., same old, same old. But this is new for me, actual flying squadrons." He showed her his one-sided grin. "Airplanes and everything! It'll be my first flying base."

He looked at the map. "Where's the G.C.I.? The AC&W unit?"

"Oh, it's not on the map, it's outside the base. I should 'ave told you. You have to catch a vehicle, I think at the main gate. If you phone them they'll send transport. Your barracks are here on the station, though."

The L.A.W. left her desk and came to a nearby file cabinet. She looked toward them, then returned to her desk.

Josie saw Russ looking past her, over her shoulder. She glanced back. "Oh. She's Olivia. We call her Ollie." She turned. "Ollie, come here. This is Danny's friend, Russ Knight."

She's Ollie? Christ almighty, she's a dream! Tanner, you wonderful sonofabitch!

When Ollie approached them he played it cool. "So you're Ollie. I think Dan mentioned your name. Glad to meet you."

"Glad to meet you, too, Russ. Any friend of Danny's...and all that."

Josie suggested, "Maybe after work we could get together, at the Wets or the snack bar..." She felt Ollie's shoe press on her foot behind the counter. She slipped her foot from under the shoe and stepped, not too gently, on Ollie's. "We can at *least* make you feel welcome, Russ. Ollie, you would love to come. Wouldn't you?" More pressure with the foot, while she ignored a dirty look.

"Oh, yeah, sounds like fun," said Ollie. She turned and started back toward her desk, saying over her shoulder to Russ, "Well, guess I'll see you later." She glared at Josie.

Russ said, "Let's make it the Wets, then. I'll probably *need* a beer or two after slogging all over the base with this." He waved the signing-in papers.

She pointed out a spot on the map. She said, "The Airmen's Club is..."

He interrupted, chuckling; "You don't have to show me. I've never had any trouble finding the Wets—on *any* station. What time are you gonna be there?"

"How about seven?"

"Sounds good. Make sure you bring…you know…" He indicated Ollie with a nod.

*   *   *   *

Russ was waiting in the men's side, sitting with a couple of FighterCops from 51, when the girls got to the Wets. Josie looked in from the other room and he quickly got up and joined her where she and Ollie were sitting at a table with two girls and a guy. He held a chair for Josie before he sat down.

There was no chair open next to Ollie, so he sat beside Josie, who introduced him to the others; Michelle Kobiashi, a cute Japanese-Canadian introduced as "Mitch," Carrol Menzies, a heavy-set blonde, and Jake MacDonald, a redhead with an obvious Cape Breton accent. Mitch and Jake were FighterCops at 51 Squadron. Carrol was a Supply Tech.

Russ soon became aware Ollie was making a point to appear uninterested in any conversation with him. He had noticed the look she gave Josie in the Orderly Room earlier. When he asked where she was from, a common question when Air Force people met, she replied, "Back east." Asked where back east, she said, "Ontario." Russ countered by claiming he grew up "in a houseboat on the ocean in Saskatchewan." *Screw you, babe.*

Josie could see Ollie had decided to be difficult, so she said, "Russ, she's from Sault Ste. Marie." Looking sternly at Ollie she said, "Okay?" She knew the problem—Ollie disliked having anyone line her up with male company, preferring to choose her own. For her part, Josie was anxious to hear all she could about Danny, and here was his friend of three years. She expected Ollie, as a friend, to be a little more helpful. It wasn't as though she was being asked to date him.

"So, Russ, you were at Clinton, St. Margarets *and* Moisie the same times as Danny?" she asked.

"Yeah, I get all the bad luck. And now I'm stuck on the same coast with him."

Jake asked, "Did you know Gus Grayson? He was at Moisie and St. Maggies. I'm not sure just when…"

"Oh, yeah. Gus and Danny and I were drinking buddies. I've never met anyone as haywire, or as intelligent. He's a hell of a good FighterCop, knows his stuff. Where'd you know Gus?" He lit a Players cigarette and offered the pack around. Jake and Mitch each took cigarettes.

"I was up at Moisie," Jake said, "I got there right after you were posted out to Foymount. R.J. Lang? He was at St. Margarets, too."

"Crazy little fart. Another good FighterCop, though. I hear Tom Hanley's here, and he's a Sergeant now? And Gil Potter, came here a few months ago, from Foymont?"

"Sergeant Hanley was posted out. He's instructing at Clinton. Gil's on my crew. There's probably a lot of people you know here."

"Right, there usually is. But Jake, here we are, sitting with four lovely babes, and all we can do is tell 'I-know-him-he-knows-you' stories?" Russ knew there would always be someone in the FighterCOp trade he knew, or had heard of, as he got transferred around the country.

He turned to Carrol and Mitch. "So, are you two Scope-Dopes, too?" When they replied, he turned to Josie and Ollie. "I know you two are far superior beings—Clerk Admin! You're the ones who get to read all our dirty little service records. Ooh, scary!" He noted the faint smile on Ollie's face. "And you, Josie, cannot wait for me to start talking about the love of your life, can you?"

"I want to know *everything!*" she exclaimed.

"Everything? You sure about that? I know some pretty nasty stuff, y' know. Like, what about all the girlfriends?"

"Not them! Yes, them, too. Does 'e 'ave lots?" *Does he still have lots*, she didn't ask.

"Nahh. He's too friggin' ugly. All he ever got were my rejects anyway. You're the first good-looking babe he ever met on his own, and I bet he had to chase you till you caught him, right?" He saw Ollie's smile crack a little wider.

"I guess I'll 'ave to be happy to be his 'good-looking babe' for now." *Is every girl a 'babe' to these two?* "And you're right. I chased him for three thousand miles! Up and down a train, from one end to the other! He got away for a while, but I caught 'im again."

Ollie contributed her first comment. "Right! Then I suppose she lures him over here from Vancouver every weekend. Russ, your buddy couldn't wait to see her again."

Russ shined a smile at her. He was glad to see her join in. "Can't say I blame him."

Russ began the story of Danny Tanner through the eyes of his best friend. As he went from one episode to another, Josie hung on every word. Ollie soon became as gripped as Josie with his telling of it. It was obviously partly truth and partly fiction, but no less fascinating. It was obvious, too, that Russ and Danny were close. She was impressed with the way he told it, how he tended to minimize his own role in events, seeming to idolize Danny. The stories went on for over half an hour…

"…I come out of the hotel and I see this guy I'd seen around the base at Clinton, holding his own against half the city of Stratford. So I jumped in. You know, a fellow Air Force type and all. As I was takin' on one guy, Tanner *flattens* two more! After I joined the dance, they all took off on the run. Then we found another beer joint…"

"…there we were, both flat-ass broke after three days in Montreal, so Tanner tells the driver this B.S. story about us poor Air Force types, just in from 'special *Arctic* duty,' no less! So we get a free taxi ride all the way from Lachine to St. Huberts. We caught our skid flight to Moncton with minutes to spare. Then they weren't gonna let us on the plane because we were both smashed…"

"…so, if it wasn't for him finding me, I would have froze stiff and never been found till spring. Not that I'd be missed very much…"

"…anyway, he gets talked into this boxing match and he decks his guy in the first round and they stop the fight. Then he says to me, 'Routine, Russ, I didn't work up a sweat.' I said, 'Neither did the other guy, you didn't give him time!' That's when I found out he was in the Golden Gloves before he joined up…"

"…so, anyway I gave her the ten bucks and the next morning he tells me, 'I dreamed I was sitting with a four hundred pound Negro woman on my lap!' I told him, 'She was no more than about three ninety, and guess what, Tanner— you weren't dreaming!' I thought he was gonna kill me…"

"…there I am, stretched out on the ice, thinking I'm never gonna see him again, when he comes up through the hole in the ice and *tosses* the little girl to me. I hold out my hand to help him out of the water but he says, 'Russ! There's another one!' And down he goes again. He went down three more times. When we finally got him out, he could barely breathe, or even move, and he was crying like a baby—because he never got the other kid out. I sat there and cried with him, holding the little girl inside my jacket to warm her up till an ambulance arrived. They never found the other kid. Dan gets letters from the little girl's mother. Don't tell him I told you, okay? He never wants to talk about it…"

"…so there's me, hung over and airsick as hell, and the son of a bitch, pardon my French, he takes me into this hot, greasy-smelling diner, it was one of those old streetcars, and orders me a big bowl of clam chowder! I just barely made it to the washroom. Thought I'd never quit barfing…"

The response to this last story was subdued. Everyone at the table was still thinking about the one before.

"Had enough, Josie?" he asked. "I hope so; I could go on all night, but I might start lying about the S.O.B." At that, he winked at Ollie.

Josie was solemn. "I could listen to you tell about him forever."

Ollie asked, "Are you telling us you haven't *already* started lying about him?"

He grinned the lopsided grin. "Just some small embellishment, honest."

Still solemn, Josie said. "Not about the little girl, though!"

"No. Unfortunately, it really happened. Just like I told it. Please don't ever let on I told you."

Ollie said, "Quite a guy." *Quite the guys, I suspect!* she thought.

Russ, serious now, said, "I know this—nobody could ever have a better friend than I have in Dan Tanner. I'd do anything, go anywhere for the guy."

Jake said, "I heard all about you guys. They say you're both crazy as hell! It's a wonder you're still both alive…"

Russ looked thoughtful. "Hey, what the hell; might as well enjoy life, Jake. Any day now, Ol' Malenkov, or whoever else is in charge over there, could send the balloon up. Don't kid yourself, those radomes here at 51, and at all the other G.C.I.s? They're gonna be one of the first targets. Shit, some little fishing boat off the coast has probably already got us zeroed in with a missile right now. It's got our name on it, man." He grinned, "Don't expect the Navy to help—they don't know port from friggin' starboard. So, me an' Tanner, we're gonna have some good times while we can. If nothing bad happens, well that's a bonus and we'll have great memories."

Jake said, "I suppose."

Josie looked solemn. "Do you believe it could 'appen?"

"They're all maniacs, the so-called leaders on both sides."

A little later, they saw the usual crowd of FighterCops from 51 gathering by the piano in the corner.

Ollie said, "Shall we join them over in Scope-Dope corner?"

On this night there was no one to play the piano. The jukebox was playing popular songs from the past four or five years.

Russ was able to get a seat on the leatherette sofa beside Ollie. After a round of introductions, he leaned over and peered closely into her eyes.

"What the *hell* are you doing, Knight?" she asked, as she pushed him away, hands on his chest.

He grinned. "Oh, just trying to see if I can tell—by looking at your eyes."

"And just what is *that* supposed to mean, for Chrissake?"

"Well, this real good friend of mine, a guy you all admire so much, had me lined up for Friday night, with what he called a 'blind date.' Her name is Olivia, sometimes known as 'Ollie.' So I'm checking it out. I've never been out with a blind person." He waved his hand in front of her eyes.

Ollie laughed as she pushed his hand away. "Oh, shit! He did, did he? The smartass. You tell your buddy I pick my own dates—okay, Russ?"

"Roger that. By the way, I *am* available for Friday night. Keep me in mind when you're picking, okay? Add me to the list or whatever."

"I'll keep you in mind."

The jukebox was playing Nat King Cole singing *Somewhere Along The Way*. Two couples were up dancing.

Ollie asked him, "Do you dance, Mr. Knight?"

He replied, "Only the slow stuff."

"Well, that's just what I'm hearing. Come on, let's do it."

On the floor as they danced, Ollie said, "Russ, I have something to ask you. It's about Danny Tanner. I know he's your friend, but can you be honest with me? How much truth is in those stories, anyway?"

"It's pretty much all the truth. Really."

"You think he saved your life."

"Absolutely! The only way I could survive would be if someone found me, and it wasn't as if I was out in plain sight." He turned his face to one side. "Look at my ear, it was the night it got frozen, Ollie." The earlobe was purplish and slightly shriveled. "I've got a couple of toes that look the same. I'm not saying anyone else wouldn't have done it, but he had a-a feeling I was in trouble somewhere. He got out of bed and went looking for me—at three A.M."

"And the little girl in the lake? I hope I don't have to ask, you couldn't make that up!"

"Look, if he didn't dive in, I believe I would have—I don't know. It all happened so fast. We both just reacted. The poor bastard has bad dreams about it." He pushed her out to arm's length. "I suspect this is about you all worried for your friend, for Josie, right?"

"Yeah. She's a sweet kid, and my friend. Is she gonna be okay with him?"

"I have never known Danny Tanner to intentionally hurt any girl."

"But he's had a lot of them, right?"

"He has, he's a damn good-looking guy. I'm not gonna apologize for him having women. From what I've seen, he has nothing but respect for women—all women. We've talked about it." He grinned. "He has me acting the same way…well, almost."

The song on the jukebox ended. They stayed on the floor.

Russ spoke again. "Another thing. In Vancouver the other day, he came closer than he ever has, to telling me he's fallen for someone and I don't think it was easy for him to say it. I think your little friend's gonna be fine."

"Yeah. You know, she's tougher than she seems. I think I've been underestimating her. Look, I'm sorry I bugged you about this. An' y'know what? I believe I would love to be your date on Friday, if you still want." She felt better about Josie and Danny now, and found the dark-eyed Russ somehow intriguing.

On their way back to the group, Russ said, "How about Danny, the S.O.B.? Sticking me with a homely date like you! I'll have to think of some way to get even."

"Yeah, how about that? If you need help, let me know."

The FighterCops, meanwhile, started the first round of the old standby songs. With no piano player in the club this night, their renderings would have to be a Capella:

"…*Gee Ma, I Wanna Go…Back To Ontario…Gee Ma I Wanna Go Ho-o-ome…They Say That In The Air Force The Women Are Divine…I Asked For Marilyn Monroe An' They Sent Me Frankenstein…Oh I Don't Want No More Of Air Force Life…Gee Ma, I Wanna Go…*"

"…*There Were Rats! Rats! As Big As Alley Cats…In The Stores…In The Sto-o-o-res…In The Quarter…Master's Stores…*"

"…*Oh, I's The Bie What Builds The Boats—An' I's The Bie What Sails 'Em…*"

Russ contributed one they hadn't heard:

"*The Liquor Was Spilled On The Barroom Floor…And The Bar Was Closed For The Night…When a Little Brown Mouse Came Out Of His Hole…And He Gazed And He Gazed At The Sight…Well, He Lapped Up The Beer From The Barroom*

Floor...And Back On His Haunches He Sat...And All Night Long You Could Hear His So-o-o-ong......BRING ON THE GODDAMNED CAT!"

The disharmony was so bad it was beautiful. On it went, till by ones and twos, the choir members departed, to stagger back to their various barracks for the night.

*   *   *   *

Danny called Josie on Friday morning to say he would arrive earlier than usual. He had got the afternoon off and would arrive about six thirty.

"Good! Ollie wants you to meet the guy she's dating."

"She's dating a guy? Oh, well...Russ'll have to wait."

When Danny arrived at the Wets at six-twenty, he saw no sign of Russ in the men's or lady's sides. He joined Josie and Ollie at a table near the door to the men's side. After he kissed Josie, he said, "Couldn't you find a better table?"

Ollie replied, "This is all there was when we came in."

"So, you're dating somebody, Ollie? Must be a total geeko."

"Well, Tanner," said Ollie with a shrug, "A girl has to grab what she can get."

He noticed Josie hadn't been looking at him since they kissed. Then he saw she was grinning, and seemed to be on the edge of laughter.

"What's with you, Hon? Is my friggin' fly open or something?"

She could barely suppress laughter. Before he could say anything more, she pointed at Ollie and giggled aloud. Ollie put a paper bag on the table. She pulled out a leather dog leash and a can of dog food. She looked matter-of-factly at him and asked, "What should I do with these, Tanner?"

He knew at once what was going on. "Son of a bitch! You met him..."

He heard Russ behind him say, "So, I'm a total geeko am I?" He had hidden in the washroom when Danny arrived and then waited just inside the men's side, listening for his cue.

Ollie said. "Tanner...meet my date! Russ Knight, meet Danny Tanner."

Russ said, "That is a gotcha, Champ!"

Disgusted, knowing he had been had, Danny didn't even turn around. He said, "Yeah, yeah, it's a 'gotcha.' Jesus, small minds or what!" He grinned and waved Russ to the table. "Sit down, shit-for-brains—I'll buy you a beer."

Josie giggled. Ollie laughed. Russ smirked.

Josie, Ollie, Danny, and Russ—dubbed that night by Ollie "The Fearsome Foursome" stayed in the Wets till closing time.

*   *   *   *

After a week of day shift, Russ was assigned to B Crew. He had met a couple of the crew's members at previous postings, including the Crew Chief, a dumpy female Corporal named Jackie "JJ" Johnson. She had been three courses behind Russ in Clinton. The officer in charge of the crew, the Crew Controller, was a former navigator from Transport Command, disgruntled at having to serve a tour of ground duty.

Russ shrugged off the manifest laxity on the crew. They obviously put more interest and effort into card games in the lunchroom than they put into anything in the Ops Room. Without regard for what went on around him, he was determined to do the job as he knew it should be done. Like his friend Danny, he had learned his craft well and believed work was work and play was play.

*   *   *   *

Danny traveled to Comox every weekend. He and Josie got together whenever they could with Ollie and Russ, who became much more than friends to each other. Ollie explained, "Shit, somebody has to look after the crazy sonofabitch!" Russ stated simply, "She drinks and smokes my brands."

Many of the young men and women recently enlisted in the Air Force went through periods of acute homesickness when service careers sent them many hundreds, if not thousands of miles from home and family. The initial sense of freedom from parental control soon paled, and the fun and partying became just so much bravado. It was the principal reason many of them did not reenlist after their initial three-year term.

Danny had abandoned his hometown roots when he joined up, didn't care if he ever returned. He got together with his mother or sister only occasionally— never at the family house in Victoria. Josie, too, had forsaken family; she and Paul Connor sometimes exchanged short notes enclosed in seasonal cards, but had no other communication. (She called them "semi-annual reports.") Ollie loved her family, but dropped in only for two or three day in-and-out visits when on annual leave. Russ, as we have seen, had no parents and had long ago lost track of his siblings, and really had no home to go back to. So the Fearsome Foursome suffered none of the angst of separation so prevalent in most of their fellow enlistees.

It was just one more thing that drew them together.

*   *   *   *

The four friends found no shortage of entertainment that summer of 1955.

With the arrival of warm weather, the FighterCops held almost nightly parties at 51 Beach. A large bonfire would be lit and couples or singles sat around on driftwood logs, drinking beer kept cool at the edge of the water, or liquor mixed with soda pop or juice and passed around the circle in quart ginger ale bottles. There was no closing time at the beach, which meant morning hangovers were often evident in the 51 Ops Room.

There were twice monthly Friday night dances in the old wood frame hall at Union Bay, a town south of Courtenay, soon dubbed "Onion Bay," possibly by Ollie Conti. Carloads of FighterCops and others from Comox would head down the highway, after gathering in the Wets. A local swing band provided the music, playing old standards from a decade earlier. Beer was sold in large paper cups and hard liquor was smuggled in under shirts or dresses. At midnight the "home waltz," always *Blue Moon,* signaled the dance was about to end and precipitated the final pairings-off for the night, with couples locked together, in demonstrations of love—or something like it. Then the jam-packed cars would travel the twenty or so miles back to the base.

There was the marriage of one of the Orderly Room staff to a civilian girl from Victoria. The wedding and reception were held on a warm and sunny Saturday in the seaside town of Parksville. Ken Bromley, the groom, was a quiet guy and not much of a party animal. The bride, Sondra, and her family were Oak Bay "old money." (Which, according to Danny, just meant Sondra likely was descended from rumrunners.) Ken's co-workers from the Orderly Room were invited to attend.

The Fearsome Foursome dressed in their best for the occasion. Josie wore a flower print dress in predominately pale blues, with off-white pumps and gloves. Ollie chose a coral dress and beige accessories. Danny wore a light gray suit in a muted windowpane material and Russ went with a charcoal blazer and light gray slacks.

They arrived in Parksville late for the marriage ceremony, having made refreshment stops at several beer parlors along the Island Highway.

The reception was at the estate of a relative of the bride, and none of the four had ever been in such a place! The large house, of Tudor design, appeared to have at least twelve rooms. The grounds took up more than an acre, terraced and groomed immaculately by Chinese gardeners. Scattered around the lawns, shaded by shrubbery, were small groupings of wrought iron furniture. Near the house two large canvas pavilions were set up, one as shaded seating for guests, the other for catered food and a liquor bar. The wedding guests were informed there were facilities for guests located in the beach cottage behind the main house—a cottage the size of a three-bedroom home. Ollie explained to Josie that "facilities" meant washrooms.

The foursome stayed near the bar at first, taking full advantage of the free drinks. Josie and Ollie tried the champagne, both for the first time. They loved the stuff.

The girls were using the washroom in the cottage when Ollie declared they just had to see the inside of the main house.

Josie said, "Ollie! We can't go in there…can we? How? You go first." She was becoming aware champagne packed a wallop—and she was becoming severely walloped.

They found the front door of the house carefully watched by two servants, stationed there to turn away the curious. They replenished their champagnes at the bar before going around to a rear door, where they had spotted a man of about their own age on guard. Ollie approached him.

She smiled coquettishly. "Hi there. Gee, you must be awfully warm, stuck out here. I wonder if you could show me to the telephone? They said it's just inside the door?"

This young man was not as diligent as the two at the front door, especially when approached by two beautiful girls. "The phone? I think there's one by the kitchen…"

"That's just what Sondra told us. The bride, Sondra—she's my cousin—said this way would be easier. She said you'd understand. We're up here from Vancouver and we have to get a taxi so we can ditch some real dumb dates—a couple of genuine Victoria snobs. You know the type; never had to work a day in their lives. Perhaps inside I could get you a nice drink of water?"

He said, "I'm not thirsty, but thank you anyway. Go along the hallway, then turn left.

"You're so kind. Thank you so much"! She waved Josie toward the door as she went in. "Come along…Marie."

Twenty minutes later the exploration took them to an upstairs hall. As they turned a corner, they encountered a large, extremely irate woman.

"HOW DID YOU PEOPLE GET IN HERE?" she screeched. "THIS IS OUR HOME! YOU HAVE TRESPASSED IN OUR HOME!"

Ollie asked, innocently, "Oh, isn't this the Beach Cabin? We're looking for the powder room…"

It might have worked if not for Josie's giggling.

They were escorted unceremoniously out through the front door, both laughing helplessly. Some of the other guests were staring and whispering so Ollie led Josie away from the house. They looked about for the boys, who were nowhere to be seen. They sat at a secluded lawn table as far from the house as they could, where they were hidden by high rhododendron bushes.

Through tears of helpless laughter, Ollie said, "Jesus! The old bag sure got excited."

Josie said, "She was so red I thought she would 'ave a 'eart attack or something. But, you know, we were in her house. But what a place, Ollie!" She giggled. "You were so funny—'Oh! Isn't this the cabin?' I thought I was going to pee my pants!" They both laughed again.

Ollie managed, "Yeah, like a *cabin* all right, with what, twenty rooms? Oh shit, the stuff you get me into, Josie. I could die of embarrassment. We have to find the guys and get away from here!"

"Maybe we could sneak out and get more champagne?" Josie suggested.

"No!"

They hid there for an hour, occasionally peering out through the shrubs for any sign of Danny and Russ. A middle-aged couple came by and attempted to start a conversation but Ollie was in no mood for polite chitchat and they soon moved on, outraged when she told them to bugger off. As they left, Josie shouted, "Hey, Mister, your wig 'as slipped!" causing him to grab for it and knock it truly askew.

They were still laughing when Danny found them five minutes later.

"Hey," he said, "I've been looking all over for you two. Have you seen Russ? This whole thing is the shits—like bo-ring!" It was obvious by his demeanor he had spent quality time at the free bar. "What the hell you two laughing about?"

Ollie replied, "We'll tell you later. Let's find him and get the hell *out* of here."

Russ appeared a few minutes later, trotting across the lawn, arms folded across the front of his blazer. They could see that he, too, had taken full advantage of the bar. He looked furtively around, then spread his blazer open, exposing two large bottles of champagne. "Ta da!" he exclaimed.

Josie said, "Russ! What did you do? That's *stealing!*" She giggled, "Is it nice and cold?"

"Oh shit," said Ollie, "we're gonna go to jail! Let's get out of here."

Danny said, "How to *go*, Q! Stay here, I'll be right back." He started away, toward the tents.

"Now, where in hell is he going?" asked Ollie. She shouted after him, "We'll meet you at the car, Tanner." She, Josie and Russ headed for the gate.

Danny arrived at the car with his own "Ta da!" Opening his coat, he exposed four champagne glasses.

Russ said, "Pathetic effort, Champ. Friggin' little wine glasses?"

"Can't drink outta the bottle, not classy."

They piled into the Ford and Danny drove north to Qualicum Beach. He parked on the side of the road and they clambered down a low bank to a deserted stretch of beach. He spread a blanket from the car. The mid-afternoon sun shined brightly.

Russ hefted the two bottles. "Look at this stuff. Probably costs ten or twelve bucks apiece!" he said.

Danny passed the stem-wear to Josie and reached for the wine.

"Here. I'll show you how it's done so you don't waste half of it." He started working at the cork while both girls eagerly held glasses out to him. Russ went to the water's edge and stuck the other bottle into the wet sand.

They sat on the blanket; coats and shoes removed, and sipped the cool bubbly. When they finished the first bottle, the boys had to roll slacks up and wade up to their knees to search for the second, having forgot about the incoming tide.

As they waded about, searching, the girls heard Danny loudly declare, "No, numb-nuts, we did *not* already drink the second damn bottle! Keep looking!"

And Russ, "Don't yell at me. Not my fault the stupid ocean can't stay put where we foun' it."

With the second bottle finally rescued from the sea, they continued the champagne picnic. At least four times Josie was heard to say she would have only "one more little one, because I really don't drink very mush," followed by a snort from Ollie. Danny twice tried to explain to Russ how the ocean tides work. Russ commented how champagne was a "sissy woman's drink that tastes like friggin' Canada Dry"—which was shortly before he started to loudly sing, "Oh, I Could Go From Rags To Rishes...If You Would Ow-nlee Shay You Care!"

When they left for home, both bottles empty, the girls joined Russ in song. Danny drove them all the way to the Lantzville road, on the outskirts of Nanaimo before they realized he had gone the wrong way.

Ollie said, "We're lost, Tanner. I s'pected we were lost 'cause we didn't go pas' Onion Bay or Fanner Bay or Blowsy..."

"It's Fann-*ee* Bay, stupid, and Bows-*er* with no L, not *fanner* and *blowsy*!" said Danny. He was embarrassed and annoyed at having gone the wrong way. "If you were so s'*picious*, why didn't you say something 'fore we got so damn far?"

"Cause I knew you'd get irritalable…arritible…iterated, 'at's why. I dunno if I ever told you, but you get iterated quite a lot, Tanner."

"That place shounds like a dog name." mumbled Josie.

Ollie got that wrong, "Yeah—sit Fanny, here Fanny, roll over Fanny."

When they turned and headed north, they passed through several hamlets, including Bowser, Fanny Bay and Buckley Bay. Josie chose Buckley Bay as a fine place to get out and be sick at the side of the road.

The rest of the way home, Josie hung her head out the window, Russ slept, and Ollie regaled Danny with the story of their home invasion.

*   *   *   *

Two weeks after the wedding on a weeknight a few of the girls, including Josie and Ollie, were in the laundry room in barracks, some doing wash, some ironing and the rest just sitting and gabbing. Josie was sitting on a sorting counter while Ollie ironed clothes. Ollie was telling them about the reception in Parksville.

"So, there we are, half smashed on champagne and hiding in these friggin' bushes, totally embarrassed. Along come these two old farts, with their noses up in the air as if we smelled bad or something. The guy's actually wearing a tweed suit, for Chrissake! The last thing we want is to get into a conversation with a couple of old snobs, when they start, 'Oh, hello you young people. Are you with the groom's party?' and crap like that, you know…" She turned to Josie, "Jo, say it like they did. She's got it down pat. Listen to this. She breaks me up every time I hear it."

Josie said, "Well, it sounded like…" She jumped down from the table so she could demonstrate. She stuck her nose in the air, put her hands on her hips. "It sounded like this: 'Ew, are yew with the grewm's party?' Ollie told them to leave us alone and the fat lady said 'Ew. Yew are sew rewd!' So then Ollie said, 'Screw yew' Then she said, 'Ew, yew must be thews Ear Force people.' So, then Ollie got real mad and told them to, you know—ew-ew off!"

Everyone was laughing. They had rarely seen this side of Josie.

"Ollie! You told them to like eff off?" choked Bobby.

"No. I didn't say it—I should have, though. I said *bugger* off!"

"Yes," said Josie, "then the woman said 'Ew, ew, ew, what 'orrible persons. Pay them new attention, Monty. Ew!' Then they 'urried away."

"The guy's name is Monty, no kidding!" said Ollie. "Anyway when they're walking away, stupid here yells, 'Hey, mister! Your wig is slipping!' Shit, the guy grabs for it and now he does knock it all crooked! Sure enough, he had on a wig! They both started trotting away. I'll never figure out how Jo spotted the guy's rug."

"Jo—you did that? Really?" asked Vera.

"Yes! It was so funny," said Josie between giggles. "The last we heard was, '*Ew, ew, ew!* With him trying to rescue his *hair*. I was glad when Danny and Russ showed up."

"Russ stole two bottles of champagne from the bar of course," said Ollie. "Then we got the hell out of there. In a big hurry."

The girls were all laughing when Lenore Alderman from A Crew came in with another girl. She waited out the laughter before speaking.

"Ladies, and you, too, Bobby Gaines; this is Nicole. Call her Nicky. She's just posted here from Station Van."

✳   ✳   ✳   ✳

Nicole St. Pierre was a plain, unprepossessing girl, with an especially monotonous demeanor. Her pointed features showed signs of past and present skin problems, her straight, mousy brown hair was cut short, and her personal hygiene suspect. Her Woolworth and Kresge's wardrobe completed the drab picture.

Her barracks mates would belatedly learn she was a malicious and dishonest gossip. She made a point of hearing as much as possible of what was being said around her, a habit that accounted for her constantly distracted air. She felt no obligation to check the accuracy or the currency of the tidbits she passed on, and needed only all or part of some overheard conversation, which was often many months dated, and a willing listener

One of the many bits of "news" she eagerly tossed about soon after her arrival at Comox concerned Danny Tanner. Her story went it was well known over at Jericho that he was currently seeing and sleeping with not one but two girls; one was a FighterCop, the other a civilian on the base, and there was possibly a third lover—"so I've heard." The fact that this news was something she heard five months ago never saw the light of day. Danny would not even recall knowing a Nicole St. Pierre at Jericho. She certainly wasn't ever in his circle of friends.

Before the tight enclave of Airwomen at Comox thought to question it, the story was expanded and embellished. After all, there were *names*, weren't there?

He had the *reputation*, didn't he? The girls were all genuinely fond of Josie, and the bastard was screwing around on her over there in Vancouver!

In a week the story had gained momentum and had spread beyond the Airwomen's quarters, so Roberta Gaines decided to talk to Ollie.

"Yeah, Bobby, of course I've heard," said Ollie, disgusted. "What's the latest, by the way, is he married with six kids yet? You know him—what do you think?"

"I really don't know him so well…"

Ollie erupted, "Well I *do*, goddamit! And I don't frigging believe a word of it."

"Christ, don't get mad at *me*. I just know Josie'll be hurt. We're her friends, Ol. Even if it's not true, do you think she can handle this? She *worships* the guy! Do you think she's heard anything?"

Ollie put a hand on Bobby's shoulder. "I'm sorry, Bobby, I'm not mad at you. I don't know if Josie's heard. I don't think so, she probably would have told me. I do know, or I'm pretty sure, and so is Jo, by the way, that he used to go with a FighterCOp named Christine over there. Jo and I have met her. Shit, we spent the better part of a day with her. Maybe whoever started this has picked up some old news. Another thing—I'm seeing Russ Knight—going with him. Did you know?"

Bobby grinned, waggled a hand from side to side, and rolled her eyes. "Well, everyone sort of suspected. Shit, you've been with him every day since he arrived. Of course I know, we all know."

Ollie actually blushed before she said, "Yeah…well, now you know it from me. Anyway, Russ told me something about Tanner when I first met him that makes me believe there's nothing to this story. Also, I happen to like Tanner a lot. We have to assume there's nothing to it, Bobby. I'm going to talk to Russ, then I'm going to talk to Jo. You know, she's a lot tougher than you think she is—if it's true, she'll be hurt, yeah, but she'll handle it. The most trouble would be because it's *not* true. Somebody's gonna, pardon my French, fucking *die*! After I talk to Russ, you and I have to tell all these little hens around here it is definitely not true, then we can only hope the sensible ones will help make it go away. I'll be seeing Russ at midnight. He's on the evening shift." She smiled. "I'm glad you came to me, Bobby."

The next day, Wednesday, Josie did not go to the mess for supper after work. Ollie found her at five-thirty, in her bed with her back to the room.

"Hey, kid, you sleeping?" Josie didn't reply so she sat beside her on the bed. "Hey, Jo, what's up?"

Without stirring, Josie said, "Nothing's up, Ollie. I don't feel too good."

"You sick?"

"No. Just don't feel good."

"Isn't that the same thing? Do you want to talk, Buddy?"

"No"

"Josie, look at me, please! I'm talking to the back of your head and it's not very nice—your roots are showing and everything. Come on, turn around." She started tickling under Josie's arms. Josie squirmed frantically—she couldn't stand being tickled. She giggled and squirmed and kept her face to the wall, but Ollie kept it up.

Josie finally had to turn and sit up to stop the torture, "Okay, okay, I'm up, and I do not 'ave roots! You know it's all me. So shut up, Olivia Conti!"

"Ooh, you're calling me *Olivia*! Now I'm worried." She smiled. "You're honestly not sick?"

"No. Just tired. I was thinking a lot last night and I couldn't sleep, you know…"

"Been crying?"

Josie was emphatic. "No! I said…just thinking."

"Touchy, touchy. Want me to leave you alone?"

"No. You're my friend. If I wanted to be left alone, I would tell you."

"What were you doing all the thinking about last night?"

"Oh, just stuff." She thought it over. "About…me and Danny."

"Have you been hearing the stories?"

"Yes I have. It's not true, Ollie."

"It's total bullshit, Jo. I talked to Russ last night. He knows. It's crap, believe me."

"I know it is. Danny loves me. He wouldn't do that."

"Soo—*what* then?"

"I just have to make sure he will always love me and won't want anyone else. That's what I was thinking about. Also," she added angrily, "also, I am going to make whoever is saying those things pay for it."

Relieved, Ollie said, "Attagirl, Jo." She stood up. "You're fine. So what the hell are you bothering me for, anyway?" She stretched out on her own bed and grabbed a magazine.

Josie's pillow just missed her head.

＊　　　＊　　　＊　　　＊

Nicole St. Pierre had never had a real friend. She was alone at a table in the Mess Hall when Josie joined her for lunch.

"Nicky, I want to speak to you. It's about something you 'ave done." In terse sentences, Josie explained the harm unfounded rumors caused on a base such as Comox. She told her, too, how unpopular the bearer would be. Afterward, they walked to the barracks together.

Nicky found her only friend at Comox that lunch hour.

CHAPTER 11

▼

The first time we made love…

COMOX

Russ arranged for Josie to get in touch with Danny over the landline. A female voice at the other end said, "Fifth Air Division."

"Oh, hello, could you put me through to the Liaison, please?" Josie was nervous. She had never used the landlines.

"You want Five Div Liaison?"

"Um…yes. Thank you." She heard a single ring then a man's voice.

"Liaison, Flight Lieutenant Morrisey here."

"'Ello. Is Da…L.A.C. Tanner there please?"

The voice said, "For you Dan."

Danny came on, "L.A.C. Tanner."

"Danny. Hello! I'm calling on the land phone—at 51. Russ put it through for me."

"Hiya, Hon. It's good to hear your voice. It's land *line,* Jo." He was not concerned about the unofficial use of the line.

"What? Oh…yes." She sounded on edge. "I called to see if you're coming this Friday."

He teased, "Do you want me to?"

"Shut up, you. Of course I do! I always do." She was impatient, "Well, are you, or not?"

"Yes, Honey, I'm coming. I'll be there about eight-thirty, I guess. Is there something special on? I hope there's no ClerkAdmin weddings, I don't need any more of those!"

She countered, "Why not? It was fun and I got to try champagne. There's nothing special on. Just make sure you come."

"Roger and wilco, I'll be there."

"Good. Well...I 'ad better hang up now. Good bye, Darling. Are you sure you're coming?"

"Yeah, yeah, I'm positive!"

"Okay, I'll see you Friday then, 'bye."

*   *   *   *

Josie had been waiting at the main gate for almost an hour when he arrived at Comox on Friday. Before he could get out of the car she jumped onto the seat beside him. She threw her arms around him and they kissed.

He pulled back. "Hey, nice welcome! What's up, Jo? I know I'm simply marvelous and all, but meeting me at the gate? What's the occasion?"

She sat on the seat close to him in her usual fashion, with her feet tucked up under her. "Well, Mister Marvelous, are you too tired to drive some more? Just a little way."

He was puzzled. "Yeah...I mean *no,* I'm not too tired. Where we going?"

"Royston."

"Royston? What the hell's at Royston?"

"You and me—if you ever get going. Push the gears in and get driving." she urged.

"Push the gears in?"

She punched his shoulder. "Push whatever you *'ave* to push. Get going. Royston!"

As he backed the car out and turned back toward Courtenay, he could see she was in a strange mood. She seemed excited, keyed up. If it were possible, she was more beautiful and vivacious than ever. She wore a gray skirt, pale yellow short-sleeved pullover, dove gray neckerchief and low, open sandals. She slid over on the seat till she was against him.

"For you, Jo, what the heck...even Royston!" he said. "What's going on? Where's Russ and Ollie?"

"I told Ollie we're going to Victoria, for the weekend." Her words were rushing out. "She'll tell Russ, too. They'll be fine without us for one weekend.

Besides, Ollie told me Russ 'as to work for a guy tomorrow on afternoon shift. But, we're not going to Victoria…"

"Uh uh. We're going to Royston. That'll put 'em off the track!"

She said, "Shut up, you. Don't tease me." She became serious. "Danny, listen to me please. I 'ave to tell you something important."

He thought, *Somebody's nervous, she's losing her H's.* He said aloud, "Okay, Hon, I'm listening."

She looked down at the seat, choosing her words. "Danny, I want you to love me…"

He interrupted, "Too late, Hon. I already do." He put his right arm around her.

She leaned her head on him. She spoke softly. "I want you to make love to me tonight…make love *with* me. Tonight."

"But…"

She put a hand over his mouth to stop him. "My Danny, I told you I 'ave loved you ever since the train. I also wanted you, um, you know, *wanted* you—since the night in my berth. I was afraid then, but now I'm not afraid. I want it with you." She looked straight ahead, down the road. "This is 'ard for me…to ask you. Of course I 'ave never asked anyone like this…"

He tried, "But Josie…"

"Shh!" She looked up at him. "I am not a…a virgin, Danny. I tried it twice before I knew you. It was no good because I was just trying. With you, because I love you so and you love me, it will be good. I know it!" She took a deep breath before continuing. "I want you, and I know you want me. I rented a cabin. It's at a motel in Royston. I took it for the weekend. Oh, Danny, I do love you!"

They drove in silence for a full five minutes, till they were nearing Courtenay on the dike road.

She broke the silence with a tremor in her voice. "You 'ad better say something…please, Danny?" She looked at him intently.

He stared ahead as he spoke. "Jo, you can't know how much I've wanted to make love to you. I believe we, you and I, will never be complete until we do." She started to say something, but it was his turn to stop her. "Let me finish. The question is—are you sure you want this? I promised you it would be your call. You have to do this because you truly want to." He turned to her.

She said, with certainty, "I do! I *am* sure. And I am ready. We 'ave waited so long."

It was again quiet in the car as they drove through town.

*   *   *   *

The *Ocean View Auto Court* was between Courtenay and Royston, just off the Island Highway. He pulled up in front of the office.

Josie said, "I already got the keys. It's number seven. I told them I'm your wife. I just came from Quebec and our furniture didn't arrive yet." She giggled. "That's what I told them." He drove on to number seven, where she jumped out. He took his Gladstone from the back seat and followed her in.

Inside number seven, he saw her suitcase was there. Some of her things were placed on the dresser. She had even brought her Baby Champ radio.

She explained, "I came by taxi after work." She surveyed the room. "It's not so bad, eh? Do you need to use the bathroom...I 'ave to change."

"No, you go ahead."

She took her bag and went into the small bathroom. Danny kicked off his loafers and threw his jacket over a chair. He turned when she came out. She had put on a short, pale blue nightgown. She approached him awkwardly, a little flushed.

"Be gentle for me, please, Danny, and be patient. Teach me...teach me 'ow to be good for you." When she removed her dog tag over her head, the chain caught in a couple of hairs. She giggled helplessly and shrugged as if to say, "Something had to go wrong." He reached and untangled it and put it in her hand; she tossed it to the bedside table. She murmured, "Thank you," and stood uncertainly before him.

"Gosh, Jo," he choked, "you don't know do you? How beautiful you are!"

Before he knew it, she was in his arms. Her body felt voluptuous through the diaphanous material of her nightgown. Her waist was impossibly narrow, and where his hands touched, her skin impossibly soft. He felt her breasts warm where they pressed against him. They kissed passionately.

She wanted this now more than anything; as he had felt her breasts pressing, she felt his erection touching her. She pulled back, looked down at him, and giggled nervously. "What the 'eck are you waiting for? Get those clothes off!" she said.

He undressed and stood before her. Inexplicably, he felt awkward with her. They kissed again and then he turned her and laid her on the bed. She reached up and removed his dog tags and put them on the table with hers. She brushed at his wayward forelock. Danny pulled her to him. As his hands explored under her gown, he wondered once again at the softness of her. He kissed her lips, her throat, her breasts.

Josie grew impatient with the foreplay. She pressed her body to his.

"Now...Please." she whispered.

He was over her. "Put me in, Jo."

"Hmm? Oh...yes."

She was tense at first, as he gently entered her, but soon relaxed. Moving with him, she was surprised at her immediate gratification. *Oh, oh—this is wonderful! As Danny increased the tempo in his own excitement, she smiled with pleasure. Ah. Ah, yes.*

"Ah! Ahh..." She didn't know she said it aloud.

Danny stopped. "Did I hurt..."

Don't stop! She thrust her body at him, pulled him tighter to her. "Don't stop!" she whispered hoarsely.

They soared! They went to places they could never dream of. High places. Higher and higher!

Oh! Oh, this is so good! What is he doing—doing to me? Oh, Danny, Danny! "Danneee ohh! Danny Danny Danny! Yes! Yes! Yes*!" Merde—I said that out loud! He'll hear me. I don't care.* "Oh, yes! Yessss!" she shouted

Danny grinned happily at her expression of joy. It stimulated him. He joined in her chorus, "Yes! Josie! Yes! Yes!" In an explosion of pleasure, he moaned, "Oh, my Honey! Yes!"

After their first lovemaking, spent for the moment, they lay resting. He lay on his back with an arm around her, she on her side, arm propping her head. She rested her free hand on his chest. They were both grinning like little kids.

"Danny, I-I didn't know it could be so wonderful! Will it always be? Was I...okay for you?"

"You were great. God, how I love you, Jo!" For all his experience, he had never enjoyed sex as he just had! He was surprised at how well they matched in this first coupling.

"I hope I was good for you. I want you to always enjoy it with me," she said.

"You just enjoy it yourself, Hon, your enjoyment will make mine. You were fine. It's gonna get better."

"Can it? Be *better?*"

"You'll see."

She asked in a small voice, "Danny...am I, um, pretty to you, really?"

He smiled. "Nope. You're an ugly hag."

"Shut *up*, you!"

"You're not just pretty to me. You are beautiful. Everything about you is perfect."

"Not *perfect!* Not *me.*" She was not above false modesty this day.

"Perfect. Everything!" said he.

"How am I that?" Pleased beyond imagining, she wanted to hear more.

"As I said—everything. Your face. Your eyes. Your breasts...now they're real perfect." She looked down at herself; then quickly up, blushing, and he chuckled. "Your lips, of course. Your little waist. And your, you know...behind? I thought so the first time I saw it in Montreal. It was the first part of you I saw."

She giggled. "Not *that!*"

"That!"

"Can my...that...be pretty? No it can't." *This is fun!*

"How do you know? You can't even see it. All you do is sit on it."

"I for sure will see it, now! Now I know it's perfect, I'll buy a special mirror." She became serious. "And you, my Danny, are so beautiful. I-I swell all up when I look at you." She smiled naughtily. Leaning across him to look, she declared, "There! Now I 'ave seen your...that. It's beautiful, too. So there." She played with the hairs on his chest, bent and kissed him there, ran her fingers down his abdomen. She looked down at his penis.

"So. This is my friend. My very little friend, now." She giggled. "Ollie would want to give him a name."

"How about...Peter. Is that a good name?"

"*My* little Peter!" She bent close to the newly named. She took it in her hands and kissed it. "Little Peter. Ooh! 'E's getting *bigger!* Big Peter!" Danny, aroused, was moving over her, pulling her to him.

"Oh, again? Now?" *Okay! Dieu, Twice!*

They soared again.

Two, three, four times, brave Peter rose to the call. Thrusting into the fray with wild abandon.

*   *   *   *

It was well past midnight when Danny did the male thing—he dozed off.

Josie lay back. Her nightgown was balled-up at the foot of the bed. She knew she was grinning like a fool, but couldn't stop. She had never known such joy. She thought, *It is so good I almost can't stand it. Yes I Can!* Her whole being swelled with feeling. *I could burst!* She looked at him where he slept on his side. She was excited just looking at his body. She reached down and almost touched his buttock before she stopped herself. *He is beautiful! And it's like…we fit! It's perfect. As though he were born in B.C. and I in Quebec, but for each other.* She looked at the ceiling, as if to heaven. *And I wanted gentle? I don't think so.*

She lay down against him with one arm over his waist, bodies nestled spoon fashion. She slept.

The sun was high outside the drawn curtains when she awoke. She looked around the room and had to smile when she saw they had somehow managed to switch sides during their lovemaking. She reached carefully across him to look at her watch on the bedside table. Nine fifteen. She got up and went into the bathroom. When she returned, she opened the curtains a crack and sat on the bed wrapped in a blanket, looking out. After five minutes she felt the bed move. Danny lay on his back with his arms behind his head.

He smiled up at her, and with sleep still in his voice said, "G'morning, Hon."

"Hello, my love, you slept well," she said. "I'm very hungry. We will have to find some food!" She bent to kiss him. The blanket fell open.

He pulled her down to him, felt the warmth of her skin on his chest. "Bullshit we will."

As they reached for the heavens again, she thought, *Who's hungry!*

Afterward however, she insisted, "Well, L.A.C. Danny," she looked down, "and you, too, AC-2 Peter, this little girl is starving. I'm going to get dressed right now. I will 'ave to walk—or maybe crawl—to some place where there's food if you won't take me!" she giggled. "I warn you, if I don't eat soon, I will have no energy and be no good to you…I need food to keep up my strength!" She got up and went into the bathroom.

He called, "We certainly can't have you getting weak, can we. There's an A & W on the highway just down the road." He heard the shower start.

She came out with a towel around her. She smiled at him. "They won't serve us at the A &W if you go there naked. You 'ad better get dressed." He grabbed his bag and went to shower.

When he came out, she was dressed in off-white pedal pushers and a big, floppy sweater with a loose turtle neck, dark gray with minute purple and blue flecks.

"You're a knockout!" he said.

"Like it? I just bought it this week." He came for her. She backed off quickly. "Danny! No! Okay, one little kiss, then get moving!"

He put on his Levi's from the night before and a maroon polo shirt.

When they got to the drive-in, they found it wouldn't be open till eleven.

"Shall we go somewhere else?" asked Danny.

"No. Let's come back when it's open. It's only an hour."

"Sounds good." In that last embrace before leaving the cabin, he discovered she was not wearing a brassiere this morning and it turned him on again. He couldn't know that she, too, was aroused, so it was eleven forty-five before they got back to the A & W. They both ordered Papa Burgers, fries and large root beers. The carhop hooked a tray in the driver-side window and started to place their order on it.

Josie said, "Do we want to eat here, Danny?"

"Oh. I suppose not." To the carhop he said, "I'm sorry, but I should have ordered it to go. Could you…"

"I'll have to get you paper cups. Or, it's fifty cents each for the mugs."

"It's okay. I'll buy the mugs." He gave her four dollars and they drove back to the motel.

Because other matters took precedence, it was two-fifteen before Josie got to eat her cold Hamburger and fries, then she wrestled with Danny for his, both thrashing about the room naked. She managed to get a couple of large bites in her mouth and mustard and relish on her person before he got it away from her and locked himself in the bathroom to eat.

Their meal times were all similarly inconsistent over the next two days.

*   *   *   *

Sunday afternoon came and it was time to leave. Danny stood by the open door with their bags.

"Got everything, Hon?"

"Yes." Her voice was small, hesitant. "Danny?"

"Right here…"

"Come back in for a minute. Okay?"

He stepped in, closed the door. "What?"

She stood close, looking up. "Danny…you said 'ere this weekend that you love me."

"I love you, Josie, believe it."

"You know I loved you since we met. It shouldn't be possible, but now you 'ave made me love you even more. I could not live if we were apart…if you ever left me. If you will ever leave, Danny, do it now. Say it to me—and do it right now!"

"Jo. Honey. You're stuck with me. I could never leave you, ever."

"I want you to promise. Promise it to me now, Danny."

"I promise. I'll never leave, Josie!"

"Oh, thank you." She put her arms around his waist. "You will never be sorry."

It was a promise he kept. Danny never left Josie.

There would be two occasions, however, when Josie would leave Danny.

✳   ✳   ✳   ✳

They were back on the base at four o'clock.

She said, "Drive right up to the gate. It's Oscar. He's nice." She leaned across Danny to talk to the elderly Commissionaire standing by the barrier. "Hello, Oscar! Could he drive me to the barracks? He'll only be a few minutes inside."

Oscar lifted the yellow and black barrier, waving them through with a smile and a mock salute

They kissed goodbye outside the barracks. When she left the car, she did not want to let his hand go. They hugged once more.

"Will I see you next week?" At his nod, she said, "Please drive carefully. I love you, my Danny!"

She watched him drive away before going inside. She just now realized she was tired and a little sore—but content.

Ollie was in the room. "Hi, pal. How'd the trip go?" she studied her friend. "Boy, you look beat."

"I am a bit tired. I didn't sleep much." *I surely didn't—that part is so true.* It took some effort to not giggle.

"What's his family like?"

"Oh, 'is mother is nice." She hated lying to Ollie. "His father and brothers, though, they don't seem so nice." It was something she had learned from him in their conversations. "I think I'll go to bed for awhile. Then I'll have to do a laundry."

"You get to bed, Jo, and I'll get your laundry. I've got a few things I have to get done anyway. You'll owe me one." She took some clothes from their dirty laundry drawer.

"Okay. Thank you. I'll pay you back." She sat on the bed, took off her sweater. "There's stuff in my bag, too." She got up quickly and took clothes from her bag. She didn't want Ollie to see the root beer mugs—or the tube of gel.

When Ollie left, she lay back on the bed with a secret little smile. She was remembering the lovemaking, feeling it all over again. She knew there could be nothing in the world as natural as she and Danny Tanner. She thought, *And to have fun, to joke about our bodies. I think I'll laugh every time I hear the word "that," or meet someone named Peter.* She hugged herself. *I'm alive. I'm so alive! Peter the Great.*

She slept till the next morning.

*   *   *   *

The summer was a warm, sunny one in the Comox Valley. Danny drove the Ford to Comox every weekend. He and Josie could not get enough of each other. She could not believe the depth of her own passion or the way their lovemaking had become so natural. Even on the days following their first lovemaking she had felt in no way "sinful" or at all contrite. She had felt no more than slightly naughty and she soon got over it. Her apparent off-handed attitude had nothing to do with sophistication or liberal morals; it was simply that she knew, with absolute certainty, she and Danny Tanner would be mates for life. They were too much meant to be together for it not to come true.

For his part, Danny had no regret whatsoever. Sexual encounters had long been a matter of course for him, and he considered sex just one of many wonderful manifestations of their love for each other. He just knew he had never wanted to be with anyone as he did with Josie. His only care was his concern for her reputation.

They made love as often as possible. As for all young couples, there were obstacles. There was first the problem of time; it wasn't easy to find time alone, away from friends, with Danny arriving from the mainland as late as nine P.M. on Friday, and leaving on Sunday afternoon. Then there was the problem of place; they used the Ocean View twice more, but the lies needed to explain the overnight absences were wearing on Josie, who hated lying to Ollie. She discovered a small, mossy clearing, in some thick woods, a few hundred yards from 51 beach and they would sneak away there with a blanket. Of course, as desperate couples have since the invention of the automobile, they did it in the Ford; it was Danny who had a problem there—he was so protective of her reputation he was bothered by the thought of someone spotting them.

They were going through a period of discovery, and no two lovers were more attuned to each other's needs and moods. Danny, especially, knew when to be gentle and slow, and when to love her with abandon.

They spoke freely to each other of their love and feelings: "Remember that night in my berth, Danny? I was already so in love with you…I only met you the day before but I knew. Anyway, in the berth I, you know, I, um…came! Just from your kissing and touching! Is that crazy?"

"It's not crazy, it's beautiful. It makes me happy for you." He grinned and added, "And kind of proud of me. I must be one of the world's greatest lovers!"

"You are! Come, show me again."

Her capricious nature surfaced as never before when they were naked together. All her reserve fell away. Some of their private jokes, which they found hilarious, would have shocked even Ollie Conti. One of their favorites was to bestow "awards" upon Peter, who soon became the most decorated organ in history. One night Josie suggested they recognize the esteemed member with a knighthood. Danny quickly vetoed her, saying any thought of a sharp sword near *that* head was far too scary, regardless of how deserving old Pete might be. They laughed so hard they affected his ability to perform.

She always tried to keep the lovemaking light. When he, the experienced lover, showed her for the first time how having her on top facilitated the act in a back seat, she imitated a gruff male voice saying, "Me Tarzan, you Jane—me on top, you on bottom!" and then fell off him, giggling helplessly. She tried again however, and they soon managed quite well.

In spite of the obstacles to their lovemaking, they fell more and more *in love*. If the problems of time and place made it impossible to make love, they were happy just to be together. When they were apart between weekends they longed for each other and thought of little else.

Those warm summer months of 1955 were, until then, the happiest of young Josie's life. She wistfully compared it to her joyful years as a little girl in Cornwall, a time she remembered so fondly. In her mind she shared her happiness with her mother: *Oh, Mama, this boy is so beautiful. And he loves me. It is just as you told me, nothing matters but to be with him—to love him! Mama, I wish you could know him. I know you would love him as I do!*

She was soon to receive news that would make her, if it were possible, even happier.

CHAPTER 12

▼

I had great news…

COMOX—JULY 26TH

It happened Josie answered the call. "Orderly Room, AW1 Connor 'ere."

"Josie? Hi, Hon." It was Danny.

She glanced to the back of the office. Sgt. Wilson had left, probably for the day.

"Hello, Honey! I didn't expect to hear from you today," she said.

"Well, I've got some news. Can you talk?"

"Yes, I can. Old Willie isn't here. Is it good news?"

"I'll let you judge. Are you sitting down?"

She wasn't but she said, "Yes. Danny, you're making me scared. What is it?"

"Well…the damn Air Force has transferred me out of here."

She groped for a nearby chair, pulled it to her and sat.

"Jo? You still there?"

Her face paled. "Oh, Danny," she said in a small voice, almost a whisper, "Where?"

"Have you ever heard of a place called…" he paused, "a place called…Fifty One friggin' AC&W Squadron? At Comox, B.C.?"

It took a moment before it sunk in. "Danny, don't fool me. Is it for sure?"

"Yeah! You guys should be getting the signal from Command. I just got it fifteen minutes ago! It's effective August sixth."

She squealed, "Danny! I'm so happy I could just…" She turned from the phone and yelled, *"Ollie!* Ollie, he's *coming 'ere!* Danny!" Unthinking, she hung up the receiver. She raced across the room to Ollie's desk. "Ollie did you 'ear me?"

Ollie held a hand up to tone her down, "Josie, he always comes here, every..."

Josie ran back to the phone. She grabbed up the receiver only to find the line dead. "Hello? Danny? The big dope, he must 'ave hung up on me...hello?" She put the receiver down again. "He's transferred here, to 51! Next month, Ollie!" She grabbed poor, newly married Ken Bromley and waltzed him across the office to Ollie's desk.

Ollie was beaming. "He's transferred here? Great! I'm so happy for you two."

At Jericho, Danny heard the line go dead, he tried, "Jo? Hey, Josie! Shit." *What the hell?* He hung up and called Russ at 51.

A few minutes later Russ called the Orderly Room. "Ollie, Did you hear?"

"Yeah. Isn't it great? Jo's bouncing off the frigging walls. Shit, now we can *really* get in trouble!"

"Y'know what, Ol, I think we were already doing that just fine. Put Josie on." Ollie signaled Josie to pick up another phone. "Jo, it's Russ."

Josie screamed, "Russ? Yes, I heard! He phoned me. Russ, I'm so happy! You, too, eh?"

"Oh, yeah. This is great!" he said.

*   *   *   *

51 AC&W SQUADRON, COMOX—AUGUST, 1955

Danny Tanner was back at a G.C.I.

51 AC&W Squadron was a key unit in the air defense of Western Canada and Northwestern U.S.A. Under the command of 5th Air Division of the R.C.A.F.'s Air Defense Command, 51 Sqn. was responsible for the surveillance, identification and control of all air traffic approaching the continent from the North Pacific and Western Arctic. The traffic processed by the unit came from its own radar and six other bases, located in remoter areas of B.C. and Alberta. The units at Tofino and Holberg were R.C.A.F. Stations. The U.S. Air Force operated those at Puntzi Mountain, Kamloops, Baldy Hughes and Beaverlodge. The range of the Sector's surveillance capability was further extended by U.S. Navy radar "picket" ships and early warning aircraft flying fixed patterns over the Pacific.

5th Air Division's Combat Operations Center at Jericho—Station Vancouver—was Headquarters for the westernmost Sector in the Pinetree Line radar chain. (Danny's former station, St. Margarets, housed the easternmost Sector HQ.)

Targets or "tracks" from all the radars of the Sector's units, each reaching hundreds of miles in radius, were reported in to 51 for identification as friend or foe. Interceptors of 409 Squadron at Comox were on various stages of readiness. They could be "scrambled" under radar control of the G.C.I., to intercept targets.

All newly detected tracks reported to Comox started life classified as "unknown." The designation would change to "friendly" or "hostile," according to information in the hands of the unit's Identification Section, called Ident. Every aircraft aloft, anywhere within North American airspace, must file a Flight Plan. For control and identification purposes long-range flights fly along pre-designated "highways" in the sky, called Airways. Enroute, every flight must radio in its position and time as it passes over certain checkpoints. All original Flight Plans and checkpoint reports were provided to the G.C.I.s along the routes via Teletype. The information was matched with the radar tracks to determine a flight's identity. In those days of largely propeller-powered commercial and military aircraft, 5 Air Div's coverage area was one of the busiest air traffic zones in North America. Hundreds of flights flew through the sector daily. They could be east and west, inbound and outbound for Vancouver and Seattle-Tacoma, or north and south to and from Alaska. Added to these were all the Trans-Pacific traffic and dozens of local and military flights. The Ident Section personnel at Comox operated in a highly intense atmosphere.

Typically, an AC&W unit consisted of several parts. There were the two search radars (one was a backup), and a heightfinder. These were housed in three large structures, the towers. Each huge antenna was protected by a "radome"—a fibreglass geodesic dome. (The domes represented one of the world's first practical uses of Buckminster Fuller's geodesics, replacing the original rubber and fabric ones that were held up by air pressure.)

The Operations Building housed the Ops Room, offices, workshops, radio rooms and switchboards for internal phones and external landlines. The center of all activity at 51 was the Ops Room, where were located the radar consoles with their fifteen-inch diameter scopes, large plotting boards, radio and landline terminals, intercept control stations, the Ident Section and the Duty Controller's station.

Crews of Fighter Control Operators and commissioned Controllers manned the Ops Room in three shifts—twenty-four hours a day, every day of the year. The crew personnel were also known as FighterCOps, FCOs and, demeaningly by other trades, as "Scope-Dopes". (The perverse nature of most FighterCOps was such that they embraced the name Scope-Dope and used it with pride among themselves.) The Ops crews were supported by the various technical trades and administrative personnel.

The Operations at a G.C.I. were under the command of the Chief Operations Officer, or Senior Controller. In addition, as a "lodger unit" at Station Comox, 51 Squadron had an Officer Commanding who held the rank of Squadron Leader. On a typical 51 crew, there were a Corporal as Crew Chief and one or more Controllers, including the Duty Controller, the officer in charge of a shift. The most experienced FighterCOps, some junior NCOs, but all at least Group 3 tradesmen, served as 'Ops-B' (right-hand man to the Duty Controller), or as NCO i/c Ident (NCO in charge of the Identification Section). The next in trade group level and experience filled positions such as Intercept Plotter, 'Ops B-1' and Ident Clerk. The least experienced, often fresh out of Clinton, served as scope operators, plotters, forward landline tellers, tote board ops and radio monitors.

It was typical in that time of rapid expansion of the trade, when promotions couldn't keep up with demand, many positions of responsibility were held by ranks far lower than officially mandated. It was not uncommon that a Corporal Crew Chief, for instance, may be filling what was on paper a Flight Sergeant's position, an L.A.C. was often in a Corporal or Sergeant's job. In 1955, 51 Squadron had just one senior NCO, a Sergeant, and five Corporals in the FighterCOp trade.

✳   ✳   ✳   ✳

Danny spent his first week on the day shift, "floating," getting familiar with 51's Ops Room before being assigned to one of the five crews. After the week, he was assigned to D Crew. He found he had already met most of his new mates, they were known as a bunch of party animals, and he and Josie had often partied with them on weekends. He knew from past experience a crew's off-duty behavior had little to do with its operational efficiency. His early read was that this bunch, who proudly dubbed themselves the "Wild Dogs," was pretty good on the job, if anything lacking in experience. The name came from the out-of-date British-American alphabet code: Able, Baker, Charlie, Dog—D for Dog Crew, hence Wild Dogs. (He supposed "wild *deltas*," using the newer code, would lose something.)

The Crew Controller was Flying Officer Pat Donahue, a former World War II Mosquito Pathfinder pilot. "Paddy," as fellow officers (and FighterCops out of his hearing range) called him, had left the service at the end of hostilities, and had come back to the Air Force in 1953. He was not a strict disciplinarian, preferring to have his people serve with, rather than under him. The Crew Chief was a Corporal named Ellen Schmidt, an attractive brunette, who planned to make the Air Force her career. She had most recently been stationed at Air Defense HQ, in St. Hubert. She knew her craft, but lacked field experience at a G.C.I., a fact she readily acknowledged. It was not the first time Danny had found his Crew Chief less experienced than he was.

Corporal Schmidt took Danny aside at the beginning of his first shift.

"Tanner...can I call you Dan?" At Danny's nod and smile, she continued, "You don't know how pleased we are, Flying Officer Donahue and I, to get someone with your experience! We've been bugging the C.Ops.O. for months to get someone like you. I'm hoping you can take over at NCO Ident right away and still help me with training. Based on your seniority and experience, we can plug you into Ident without hurting anyone's feelings."

"Sounds good, Corp."

"Dan, these kids are a good bunch on the job. They just need help—training from an experienced guy like you." She paused, "If there's no big wheels around, please call me Ellen. Come up to the ivory tower, I'll introduce you to the Controller."

After the introductions, Donahue said, "Tanner, Dan is it? Welcome aboard. I've looked at your trade record. You have a ton of experience, how is it you're not a Corporal by now?"

A little abashed, Danny replied, "I can't say, Sir, I guess..."

"Been in a little trouble, have you, Dan?" Donahue was smiling.

Danny smiled back at him. "Yes, Sir. They keep my service record on a roller! It was all off-duty stuff. The Air Force is in need of a better sense of humor. Been a good boy for almost two years, though."

"Well, you come highly recommended by an old friend of mine, Moe Morrisey."

"I appreciate that, Sir."

"Hell, don't say 'Sir' with every sentence. About once at the start of a shift will do." He lowered his voice. "Unless the Old Man's around, of course then you'd better Sir me to death!" He grinned as he went on, "I'm sure Moe didn't like to lose a good man. Listen Dan, together, you and I and Ellen here will whip this crew into shape—then there'll be a promotion for you, I'm sure. Training is important for this crew right now and I want to give it top priority. We just got a new C. Ops. O. last month and I have a feeling there'll soon be a shake-up. Have you got lots of experience at Ident? The traffic in this Sector is as heavy as you're ever going to see."

Danny replied, "The heavier the better—makes the shifts go by quicker. Just to straighten one thing out, I'm not concerned, one way or another, about promotion. I agree with you and the Corporal about the training. I don't know if you were aware, I helped instruct a couple of these people for their trade exams back in May, Gil Potter and Gerry Henderson."

"Then, you'll be happy to know they passed their exams," said Donahue. "You know, there's nothing wrong in hoping for advancement. You work hard, you learn your business, and you deserve it. It's recognition, Dan."

$$*\qquad *\qquad *\qquad *$$

So Danny became a Wild Dog.

He soon found that the crew—the whole unit—had a higher than acceptable number of PE's—Personnel Errors. At his other units, Danny's crews went months between P.E.s. Here at Comox, D Crew committed three and four every month, and the other crews averaged about the same. He considered it unfathomable for any C. Ops. O. to tolerate such numbers.

Ellen introduced him to Jake MacDonald. Despite his inexperience and only being a Group 2 tradesman, Jake had been holding down NCO i/c Ident before Danny's arrival.

"Do you mind if we take a ten minute coffee break, Ellen?"

"Fine. I'll hold down Ident for you. I'll call you if I get into trouble. Okay?"

"Just don't lose any Russians, Ellen." He replied, with a grin.

In the lunchroom, he asked, "Jake, you got any problems with me taking over Ident?"

"Not at all, Dan. I'm glad for it. Hell, I'm only a Group 2. My only other posting was Moisie, and you know there's no Ident function there, the G.C.I. at St. Margarets did it all. I just hope you'll keep me on with you for awhile. I want to learn."

"Good. I want to start a log of regular flights…all the scheduled stuff that comes through the sector.

"Never heard of it."

"We'll start logging everything coming through regularly from the Flight Plans; I'll get a log book. One other thing; each month, on nights and evenings, Donahue wants us to rotate one of the Group 1 or 2 people through Ident. They won't get to make decisions, but they appreciate the change and it's good training. You'll be helping to train them, Jake. It's amazing what you learn when you have to teach it to someone else."

As the crew worked through the next round of shift changes, Danny got to know his fellow Wild Dogs. Besides Ellen Schmidt and Jake MacDonald, he had already met Vera Cromwell and Bobby Gaines and knew Gil and Gerry from the Trade Group course. The others were Marianne Coles, Todd Granger, and Dave Nickerson. The only Group 3 tradesmen were Danny, Ellen and Gil, who had just passed the exam in June. There were three Group 2 people, and the remaining five were all Group 1—green FighterCOps on their first field posting.

$$*   *   *   *$$

At the start of a round of graveyard shifts, Ellen told Bobby to report to Danny at Ident.

"Welcome to the mysteries of Ident, Bobby," said Danny. "When the traffic slows down, after about zero-one-thirty, I'll give you the two-bit tour. Meanwhile, sneak upstairs for the first break, if you want."

"Can I go up a little later, Dan? I'll just watch you geniuses at work for awhile."

"No sweat." He turned to Nickerson. "Dave, you want to take your break now?"

"Sure do. See you later, folks. Want the usual, Danny?" said Dave. He knew Danny was holding off on taking breaks during busy periods. He mistakenly thought it was because he didn't trust anyone else to perform while he was away. In truth, he was protecting them from P.E.s, till they were sure of themselves—anything going wrong in his presence would fall on his shoulders.

"Thanks, Dave. Double sugar, eh?"

"Roger-D."

Danny turned to Bobby, "Okay, Bobarino, my first question is, do you want to learn this stuff, or should we just sit in a dark corner and neck?" said he with a smirk.

She smiled back. "Yeah, right, Romeo. But I do want to learn." She hesitated. "Will we get a chance to work with the Ops B, too?"

"Surely, you don't think you'd prefer to be up there, with the officers?" he asked.

She whispered her answer. "No. But you-know-who is always at Ops B."

"Ah. So you're hot for Gil? That's why you wanted your break later!" Bobby was a pretty girl with curly auburn hair and a smattering of freckles.

She whispered, "Shit yeah, but he won't even acknowledge I exist."

Danny lowered his voice. "He must be blind. How about we try to work your breaks with his."

"Sounds good, thanks. Don't say anything, please, I'd die!" She turned to the nearby Teletype receiver. The machine was chattering noisily as always with incoming flight plan data. "I always wondered what this loud beast is all about."

Jake answered her. "Well, this is where it all starts. Those are the flight plans we work from.

*   *   *   *

And so, the "shaping-up" of the Wild Dogs began. D Crew was charged with only one P.E. the following month. In the next three months they would have none. Flying Officer Donahue was pleased, a fact he asked Ellen to pass on to the crew.

In the lunchroom Ellen gave Danny a big hug. "How to go, big guy, you did it! The boss-man is happy as hell and…"

He interrupted, "We, Ellen! We did it, not me, *we*. All of us. You were right when you said these are sharp people, they learn fast."

She replied, "Okay, *we*. Thanks, that's nice of you. You know, Tanner, sometimes I almost wish you weren't already taken."

Bobby Gaines rolled her eyes. "Ooh. Bad thoughts, boss-lady!"

"We all know I'm just kidding…I like Josie too much. Besides, my guy would be pretty cheesed-off."

Grinning, Danny said, "Just my luck, my girlfriend's too damn popular—shit, I couldn't fool around if I wanted to. I should get me an ugly and unpopular babe, like Bobby here." As he got up to return to the Ops Room, he said, *"Some of us have to get to work. Ta-ta, ladies, feel free to rave about me when I'm gone!"*

They threw balled-up napkins at him as he started down the stairs. Ellen stuck out her tongue at his disappearing back. Bobby muttered, "Shithead!"

*   *   *   *

On a Sunday in late August, Bobby was talking about Danny in the Mess Hall. Josie, Ollie and Gil were at the table.

"I'm telling you, Jo, your guy's a totally different person on the job. It's hard to describe…he knows, like, *everything!* I mean he doesn't *say* he knows it, he just does! I don't mean he's not still a great guy or anything, we have a lot of fun on crew, but he makes us want to learn. Our Controller, Donahue, wanted him to train the crew. Shit, I almost want to call him 'Sir' sometimes!" She paused, "Then, after work, in the Wets or whatever, there's the same old crazy Danny we all know and love—and sometimes want to murder."

Gil added, "She's right. He's one of the sharpest guys on the job I've ever seen. He's…what would you call him, um…systematic? He's got everything down to a tee. No room for error. And he's a natural teacher."

"Yeah," said Bobby, "he makes it so easy to understand."

"I'd hate to be the guy, or girl, that causes our next P.E. The rest of the crew'll lynch him!" said Gil.

"Or her," said Bobbie.

Ollie asked, "What's a P.E.?"

Bobby replied, "Personnel Error. We used to get them all the time, mostly at Ident. Everyone always blamed it on the heavy traffic. Even our Controller, old Donahue, thought so. Now we've just gone a whole month, without even one! All of a sudden, the whole crew's proud as hell. Everyone's determined now to get zero P.E.s! It's kind of more fun to be at work this way. I know it sounds weird…"

"It's not weird," Said Ollie, "but, shit-all-to-hell, I'm glad we don't have someone looking for P.E.s in our place, hey Jo."

Josie said sardonically, "We *do!* We 'ave old Sergeant Wilson!" She went on, "Danny told me about his friends back east, the guys who taught him and Russ about their trade. His heroes."

Gil said, "Jake MacDonald told me a good one. Get this—the other night Dan's sitting there reading a book, no sign he's even looking at the plotting board, and he hears Jake say he's not sure about a track. Well, Danny's about forty feet away in the corner. He says to Jake, 'What's the speed and height on it?' He doesn't even look up from the book. Jake tells him whatever the speed and stuff is, and Danny looks at the clock and says, 'That's Northwest flight forty-two, DC-4. Fairbanks, Anchorage, Seattle; it's late because there's weather up at Anchorage. You'll get a corrected Flight Plan in a few minutes. Just tell the boss-man what's going on.' Sure enough, about five minutes later, in comes the correction. Jake just about had a baby."

Bobby exclaimed, "Yeah! I was on Ident with him and Jake that night. It was as if it was just *normal* for him. Then of course, you know Danny, later he brags it up, 'Just routine for the Ident Wizard!' or, 'I'm so bright, my Dad calls me sunny.' The shithead!"

They all laughed.

"Yeah, nothing modest about our Tanner," said Ollie. "Russ told me he wasn't so much into your trade when he first finished training, but Danny and those other guys got to him, and now he loves it. He calls it the 'Tanner Scope-Dope Disease.' Sounds like you guys are getting infected."

Gil said, "It's funny you said that. Russ is a hotshot, too. I was at Foymont with him for a few months. Now those two have started a competition between B Crew and us. So far, we're kicking their...you know."

Ollie said, "Russ says you guys are the only trade in the Air Force that has to work in the dark and write backward. What's *that* all about?"

"It's true!" said Bobby. "The Ops Room is dark, it's for the scopes. Everything's in the same room and it has to be dark so you can read the scopes. And watch this..." She took a pen from her purse and quickly printed on a napkin the first ten letters of the alphabet, J to A, and the digits 9 to 1, all backwards and perfectly legible. "You do it because you're writing behind the board, so it can be read from out front. I wrote a whole letter backward to my sister, just to show off."

Ollie said, "That's quite a skill, Bobby. It won't get you far on civvy-street, though." She looked closer, squinting. "Actually, it kind of looks like Jo's frontwards writing."

"Shut up, you," said Josie.

"There's one thing about Danny—as a joke he may like to brag it up, but otherwise he's no bullshitter." declared Gil.

Josie had taken all this in, proud of her man. When she heard the last statement, however, she jumped in loudly, "HAH! Danny no bullshitter? Hah!"

They all looked at her in surprise.

Bobby said, "He isn't, Jo." She saw Josie's head shaking. "Is he?"

Josie looked at Ollie. "Should I tell them about the first time I ever met him, at Montreal?"

"Oh, yeah," said Ollie. "You guys have got to hear this. Tell them, Jo."

Josie set about telling them the story of Danny and the soldiers at Windsor Station. She exaggerated, of course, puffing her chest, strutting back and forth and giving her best impression of a gruff male voice as she spoke Danny's parts.

"Well, I saw this big, mean *L.A.C.*—that was Danny. Remember, I was just fresh from my training so I was scared of his rank, but I thought maybe he could rescue me from those army guys, so I asked him. He told me, 'Okay, little AW2, I shall take care of those army guys for you!' He went over to them and starts to give them...like this: 'You army guys hold it right there! You are talking bad to that *nurse* over there, and nurses are *officers!*' He was pointing to *me!* I had to go over to see this! Then when he saw me coming, he said, 'Now you two move along, quickly now, get moving or I'll make you shine all the garbage cans in-in Canada, you bad soldiers!' And they *left!* In a big 'urry."

Everyone at the table broke up at the story, and her hilarious impersonation.

Gil said, "No way, Josie!"

Bobby said, "Oh, shit, I think I believe it. That is so funny."

Josie nodded her head. "Uh, huh. It's true, he *did* it! And me, I was so stupid. I said 'But, L.A.C., I'm not a nurse!" She said it in a simpering female voice. "Then he gave me '*ell*, for not watching his bag! But there's more..." She looked at Ollie. "You didn't hear this one. After the soldiers ran away, he looked at my ticket." She used the male voice again. "'Well, little *AW-2*, that Comox place, it's way out across the ocean! You go there on a boat!' Then he looks at my ticket again, 'This is no good. Come with me.'" She did the comical swagger, jabbing a finger at the floor. "'You wait right 'ere, *AW-2*. And don't you move!' He talked to the, um, ticket lady, 'Hi, there, nice lady, you remind me of my mommy. That's my nurse over there, I'm her *escort*. She is an officer and there's a mistake. Somebody gave her an *upper berth...*"

They were all laughing again. Josie started to laugh and couldn't finish. She had to sit down.

"Oh, Jesus, I can see what's coming," said Ollie, "his mommy. Stop it, Jo! His friggin' *mommy?*"

"Yes!" Josie managed. "He came back with a *lower* for me! I 'ad it for the whole trip to Vancouver. He still doesn't know I heard every word he said! And you say he's not a bullshitter?"

She didn't see Danny a few feet away, carrying a tray and talking to some people at another table.

Bobby doubled over laughing. "Jo! You're *lying!* You have to be."

Gil added, "Yeah, it's too crazy, Josie."

"What's she lying about, now, Bobby?" It was Danny. He sat beside Josie.

She looked up at him in wide-eyed surprise. She clapped her hands over her mouth. "Oh, oh," she said, behind her hands.

Bobby answered him. "About the train station in Montreal, Danny?"

Gil said, "Tanner, you are haywire!"

Danny smiled broadly. "Hey, I got the girl didn't I? Whatever works, people." He put an arm around her shoulders.

*   *   *   *

51 AC&W SQUADRON

Danny was on D Crew for two weeks when the new C Ops O of 51 AC&W had seen enough. He ordered the anticipated shake-up of the unit in late August. Suspecting members of the various crews were becoming complacent because of familiarity and some weak leadership, the C Ops O ordered a realignment of the unit's crew personnel bringing top-to-bottom changes to some of the crews, and an ongoing training program. D Crew was not in the least adversely affected by the realignment. Russ Knight was transferred to D Crew, in exchange for Dave Nickerson who was engaged to a girl on B Crew and had requested a transfer so he could be on crew with his fiancée. (Neither the Crew Chief nor the Crew Controller of B Crew had been comfortable with the presence of L.A.C. Knight, who they believed displayed "a know-it-all attitude.") Also added to the Wild Dogs were a tall, angular L.A.C. named Herman Melville Zachary nicknamed "Zack," transferred from C Crew, and "Mitch" Kobiashi from A Crew. The changes brought the crew up to a full complement of twelve.

Flying Officer Donahue fought vigorously against the transfer of Corporal Schmidt. He pointed to the crew's performance over the past months under her leadership. Corporal Schmidt stayed with D Crew, and the Wild Dogs were favorably impressed with his display of loyalty—by an officer, no less.

When Donahue commented on the acquisition of one more Group 3 type in Russ Knight, Danny said, "Hell, boss, you'll soon see we just traded off a bench-warmer and got Willie Mays!"

Ellen began rotating Danny, Russ and Gil through the key Ops-B, Intercept Supervisor and NCO Ident positions. She jokingly declared to the Controller, "You won't be needing me anymore, Sir. I'll just spend the rest of my tour up in the lunch room!"

*   *   *   *

For the third time since they enlisted, Tanner and Knight were on the same crew. The Fearsome Foursome became just a bit more fearsome, and the Wild Dogs a bit wilder.

The two couples continued to go places and do things together. Danny's old Ford was a godsend to them, in those times when only a few Airmen could afford to own a car and keep it running. Whenever the Ford required repairs, the four of them pooled their cash and shared the cost. They took turns buying gas—three or four dollars would top up the tank. (If short of cash between paydays, Danny and Russ weren't above occasionally siphoning a little gas from parked vehicles, using the short length of garden hose they kept in the trunk. Their favorite source was the 51 shuttle vehicle.) Danny, Russ or Ollie, whoever was in the best shape, did the driving. They called it "taking the con" or "pilot duty." Ollie, with her penchant for naming people and things, dubbed the Ford "Prince Henry." One weekend, when they were all broke and the good Prince took ill, leaving them stranded on the base, Russ temporarily renamed him "Henry the Royal Prink," the linguistic and anatomical meanings of which Ollie had to explain to Josie. As a compromise the name became "Just Henry" and finally, "J.H."

On nice days the two couples would pile into J.H. and explore their part of Vancouver Island. Josie and Ollie especially liked the Provincial parks and the many beaches. If an activity involved all the Wild Dogs, they would cram as many as four couples into the car and hit the road. Jake MacDonald owned the only other car on D Crew, a '47 De Soto wood-sided station wagon that could accommodate as many as six couples—if neatly stacked. The De Soto was named the "Dog Pound." It wasn't uncommon to see J.H. and the Dog Pound barreling along the district's roads, arms and legs sticking out of windows, on the way to or from some party site or other. If there was reason to transport some of the girls around, Ollie borrowed either J.H. or the Dog Pound. (Jake commented she drove his car as much as he did.)

Josie and Ollie were accepted into the Wild Dogs as "Lifetime Associate Members Under Continuous Surveillance" in a riotous impromptu ceremony presided over in the Wets by Jake and Gerry. Gerry tried to charge the girls a fee for their membership but was voted and shouted down. A chorus of "Speech, speech!" followed the induction. The addled Gerry rose from his chair, only to be shouted down again, "Not you, idiot! Siddown, stupid! Boo, hiss!" Ollie, of course, spoke for both girls: "This is a day I'm sure Jo and I shall forever remember, much as if we broke a hip, or contracted the black plague." Which brought, "We want Gerry!" from the fickle membership.

*   *   *   *

OPS ROOM—51 AC&W

On a tense Saturday morning, Danny demonstrated the training and versatility of Canadian Air Defense personnel and tested even his innovative imagination.

It happened as the Wild Dogs relieved B Crew at 0750 to start a day shift. There was an Unknown track on the plotting board when Danny came into the Ops Room. The target was "strength four plus"—four or more aircraft—out over the North Pacific, incoming on a south-southeast heading. It was presently on 53 AC&W's radar, near the outer limits of the sector's coverage. It's multi-aircraft strength and speed of 480 knots ruled out any civilian traffic of the day. The speed would bring the planes over the Vancouver-Seattle population centers in about an hour and a half.

Dave Nickerson, Bravo's NCO Ident, said, "Dan, am I glad to see you! Holberg reported this track five minutes ago…we've got nothing on them, no paper at all. Christ, you know the Yanks!" They often joked that the Americans were liable go to Red Alert and scramble their entire air force against an unidentified civilian Piper Cub.

"The Crew Chief up at Consort says he checked the scope. He says the strength is at least four, maybe more. I'll stick around if you need me."

Danny said, "Good. We can use you. Let's see what we can do about this track." He could feel the tension in the room. The word had spread to the arriving Wild Dogs. Everyone was alert and wide-eyed, and there was no unnecessary conversation. It was not hard to imagine in 1955, that the Soviets could launch a preemptive strike—it was the reason Air Defense Command existed.

Corporal Schmidt was assigning her best people to key positions.

Danny called to her, "Ellen, can I have Knight up here till this is figured out? I need him."

Ellen replied from down on the floor, "You got him. Did you hear him, Russ?"

"I'm on my way, Dan."

"Okay," said Danny, "Russ, you sit down and go over every flight plan and position report. Everything that came off the printer—right back to yesterday. Dave, think hard. *Anything* with multi aircraft?"

Dave said, "No…oh, wait a minute. Shit, yeah! We had a flight of B-47s from SAC. Just after we took over last night. They were headed out, north-northeast, and that was the only flight plan, nothing saying they were coming back this way. There were six of them."

"See if you can find that original flight plan, Dave. Russ, you help him. Get any follow up on it, checkpoints, anything. Russ, take over here for a few minutes—you're in charge." He bounded up the short flight of stairs to the Duty Controller's dais. The B Crew Controller, F/O Quinn had stayed behind, too. Danny spoke to Donahue.

"Sir, we're working on something. How long before we have to go Hostile on these targets?"

Dave tapped him on the shoulder and passed him some green teletype copies. Danny glanced at them and then turned back to Donahue.

Donahue said, "The Americans just went to Yellow Alert, Dan. The decision's out of our hands. The Sector Commander was just on the line, getting antsy. What can I give him?"

"A SAC flight—six B-47s out of Mountain Home. They went outbound earlier. We have nothing, and I mean *zilch* paperwork, about any return leg. Just the outbound flight plan. I've got an idea I want to try…"

Donahue interrupted him, "Hold on, 5 Div's calling again." He took a handset from Gil, the Ops-B, saying, "Waterfall—Duty Controller here." He listened to the phone and then said, "Yes Sir…our best people are on it. They've checked everything. They've got a possible but no paper. Roger Sir, he's right here. I'll put him on." He pushed a second handset at Danny. He mouthed *Wingco,* for Wing Commander. "Here's L.A.C. Tanner, our NCO Ident…"

"Sir?" said Danny.

The voice of the Wing Commander, the man in charge of 5 Div's ADCC, said, "Tanner, I understand you have a possible?"

"Roger. I have a good possible, just no paperwork or anything. We think it's a SAC flight. Six Bravo four sevens, that went out earlier from Mountain Home in Idaho."

"I'm just told the Americans have gone to full Red Alert. Their whole West Coast is on Red. I'm holding us at Yellow up here." He chuckled and added, "If we don't get something quick, you and I may be drinking in the same mess tomorrow! I know you're busy, son, so I'll let you get to work."

"One question, Sir, is Flight Lieutenant Morrisey in the Ops Room? I need to talk to him."

"He is. I'll put him on."

In a few seconds, Moe's voice said, "Morrisey here."

"Sir, it's Danny…anyone else listening?"

"Not right now. What can I do for you?"

"See how fast you can get me the callsign and landline routing to Mountain Home AFB and the name of that SAC guy from Texas, the Colonel. We listed all the contacts in the SAC EWO file…"

"I remember. Stay on, I'll be right back."

In two minutes Danny had what he needed. As he handed the handset to Gil he said, "Russ is going to take Ident for a few minutes. I'm gonna try something. Definitely not by the book but it just might work."

He knew Strategic Air Command was not always prompt in giving flight information to Canadian units over the landlines. He knew, too, that if he used proper channels, he might never get results in time to affect the escalating situation. Red Alert meant SAC Wings were already mustering a counter strike. He ran to the switchboard room just outside the Ops Room. Vera was on duty at the PBX console.

"Vera, if you're smart, you won't hear anything I'm saying." She looked confused but nodded her head, trusting him. "Get me through to the Jericho switchboard, then cover your ears!"

She asked, "What's Going on, Danny?" She pushed a jack into the console and toggled a switch.

"Nothing much—just your normal everyday Red Alert. Right now there's sirens howling all the way down to friggin' Mexico. Shut the door." He stood over the PBX with a handset to his ear. "Am I in your way?"

"No, I'm okay."

While he was occupied with his call, the Sector Commander ordered two flights of interceptors, four CF-100 fighters, scrambled on Combat Air Patrol—C.A.P. They would circle over a point northwest of Comox, awaiting further orders. The U.S. 25th Division scrambled six F-89s to fly C.A.P. farther south.

Danny purposely used a roundabout routing of the landlines. When he got Mountain Home, he spoke in a thick Southern accent.

"Is that theyuh Wagontrain Operations? Who am Ah talkin' to?"

"Wing Operations, Staff Sergeant Jefferson here."

"Sahgint, this heuh's Colonel Rawlins." He pronounced it Cunnel. "Git yoah seniuh supervisuh on this lan, rat away."

After a few seconds a voice said, "Captain Jamieson here."

"Cap'n, Cunnel Rawlins heuh—listen good now son. Ah'm ovah heuh at Waterfall, in the Fifth Air Division, in Canada. Yew already know we got us a big ol' alert goin' on. The boys up heuh, they tell me theyuh's a SAC flight from yoah Wing…six Bravo Four-Sevens, went outta theuh 'roundabout last midnat. We s'spect we got em rat now comin' home on a return leg. They was last plotted by Consort control at about fifty-fav-ten north an' one-thirty-seven west on a headin' of one-fav-fav. Ah want y'all t'check it out pronto and git the info on those airplanes onto the net, son—rat away! Ah would surely hate t'see yore boys git shot up by some hotshot Canadian, jes because some fool didn't forward a flat plan. Git movin' son! Ah'll hold on heuh."

"Yes Sir, Colonel. I'll get right on it." The line went quiet.

Danny looked at Vera and gave her a wink.

The Captain came back on the line. "Colonel?"

"Ah'm rat heuh, Cap'n, what y'all got for me?"

"The flight plan is on the net right now, Sir. The Canadians are right, it is our flight. Callsign is Wagontrain Two Seven. I don't understand why it wasn't filed earlier. Could you spell your name for me, Colonel…?"

Danny interrupted, "That was rat good work, Cap'n. Stand by for me to call y'all back, ol' son." Danny disconnected the jack and handed the headset to Vera. He thought, *Yeah, Yank—if you ever hear from me again, I'll be in friggin' handcuffs!*

He admonished Vera, "Remember, for your own sake, you weren't in here. If anyone asks, say I threw you out."

Ten minutes later the teleprinter on the ident dais clattered out the flight plan information on the B'47s—callsign *Wagontrain 27*. Russ made an ID as friendly after an IFF check and identification vector by a Controller. The interceptors were all recalled and within half an hour the alert was stood down.

When the B Crew people had left for home, Donahue bellowed, "Tanner and Knight, out in the hallway, please—NOW!"

In the hall he declared, "Okay, Danny, I don't mind taking some flak, but I want to know what for. What's this 'not-by-the-book' procedure of yours?"

Danny explained to him and Russ what he had done.

Donahue shook his head. "I guess that's the job, isn't it. Getting the damn planes identified. It's what we're here for, but Jesus H. *Christ*, Dan!"

In the Wets after their shift, Russ asked, "Shit, Champ, how come you didn't tell them you were General Curtis Lee-may himself?"

"I didn't know Lemay's accent, Q, but every SAC type would."

On Monday they were informed there was to be an inquiry into the incident. Flying Officers Donahue and Quinn were to attend, along with Corporal Schmidt and L.A.C.s Nickerson, Knight and Tanner.

The inquiry was held at 51, in the lunchroom. There were only four non-commissioned people at the table. The Wing Commander chaired the proceedings with a U.S.A.F. Brigadier General sitting beside him. Danny had trouble swallowing when the Wingco looked directly at him as he reported he had been "fully briefed" by the 51 AC&W Controllers. It turned out a SAC Major at Mountain Home had put the flight plan in a desk drawer and gone home for the weekend. All present agreed the incident called attention to a need for closer liaison between the two air forces. The American General hinted that within a couple of years there would be a unified command in place for air defense of the continent.

The only unresolved matter was a landline transmission of mysterious origins logged by the Duty Ops Officer at Mountain Home.

After the inquiry Danny and Russ were in the hallway talking to Moe Morrisey. Danny felt a hand on his shoulder. He turned to see the Wingco.

"Walk with me, L.A.C. Tanner, would you? You too Knight."

They both said, "Yes Sir" and fell in beside him.

With a hand still on Danny's shoulder, the Wingco asked, "Tanner, you didn't really impersonate a Yank General, did you?"

"No Sir…just a Colonel."

The Wingco shook his head. "I'll be damned," he muttered. "Carry on, fellas." He walked away chuckling.

As they walked back to the Ops Room, Danny looked at the ceiling. "Thank you, Gus, R.J. and Jack!" He referred to some of the veteran FighterCOps who had showed him the ropes.

"Amen," said Russ.

CHAPTER 13

▼

51 BEACH, COMOX

An unfortunate incident occurred at the beach late one Friday night as the Wild Dogs were partying. An Aero-Engine Tech from 407 Squadron, named Tucker, known as "Tuck," came to the party with Vera Cromwell. Danny had heard of him and of his reputation as a troublemaker, and he had apparently heard of Danny, too.

Danny and Josie were seated on a driftwood log with Ollie and Russ when Tucker came and sat beside them. He was a stocky man, not as tall as Danny but well muscled.

"So how're you two?" he asked. He smiled as he spoke.

"We're good." answered Danny.

Tucker leaned over to look at Josie, still smiling. "How about you? You good, too?"

She shrugged and smiled, not sure what to say.

Danny said, "I already told you, *we* are good. That's *we*—both of us, okay?" He, too, had a smile on his face, but there was an edge to his voice.

"Hey, no sweat, man. Just asking. We've never met, I'm Tuck, Craig Tucker." He looked at Josie again. "An' what's your names?"

"I'm Josie and this is my...boyfriend, Danny." Danny was looking down at his feet.

"Josie what? Danny what? Have you got last names? I told you mine."

She was more than a little flustered. "Oh. Yes we 'ave, I'm Josie Connor..."

Danny cut in, "And I'm Dan Tanner. I think you already knew that, didn't you." He was still smiling.

Tucker smirked. "Why, you famous or something? Should I know your name?" He feigned concentration, then said, "Wait a minute, of course! You're the guy from the radar squadron. Supposed to be a tough guy. Is that you—the tough guy? You don't look tough."

Danny patted him on the shoulder as he stood up. "Sometimes appearances can fool you. We're going to join our friends over there. Nice to meet ya." He stood up with his beer and took Josie's arm. Russ and Ollie followed and they went to another log, where Gil, Gerry and Mitch were sitting.

Gil said, "Fun guy, eh?"

Josie whispered, "I don't like 'im. Is he from 51?"

Gerry said, "Nah, Jo, he's 407 and he's big trouble. Beat the hell out of a guy outside the Wets the other night."

"Yeah, I figured," said Danny, "we'll just ignore him, maybe he'll go away."

Gil said, "I think you should know, Dan, he's been asking about you. I think he wants a fight."

"His problem," said Danny.

A little later, Tucker arrived at their new log. "So, Mr. Tough guy, I guess you never heard of me, eh?"

So it went; the foursome twice more moved to a new spot only to have him join them with more fight talk.

When they moved a fourth time, Tucker called after him, "I believe I'm right. You don't look tough, you look scared! Are you scared, Mr. Tough guy?"

Danny sat down between Josie and Russ. "Ignore him. Looks pretty harmless,"

Russ muttered, "He ain't gonna be happy till you deck him, you know, Champ."

"Too bad. I'm here for a good time, not a hard time—there'll be none of that when I'm with Jo, not if I can help it."

Russ was right, Tucker didn't give up. He stood up by the fire and spoke loudly. "Is the scared tough guy over there somewhere, hiding behind his little girl friend? I love tough guys, but I guess this one is too chickenshit to give me a try."

Josie started to say, "Danny, let's just go…"

Danny spoke across the darkness in a deliberate voice, "I really don't think you want to push this friend, that would not be smart. Now, why don't you cool down—maybe go and find another party."

Somebody suggested, "Shit, Danny, why don't you kill the jerk? Y'won't even work up a sweat."

Tuck said, "Ah, so the tough guy's got fans, eh? Face it, you all know he's too chicken to fight."

At this, a couple of the girls protested, "Come *on,* don't be such a jerk." And, "Sit down and shut up, or go away, you idiot!"

Russ spoke up. "Hey, Danny, don't worry about this jerk. He's just trying to show you how far he can piss. If he's smart, which I doubt, he'll go away. We don't have time for stupid people."

"Oho, the little twerp's got more guts than his buddy! Where are you little man? Maybe you and me are gonna dance," said Tucker.

Russ started to rise. "Any time, you ugly prick..."

Danny pulled him back to the log. "Sit down, Russ."

Tucker said, "Yeah, sit down little man. I don't want you, anyway." Determined to rile Danny, he went on, "Hey, little French broad, seems I recall sleeping with you—remember? You loved it, didn't you."

Russ again started to get up. *"Son of a bitch!* That does it..."

Danny pulled him back again. "Hold it, Russ. This guy wants me and now he's gonna get me." He stood up and walked into the firelight. He spoke quietly. "Okay, *Greg,* you seem to want a beating, and that's what's gonna happen if you stay here. Either take off, right now, or take the beating. Your choice."

"You couldn't beat your grandma, Scope-Dope. I ain't going anywhere." He came at Danny in a crouch, fists in front of him. The crowd around the fire jumped up and moved back. Danny stepped past the man's first punch, drove an elbow into his ribs and threw him hard to the sand. He pressed a bare foot onto the man's neck, forcing his head into the loose sand.

"One more chance, Greg. You gonna leave?"

"Go to hell. You're dead, man."

"You're *sure?* Get up then, and show us just how stupid you are." He lifted his foot.

As soon as Tucker got to his feet Danny threw him down and used the foot on his neck again. "Come on, *Greg,* don't just lie there, *get up!"* The foot lifted.

And get up he did. He rushed Danny, head down, attempting to get a hold on him. Danny sidestepped and, with a hand on the back of his neck, drove Tucker into the sand again. This time he jerked him to his feet with a grip on his shirt-front. He drove three hard punches to the gut and a stunning right to the face. He took him in a hammer-lock, painfully twisting one wrist, and dragged him over to where Josie was sitting.

"Now, *Greggy,* apologize to the lady—nice and loud, so everyone can hear you!"

Tucker had never been beaten so handily. He muttered, "Okay, I'm sorry..."

Danny wrenched the arm almost to his neck. "Louder! Damn you!"

Tucker shouted, "I'm SORRY!"

"Now tell everybody when you've ever met Josie before tonight. Nice and loud...do it!"

"Never...I'VE NEVER SEEN HER. I'm SORRY!"

Josie said, "Okay, let 'im go now, Danny?"

"Okay, Jo. But I've gotta cool him off first." Maintaining the hammer-lock, Danny ran him into the nearby surf and shoved him sprawling out into deeper water. Then he turned his back and walked to shore. Over his shoulder, he said, "Now, Greggy, take off!"

The completely subdued Tucker gave Danny a wide berth as he sloshed past the group and headed up the path to the road. He couldn't believe how easily he had just been handled.

When the beaten man was out of sight on the path from the beach, Danny said, "I apologize, everybody! I just couldn't avoid it. Vera darling, he was your date and I am sorry, but he was determined he was gonna fight me."

A quite drunk Vera answered, "S'okay, Danny. He's a pain inna ass, anyway."

"Roger, Vera! Good attitude." He hugged himself and shivered. "Damn! Water's cold—anybody got some hard stuff?"

Vera said, "Right here, Danny. Bacardi an' Coke. And guess who brought it?" She started the bottle around the circle to him.

"Thanks, Vera. That's kinda justice." He felt the liquor warm him inside. He sat next to Josie, put an arm around her and spoke softly. "I'm sorry, Hon. You shouldn't have to see that stuff."

"Are you all right, Danny? Why did you let him make you mad?" she asked.

Ollie said, "It's not Dan's fault, Jo. The guy wasn't going to leave it alone."

"I know...I just worry. I hate fighting." She leaned on Danny.

The party broke up a little after one o'clock. Danny and Josie dropped their passengers off at the barracks. He drove to a spot at Point Holmes, along the Lazo Road, where they got out and walked the shingle beach. A three-quarter moon, low in the sky, was reflected shimmering brightly on the water.

After some minutes of silence, Josie asked, "Are you sure you're okay, Danny?"

He had been hoping the fight wouldn't come up again. "Yeah, I'm okay. The guy's all talk. Booze talk, mostly."

"Well, maybe so. But I get scared for you. I 'ate trouble and fighting. It's stupid."

He replied defensively. "It wasn't much of a fight, Jo."

"That isn't the point. Maybe we should 'ave just left..."

"Didn't you hear what he said about you? No way he gets away with it!"

"We could have left before he said it."

"We could have, but it would just happen some other time. I'm sorry you were there."

"Next time, we'll just leave. Walk away." She stopped walking and turned to him, putting her arms around his waist. "I hate it. I was so scared...not just for you getting hurt...you might get in bad trouble."

He took her into his arms. Her hair smelled wonderful, of perfume and soap and salt air. He said, "Okay...I'll try. I'll try to walk away. I promise."

Tucker surprised Josie a few days later, when he came to her table in the Mess Hall to apologize again for what he said; this time with no arm-twisting.

He told her, "I was way out of line and I'm truly sorry. I deserved what I got."

CHAPTER 14

▼

Our secret was out...

COURTENAY

The foursome liked to take in a movie in Courtenay one night a week if the boys weren't working a night shift. Afterward, they would go for drinks, then end the evening at a restaurant, before returning to the base.

There was a Thursday night, Josie's nineteenth birthday, when they went to the nine o'clock movie at the E.W. Cinema to see Guys and Dolls. Josie wore a pale blue sweater Danny had given to her for her birthday that afternoon. After the show they went to the Arbutus for drinks. Inside the lounge, Danny excused himself to go to the washroom.

"Do you want me to come with you, dear?" Russ asked.

Danny replied in a falsetto. "No thank you, sweetie, I'll be fine." It was a standing joke with them, mocking the girls practice of always going to the washroom together.

Russ and the girls could only find a table with three chairs. Josie spotted an empty chair at a nearby table.

"There's one over there. I'll see if those people need it," she said as she started away.

At the other table were seated two men and a woman, obviously local civilians. Josie gestured toward the empty chair as she approached.

"Is anyone using this?" she asked with a smile.

A large red-haired man with a beard leered at her. "Just you, now, sweety." He started to pull the chair out from the table.

She tried to conceal her pique and embarrassment. She smiled stiffly and said "Thank you. Then I'll take it. We 'ave only three chairs, for four of us." She started to lift the chair.

The redhead clamped a big hand on the arm of the chair and forced it from her hand and to the floor with a bang.

"I said you could sit on it. I didn't say you could take the fuckin' thing anywhere. Don't you want to sit with me and my friends, little Frenchy?"

She heard Russ. "Hey! Come on, man—watch your mouth!" He started toward them.

The man grinned at Russ and said, "Well, lookee here, a little pigeon coming to Frenchy's rescue!"

The other man at the table spoke up. "Hey, come on, Red...we don't need this. Just give them the damn chair."

The bartender had been watching. He came around from behind the bar, pointing a finger at the redhead.

He said, "Carlson, I don't want any crap from you tonight! Understand? Don't you be making any trouble in here."

"Okay, okay! I was just kidding around. Whatsamatter anymore...can't people take a joke?" The big man smiled, turned to Josie, and shrugged. "I'm sorry. Okay, sweety? Take the goddam chair." Then to Russ, "Okay, little man?"

Josie went back to the Foursome's table, leaving Russ to pick up the offending chair.

With a hint of sarcasm, he asked, "You folks are *sure* you won't need this?"

The woman shrugged and said, "No problem. It's all yours. Sorry about...you know. Okay?" Russ didn't reply.

When Josie sat down, Ollie muttered, "What a complete dork."

When Russ came back with the chair, Josie said, "Let's not tell Danny what happened...what that guy did. Just don't say anything to 'im."

She was too late. Danny heard the last part of her remark as he returned from the washroom.

"Don't say what, Jo? What did *what* guy do?" he asked.

Russ was putting the chair in place. "Nothing, Champ."

"Well, somebody did *something* to *somebody!* Right?" He looked around the room

Ollie gave Josie's thigh a poke. She said, "Aw, Danny, it's nothing. Some jerk didn't want to give Russ a chair. That's all it was, don't worry about it."

Danny noticed the redhead looking sullenly their way. "Those guys over there?" He stared back at the man for a moment, then, remembering his promise to Josie, he looked away. "Okay! Let's order. What are you girls having?"

After two drinks at the Arbutus, they decided to go for Chinese food. It was a fine evening so they walked the four blocks to the restaurant on Fifth Street.

"STAR CAFÉ—CHINESE AND CANADIAN FOOD"

When they got inside the crowded restaurant, they found they would have to wait for a booth.

Russ suggested, "Should we go somewhere else?"

Josie cried, "No! Please? Can we wait? I really want Chinese tonight…"

Ollie joined her, "Yeah, yeah! I vote we wait. Sweet an' sours, chicken chow mein, sweet an' sours…"

"You said that twice, that twice," said Russ.

"Because I like 'em, I like 'em."

Danny just grinned and shrugged. The guys would lose this one.

Russ said, "All right, already! You win! And, by the way, Ollie and I are buying this time. It's our birthday present for Jo—no argument allowed!" The Foursome's agreed rule was each paid for his own meals and drinks.

Josie reached up and kissed his cheek. "That's so nice! Thank you both. But you don't 'ave to…"

"Yes we do."

"So shut up, squirt. Done deal." said Ollie.

They spotted a couple from Charlie Crew, already seated, and stood around joking until a booth opened for them. Once seated, they waited five minutes before they received menus from a harried waitress who left them, saying, "Be back as soon as I can." As soon as she could turned out to be ten minutes. They decided on "dinner for four," and she told them they would have a long wait. While they waited they carried on the usual banter, including Ollie giving a name to the red bearded man. She dubbed him the "SLUG," and explained it stood for 'Slobbery-Lumbering-Ugly-Galoot.' They didn't tell Danny about Josie's involvement in the incident.

When they had waited twenty-five minutes, Josie complained, "I hope it's not much longer. I'm so 'ungry!"

Ollie declared, "Shit-all-to-hell, Jo, when in hell *aren't* you '*ongree!*"

"Well, I can't help it." She grasped Danny's arm and laid her head on his shoulder. "My Danny is giving me too much exercise—it makes me hungry."

In the stunned silence that followed, she suddenly realized what she had said. Blushing crimson, she buried her face in his jacket. In a moment, she looked up, still red-faced. "I didn't mean...you know..."

Ollie looked from her to Danny, to see him also blushing. "I...shit-all-to-h..." She didn't finish.

Josie tried again. "Ollie! Russ! I didn't mean..." She became resigned. "Oh, merde! Yes I did mean...that." She looked pleadingly at Danny, as if for his forgiveness, then back to Ollie and Russ. "You won't tell anyone? *Please!*"

Danny, Ollie and Russ were looking down at the floor, all red-faced.

Josie tried, "So, now I told you. It's not so terrible. We love each other and...Oh, merde..." She was miserable.

Danny, head still down, started to chuckle. Russ joined in.

Ollie placed a hand on Josie's. "It's okay, Jo. Just a surprise—though I don't know why it should be. So long as you're okay with it, you two are good for each other." She looked at Russ. "As long as *they're* 'fessing up...Russ?"

Russ moaned. "Jesus Christ, stupid! We hardly need to say anything now!" His face was crimson.

Danny laughed. Josie giggled. Russ and Ollie blushed.

"Oh shit," said Ollie. She took Russ' hand, "Well, now it's out, guys. Though I'm sure by now the whole frigging base suspected it!"

Josie stopped giggling long enough to blurt, "We are so bad, aren't we? The Fearsome Foursome is the *'Orny Foursome*, I think!" That brought more laughter. "When, Ollie? When was the first time for you two? Oh, don't answer; it's not my business."

"Can I tell her, Russ?"

"Shit, why not. But I didn't keep a log, did you?"

"But, Jo, you have to tell me, too."

Josie nodded, "Okay, you first."

Disgusted, Danny said, "Jesus! Girls! Do you mind?"

But there was no stopping them now. Ollie said, "Well, it was a week after you went to see Danny's family in Victoria. We..."

Before she could say any more Danny was snickering and Josie was giggling.

"What!" she exclaimed. "No!"

Between giggles, Josie blurted, "Oh, Ollie! I 'ave never *been* to Victoria!"

"You sneaky *shits*."

Danny said, "Well, Ol, you insisted on knowing."

"Yeah…so I did. But, you know, you said we're bad, Jo. I don't know about you guys, but I don't feel bad at all. In fact I feel damn good. I feel…*right* about it." The others nodded in agreement.

Josie had a thought. She giggled again. "Do you mean you feel good after, or just during?"

"You know what I mean, you little shit."

"Anyway," said Josie, "I am still hungry!" She was glad the matter was out into the open.

The waitress came by and told them, "We haven't forgotten you, folks. Won't be long now. We're busy, busy, busy—and one girl didn't show up." She placed two plates on the booth across the aisle, chow mein and spare ribs. There was nobody in the booth. The woman muttered, "Jeez, I hope this guy didn't get tired of waiting and leave!" She hurried away.

Ollie looked longingly at the plates. "Ooh, look, Jo. Sweet and sours. I'm tempted to steal one! I wonder where the guy went."

Danny had seen the man heading to the washroom. He reached across with a fork and speared a sparerib.

"Here, Ollie. He's probably gone. He won't miss one anyway."

Ollie looked guiltily around. She took the proffered morsel and popped it into her mouth.

Josie looked around, too, eyes wide and a hand over her mouth.

"Danny! Ollie! Russ, don't let them."

Danny speared another rib. "Here, Hon, one for you."

Her hand still covering her mouth, she shook her head from side to side.

"Come on, Jo, hurry up!" He pushed the fork at her. "C'mon, you're gonna get me caught!"

She quickly took the rib and put it into her mouth. "Mmm, it's good." She giggled. "We are *so awful*. Quick, get me another one?"

He speared a couple this time. Russ, using two forks, snared three. Josie got Danny's two, Ollie the three from Russ. They stuffed them into their mouths, chewing mightily. Their cheeks were bulging.

Ollie tried to speak. "Mmm. Make slure lou hide lour blones, Jlo."

Just then, the man whose food they were enjoying returned to his booth. He appeared to be blissfully unaware anything was missing as he dug in. The girls were sitting wide-eyed, cheeks bulging, faces turned to the wall. Josie could barely stifle her giggles as Ollie frowned intensely at her.

Danny winked at Russ. He turned to the man. "Hi there, how are you doing tonight? I'm Dan and this is Russ, and those two are Josie and Olivia."

Russ leaned across the aisle and shook the man's hand. "Very pleased to meet you, sir."

"Pleased to meet you, too." He took Danny's offered hand. "I'm Arthur."

Danny said, "Say hello to Arthur, girls. C'mon, don't be shy, say hello."

Both girls stopped chewing. They couldn't speak. They turned and nodded briefly at Arthur, both red-faced and smiling weakly.

Russ managed to look serious as he told on them, "Arthur, you seem like a nice guy. It hurts me to tell you this, but these ladies…these *women*…well, Art, they've been stealing your spareribs while you were away in the john. They've got some in their mouths right now. Your food, man."

Danny jumped in. "It's the truth, Art. It's just terrible! I gotta tell you it's terribly embarrassing for us, being here with them."

In utter disbelief of this betrayal, the girls were wide-eyed.

Arthur, seeing the obvious guilt in their faces (if not the bulging cheeks) and the wide grins on the boys, picked up his plates and looked around for somewhere else to finish his meal. He departed to a stool at the coffee counter, grumbling about "goddamned Air Force smart-asses."

Josie hadn't been breathing. She expelled much air and three rib bones across the booth. Danny and Russ were doubled over with laughter.

Ollie's eyes were bright with fury. Forgetting about the bones in her mouth, she rasped, "Lou SLONSLABLITCHES! I'm gloing tloo klill lou bloth!"

"What's that, Ol? I can't understand a word—can you, Dan?" said Russ between laughs.

Spitting her four bones into an ashtray, she hissed, "I—am—going—to—KILL both of you clowns! BASTARDS! Shit. SHIT! I have never, *ever*, been so embarrassed!" They were laughing harder. "NOT funny…you JERKS!"

Josie contributed to the death sentences. "And I am going to 'elp her kill you! That was just so *mean!* How could you *do* such a thing? We were…we were…" She started to laugh with the boys. She pointed at Ollie. "Oh, Ollie, you should 'ave seen yourself. You looked so dumb! And the guy, Arthur? It was so funny."

Ollie hissed, "Dumb? *Dumb*, am I! I'll kill you, too, you little shit." She turned to Russ and punched his arm. "You ignorant *bastard*, Russ "I hate you…" Then, in spite of herself, she grinned, then she chuckled and shook her head. "Okay, jerks, good one. You got us good. But remember—we'll get you for this! We'll get you big time!" Smiling at Josie, she added, "You didn't look so damn brilliant yourself, by the way, bitch."

When their own orders arrived, none of them spoke while they ate, but in turns one or the other couldn't stop a laugh. Poor Arthur, the victim of the prank, finished his somewhat diminished meal and left the premises; witness to yet another example of the sad state of Canada's armed forces.

CHAPTER 15

▼

Remember how Ollie tried to gut out her problem...

It was a couple of weeks after "the great sparerib caper," as Russ referred to it, when Josie first noticed a change in her friend.

Josie had always taken Ollie's unceasing good humor for granted. That was Ollie. It was why she had so many friends and was one reason why Josie loved her. Surely, she sometimes lost her temper, but her pique was always quickly followed by an apology or a joke saying, "It's okay, everyone, I'm over it! We're still friends."

The change in Ollie was subtle at first, not seen by anyone but Josie, who was tuned in to every alteration of her friend's temperament. Where in the past she displayed infinite patience with Josie, now she would grow peevish if she had to explain something, or if Josie failed to reply to a question. Where she always saw the humor in a situation, now she seemed solemn or preoccupied. Where she had tolerated criticism, now she often snapped back at the slightest hint of it.

*   *   *   *

Ollie's new moodiness was plainly apparent to all at a dance in the Rec Center on the Saturday before Labor Day. The Wild Dogs of D Crew were howling, despite having to work the 0800 to 1600 day shift the next morning. Everyone except Ellen started drinking in the Wets long before the Dance started. By nine o'clock those who weren't totally "smashed," to use their favorite description, were somewhere between "half smashed" and "three-quarters smashed."

The music was from records, seventy-eights and forty-fives, played by one of the Rec Center staff. Each crew member in turn found a way to make a fool of him or her self as the evening progressed. Vera and Bobby performed their version of a Cossack dance to the beat of Mitch Miller's *Yellow Rose of Texas*—no easy feat in semi-formal dresses. Zack wandered around the room, soliciting people to sign a petition to have the disk jockey removed because his demand for "some good Canadian music like Hank Snow or Wilf Carter" was denied. Gil was threatened with expulsion when he demonstrated a handstand on a nearby table. Gerry, who could do "any damn thing Gil can do," tried the same stunt, with less success when he crashed off the edge of the table and was expelled. (He sneaked back in later, wearing sunglasses.) Jake slept through most of the evening with his head in his arms. Ellen's date, Ken Baxter from 409 Squadron, fell asleep, too—for over an hour on a toilet in the men's room. At one point, dozens of people stopped dancing, to stand in a circle and cheer for two couples putting on a spectacular jive show to Bill Haley's *Rock Around the Clock*. One couple was Ollie and Danny, the other Josie and Bobby. The disk jockey played the number over twice.

The trouble between Ollie and Russ occurred midway through the evening, when Ollie, who had been truculent all evening, and was drinking far too heavily, decided it was a good time for Russ to learn how to jive, and dragged him onto the dance floor. Uncharacteristically, she flew into a rage when he acted up during the "lesson," by twirling clownishly around her. She knocked the wind out of him with a well-placed and unexpected uppercut to the solar plexus, called him an "ignorant son of a bitch," and stormed out of the Rec Center in tears. It took five minutes for a worried Danny and the others to get Russ breathing normally.

A sober Josie would have gone after her friend to console her, but she had decided at the start of this night she would try to keep up with the serious drinkers. An hour before the incident she had reached the plateau (or deep valley) of "utterly smashed," so this Josie just sat bemused in her chair and asked, "Why's Rush sittin' onna floor all red in the face? Can I sit onna floor with you, Rush? 'At looks like kinda fun."

Russ, finally breathing properly, asked, "What the hell was that all about? Ollie just blew up! Shit, that friggin' hurt."

"Aw, she just drank way too much," said Danny, "in the morning she won't even remember blowing her stack."

"Oh yeah? If she doesn't, I'll remind her!"

"Hell, Q, just let it go…"

"Yeah, maybe you're right. I need a drink…mine got knocked over or something."

Later, a half-hour before the dance ended, Josie looked bleary-eyed at Danny, smiled sweetly, and said, "Wanna go outside, you?"

Danny said, "Go outside? It's raining and cold out there, Jo."

"Good. Need some cold, s'too hot in 'ere. C'mon!"

He thought she wanted to go out to be sick. "Okay, let's go." He put her coat over her shoulders and hurried her to the exit. Outside, it was raining hard. He asked, "Gonna be sick, Hon?"

She pressed against him. She whispered, "Not gonna be sick…gonna be horny! Wanna screw you." Looking at him defiantly, she then added, "Wanna screw you right now, you bew'ful man."

He was dumb, surprised at language he had never heard her use.

She said, "S'matter, don' unnerstan English? C'mon! We'll get in your car an' I can be Tarzan!" She tugged at his sleeve, pulling him along.

He said, "Honey, calm down. You're drunk. The car's not here, it's at the barracks."

"Good! C'mon!"

He decided to humor her. It took them five minutes to reach the car in the cold rain. She was shivering as she got into the back seat.

Accusingly, she said, "Josie's all *cold* now. All wet, too. Can I snuggle up?"

Danny got the heater going and held her close. In five minutes she was sound asleep. He shook his head as he covered her with her coat and the car blanket. He drove to the Rec Center to fetch Ollie.

But he had forgot Ollie left the dance. So he prevailed on Bobby Gaines to get Josie to her room.

*　　　*　　　*　　　*

In the 51 Ops Room the next morning, it was obvious to F/O Donahue that most of his crack crew of FighterCops were suffering from hangovers. He commented on the fact to Ellen.

The Crew Chief winced in pretended pain. "Sir, I wonder if you could not speak quite so loud? You're aggravating this big split in my head." She gave him a shamefaced smile

Donahue roared with laughter. "God help us!" he said, "Even the fearless leader? It's a good thing this is a Sunday. Well, we'll just have to keep the coffee-pots full, and please—make sure whoever you put on the scopes can see!"

When he checked the lunchroom later, he saw those Wild Dogs on their breaks sprawled sleeping on lined-up chairs, a table, and even the floor.

The Soviets didn't attack North America that day. They might have missed a wonderful opportunity.

*   *   *   *

In the Airwomen's barracks, while the rest of the Wild Dogs were only suffering, Josie was dying. She knew it with absolute certainty. The horrible nausea began the moment she laid her head down and the room started its spinning. The agonizing headache waited in hiding and ambushed her in the morning. When she vomited, it made the headache worse, and when she tried aspirin for the headache, it made her vomit. If she didn't expire from the headache or the nausea, she knew it would be from starvation, for she fully intended to never again touch any food! *Oh, God...help me!* When she managed to drink a little water, it tasted exactly like the rye and ginger ale she had been drinking, which just nauseated her again. *Dieu! Am I to die of thirst then?*

"Come on little buddy, time to get up. The mess hall's open for lunch," said Ollie, who had just come in the door.

Lunch? Ulp..."Please, Ollie, don't talk about lunch. Don't talk about *any* food!"

"Oh oh. Life-of-the-Party's a bit sickly, is she?"

Josie sat up in the bed. *Ow, oh! I'll be okay. Just don't move.* "Ollie, how can a person *do* this to herself? It's...insane."

"It's the price you pay for having a great time, Jo."

"I *didn't* have a great time. I was awful, acting stupid, and I was so out of control! I said horrible things."

"I wouldn't worry too much about it. Shit, at least you didn't try to kill your boyfriend. I didn't have a very good time, either," said Ollie, her chagrin evident. "So, anyway, what about lunch? If we're lucky they'll probably be serving leftovers from about only last Thursday."

For the first time since the early morning Josie's eyes showed life; they glared murderously at Ollie. "You are a *bitch*, Olivia Conti. You're an evil, cruel bitch! Ulp. Oh, no! Excuse me. I 'ave to go to the...ohh..." She ran down the hall to the washroom.

She promised herself she would never again try to drink with the drinkers.

*   *   *   *

A couple of days after the dance, Josie walked in on the tail end of a heated argument between Ollie and Russ in the snack bar. She heard Ollie say, "Jesus, Russ, I *said* I'm sorry. What the hell do you want from me?"

"I just want to know what the hell is eating you lately, Ollie!" Russ's voice was raised.

"Nothing is eating me, damn it. Screw this, I came here to apologize, and I get the third degree. I'm going back to the barracks. I'm tired of your crap." She got up and stormed out past Josie without a word of greeting.

Josie spoke to her back as she passed, "Hi, Ollie..." she shrugged, "Goodbye, Ollie?" She was puzzled. She bought a Coke at the counter and sat down with Russ. "Hi."

"Hi, Jo. Did you hear that?"

"Just a bit...the last part. She didn't even say hello to me." They both glanced toward the exit.

"What the hell *is* eating her lately? Do you know if it's something I did? This started before the dance, you know."

She didn't know how to answer. She and Ollie always kept confidences, so she didn't want to share her own concerns. She honestly didn't know what the problem might be, or if indeed there even was a problem.

"I don't know, Russ."

"Haven't you noticed, or is it just me?"

"I know she hasn't told me anything..."

He said, "How about her little scene at the dance? She was like...man, she got *mean*, Jo."

"She 'ad been drinking, we all were. Didn't you see *me*?"

He shrugged. "Ah, hell, never mind—it's probably nothing."

Josie didn't think it was nothing. She determined to have a talk with Ollie.

Danny arrived to join them and they changed the subject.

In the room the next evening Josie was taking her turn doing laundry and had just returned from starting her first load. She could see Ollie was in a better mood than she had been in for weeks.

"Phew! It's hot in there tonight." She flapped the front of her tee shirt.

"Yeah, sometimes it can be unbearable. It's those girls from downstairs, they have the heat turned up already. Want me to do the next load?"

"Oh, no. I was just mentioning it. I would like to talk, though…could we?" She was nervous.

"Sure. What's up?"

Josie hesitated. This was a reversal of their usual roles. "Well, Ollie—is there anything wrong? Is something bothering you? Are you feeling…"

"Jesus, you've been talking to Russ!" Her good mood disappeared instantly and there was an edge to her voice. "No. There's nothing wrong, nothing bothering me, and there's nothing *eating me!* I feel just fine, okay?"

Josie considered the answer both untrue and out of character, thereby justifying her concern. For the first time since they had met she raised her voice at Ollie. "Listen, you, I remember a good friend, my very *best* friend, once said to me, 'Don't tell me it's *nothing!* Don't…*effing* bullshit me. It's insulting!' Do you remember? Maybe I am not your *only* friend, as you were mine, Olivia, but I *am* your friend and I think I deserve a better answer. And don't blame Russ. I 'ave been meaning to talk to you for over a week. But, yes, he 'as noticed it, too, and he's worried for you like me. Something *is* bothering you." She was furiously stuffing clothes into a pillowcase. "I'm going to take this load, then I'll be back if you want to talk—I am not finished!" She picked up the clothes and left.

When she came back to the room, Ollie wasn't there. She saw that one of her coats was gone.

The next day during their morning coffee break, they were alone in the lunchroom. Ollie reached across the table and grasped Josie's hand. "I'm sorry about last night, buddy. I shouldn't have got pissed-off at you. I don't—wouldn't want to B.S. you—not you or Russ. Honestly, everything's fine. Don't worry about me, Okay?"

Josie looked directly into her eyes for fifteen seconds. She shook her head, took her cup to the sink and left the room, she could think of nothing to say in reply to the obvious dishonesty. One step outside the room, she turned and went back to the doorway.

"Ollie, I don't believe you. I respect your decision to not tell me what's wrong; but to say it's nothing, that's still not true, still insulting. It's as if you don't trust me to keep your secret and you know better! As you once told me, maybe just talking about it will help you. I learned from you, Ollie, not to keep things inside me. I *will* worry about you, until you convince me…" She threw her arms to the side. "Aw, *damn* you, it's not my business! Do what you will." She walked out the door again.

Ollie said after her, "You're right about one thing. It *is* none of your business."

Josie spun around and came back into the room. Her eyes were blazing. She walked to the table and put her face close to Ollie's. "That was *rotten*. I cried for you last night." She turned and left, tears sparkling in her eyes. *Oh, good for you, Josie, losing your temper—that will surely help!*

Ollie booked off sick at noon, claiming a headache.

She was waiting in the room when Josie came in after work. It was apparent she had been drinking heavily. Josie stood in the doorway.

She said, "Hello, Ollie, feeling better?"

"Hi, lil buddy—yep, feelin' no pain. No pain whatever!"

"Good. I'm glad." She stepped into the room. "It's not like I *worried* about you or anything." The jab was wasted.

Ollie produced a mickey of vodka. "Wouldja have a lil drink with me, Jo?" She tipped the bottle back, took a swallow and made a face.

"No, thanks. I'm going for supper. I'm meeting Danny." She started to take off her uniform.

Ollie mumbled. "Screw you then. I've drunk alone before...don't need you. Don't need your Danny either and sure as hell don't need Russ Knight. Think I'm gonna find somebody to sleep with."

Josie shook her head. "Why did you get drunk? It won't 'elp anything." She looked in a drawer for a blouse.

"Well, well, listen to Sister Mary Goodycrotch. I don' need no *elp!* From you 'specially, so mind your own business. Go an' *elp* somebody else." She looked owl-eyed at Josie. "Y'unnerstand? I can look after myself!" She dropped the bottle and fumbled on the floor for it while still looking drunkenly defiant at Josie.

Looking askance, Josie said, "Yes, I'm sure you'll do a good job of it." She was pulling on her slacks.

Still fumbling, Ollie mumbled, "Damn shur I will. Can you see my bottle, Sister Mary?" She giggled. "Ah, there you are! Gotcha." She picked up the bottle. "An' if you wanna be my friend, you mind your own business."

"Yes. You already said that. You made it very clear." She buttoned her blouse.

"I know people like you. Y'can't even look after yourshelfs, but you wanna look after everybody else! Don' need ya."

"I see." She brushed her hair.

"You see! Well *fine-a-lee!* S'about time. Took you long enough t'*see!*"

Josie went out the door. "Bye, now."

When she returned after supper, Ollie was asleep on top of the bed in her slip, clothing strewn on the floor. She put a blanket over her, and hung her clothes in the closet. She sat at the dresser and put on her makeup. When she finished, she got up to leave. She looked down at Ollie and whispered, "Goodbye." Then she went out to meet Danny.

At the snack bar, Danny could see Josie was somewhere else. He was telling her about something that had happened at 51 and realized she wasn't hearing. "Did you hear a word I said, Jo?"

"No. I'm sorry, Danny…I didn't." She smiled ruefully and put a hand on his. "Tell me again."

"It's nothing. I must be losing it, getting boring. You and Russ both haven't heard me today."

"Danny Tanner, you will never bore me."

"Do you want to tell me what's got all your attention then?"

"It's Ollie…something is bothering her." She was nervous about telling him. Would she be betraying a confidence? "But I can't get her to tell me anything."

"Russ told me the same thing. He said they might even stop seeing each other. When he calls her he has to leave messages. Then she takes her time about calling him back. Any idea what it is?"

"No. I saw them fighting…arguing at least. She walked out on him, here at the snack bar. She went right past me without saying a word. Russ says it started before the Labor Day dance."

"Maybe she's tired of him and wants to break it off."

"Oh, no! I 'ope not. We have so much fun!" She grew pensive. "I don't think that's it, Danny."

"Well, whatever. Tough on him, though. There's nothing worse than being with someone's moods and not knowing what's going on. She'll work it out."

"I hope she will," said Josie. She looked up, "Here's Russ now."

Russ pulled up a chair. "Hi, Jo—Champ. Have you guys seen Ollie?" he said.

"She's in bed asleep, she's tired. I didn't want to wake her up." She didn't tell him she likely couldn't wake her if she tried.

"Yeah, okay. Did you ever find out what the hell's going on with her?" said Russ.

"No."

He looked away for a moment and then he said, "I'm going over to the Wets. You guys want to come?"

Danny answered. "Naw, not tonight Q, we're going into town for a movie. You're welcome to join us…"

"Thanks anyway, Dan, but it's the Wets for me. Have fun, see you later." He started to leave, but turned back. "If you see her, tell her where I can be found, will you? That's assuming she would want to find me."

*   *   *   *

The next day after supper, Josie found Ollie sitting in the room. They had not spoken all day at work. Without a word, Josie went to her closet and started taking off her uniform; she had her back to Ollie.

Behind her a small voice said, "Did you really cry for me, Jo?" Josie nodded. "Jo, I *would* like to talk...I want to tell you about it, okay?"

Josie turned. With a smile, she said, "Good! Let me phone Danny first, he'll be waiting for me."

"Later's okay, Jo, if you want..." Ollie rushed her words.

"No. Right now is fine! Just wait for a minute. I'll be right back." She went out to the hall to make her call.

When she returned to the room, she sat on the bed beside Ollie. "There. We 'ave all the time we need. Um, as you always say...*shoot!* Remember, I'm your friend and I love you."

Ollie began, "I want you to promise you'll never tell Russ what I'm going to tell you. He'll go nuts and get in real trouble. Will you promise?"

"I promise. Wait, I'll shut the door." Their room had become a favorite meeting place and she didn't want them disturbed.

There were tears in Ollie's eyes as she haltingly told her story.

Her problem had a name—he was Flight Lieutenant Blair Watson.

Watson was the son of an Air Vice Marshal and a graduate of Royal Military College at Kingston; one of those officers that believed enlisted personnel existed only to do his bidding. He saw himself as not only a superior officer to those of lower ranks but also a superior being. The military college officers were generally despised and mistrusted by the non-commissioned ranks. Danny Tanner had an appropriate saying—"All the other ranks serve for queen and country, R.M.C. officers serve for R.M.C. officers."

She had been a twenty-year-old AW1, and he a Flying Officer, when they were both stationed at Trenton, Ontario. He was handsome in a patrician way, slim in body, with a narrow face, square jaw and trim military mustache. He told her she was the loveliest girl he had ever met. They dated for three months. Sometimes another officer and his date went with them. She believed she loved him and he told her the love was mutual. They began sleeping together.

She missed him terribly when he left for a month on annual leave, "to see the family in Edmonton." A week after his return, on what turned out to be their last date, they spent the weekend together in a Belleville hotel.

She learned the awful truth from another officer. Blair had gone home on his leave to marry the girl that had been his sweetheart since high school and his fiancée for two years. He had spent a good part of the month honeymooning in Hawaii! His bride would soon be arriving at Trenton to take up residence with him in a rented house in town. Heartbroken, she phoned and told him she knew of his marriage and didn't wish to see him again.

A Belleville doctor confirmed her pregnancy three weeks later. Joe Conti sent her money when she told him she wanted it to buy a car. A man of questionable profession performed the abortion in a shabby apartment in Toronto.

After she ended the affair Watson's interest became obsession. She didn't hear from him for two months and then the torment began. When his persistent phone calls to her barracks got no response, he began haunting places on the base she frequented. He invented reasons to call or visit the HQ building, asking for her at work. He showed up in civilian clothes at the Wets and Airmen's Mess, both out-of-bounds to officers. He would not be discouraged despite her determined efforts to avoid him. One Saturday he waited outside her barracks and caught her by surprise on her way to breakfast. She turned to go back inside but he caught her by the arm and started to make a scene. She agreed to meet him later for lunch in Belleville. She would tell him once and for all that she was not interested in him any more and he must stop harassing her.

After lunch, on the pretense of driving her back to the base, he parked and tried to persuade her to change her mind. His approach went from pleading to demanding to pleading again, and ended with him trying to force himself on her. She managed to escape and took a taxi back to the base. When she later phoned and threatened to report him, he reminded her they had sometimes double dated with his officer friend. If she tried to report him his friend was prepared to say she had been the one pursuing him, and it would be a case of her word against the word of two officers. She was convinced, whatever the consequences for him, the affair would mean the end of her career in the Air Force. She had been in a licentious relationship with a commissioned officer and she knew the service placed a much higher value on his career than it would on hers.

Just when it appeared she would have to leave the service to be free from him she was ordered on transfer to Comox.

Now, two years later, Watson had arrived at Comox—and he brought his obsession with him. On his second day at the base he phoned her to tell her his marriage was failing and he loved her and wished to resume the relationship. The harassment started again. She felt trapped. Requesting a transfer or, more likely, leaving the Air Force, were the only options she could see now. She had prepared the memo requesting a transfer but had not yet submitted it—the prospect of leaving behind her career and people she loved desolated her.

As her story unwound Ollie stopped several times to regain her composure. When she finished there were tears in Josie's eyes as well as hers.

Josie said, "Oh, Ollie I 'ave been mean. Why didn't you tell me it was...something like that? He's the guy who's been phoning you at work, then?" She had taken some of his calls at the office.

Ollie begged, "Please, Jo, you must never tell or even *hint* at this to Russ."

"I promise. I won't. But there *is* someone we should tell, you know."

"Who?"

"You know who, Ollie."

"Shit, you mean Tanner, don't you. What can he do?"

"I don't know, but if anybody can think of a way I know he can. You know how he, um...figures things out."

"He'll just tell Russ, won't he?"

"Not if I say don't. He won't want Russ to get in trouble any more than we do. It's up to you...you know Danny loves you, Ollie. Loves you as a friend."

Ollie had to smile. "Yeah. I love him, too, as a friend. Okay, tell him. I don't see what he can do, though."

"He'll surprise you. I know it!"

"Okay. I suppose it's worth a try, but don't let *him* get in trouble. I just want this sick creep to leave me alone!"

＊　　　＊　　　＊　　　＊

Three evenings later, while F/L Watson was attending a function at the Officers' Mess, Mrs. Watson received a phone call at their Courtenay home at ten P.M.

"Hello," she said.

"Can I speak to Joanne, please?" A woman's voice.

"I'm afraid you have a wrong number, there's no..." Click. The connection was broken.

Two days later, in the afternoon, the same female voice said. "Hi, Joanne...?"

"There's no Joanne here...you have the wrong..."

"Oh, oh!" Click.

Then, on the next Friday a man's voice. It was nine-thirty. "Hello. This is the Station Hospital, could I speak to Nursing Sister Pierce, please?"

"I'm sorry, you have the wrong number."

"Oh. This is strange. She's on call at the hospital—that's where I'm calling from. She left word she would be with a Flight Lieutenant Watson for the evening. I tried her quarters and the Officers' Mess but she's not there."

"This is Flight Lieutenant Watson's home number. He's at the base for the night...he's the Orderly Officer tonight."

"Hmm. There is another number she gave, but when I tried it, they said it's a Motel. Must be a mistake."

"Oh? I'm afraid I can't explain..."

"Yes, well...this is embarrassing, I'm sure there's, uh, been a mistake. I'll have to get one of the other nurses to come in. I'm sorry to bother you like this. Thank you for your trouble." The words were rushed.

At eleven-thirty, she received another call.

A female voice inquired, "Joanne?" She could hear laughter in the background.

"There is no Joanne here, who is..."

"Oh, is Blair there, then?"

"No. He's not in. This is his wife. Who is..."

"Oh, shit!" Click. The line disconnected.

At the 51 AC&W switchboard, Bobby Gaines asked, "How'd we do, Danny? Academy award time?" She was there with Danny, Vera and Gerry Henderson.

Dryly, Gerry remarked, "Sure, Bobby—'Best Actor' for me, the star. All you and Vera get is 'Best Supporting Actress."

Danny said, "I think you all should keep your day jobs and just settle for the beers I'm gonna buy you."

*   *   *   *

Events proceeded better even than Danny anticipated. He had done his homework well. He correctly figured Watson had had other affairs—once a philanderer, always a philanderer.

There actually was a good-looking nurse named Joanne Pierce who had a reputation around the Officers' Mess as a chaser of married men.

Mrs. W's phone call to her husband's father, Air Vice-Marshal Watson, followed by the senior Watson's call to the Commanding Officer at Comox, resulted in a transfer to Gimli, Manitoba for Mr. W. "For his own good, in consideration of his marriage, family and career."

The innocent Nursing Sister Pierce also received a sudden transfer, to Bagotville, Quebec.

Ollie's first news of the events, and first suspicion of Danny's involvement, came when she read the paper work on Watson's transfer. The next time the Foursome went out, she leaned over the seat of the Ford, kissed Danny on the cheek and whispered "Thank you, Tanner."

She waited till Watson was off the base before she told Russ about him.

CHAPTER 16

▼

You showed me your wisdom on a September afternoon, just as you did so many other times. If I had only been listening! In my ignorance I believed I had done a noble thing—instead I once again just hurt and disappointed you!

COURTENAY—SEPTEMBER, 1955

The Foursome had just come from the movie at the E.W., and they were in the Arbutus for the usual after-movie drinks and discussion of the picture. That night it was *Rebel Without A Cause,* with James Dean and Natalie Wood.

When their drinks arrived Ollie commented on the movie, "Well, they sure weren't *Blackboard Jungle* teenagers and they weren't David and Ricky Nelson…somewhere in between? Middle class delinquents."

"What about that guy, the hero, bitching about his parents," said Russ. "Shit, it was them that got him all his good stuff. Sharp car, clothes like crazy, new stuff to wear every damn day, and all he could do was put his old man down. The father was probably overseas during the war, getting his ass shot off! He was lucky to *have* any parents…" He realized he was getting close to home, and looked down at his hands in his lap. They all knew something of his life before the Air Force. Ollie reached under the table and took his hand.

Josie said, a little self-consciously, "I think maybe I am, or *was,* one of those 'middle class' kids. My father is a manager of a big place, a textile company. I think there was always lots of money. But, you know, *I* wasn't always happy. Even with all I took for granted I had problems—not like needing food or clothes or anything, but they were real problems to me." She thought for a moment, then added, "For instance, I think I should love, or at least respect my father more. But I'm not sure he *deserves* my respect, and I don't think I like him much. I know it's awful to say, but it's 'ow I felt. How I still feel."

Ollie commented, "Maybe that's what it was supposed to be about. Kids of all kinds *think* they have troubles. Even the, uh, middle class kids—whatever the hell that means. My dad makes more money than some so-called 'middle class' people do and he works in a friggin' steel mill. He got to be a foreman of some kind, later, but he's still just a steel worker."

Russ had been looking intently at Josie. He quietly said, "You be careful, Jo. One day your dad won't be there." Then he shrugged. "Aw, it's none of my business. You gotta do what you gotta do...you can't help what you feel." He smiled apologetically.

Danny said, "That James Dean's a good actor...convincing."

Russ showed the lopsided grin, "You can have him, I'll take Natalie Wood. Hot stuff!"

Ollie jabbed him with an elbow. "Sure, Mister Hornydork, it figures!"

Later, as they were leaving the hotel, they found it was raining outside. The car was parked a block away on another street.

Danny said, "You guys wait here. I'll bring J.H. around." He went off at a trot, hunched over against the rain, jacket collar turned up.

Russ and the girls huddled in the hotel doorway. When they saw Danny pull up they started toward the car. They didn't see the large red bearded man, Carlson, coming out behind them. He was the same man that made trouble on an earlier night in the Arbutus. He was with the same couple again and he recognized Josie and Russ.

Carlson shouldered past Russ, who was between the girls, pushing him into Josie and knocking her to the concrete, bruising and scraping an elbow and knee. He barged past them and continued on his way.

Russ shouted, "Hey! Watch it, you big clown!" He and Carlson's companions bent to help Josie to her feet.

The woman asked, "Are you okay? Can you get up?" Josie nodded and stood up.

"Thank you. I'm not 'urt..."

The woman said, "Your knee's cut." She shouted after Carlson, "You're a real horse's ass, y'know, Red!"

He looked back and sneered. "Yeah, yeah. Tell your Air Force friends to watch where the hell they're going. C'mon, for Chrissake! I'm getting soaked." He walked on.

Then they heard Danny's shout, "HEY, YOU! *FAT-ASS!*" He was striding rapidly after the man. The Ford was double-parked a few feet away. "HOLD IT RIGHT THERE!"

Carlson stopped and turned. He stood a good six feet four, and weighed at least two-forty. He had a bit of a paunch, but otherwise looked strong as an ox.

He sneered at Danny. "You talkin' to me? What the hell do you want?"

"I want a piece of you—*LARD ASS!*" said Danny as he approached. He walked deliberately up to the man and slapped him hard across the face, first forehand, then backhand. The big man drew back to throw a punch but the slaps were followed by a lightning-quick series of solid right and left-handed blows. The force of the punches drove Carlson backward against a parked car, breaking his fall and enabling him to lunge forward. He wrapped huge arms around Danny in a bear hug. Danny was bent forcefully back in the powerful grasp. In just seconds he was having trouble breathing.

Josie cried, "Danny! No…" She looked away.

Just as it appeared he was in real peril, Danny demonstrated his skill. He let his whole body relax, sagging as if he were finished. Then with lightning-quick moves, he rammed his forehead into the man's nose and stomped a heel hard into his instep, feeling the small bones give. In pain, Carlson relaxed his grip, allowing Danny to take advantage by dropping quickly down and out of the bear hug. He came up swinging with a barely audible, keening snarl. He landed three fast blows to the mouth, smashing Red's lips. He grasped the big man's windbreaker, jerked him forward and then threw him back and down to the sidewalk. Still snarling, he was on his man in a flash. He landed blow after blow. Under the cruel assault, Carlson's face was raw flesh and he was barely conscious. The fight was over, the man obviously beaten, but Danny kept banging away.

Russ had been watching Red's friend in case he interfered. Now he yelled, "Dan! No more! It's over—he's beat." He tried to pull Danny off, but he ripped loose and landed still more blows. Russ shouted to Carlson's companion, "Help me get him off!" the two of them and a bystander were able to pull Danny off and away from his victim. "Calm down, Dan. He's finished!"

Danny stood, legs apart, chest heaving. He was unable to speak. Rain ran off his hair and face as he pointed down at his victim. A small crowd had gathered but he was oblivious to everything and everyone around him. Carlson lay on his back on the wet sidewalk, only his arms moving, waving feebly as if to ward off further blows. His face was ruined, eyes already swelling shut. Bloody froth gurgled from his nose and mouth and blended with the rain on the pavement in little pink rivulets.

It had been barely two minutes since the first blow was struck.

Danny, still pointing, sobbed in a small voice, "Don't ever...don't you God-dam *ever*..." He couldn't finish.

Ollie stood frozen, eyes wide in fascination, looking from Danny to Carlson. She whispered, "Jesus Christ!"

Josie turned to look. Quietly, she again said, "Danny. Oh no."

Russ spoke. "We'd better get to the car." To Carlson's awestruck companions he said, "You should get him looked after. Right away."

The four of them went to the car. Russ murmured, "Shit, Champ, that guy's kind of *huge.*"

Danny rubbed bruised knuckles. His face was unmarked. "Yeah, Russ, he scared the shit out of me." He got in and started the motor. Russ never knew just how to take the remark.

After only two blocks, Danny pulled over to the curb. He couldn't control his trembling.

"Russ, you better drive." He got out and stood leaning on the roof, head buried in his arms. Russ helped him into the back seat.

Ollie got out on her side. She said, "Jo, get in the back with..."

Josie interrupted her, "No. You sit with him." She stared straight ahead.

All the way to the base, Danny sat hunched over, head in hands, and occasionally rubbing his knuckles. Ollie kept her arms around his shoulders. She could feel his trembling.

At the base, Russ parked in front of the girls' barracks. They sat. No one spoke for several minutes.

Danny, his head still down, broke the silence. "I'm sorry...I lost it. I went way too far..."

No one was inclined to disagree. They all sat silent for five more minutes.

Russ spoke up. "He had it coming, Dan."

Ollie looked at Russ. "Jesus Christ." she whispered.

Josie opened her door. "I'm going in now." She hadn't looked at Danny. He reached over the seat for her hand but she pulled it away. She left the car and without looking back headed into the barracks. Danny stared after her. Ollie patted his shoulder and he looked at her blankly, then got out and walked up the road toward the men's barracks.

Ollie and Russ sat without speaking for another two minutes before she said, "Russ...Jesus...at first I thought he was gonna get killed, but he almost did the killing!"

"I've never seen him like that...so out of control," said Russ.

"But, why?"

"The guy knocked Josie down, that's all. It was enough."

She whispered again, "Jesus Christ."

*   *   *   *

D Crew worked the 0800 to 1630 day shift for five days after the incident. He didn't see or hear from Josie during that time and for three more days after. When he attempted to call her at work or in the barracks, he was told she was not in or not able to come to the phone. He left messages for her to call him but got no response. None of the girls, when he asked, would tell him anything and refused to pass-on his messages. They were rallying around Josie, supporting her decision to not see or speak to him.

He didn't see her in the Mess Hall; the girls were taking food to the barracks for her. He haunted the canteens and other places she and he usually went to together in the hope of running into her. On the fourth evening he called Ollie for the sixth time.

To his frantic questions she told him, "Let it go, Danny; everything's going to be okay, you'll just have to wait for her. She's hurt and angry."

On Saturday, his third day off, he was playing cribbage in his room with Russ, Gerry and Gil after returning from lunch in the mess hall. Somebody in the hall yelled, "Tanner—phone! It's a broad." He ran to the phone in the hallway.

"Hello, Tanner here."

"Danny?"

"Jo…Hi."

"Danny, could you meet me at the car?"

"Right now?"

"Yes. If you could."

He was waiting at the car when she arrived. He was apprehensive. It was a warm day and she was wearing a yellow blouse, pale blue pedal pushers and white sandals. She had a white cardigan tied around her shoulders, and had never been more beautiful. He felt his throat constrict at the sight of her.

Three feet in front of him, she hesitated, then rushed into his arms. Her feet lifted off the pavement as they clutched in an urgent embrace.

"You okay, Honey? Am I glad to see you!" He set her back to the ground. "I missed you, Jo."

She didn't answer. She went to the car and sat with her feet tucked under her. He got in and started the engine.

"Where to? Your choice, Josie." he said quietly.

She said, "Maybe the beach. Would Kye Bay be okay?"

"You got it."

He glanced at her once or twice as they drove along Knight Road. She moved over on the seat till she was sitting against him. He negotiated the steep switch-back down to the bay and found a place to park. He went to open her door but she was out before he reached it. She kicked off her sandals, placed them on the seat and started walking toward the beach. He removed his loafers and socks and caught up with her.

They walked the sandy shore close to the water's edge. The tide was halfway out, the water mirror-calm. The September sun made a kind of bright haze over the sea. They could hear the calls of gulls and the faint laughter of children playing. It was the kind of day when everything seemed to move slowly. They walked a few hundred yards and stopped at a spot where there were no other people. He turned to her and took her into his arms.

"Jo, Honey. About the other night, I am so…"

"We do not 'ave to talk about that. Kiss me, Danny." He did.

After the kiss, he persisted, "Hon, I have to tell you—the guy…"

She interrupted, "Please, let's not talk about it, Danny." She turned away and looked out at the water.

"I have to talk about it, Josie. I broke a promise. I want to explain."

She turned back to him, sighed, and said, "Okay, Danny, I *will* talk about it, but only one time!" She took a half step back from him. "I was so scared, Danny. I was…I was terrified!" He started to speak, but she put her fingers over his mouth. "No! I 'ave to finish this. Then I will never speak of it again." She took a deep breath. "I never before saw anything like that. I never saw *you* like that. I didn't know you. I didn't know *who* that was. Ollie said you could 'ave killed the guy…"

He blurted, "Jo! I did it for you. Nobody's going to…"

She stamped her foot in the sand. Her eyes flashed angrily. *"No!* You might believe that, but it is just not true! Since I first met you, whenever I have trouble or a…a hurt, I always look for my Danny for help. You're my *hero*, Danny! So I looked for you when I was knocked down. Looked *at* you, Danny. You just went right after the guy. I don't know if you even looked at me! If you wanted to do it *for me*, as you say, there I was, wasn't I? Right there on the wet sidewalk on my 'ands and knees!" She took in another deep breath. "Okay to knock the guy down or something but to hurt him so bad as you did…I didn't know the person doing that." Her tears were flowing. "You should 'ave come to *me!"*

She put her arms around his waist, laid her head on his chest. "Danny, I love you so much!" she murmured. "I love you too much, I think." She sobbed wretchedly into his chest.

He held her tightly. He could feel her wracking sobs. He turned his face to the sky, silently crying with her. He wasn't sure he understood what she wanted of him, for until now he had believed his action was appropriate.

They stood locked together for five minutes. When she looked up at him, tears still wet on her cheeks, she said, "I never want to be away from you again. How I missed you. It was only one week, I know, but…"

He corrected her, "It was eight days."

She thought that to be funny and sad and sweet. Smiling through tears and sniffles, she said, "Eight days then. I never thought love would 'urt so much!"

She led him to a log and they sat down. Dabbing at her eyes and nose, she asked, "How is your 'and? I saw you rubbing it in the car." He didn't answer. She took his hands and kissed the knuckles.

They sat and looked out over the bay. They couldn't make out the mainland across the strait. The line where sea and sky meet was not discernible in the hazy air. The gulls swooped and soared and called overhead. At the water's edge, a sandpiper darted busily about, doing whatever sandpipers do on warm September days.

When they returned to the car she stopped, turned, and stared back in the direction of the beach before getting in. He stopped and waited beside her.

"Do you want to stay here for a while longer?"

She looked thoughtful. "No…no, let's go back now."

"You're the boss."

The incident with Redbeard was never again mentioned between them.

CHAPTER 17

▼

You found our cabin at the beach...

SEPTEMBER–OCTOBER, 1955

As they were leaving Kye Bay on that Saturday after his fight with Carlson, Josie had spotted something that gave her a crazy idea. The next Thursday she was talking to Ollie during coffee break.

"What would the Air Force do about someone if they moved off the base to live?"

"I don't know, Jo," said Ollie. "I don't think it's illegal or anything. I guess as long as he, or she, was willing to pay the expenses...hell, I really don't know. I'd have to read Q.R.s to see if it's allowed. I think some of the single officers do it. Why do you ask?"

"Oh, just thinking out loud. You said he *or* she...what about a he *and* she...?"

Ollie was alarmed. "Jo! What the hell are you thinking? Is this something Danny..."

Josie cut her off. "No. Not Danny. He doesn't know...honestly. I was just *wondering* anyway, Ollie."

"Wondering about what, for Chrissake?" She was even more alarmed.

"Nothing. Really. Just a stupid thing I was thinking about. Just wondering."

"Bullshit! You're doing a lot more than wondering. Did you mean an *unmarried* he and she?"

"Well...just for fun...what about the couples who get married, then both stay in the service? They get places in town, don't they."

- 174 -

"Jo, they get marriage allowance, so they can afford to live off the base. They have to pay rent, buy food, there's electricity, heat…all that."

"So if people are in love and want to be together? They can't do it…be together?" Josie was trying to sound casual, dismissive.

"They'd have to figure out some way to cover their tracks—get around the rules. If they were ever caught there'd be hell to pay. The Air Force can be *moral* as hell and that kind of thing is frowned on, big time. A good little Airwoman is not supposed to sleep with her guy, even if they're in love. They would be charged…with something, and the girl, at least, would likely get kicked out of the service. Why do you suppose the guys aren't allowed up to our rooms? I'm telling you, kid, the more I think about it, it just wouldn't be worth all the hassle, or the risk!"

Josie looked thoughtful for a minute. Absently, she said, "I suppose you're right…"

Ollie's feeling of alarm didn't go away.

When she was alone, Josie zeroed in on one thing Ollie said: *They would have to figure out some way to cover their tracks. Get around the rules!*

＊   ＊   ＊   ＊

Friday after work she begged a ride from Jake MacDonald and went to Kye Bay. She made him promise not to say a word to Danny about the trip. They were back on the base in an hour.

On Saturday afternoon she and Danny were alone in the Snack Bar.

"Can we go for a ride? I 'ave something to show you," she said.

"You're not planning to drag me off to Royston again, are you?" he answered playfully.

Smiling, she said, "Shut up, you. Please be serious now. There's something I want you to see."

He playfully pulled down the corners of his mouth with thumb and finger. "Of course. There, see? I'm all serious—where are we going?"

Grinning at his antics, she said, "Kye Bay."

"Not Royston this time?"

"Shut up, you. Finish your coffee and let's go."

At the beach, Josie directed him to turn into a short driveway and park in front of a cottage. It was the first of three identical cedar-sided cabins, situated in a line parallel to the shore. All three were enclosed by a common green picket fence, with a gravel driveway for each.

She said, "Wait here, Honey. I won't be long." She went to the door.

Danny waited by the car. He could hear a small dog barking inside. She knocked on the door and was greeted by an elderly woman. The two of them came to the gate with a blond cocker spaniel dancing around their feet.

Josie introduced the woman while she bent to pet the dog. "Danny, this is Mrs. MacKenzie. She and her husband own these three cabins…" indicating the dog, she added, "and this is Skipper."

Mrs. MacKenzie said, "Pleased to meet you, Danny." She looked to be in her mid-sixties, short and tending to plump, with a round, kindly face. Danny detected a trace of Scottish burr.

"Why don't I give you the key, Josie, and you can show the place to Danny. Just remember to bring it back when you're done, won't you." She separated a key from a ring. "Here you go, dear…it's this one."

Josie led him to the center cabin, across a lawn barely surviving its war with the invading sand. The exterior was white with green trim and in the front window was a hand-lettered sign:

"Cottage for Rent—Winter Rate. See Owner Next Door."

As she unlocked the door, she explained, "I saw the sign on Saturday when we were here. It's thirty dollars a month, but only for the winter. It goes up after the end of April. It's old, but it's not too bad, come see!"

The cabin was small, twenty-four feet deep by twenty across. The entire front half made a single large room, twelve by twenty feet. At the end nearest to the entrance were a refrigerator, small electric range, enamel sink with linoleum countertop and glass-doored cupboards. Next to this "kitchenette," by the door they came in, stood a wooden dining table covered with flowery oilcloth, and four chrome and leatherette chairs. At the other end of the room, grouped around a stone fireplace, were a hide-a-bed sofa and two comfortable looking easy chairs set on an oval braided rug. There was a floor lamp by each easy chair, and a wagon wheel chandelier hung from the ceiling. No one piece of furniture matched another in this "living room."

An oil-fired space heater stood between two doors at the rear wall of the front room. The door on the right led to a large bedroom with double and single beds separated by a portable screen, a dresser, a chest of drawers, and a wardrobe. The other door opened to a short hallway that in turn led to a bathroom and a lean-to shed. The bathroom had a basin, toilet and shower stall. Danny had to duck his head to see through a low door into the lean-to. He saw it contained a water heater, oil tank and a stack of firewood. It had a hand-hewn door leading to the outside.

All the walls were freshly painted in a cream color. The flooring was linoleum in a fake parquet pattern. Faint, not unpleasant odors of fresh paint, stove oil and cut wood permeated the place.

She said nothing as she led him through every inch of the place but kept glancing his way.

When they were outside on the small stoop again, she asked, "Well?"

"Well? Well what?"

"What do you think?"

"What I think is…maybe next summer, or spring, we could try to take our leave, or part of our leave, together. This place would be fun." He was thoughtful, "I'd guess they rent by the week after April. We would have to book ahead."

She tried not to show disappointment. "I wasn't thinking about after April, Danny…" She looked at the ground. She was beginning to have doubts about her crazy idea.

"What then?"

"Oh, it's stupid I think. It was for us to move in here—right away." She shook her head. "It is stupid. I'll take the key back."

"Jesus, Honey, move in? It sounds great, but…but I don't know if it can be done." He put his arm around her shoulders. "I don't know…"

"I'm silly, but I'll ask about the summer rate. Meet me at the car."

Mrs. MacKenzie told her she would hold the place for three days, then she would require a commitment and a deposit. Josie couldn't bring herself to say they wouldn't be taking the cabin. She wasn't prepared, yet, to give up on her original idea. She forgot to ask for the summer rates.

On the drive back to the base, she said wistfully, "It would be so wonderful if we could stay there together, wouldn't it!"

He replied, "Yeah, Honey, just imagine, waking up and being together—every morning!"

In her bed that night, she thought, *Okay, Mister L.A.C. Tanner—you always figure ways to make things happen, now you have three days. I know you'll think of something!*

*   *   *   *

It took him just two days.

Danny's fondest dream was to be with Josie every night, all night—to awake with her in the mornings. The cabin could make his dream come true. At breakfast in the Mess Hall he casually asked her, "Do you suppose that cottage at Kye Bay would still be available?"

She fought not to show her delight. *You have been thinking about it!* "Do you mean for next summer?"

"No, let's say for right away…like you said."

"But Ollie says the Air Force doesn't like it for single people to live together off the base. We could get in trouble."

"There might be a way—if you're interested." He raised his eyebrows.

"I am. I just don't want…I don't want us to get in trouble, Danny."

"I've been thinking, what if we kept our barrack rooms, kept them looking lived in. We could leave some of our clothes in the room. Russ will cover for me and none of the other guys'll say anything. We know Ollie will back you up. Is there anyone, like any NCOs, who would blow the whistle in your barracks?" Josie noticed he had gone from "would" and "could" to "will." He continued, "We'll sleep in our barrack rooms a couple of nights a Month; show up for inspections and do our share on cleanup days. We'll want to do our laundry here anyway." He was warming to the idea. "You'll want to sleep here when I'm on the graveyard shift. I don't want you out there alone at night. We'll put the rent in my name so I'll have a story to cover us." If their plan were discovered he would swear it was rented as a place to party, and Josie was just visiting.

She covered her mouth before a squeal of delight could escape. His solution was so simple. "Oh, Danny. Will that work? It would be wonderful!"

"I don't see why it wouldn't work. I'm willing if you are. If I'm wrong, don't forget we could be in deep shit. Is it worth the risk? I couldn't live with being the cause of your reputation getting hurt. We know from experience how gossip travels." He paused, wanting to cover all the angles. "It'll be pretty expensive, too."

"I don't care. Let's do it!"

"Okay! I'll shoot over there this morning to see the lady."

"Mrs. MacKenzie," she prompted.

"Yeah. Then I'll meet you here for lunch. Don't get your hopes up—it might be rented by now to someone else." She nodded seriously. He looked at the clock. "You better get to work, it's five to eight. I'll see you later."

She wore a satisfied smile as she walked to the headquarters building. She looked to the sky and said aloud, "It will not be rented, my Danny."

✳   ✳   ✳   ✳

They moved into the cabin on the first of October.

They arrived with a carload of clothes and other personal effects. Josie set about making a home of the place. She was pleased to discover that dishes, cutlery and cooking utensils were supplied. There were even flower vases in a cupboard and pictures on the walls.

When they went to bed the first night, however, they couldn't find any bed linen, just a mattress and two bare pillows. At first it brought tears—she saw it as an inexcusable failure in her domestic responsibility, but he kissed her tears, held her close, and they laughed. They made love and slept on the bare mattress for two nights. On the third day Mrs. MacKenzie brought by some freshly washed bedroom curtains and noticed the bare bed. She innocently inquired if they would be needing more blankets; if the bedding she had supplied would be adequate with winter coming.

Her words precipitated a frantic search after she left. Sure enough, they found sheets, blankets, pillowcases and towels in a cabinet each thought the other had explored, in the hall outside the bathroom. More tears, then more laughter, then pride, as she made their bed for the first time. Danny kidded that he kind of preferred the bare bed because he got to see more of her. She said, "See this, you!" and stuck out her tongue.

For Josie the little cabin was heaven. She thrilled at everything domestic. She hummed popular tunes as she scrubbed cupboards and mopped floors. On their first trip to the Safeway store in Courtenay, she learned he liked puffed wheat better than he liked corn flakes, preferred breakfast sausages over bacon, hated carrots and admitted he enjoyed liver.

Sometimes she would watch him as he did little things she had never seen— vigorous toweling after a shower, turning the tops of his socks inside-out to put them on or working on all his boots and shoes for an hour to attain a brilliant spit shine. She saw how his expression changed from smile to frown with the story's plot when he read. She was fascinated watching him shave, fitting a new blade into the safety razor, brushing the rich soap over his face, pulling his skin taut and scraping away at the night's growth. (One morning as she watched, absorbed, he turned suddenly and lathered her face and breasts, starting a shaving cream and toothpaste battle, bedaubing the bathroom and making them late for work.)

For his part, Danny was happy just to be with her for so many hours each day. The time of greatest wonder for him was waking in the morning with her beside him. If he were the first to awake he would lie still and quiet and marvel at the warmth and softness of her. The curves of her shoulder or hip, the way the light from the window highlighted the fine hairs on the back of her neck, the look of total serenity on her face. It made him smile and wonder at his good fortune. Sometimes he would watch her as she moved about the place or curled, feet up, in an easy chair. She would at times see him watching and, for no special reason, come into his arms. He bought them folding lawn chairs and they would sit outside the cabin and watch the sun rising over the mainland as they drank morning coffee or watch it go into hiding behind the bluff in the evening. On mild weekends they would take long walks on the beach, often with Skipper the cocker spaniel cavorting along with them. She loved the walks. She discovered in her explorations that the shoreline is an ever-changing thing, bringing new treasures with every rise and fall of the tide.

After dark, they would sit inside—reading, studying, or listening to popular music on the Baby Champ radio, each content just to be in the same room with the other.

Josie proved to be helpful to him in his studies. He felt especially inept at mathematics, a subject that had contributed to the demise of his formal education. She, on the other hand, had graduated from high school with top marks, math being one of her better subjects.

One evening he was at the kitchen table, working on a geometry problem. She was in her favorite easy chair, reading Edna Ferber's *So Big*. He had been at the same question for twenty minutes, and had searched through the textbook several times for a hint at the solution, but was still defeated. He dropped his pencil and stared at the page.

He looked at her over his shoulder and said, "Hey, smartass, come here and see if you can explain this one."

She came and stood behind him. "Explain what, Darling?"

"This, number six, they're saying here I can figure out the square feet in a gable—that's the pointed part of a roof—because they give me the height and width…"

She said, "Hmm, let me see." She sat down beside him and studied the paper. "Yes. Look what 'appens when you do this." She sketched a gable, a flattened triangle, in the margin, then she drew a vertical line down the center. "See? Now what do you have?"

"What do you mean…"

"You now have two…what?"

Puzzled, he just shrugged.

She touched the two halves with the pencil. "See, here and here, you have two what?"

"Two triangles." He still looked puzzled.

'What kind?'

"Aha! Right angled triangles!" he thought he was getting it. "So, I have to do the square root thing on the two known sides. That'll get me the area? I'll have to figure out both triangles and add them together…"

She was shaking her head.

"…No?" He was stumped.

"No…you're thinking of Pythagoras; for the length of the third side. But look, the triangles are identical. So, if you swing one over…"

"Swing it frigging over? What do you mean?"

"In your mind, I mean. Watch. If they were like this…" She drew a rectangle, with a diagonal line from corner to corner forming two triangles. "What happens now, Danny?"

"Yeah! They make a rectangle! Isn't that something…"

"What are the sizes they give?"

"Um…twenty-two wide by six high…I've got it! Six times, uh, half of twenty-two, that's eleven, so it equals…sixty-six. Sixty-six square feet." He leaned over and kissed her. "You are a genius—a beautiful, gorgeous genius! Want to finish the rest of these for me?"

"Certainly not!" she declared as she retreated to her chair. "It shames me to think Danny Tanner, an L.A.C., would even think of cheating." She grinned at her book, "And I know what a gable is."

He muttered, "Little fart."

"What!"

"Nothing, Honey."

∗   ∗   ∗   ∗

So, they settled into a routine.

Once a week as planned, and whenever he worked the graveyard shift, they spent their nights on the base. At first they worried about being found out. As the weeks went by, however, they were able to relax.

Mr. and Mrs. MacKenzie, Anne and Morrie, were considerate, friendly land-lords, and Josie, always so easy to love, became their favorite. On more than one occasion, one or the other admonished Danny to, "treat your darling little wife decently, the way she deserves!" They went out of their way to be helpful to the young couple. Anne would drop in apologetically on weekends or evenings when he was on shift, to see if there was anything Josie needed. Josie would make tea and they would chat for an hour or so while the landlady offered old-fashioned advice on one homemaking function or another. Morrie was always fussing around the property, keeping busy with repairs: painting, roofing, and plumbing. Danny spotted him favoring a sore back one afternoon and insisted on helping with, and then finishing, the painting of the trim on the cabins; work that earned him half a chocolate cake from Anne.

"The fool man! He doesn't know how old he is—always puttering around looking for something to do."

Two weeks after they moved in, Anne introduced Josie to Lorna Letourneau, who, with her husband Leo, lived in the third cabin. Lorna was from rural South-western Ontario, red-haired, short, just an inch or so over Josie's height and, in her own words, "pleasingly plump." Josie liked her instantly. They would come to know her as an unfailingly cheerful person.

Lorna arrived at their door with Leo one evening. He carried a case of Lucky Lager with him—"In case your old lady filled the fridge with food and crap and left no room for beer—it was all the introduction Danny needed. Leo was a Com Technician with 407 Squadron who had been in the service for seven years. He had received his Corporal's "hooks" a year earlier. In contrast to his wife, he was tall, six foot three, and angular in build, with the weathering of an outdoorsman on his homely face. They soon realized he was as cheerful a person as his wife. That evening together was the first of many for the two couples.

She became "Jo-Jo" to Leo when he asked her, "Josie? Not Josée?" He pronounced it as Jos-ay. "How come? I know you're French like me."

She confided the reason for her name change.

"Sounds fair, I'll just call you Jo-Jo."

"No! It sounds like a name for a monkey or something!"

"Too bad, you're stuck with it." And that was that. In truth she didn't mind but never told him so.

They got together regularly at one or the others' cabin, to play cards. Lorna and Leo taught them the games of hearts, whist, rummoli and euchre. Josie had played children's card games and Danny was only familiar with poker and cribbage. It was always the men versus the women and they all played to win. Ollie and Russ often visited, sometimes sleeping-over on the hide-a-bed. Some nights they would all go into town for a movie and drinks. Lorna and Leo, it turned out, enjoyed a good laugh, so they fit in well with the Fearsome Foursome.

Danny and Leo volunteered to relieve Mr. Mac of the job of gathering and cutting wood for the three fireplaces. They started going out once or twice a week in Leo's pickup truck, with Morrie's chain saw and a Swede saw. They brought the sawed lengths home and split them in the back yard. They decided that before Christmas they would get enough wood stored in the lean-tos to last the three cabins through the winter.

*   *   *   *

Later in September, Danny brought home a rifle. He ran into Jake Mac-Donald and a Fightercop from Charlie Crew named George Dukovich one morning, and they went shooting at the station's firing range. Dukovich owned a rifle, a new Savage thirty-ought-six bolt action. It was an expensive, finely crafted weapon, with an intricately carved stock. Danny and Jake signed out Lee Enfield 303s and they spent two hours on the targets.

On their way back from the range, George said, "You might be just the guy I need, Dan; they're getting strict about the no-guns-in-the-barracks thing. They want me to either get rid of it and my ammo or turn it in at the guardhouse for safekeeping. If I turn it over to those S.P. jerks I just know it'll get abused and it cost me a month's pay. If you could keep it at your place for me, it would solve my problem."

Josie was waiting on the porch when Danny parked the car and took the rifle in its case from the trunk.

When he got to the door she asked, "What have you got?"

"It's a rifle."

"Why do you 'ave a rifle? Where did you get it?"

He explained about storing the gun for Dukovich.

"Is it okay?" he asked. "I'll keep it in the back of the wardrobe. If you don't want it here, just say so and I'll tell him I can't do it. Or if you'd like, I can keep it out in the lean-to."

"No, you 'ad better keep it in the cabin, it could get damaged or rusty out there. I don't mind. I don't like them, but my father had guns, so I'm used to them. Can I see it?"

He took it from the case. "Beautiful, isn't it?"

"I wouldn't call it beautiful. Kind of ugly, really." She ran a hand over the carving. "The wood part's kind of nice, though. Does that guy go hunting?"

"Yeah...so does Leo, Jo. It's a sport."

"How about you? 'Ave you ever hunted?"

"No, as a matter of fact, I haven't. I won't be going out to slaughter Bambi, okay? I just enjoy shooting, at targets. I'll put it away now, right at the back of the wardrobe, okay?"

When he returned to the kitchen, he asked, "When do we eat. I'm hungry."

She displayed her sly smile, "Why don't you go out and shoot a rabbit...or a turkey?"

"Because, Little Miss Weak Stomach, you definitely wouldn't clean it, and probably wouldn't cook it or eat it either! Now, open a can or something, Julia Childs, I'll be in the john while you burn it."

"Shut up, you."

The rifle was in its case, in the closet, and soon forgotten.

*   *   *   *

One evening during a card game at Letourneaus' Leo invited Danny to go fishing the next morning. They would leave first thing in the morning for Little River, where they would rent a boat.

It was still dark outside when he got up. Josie kept her eyes closed, feigning sleep. She listened, as he dressed then rummaged in the fridge for the lunch she had made. She heard him and Leo outside at five-fifteen, loading gear into Leo's old truck and driving off.

Later, at eleven, she was kneading a plastic pouch of margarine to mix the color, when she heard the truck pull into the driveway.

She heard Danny call from outside, "Jo! Come out here and see this."

Danny and Leo were in the back yard, by an old workbench. Skipper came dancing over to her with a stick in his mouth. Danny was holding a salmon by the gills. She saw there was blood and scales on his hands and some on his shirt. She stopped six feet short of the bench, absently petting the dog as he jumped up on her. "Babe, take a look at this—I caught him! It's the biggest one we got! You should have seen the fight he gave me—he jumped about ten times!"

"What is it?" she asked. She came no closer.

"It's a coho! A salmon."

"Like in the tins?"

"Huh? Well, yeah. But it's way better. It's fresh, we just caught it."

"Oh. It's, um, very shiny."

Pointing at three more fish on the bench, he said, "Leo caught those three. Mine's the biggest though. Leo says it'll go about twelve or thirteen pounds." He was having trouble sounding matter-of-fact.

"Oh. Good. What are you going to do with it?"

"Leo's gonna clean it, then we can cook it—part of it—for supper! It's too big for one meal."

"Oh." She was no closer to the bench and no more enthusiastic.

Indicating the fish on the bench, Leo said, "You guys can have one of these, too. We've got lots, Lorna cans them." He picked up the smallest fish. It was dripping gore from its mouth. "This little guy's a grilse, he'll be great to eat!"

"Oh. Thank you." The disgusted look she failed to conceal belied the spoken gratitude.

Bent over the bench to hide his wide grin from Josie, Leo started cleaning the fish. He started by slitting the bellies from head to anal fin and pulling out the guts and examining them carefully before scraping the whole mess into a garbage can. Then he cut the heads off. She watched the procedure, mesmerized.

With a wink at Danny, he said, "We should save these heads, y' know, Jo-jo."

"Why?" she asked.

"For fish head stew. It's delicious!"

"Oh?" She didn't realize she took a step backward.

"Sure. You put them in a pot of water with carrots and onions and stuff, then you boil them. You know it's ready to eat when their eyeballs bob up to the top of the pot!"

"Ahgg! I 'ave to go in…and-and finish the dishes!" She turned and almost ran for the door. Leo chuckled and Danny laughed aloud. From inside they heard her, "You're mean, Leo!"

Danny cooked fresh salmon fillet for his supper—Josie made herself a hot dog.

*   *   *   *

In early October, Danny listened to the World Series baseball games on the Baby Champ. They invited Ollie, Russ, Lorna and Leo over to hear game seven. Josie and Lorna, relegated to snack-making duty, were amused by the others' passion for the game. Leo was neutral but Ollie and Russ cheered for the favored Yankees—but 1955 was the year of Danny's beloved Dodgers. "Da Bums" won the National League pennant by thirteen games, exacting revenge on the hated Giants for their 1954 win. Now the series was tied at three games each. Beer and insults flowed in steady streams as the game progressed. When the game ended and the Dodgers had beaten the despised Yankees on a Johnny Podres shutout, Ollie and Russ each owed Danny a case of beer.

After the game, Ollie warned Danny, "Look out for the Braves in a couple of years, they're in Milwaukee now and they've got pitching and a couple of guys named Aaron and Mathews that really bang it around. And your Bums are getting old, Tanner!"

The guys scoffed—but events two years later would prove she had astonishing baseball prescience.

*   *   *   *

COMOX—OCTOBER, 1955

The couple's domestic journey wasn't always smooth flying. They encountered occasional bumpy air.

In early October, for instance, she asked him to teach her to drive the car, and they had their first fight—the male ego displayed. There were tense moments from the beginning, more correctly, from the starting:

"Jo, it's just not so hard. Give it some gas as you ease the clutch out. If you don't give it gas, of *course* it'll stall out on you. Now try again..."

Start...lurch...stall.

"Jesus! You're doing the same damn thing every time. Why can't you listen?" *How can someone who jives as well as she does have so much trouble keeping her feet straight on a couple of pedals in a damn car!* "Try again...eeease the clutch out as you give it a little gas."

"I'm trying, Danny. Give me a chance!"

Her next try was a near smooth start, no lurch forward. Start...smooth roll, and then stall.

"That was better, eh?"

"It was smoother, but you let the motor die. You have to keep the..."

"Oh." She turned the key while vigorously pumping the accelerator.

"DON'T PUMP THE GAS! You'll flood it. Shit, you flooded the damn thing."

"Don't swear at me, okay? Look, now it won't start."

"That was *not* because I swore!"

"I know. Just don't swear and yell at me."

"I'm sorry but you...aw shit, Hon, I'm sorry."

And so it went. He was learning—too late—a sane man never tries to teach the woman he loves how to drive.

After a few more lessons, she was able to get the car started and keep it running. Danny now had to turn her loose on the roads of the Comox Valley. He limited her at first to a straight portion of nearby Knight Road, where she became fairly proficient at keeping the car on the right side of the road.

With a lump in his throat and fingers crossed, he took her farther afield.

So it came about that one early evening she was driving on Lazo Road at thirty-five miles per hour. Lazo Road was a back way to the village of Comox, winding around the seashore and through forest from where it joined Knight Road near Kye Bay.

Danny said, "Turn into a side road or driveway up ahead. Then you can back it out and turn around. We'll see how you do. We have to head back anyway, it's going to be dark soon."

She turned to her right into the first driveway she came to. She stopped there and put the car in neutral. It was well done, but a bad choice, they were in the middle of a sharp curve.

Maintaining his calm, Danny said, "This wasn't a good place, but we're here now. Be careful and look for any cars coming, then back out and turn back the other way. Make sure you get it over to the far shoulder, in case somebody's coming, okay? Get a good look before you move."

His caution made her nervous. Backing onto the road, she popped the clutch too quickly. The car lurched back halfway across the road and stalled.

"Okay, get it started quick, Jo."

She sat frozen. She couldn't remember what to do.

"Get it started. A car might come." Anyone coming around the curve would be doing at least fifty and wouldn't be able to stop before hitting them. In her panic and embarrassment she stalled the engine again.

"Jesus Christ! Get it moving, we're right on the road!"

She slumped back in the seat, looking lost.

"COME ON, JO—GET US MOVING!"

"Don't YELL at me!"

"Don't YELL? We're in the middle of the DAMN ROAD! Move over, I'll do it." He leaned on her roughly, cramming her against the door. He got the engine started and awkwardly backed the car to the far shoulder and stopped. At that moment a car appeared in the curve and sped by them.

"Danny, don't *talk* to me like that!" He didn't see the tears glistening in her eyes.

"THEN DON'T BE SO GODDAM STUPID! THAT CAR WOULD HAVE CREAMED US." He was frightened and angry and reacting to the close call.

She was crying now. She knew she had put them in peril, but she couldn't stand him, her Danny, talking to her in such a way. "I won't stay here and listen to you. You're a big *shit!*" She got out of the car and started walking along the shoulder.

He had only rarely heard her curse in anger. He drove the car slowly alongside her. "Jo...I wish you wouldn't talk like..."

She didn't turn her head, "It's just too bad what you wish, isn't it? Big shit!" She kept walking.

He called after her, "Jo, where are you going?"

She didn't look at him. "I'm going 'OME!" She walked faster.

Oh, Jesus, what's the matter with me? How can I fix this?

With a weak attempt at The Tanner Smile, he said, "You're pretty mad, eh, Hon?"

She stopped. She turned to him, hands on hips. "And 'ow did your stupid little brain figure *that* out?" She started walking again. Without looking back, she called, "You're a big, stupid SHIT, Danny Tanner!"

He shouted after her, "Okay—My *little stupid brain* figured out you're walking the wrong way to get home. How does *that* grab you?"

Her steps slowed. "Like *'ell* I am. You stupid...big stupid shit!" She couldn't help but look around at the surroundings.

He was out of the car, following on foot. "I'm telling you, Josie—wrong way."

Her steps faltered. She stopped and looked up and down the road. "Am I, really?"

"Yep. It's the other way."

She sat down on the gravel and wept. He knelt beside her. "I'll take you home, Jo. Get in the car." He opened the door for her.

She wiped her tears with a sleeve and got in the car. "Take me home, right now!" All the way to the cabin she sat as far to the right as she could, looking sullenly out the side window. As soon as he stopped the car, she was out and headed for the porch. With a hand on the open door, she called back, "An' I will *not* be cooking any supper for you!"

"Okay," he said, "How about I go to Bud's...pick up some burgers or something?"

"Fine!" The door slammed. From inside he heard, "Stupid shit!"

When he returned they ate the hamburgers in silence. When she finished she went into the bedroom. In five minutes she came to the door.

"Don't even think about apologizing. There is no excuse you can make up for talking to me like you did. You're a cruel man and I hate you." She slammed the door.

He went to the door, reached for the handle.

She shouted, "Don't you come in here. Go away!"

He leaned his forehead on the door. "Hon, I'm sorry. How can I make it up to you?"

"Go away!"

He went to the hide-a-bed and sat down. *I hope you're comfortable, couch. I think I'm going to spend at least one night right here.* He sat with his head in his hands.

She opened the bedroom door again. She didn't see him at first. "Danny…are you here?" She thought for a moment he had gone out.

He raised his head. "I'm over here."

"Okay. I'm sorry for what 'appened, Danny…for what I did. I could 'ave got us hurt by my mistake. I'm sorry for saying I hate you, and I'm sorry for using bad words, too. So…I'm sorry." She shut the door before he could answer.

Another hour went by. The darkness outside was complete when he heard the door open again. He looked up expectantly. She was wearing her babydolls and was silhouetted in the lighted bedroom doorway. "Do you want to come to bed, Danny?"

He looked at the wall clock. "It's not even eight o'clock…"

"I didn't ask the time. Do you…don't you want to come to bed…with me?"

He did.

They made up.

They made love.

A week later she started going out in the Dog Pound with Ollie. They didn't tell him about it. On the tenth of December she would pass the driver test and get her license.

When she told him he was proud of her.

CHAPTER 18

▼

I took you to see my Mom and she loved you just as I knew she would. I only wish you had met her sooner…

OCTOBER, 1955

Danny received a message at work to phone his sister in Vancouver. She had called the base, saying there was an important family matter. When he called her back, she told him his mother was ill; she had had one stay in hospital already and was now back in. The doctor had told Beth it was a serious heart condition.

F/O Donahue authorized three days off and Danny drove to Victoria the next day.

He didn't go to the James Bay house when he got to town; instead he drove straight to Royal Jubilee Hospital to see his Mom.

Betty Tanner appeared fatigued to him, but otherwise in fairly good health. She was overjoyed at seeing him and her spirits lifted; she seemed to be energized by his presence. She had only seen her son a few times since he joined up, and she knew how he hated the house and his father and brothers. In the year and a half since he was stationed at Jericho he had seen his mother at Beth's place in Vancouver on four occasions, and had gone to Victoria only once, to have lunch with her in a downtown restaurant on Mothers' Day. Now, in her hospital ward, she embraced him tearfully.

"Oh, Daniel. I'm so happy you could come see me!"

"Hi Mom, how are you feeling?"

"Oh, not so bad…a little tired."

"Beth said it's your heart?"

"I'll be fine, Danny. I feel better already 'cause you're here. Tell me what you've been up to…it's been months since I saw you at Beth's."

He told her about Josie—the first mention of a girl she had ever heard from him.

"She must be pretty special, Danny. Could you bring her to see me? It doesn't have to be at the house. It would make me so happy to meet her. We could have lunch…"

"Yeah, I will Mom, next weekend. I think my days off work out okay. You'd better be up and around by then, hear me?" He thought that over. He remembered how she had always been tired, always working. "Naw, come to think, Mom, you stay right here as long as they'll let you. Get lots of rest, you deserve it. Let someone wait on you for a change."

Before leaving for Comox, he stopped at the office and arranged for her to get the next available private or semi-private ward.

On Friday he and Josie drove to Victoria after her work, arriving at nine P.M. They took a room in the Dominion Hotel on Yates Street. She remarked, "At last I 'ave come to Victoria."

He managed to get around the regular visiting hours by cajoling the ward's head nurse. It helped that his mother was alone now, the only patient in a semi-private room, and of course The Tanner Smile didn't hurt his cause with the nurses.

Beth had called to tell him Betty had had another bad spell and she looked somewhat worse on this visit. She was dozing but when he kissed her brow her eyes fluttered open and she gave him a tired smile. "Danny, you came…again."

"Mom, this is Josie, the love of my life," he said proudly.

Josie forced herself to smile brightly. This woman did not look at all well. She was reminded of her own mother's illness. "Hello, Mrs. Tanner, it's nice to meet you. Danny 'as told me all about you."

Betty smiled. "Josie?" She glanced at Danny to be sure she had the name right. Then she turned back to Josie. "Don't call me Missus, Dear, I'm Betty. Or better yet, could you call me Mom like Danny does?" She looked at Danny. "I always knew you'd find a good one, Danno—but she's the most beautiful girl!" She took Josie's hand. "I'm embarrassing you! Don't be shy, Josie, it's true you are just lovely, believe it!" Then, back to Danny, "Don't lose this girl, Son. Treat her right, and always respect her."

"I will, Mom. She's pretty special to me."

Back to Josie she said, "You must feel like cattle at a fair, getting inspected like this. But I meant it, and I meant it about calling me Mom, too."

Josie couldn't stop herself. She leaned down and gave Betty a hug and kiss. In a quiet voice she said, "Okay…Mom. Thank you."

Danny said, "Josie lost her mother when she was only thirteen, Mom."

"Oh, that's terrible, Honey! Then, if it's all right with you, I'll be your substitute Mom."

Josie smiled through tears. "I would love that!"

They left the hospital at ten-thirty and returned the next day. During the afternoon Danny went to the cafeteria for coffees and when he returned, his mother was sitting up. Her face was made up and Josie was brushing her hair.

"Look, Danny!" said Betty, "Josie's getting me all prettied up. She says I'm gonna look sexy. What do you think?"

Josie giggled. "Maybe I should 'ave said seductive, Mom."

Danny thought his mother looked a little less tired. He noted, too, how easily Josie called her Mom. "Betty Tanner, you look sexy *and* seductive—voluptuous, even!" he said.

They visited in the evening and again on Sunday. On the Sunday visit, they encountered Vic Tanner as he was leaving the ward. Danny and his father exchanged terse greetings. He didn't introduce Josie.

On Sunday Josie insisted on again brushing Betty's hair and applying makeup. Betty of course demurred, but it was plain she was pleased when Josie pressed the matter.

Later, as they got in the car to leave town, he said simply, "Thanks, Hon."

She understood and moved a little closer on the seat.

*   *   *   *

A week and two days later his sister called with news that Betty Tanner's heart had failed.

Danny was granted one-week's Compassionate Leave to go to the funeral. Josie couldn't manage any time off, but would go to Victoria by bus on the weekend. On his arrival in town, he went to the house in James Bay for the first time since 1952. He saw the yard was neglected and the exterior paint was flaking. Vic and Jimmy were inside, Vic drunk and Jimmy getting that way. His father had gone down hill in three years; he was much older than Danny remembered.

Vic was maudlin. "She was a wonderful woman, Danno, I don't know what I'll do without her…"

What's new? I would bet you don't know what to do without her, you useless prick!

His father tried to embrace him. He evaded it by turning to Jimmy.

"Where's Eddie? He in the joint or something?"

"Ed moved up island, he's at Cowichan Lake—he's working at the mill there now," said Vic. "Beth's coming from Vancouver today…" He looked at the floor, "I think it's today."

Danny nodded. "When's Mom's funeral?" he asked Jimmy. "And where? What funeral home?"

His brother just shrugged and nodded toward Vic.

"Dad?"

"Well, I was supposed to see them…this morning. But I couldn't get there…"

"Did you phone them at least, when you decided to get too pissed to go?"

"I guess I should have…"

"Jesus. What about you, James? I suppose you were just too broken up. Shit—I'll go see them…"

Vic, head bowed, said, "That would be best, Danno. It's on Quadra Street, just this side of Central Park…past all those churches they got there."

"There used to be two undertakers on Quadra, as I recall…where's your phone book, do you know the name?"

"Here. I wrote it down…" He passed Danny a matchbook with two phone numbers written on it. "It's the second number, there. We'll give her a fine funeral, Son…"

"I'll go and arrange things, then I'll phone you from my hotel, I'm staying at the Dominion." He looked scornfully at the rye bottle on the table. "Why don't you two have a drink or something. I'll call later, you make sure you're here." He left the house, disgusted and angry.

At the Funeral home, he told a gray man in a gray suit that he wished to see his mother.

The man cleared his throat. "I'm afraid I can't allow you to do that. The body hasn't been, uh, prepared yet." He cleared his throat again.

"That doesn't matter," said Danny. "I just want to see her for one last time."

The throat cleared again. "There is ah, some concern about the payment." He said 'payment' as if it were a dirty word. "We are a business, after all, and ah, I must be assured of payment for our services. You father ah, didn't seem too clear about how…"

"Jesus Christ. Tell you what; I'll give you a check before I leave today. Then maybe you can turn your *concern*, from your money to my Mom and the family. Now, can I see her?"

"Yes. I believe we can, ah, accommodate you. Though it is rather, ah, irregular. Come this way."

His mother's body was in a refrigerated room, on a metal table, covered by a white sheet. Danny felt a chill that had nothing to do with the room's temperature. The mortician folded the sheet down to expose her face and stood aside.

Danny said, "Thank you. Wait outside the room, would you?"

The man hesitated.

"Look, I'm not going to steal any damn bodies. I want to be alone with her for a minute. Wait outside, for Chrissake, man." The man left, clearing his throat as he pulled the door part way closed.

Danny looked upon his mother for a minute. He bent and kissed her cold brow. "Thank you, Mom—for everything. And I'm sorry. For everything." He swiped at his eyes with the backs of his hands before leaving the room.

He arranged and paid for a "tasteful but moderately priced service." The mortician now smiled warmly as he filled out forms for Danny to sign. With the business done, Danny went to the Dominion Hotel to get a room.

Beth called him there at three-thirty. She was staying at the Douglas. Danny filled her in on everything that had taken place.

"You shouldn't have to pay the whole thing, Danny. I have a little bit, I can afford to…"

"It's okay, Beth. I can handle it." In reality the expense had all but emptied his bank account. He was thankful his loan-sharking activities of the past had allowed him to maintain a small savings account. He added, "My girl friend is coming down tomorrow from Comox. Maybe we can get together for lunch. I'll call you in the morning."

Beth said, "I'd love to meet her, Danny. Mom said she's real sweet," bringing tears to his eyes for the second time that day. She continued, "Mom told me she managed to put away a little money. She was planning to will it to you and me…only you and me. If there is some money coming, I'll pay you for half when we get it…would that be fair? I've had it kinda tough the last year or so, but I want to do my share if I can."

"You don't have to do…"

"Danny, please let me. I need to do something for Mom. Do you understand?"

He did. "Of course. I'm sorry for being so selfish." He smiled at the phone. "I'll be happy to take your money, Sis. See you tomorrow."

He picked Josie up at the Vancouver Island Coach Lines bus depot at eleven in the morning.

She said as they hugged, "Darling, I'm so sorry! She was so sweet...so kind! I wish I had met her before. I-I cried for her all last night. You must miss her so. Are you all right?"

"Yeah, Hon, I am. We have to meet my sister for lunch, okay? Then she and I have to go to the Funeral Home."

After lunch, he and Beth set the date for the funeral. It was to be two days later at ten o'clock. He gave Beth a ride to the house so she could notify Vic and pick out a dress for their mother. She would get a taxi from the house back to her hotel. Before he and Josie returned to the hotel, he parked the car by the sea wall on Dallas Road. They sat for a long time, watching passing ships and looking across Juan de Fuca Strait at the snowcaps of the Olympic Mountains. He pointed out the smoke from a mill at Port Angeles, in Washington State.

At ten the next morning, the day before the funeral, Danny stopped the car on Quadra Street, outside the funeral home. They were stopped at a yellow curb.

Josie asked, "Where do we park?"

"We're only here for a minute."

"Oh."

He stared at the building for five long minutes. There was a small gathering of people outside. He wondered if they were there to attend a "tasteful but moderately priced service."

Josie sat with him in silence, until he murmured, "Goodbye, Mom," and started the car.

They picked up their bags at the hotel and drove out of town. Neither of them spoke until they stopped for lunch at the Malahat Chalet.

Danny said, "It's done. Thanks for being there, Jo."

They arrived at Kye Bay at four o'clock.

*   *   *   *

Betty Tanner had managed to accumulate and hide from her husband over eight thousand dollars. She had named Beth as executrix of the small estate. Danny's half arrived enclosed with a letter from a Victoria Notary Public. He called Beth when he received the letter and check.

"Hey, Sis, you must have had expenses. Be fair to yourself—you don't have to give me half."

"Danny, the expenses came to just about one half of what you paid for the funeral. Remember what I asked you? Please allow me this."

He also learned from her that the old house was paid for and Betty had paid off any debts she and Vic had accumulated. He deposited the money into his account at the Bank of Toronto branch in Courtenay. The little over four thousand dollars was about twelve hundred more than he earned in a year, as an unmarried L.A.C., Trade Group 3.

CHAPTER 19

▼

Can I ever forget the night you chased off the intruders...

KYE BAY—NOVEMBER, 1955

On a day two weeks after his mother died, D Crew was working the 1600 to midnight shift. Danny arrived home at twelve thirty and they went to bed at one.

At two-thirty, while Danny slept soundly beside her, Josie's eyes were wide open. She had a vague sense something had awakened her. Still somnolent, her thought processes were fuzzy. She lay still and strained to hear, while her pupils slowly adjusted to the dark and she could make out the little alarm clock. It was three A.M.

There! A noise! Something—someone—was moving outside the cabin. *At the front? The porch?* She held her breath, concentrating. Without turning her head, fearful any movement might somehow impede her hearing, she whispered, "Danny?"

No response.

She turned to him, spoke close to his ear. "I 'eard something, I think." She wasn't yet *certain* she had heard anything. She strained again to hear.

There it was again.

"Danny? Danny!" He moved his head slightly away from her. She touched his shoulder, shaking him gently.

He stirred. "Hmmf?" He turned toward her, eyes still shut.

There—again! She was becoming more frightened. She shook him again. "Danny!" She spoke louder now. "Danny, there's a noise outside."

"Whad? Whadya say?"

"Listen! Somebody by the door…" Then certainty! The screen door squeaked open.

She screamed, "EEE! DANNY, THERE'S SOMEONE 'ERE!"

He was instantly wide-awake. He leapt from the bed and bolted for the kitchen just as the front door crashed open. Josie screamed again behind him and he saw a man outlined in the doorway. He jerked the light cord, illuminating the room. Impressions of an unshaved face, a plaid jacket and a large flashlight.

Danny yelled, "WHAT THE HELL'RE YOU DOING HERE?"

The man whirled, ran back onto the stoop, stumbled to one knee and dropped the flashlight. He regained his balance and ran out onto the grass of the yard, where he turned back toward Danny.

Danny reached the stoop. "Hey, man—I said, what are you *doing* here!" He bent and picked up the flashlight. As he started forward he felt, rather than saw, the other man to his right. This one was twenty feet away. He had come from the lean-to, and now he was moving slowly at Danny carrying a club-sized piece of firewood.

Danny stopped. He turned so he could keep both men in sight. From the corner of his eye he saw a light come on in Letourneaus' place. He shined the flashlight on the man with the club. He and the two men stood, frozen.

He shouted, in an attempt to influence the intruders, "HEY LEO! TROUBLE OUTSIDE, BRING YOUR GUN!"

Leo replied from inside his cabin. "Coming, Dan, be right out!"

Then they heard Josie shout from the porch:

"YOU GUYS—YOU GET AWAY FROM 'ERE! GET MOVING, RIGHT NOW—OR I'LL—I'LL SHOOT OFF YOUR-YOUR DAMN…BALLS!"

She was silhouetted in the doorway and had the thirty-ought-six pointed shakily at the man with the club.

Convinced this mad woman was about to start shooting, the men turned and ran for the road. Danny could see they were headed for a vehicle parked there and started after them, but they reached the car and sped away up the hill before he caught them. He turned back.

Leo called. "They're gone, eh, Dan? Who was it?" He stepped into the rectangle of light cast by a window. He was carrying a rifle.

"Yeah, they're gone. I don't know who they are—a couple of guys. They were trying to break into our place. One of them kicked our door in."

"I'll just leave my gun here," said Leo. He leaned the rifle against the wall. They heard him chuckle as he approached from the shadows, "Don't shoot, okay, Jo-Jo? It's me, Leo, and I really like these balls of mine! I'm kind of attached to them." He chuckled again as he reached the porch. "That damn rifle's bigger than you! You take care with it, now."

Danny turned now to Josie. She slumped in the doorway, her forehead pressed to the jamb. The rifle hung limply by her side.

He went to her, put an arm around her.

"I'd better take this now, Hon." He took the rifle from her, checked the safety, and put it aside.

She fell against him. He put his arms around her. She was trembling.

He whispered, "Ya done good, Babe; you scared away the bad guys—and you scared the *hell* out of Leo."

She sniffled and giggled nervously. "Shut *up*, you." She held tightly to him and shuddered. "I was so scared for you!"

Leo joined them on the porch. "You should have shot those sonsabitches, Jo-Jo!"

With her face buried in Danny's chest, she mumbled, "Couldn't shoot them. No bullets."

Danny wasn't sure he heard her right. "What did you say?"

She lifted her head and repeated, a little defiantly, "I *said*—there were no bullets! Okay?"

"Jesus apey Christ!" he exclaimed.

"I don't know 'ow to load it, anyway. I don't even like to touch it!"

"Oh, this is great!" said Leo. "So, their jewels were safe, eh? And I hit the dirt out there for nothing?"

They heard Lorna call, "Leo—what's going on?"

Then Mr. MacKenzie, "Hey, kids. It's three in the morning. What's all the noise about?" He was walking across the grass toward them. He and Lorna appeared from two directions. They plied Danny and Leo with questions.

Josie hugged herself. She remembered she was wearing only babydolls. *Dieu! If I had been in bed with nothing on, like so many nights…*

She said, "It's cold. I'll make hot chocolate. You can all come and 'ear about it inside." She looked at Danny, who had on only his boxer shorts. "I think you'll want to put something on, won't you?"

They all crowded through the door into the kitchen.

Lorna looked askance at Danny. "Nice legs," she said, "anything higher up, like under those shorts?"

He replied, "Wouldn't you love to find out." He hurried toward the bedroom to get some clothes.

"Not really," she called after him. "Got all I can handle. Right, Leo?"

Josie could see Mr. MacKenzie was not altogether comfortable with the sexual banter. She spoke up. "Okay, okay, you guys, that's enough! You will 'ave to excuse them, Mr. Mac, you know it's all they ever think about. Besides, whatever *is* there, it's mine." She added, "Is Mrs. Mac awake? She could come over, too." She put on the housecoat Danny brought from the bedroom. He was dressed now in jeans and a tee shirt.

Mr. Mac turned from examining the broken latch, he said, "No, no, Josie. Let's just leave her be, if you don't mind. She'll just get all het up." Then, to Danny, "Did you get a look at them, Dan?"

"Not very well. They were in the dark. One was a skinny guy, needed a shave. The other was bigger. Didn't get a good look, though, before they took off." He chuckled, "Hell, they were just a couple of blurred streaks after Jo showed up with the rifle." He thought for a moment. "But, you know, I've seen that car around. Old Chev panel truck. It's red—with rust paint—you know, undercoat."

Leo said, "Yeah, yeah! I know the one you mean. Seen it around town."

"I think I'm gonna be looking out for those guys," said Danny.

Leo added. "Me, too. We should have a little talk with them. The truck should be easy to spot."

Josie handed out mugs of hot chocolate. They were all quiet as they sipped.

When he finished his mug, Mr. MacKenzie rose to leave. He declared, "Well now, I'm off to bed. Dan, if you want me to call the police, or maybe you could use our phone…"

"Nah. Thanks anyway, Mr. Mac. Too late for them to do anything much now." He didn't want to give out his and Josie's names and address for fear the information would get back to the station.

"Well, okay then. I'll see you all in the morning. I'll fix up the door latch first thing tomorrow, it'll be good as new. Thank you, Josie, for the nice drink."

"G'night, Mr. Mac," said Danny, "I'll check the shed in the morning when it's light."

"Fine, Dan, good night."

When the door closed behind him, Lorna said, "Hell, I ain't gonna get any sleep after this, for sure! Get the cards out, Jo, let's beat these guys. Should I say it? Let's beat their *balls* off!

They played Whist till the sun lightened the sky outside. Danny and Leo managed—barely—to keep all their God-given parts.

In the morning, Danny checked the lean-to and found no damage. Remembering how he had suggested keeping the rifle out there, he shuddered at what might have happened if the intruder had found that instead of a club.

*   *   *   *

Two days after the incident, on Friday, Leo reported he had spotted the red panel truck in Courtenay. He told Danny about it out in the yard between the cabins.

"It was parked at the Riverside Hotel. The two guys came out just as I pulled into the lot. They got in the truck so I followed them out Headquarters Road to Merville…they went to a farmhouse on a road that branches off Headquarters. A tall, skinny guy and a bigger, better built guy. Skinny guy had a plaid jacket, like you said."

"Good. Russ and I work the afternoon shift tonight. How about we check these guys out in the morning? We can at least throw a good scare into them and make sure they know who they're screwing with."

"I'm with you, Dan. Meet me at my place whenever you're ready."

"Okay. Russ'll come, too." Danny paused, "Listen…don't mention this to Josie. She doesn't like me to get rough."

"Got it, don't worry. Same goes for Lorna."

In the morning, Danny drove slowly past the house Leo pointed out. The place sat in a muddy yard, below the level of a dirt road, with a rutted driveway leading down to the house, it was an old farmhouse with gray imitation brick siding, and bare tarpaper and beaverboard showing through in places. The windows and doors were in need of paint and some of the asphalt shingles had blown off the roof. A sagging barn and a doorless shed, both in apparent disuse, stood behind the house.

There was no sign of the red truck, so Danny turned the Ford around and drove past the house again, to a point a hundred feet along the road, and parked so they could watch and not be spotted from the house.

"We'll wait here for a while and see if he shows up. If he doesn't show, we'll go to town and see if they're at the Riverside…the beer parlors won't be open for another couple of hours."

"Sounds good," said Leo.

"I say we lay a beating on that prick and his buddy," said Russ, "We should put them both in the hospital for scaring Jo like they did…"

"You trying to get me in more shit with Josie, Q? We'll just give them a good lecture—let them know what could happen if they ever show their faces near Kye Bay again. Their turn to be scared."

"Yeah, I suppose."

Leo chuckled, "Jo-jo didn't look very scared, Russ."

"Maybe she didn't look it, but I bet she was scared shitless."

When they had watched for an hour, the door opened and a woman and two small children appeared on the porch. The woman, wearing a faded dress, carried a laundry basket to the side of the house where a sagging clothesline hung between two posts. The children, a boy and a girl, began playing, chasing each other around the muddy ground of the front yard. Both kids wore old clothing and no coats despite the chill November air.

Danny said, "Shit—wife and kids."

When the woman finished hanging the clothes on the line, she went inside, but the little boy and girl stayed out, playing now on the porch.

Another fifteen minutes went by before Danny muttered, "Y'know what? Those little kids and the woman...they've got enough troubles. I don't know about you guys but I really don't want to...you know."

Together, Russ and Leo said, "Yeah."

They rode in silence back to Kye Bay.

CHAPTER 20

▼

I was living too much to see the gathering clouds…

COMOX—NOVEMBER, 1955

All of his life Danny had been a free spirit; had gone where he wanted, done what he wanted, and had always been where the fun and action were. He didn't see why he shouldn't continue to do so. It was not that he loved Josie less, in fact he loved her more with each passing day. It just never occurred to him he should curtail his activities or change his lifestyle because he was with her, and she had never asked him to.

For her part, Josie decided after her experiments at drinking that it wasn't for her; she would have one or two weak drinks in the future, just to be polite. She was always amazed he and their friends could drink as they did and rarely show ill effects. Danny could usually get up in the morning after a night of drinking and function normally, as if he hadn't had a drop.

She never asked him to *not* "go out with the boys;" in fact she unknowingly encouraged it with her acceptance. But she worried for him. When she knew he was partying, she was afraid he might have a driving accident, or get in a fight or some other kind of trouble. She didn't tell him at first, but since the night of the intruders, she was frightened when left alone in the cabin at night.

The first time she complained about his partying was November eleventh, Armistice Day. The male members of B and D Crews, along with members of other units on the base, were nailed on one of their days off to take part in the memorial service in Comox. It turned out the ragging they took from the girls on crew was premature. They formed up with the rest of the parade and marched a couple of blocks from the Canadian Legion hall to the cenotaph, stood for a twenty-five minute ceremony, and then marched back to the Legion. To their delight, they were all invited to spend the afternoon inside the hall, partaking of free drinks. Danny and Russ, declaring it would show disrespect to the veterans to turn down the invitation, made the best of it.

Josie showed her pique when he got home at seven thirty, much the worse for wear. They had planned to go into Courtenay for groceries and he had forgotten all about it. His excuse, sure in his inebriated mind to be most relevant, was that he and Russ befriended some "genuine World War II parashooters." (Who, he confided, don't really yell "Geronimo.") He was asleep and snoring on the sofa soon after arriving home. In the morning he apologized and promised to be more considerate in the future.

There were more occasions when he forgot all about his promise as he seized the moment. What wounded her most were the times he didn't get home at all, when she would lay in the silent cabin, unable to sleep, paralyzed with fear and worry. He would later promise it wouldn't happen again, and she would again forgive him.

*   *   *   *

COMOX—DECEMBER, 1955

December arrived without a trace of snow in the Comox Valley. There were signs of heavy snowfall in the surrounding hills and mountains but at the lower elevations it was almost daily overcast and rainy.

The beach at Kye Bay was transformed. Without all the people of summer, it became a much quieter place, haunted by the ghosts of summer picnickers. Some would see it as desolate but others, like Josie, saw it as interesting in different ways. Most of the cottages were closed for the winter, even the little concession stand was boarded up, and just eight or nine houses remained occupied. When Josie and Danny walked on the beach, they were usually alone. Their walks now were on weekends, because it was dark before and after work on weekdays. She was discovering all manner of jetsam driven ashore by winter tides, keeping the more interesting pieces and piling them beside the porch. As they sat by the fire in the evenings they could hear the howl of the December wind and the crash of waves.

Early in the month Danny bought a string of outdoor Christmas lights and hung them across the front of the cabin. Josie put up some decorations around the living room. She spent time with Mrs. Mac and Lorna, cooking for the holiday. Mrs. Mac helped her bake a fruitcake and cookies, and Lorna showed her how to make tourtiere, the traditional French-Canadian meat pie.

By the middle of the month the rain had stopped and the days were mostly sunny and cool, with some broken cloud cover.

Danny said one Friday, "I guess we'll have to get a Christmas tree, won't we."

Looking away to hide a grin, she said, "Certainly not! Why would we want such a fire hazard in our house."

"We could, though, if you want…we'd be careful…"

"Do *you* want one? I don't care one way or the other. But, if you were to insist." He still didn't see her smirk.

"No…it's okay I guess."

She didn't tell him it was already arranged that they were going out with Leo and Lorna the next day to cut a tree.

Saturday dawned with only scattered clouds. She told him, "Get dressed warm, Danny, we 'ave to help Leo to cut some firewood for Mr. Mac."

"But we just cut a big pile last week——we decided there's enough for the whole damn winter!" He wondered why Leo hadn't mentioned it to him.

"Well, um…Leo says we need more. 'Urry up, they're waiting for us." Her blush told him she was hiding something. He knew something was up, but didn't say anything.

Josie and Danny rode in the open bed of Leo's pickup truck. Lorna provided a couple of blankets and a thermos of hot chocolate.

Danny grumbled, "Hell of a way to spend my day off." He had figured out what was going on and was putting her on.

She couldn't hide her excitement. "I'll bet you can't guess where we're going, can you."

"Hmm, let me see…we're riding in a truck instead of the car, all bundled up for the cold, there are two axes and a Swede saw. Hmm…groceries! We're going grocery shopping! Or maybe to a movie?"

"No…" It was her turn to catch on. "Danny, you big rat! You knew, didn't you! Did Leo tell you?"

"Tell me? Tell me what?" he teased.

"You big *rat!* I'll get you. You still don't know *where*, though."

"Okay, where?"

She blushed. Leo hadn't mentioned a location. "Okay, I don't know, either…" Giggle.

They took a back road north from Courtenay and soon started up the winding mountain road to Forbidden Plateau. They passed the snow line, and the snow along the roadside got deeper as they climbed. Leo pulled into a logging track covered with packed snow, drove in two hundred yards and parked the truck. Josie had been this far up the mountain only in summer, she could hardly wait for the truck to come to a stop. The snow in the surrounding bush was two feet deep, stirring her Eastern Canadian blood.

She leapt out and ran to the side of the road.

"Look, Danny, snow! Come and see."

He had jumped down on the other side of the truck. As he came around the cab, she threw a double handful of snow, catching him in the face and causing some to get down his neck. She giggled and ran into the woods. She hadn't reckoned on the depth of the snow—or the tangle of underbrush under it. After just three steps she stumbled and landed face first. He was on her instantly. He pushed handfuls of snow down her neck while she wriggled and screamed.

"There, smart-ass," said he.

Lorna cried, "Danny, It's cold! Don't be mean!"

Josie sat up, giggling and trying to look angry. "That's NOT FAIR!" she shouted. "I fell down! You took advantage—big RAT!" She got up and started toward him menacingly.

He didn't see Leo behind him as he backed away from her. Leo stuck out a foot, tripping him. He fell backward and Josie, joined by Lorna now, began shoveling handfuls of snow on his face as he tried to cover up with both hands.

He yelled, "Okay! Enough! I surrender!" He lay back and appeared to relax. Lorna stopped shoveling.

Josie shouted as she jumped back from him, "DON'T TRUST 'IM, LORNA! WATCH OUT—HE'S TRICKY!"

Her warning was too late. Danny snaked out a hand and grabbed Lorna by an ankle. He flipped her down into the snow, where he proceeded to pelt her. Josie collapsed to the ground beside them, giggling uncontrollably.

She managed to say, "See…" giggle…"I *told you*, Lorna," giggle…"you can't *trust* 'im. Now he's caught you!"

Leo stood back with crossed arms. "Hey, you children, when you're finished playing, maybe you can help me find some trees." That was his mistake. Lorna and Danny tackled him around the ankles, pulling him to the ground, and now all three pelted him with snow.

Josie, spent, stretched out on her back in the snow. "Oh, dieu, I'm tired! We 'ad better 'ave a truce and find some trees now." She got up, brushing snow from her clothes.

They trudged through the deep snow of the logged-out area, looking for likely trees. Josie ran ahead, dragging Lorna with her.

Leo shouted after them, "Christ, keep an eye on her, Lorna, she could disappear under a drift and we'd never find her!"

"Shut *up*, you!" cried Josie.

Then Lorna, "Yeah, shut up, Leo."

Josie pointed at a four-and-a-half foot spruce. "'Ere's a good one!"

"No good, Jo-Jo, too short," said Leo, with a secret wink at Danny.

"Oh. You're right." She ran to another. "How about this one?"

"Too tall, Jo-Jo."

She came upon a lush pine, just over six feet high. "Ooh, look, this one's *beautiful...*"

"Too fat," said Leo.

"Oh, come *on*, Leo!" Looking at Lorna beside her, she asked, "What is *possibly* wrong with it?"

Lorna shrugged, as if to say, "Don't ask me!" She well knew what was going on.

Danny looked at her, beautiful as ever, wearing slacks, a bulky sweater under one of his jackets and a child-like expression. Her face was flushed from the excitement and cold. He had to turn away to hide his grin. "Jesus, sometimes I swear I've robbed a cradle," he murmured.

"She's just excited," Leo said quietly. "Dan, You have a wonderful girl there—don't ever change her."

Josie figured out what was going on. With a grin of her own, she pointed at a scraggly hemlock. "How about this one? No, don't say it. Too, um, too *skinny*, right? Leo, you're a rat, too!"

They eventually cut three trees, including the pine, one each and one for the MacKenzies, and hauled them to the truck for the trip back down the mountain. This time, laughing, the girls quickly jumped into the cab. Lorna drove, and Danny and Leo rode in the back with the trees.

As they passed the snow line Josie looked back longingly. "I wish we could have some snow for Christmas."

*   *   *   *

Besides the Christmas holiday, December brought the 1955 Canadian Football playoffs and the Grey Cup Game, with the top teams from the East and West playing each other for the championship of Canadian football. "The Cup" and the week leading up to the actual game were a national insanity—a crazy celebration of much more than a game of football. CBC Television would be telecasting the game which, for the first time, was played outside of Toronto, in Vancouver.

The Wild Dogs lucked out, Grey Cup Saturday fell on their days off. The males of the crew watched the game in the Wets, where a TV set had been set up on the Men's side for the occasion. Danny and Russ had been making friendly bets on the Cup for three years. With Eastern wins in 1952 and '53, before Edmonton surprised the world in '54, Russ was up two to one since their first bet at Clinton. This time the loser would buy the winner's drinks for the rest of the evening. Danny bet with his Western heart again, even though he felt Montreal was the better team.

The game proved to be anticlimactic. The Edmonton Eskimos overwhelmed Montreal in a one-sided win, so convincingly that Russ started buying Danny's beers before the third quarter ended. The Easterners in the place were morosely quiet for most of the game, while the West fans were pitiless in their ragging.

The party raged till closing time at one A.M. Afterward, Danny joined Russ and some others in the barracks where they started and finished "twenty-sixers" of rye and white rum. He thought briefly of calling Josie, but didn't want to disturb the Letourneaus at such a late hour. He fell asleep on his bunk fully dressed, at three thirty A.M.

At eight-thirty he was called to the phone.

"Tanner here…"

He heard her voice. "Danny, are you all right?"

"Yeah, Hon…a headache but…"

The click told him she hung up before he could finish. He belatedly remembered his promises. *But shit, it's the Grey Cup!*

He was sitting on his bunk when Russ woke up.

"Hey, Champ, take a look for me will you, do I still have a head?" moaned Russ.

"What the hell do you think hurts so bad."

"Did you sleep here? Isn't Jo out at Kye Bay?"

"Yeah, and yeah."

"You gonna be in shit?"

"Already am in shit, Q. She just hung up the phone on me. She's most likely mad because I didn't call her…she worries."

"She's probably right. You should have called. No fun for her, stuck out there all night."

"Hell, Russ—I know that. I got drunk and forgot…"

"I would advise you don't try that excuse, Champ."

"I have to get home…Christ, did you hear me? I'm calling it *home!*" He smiled ruefully.

"I noticed."

Opening a wax paper parcel on the dresser, Danny asked, "What're these, cookies?"

"Camolies or something. Ollie's Mom sends them."

Biting into one, Danny said, "This's good…cojones?"

"Those're some kind of nuts or something, aren't they?"

Chuckle. "Nuts alright." He took another canole.

"Hey, c'mon, she gave them to *me!*"

Grabbing another, Danny said, "Ollie's Mom likes you to share, Q."

"Hey, come *on!* Aw, shit!"

"I'll see you…whenever Jo lets me out of solitary."

"Yeah, later Dan."

It was darkly overcast when he parked at the cabin. Josie wasn't inside. A check of the closets told him a coat was missing so he went across the yard to Letourneaus' cabin. She was at the kitchen table with Lorna.

He didn't want a confrontation in front of Lorna. He spoke from the door-way.

"Hi, Jo, I'm home." *Hell, let's state the obvious, shall we, Tanner?* "Hello, Lorna."

Josie said only, "Hello." She didn't get up from the table. He waited, still at the open door.

"Well, aren't you coming in?" said Lorna "Shut the door, I don't want to heat the whole Comox Valley! There's coffee on." She smiled and got him a mug from the cupboard.

He stepped inside and shut the door behind him, thinking, *This is gonna be awkward.*

"Oh, sorry Lorna, I wasn't thinking. I'll have a cup with you guys; thanks." He looked at Josie but she was looking out the window. Five minutes later, as she rose to leave, she said, "Thanks, Lorna, for the tea and the *company* last night." She gave him a pointed look.

"I'll go with you, Jo…" said Danny. "Wait up…" He was talking to her back. He had to gulp a third of his coffee. "Thanks, Lorna…I'll see you later."

She said, "Good luck, Danny. Hope you're prepared to brown-nose."

He stopped at the door. "Is she real mad?"

"Don't ask stupid questions, especially when you know the answer. Be nice, okay?"

"Yeah, I will."

Josie wasn't in the kitchen or living room. The bedroom door was closed. He knocked lightly.

"Hon?" he said, softly.

"Yes?"

"Hon, can we talk? Please." He heard her moving.

She opened the door. He could see she was tired. "Do promises mean nothing to you?" Her voice was a bit hoarse.

"No…I mean yes! Yes they do, Honey. I should have called you but it was late and…"

"I'll use your word, Danny—Bullshit! It did not matter to you that I was 'ere alone all night, did it?" Her eyes were blazing.

"It did, I…"

She interrupted, "More bullshit? It doesn't matter that we 'ave guys…bad men…sneaking around here trying to get into cabins. You just don't care." she went to the sink.

"Jesus, Jo…it was the Grey Cup game!" He knew he needed more. "I mean, it's once a year…the guys, we do this every year."

She turned abruptly to him. "Well, thank you for the explanation. How stupid can I be? To forget about such an important event in our life…and to not know a game of football goes on all night! Thank you so much for the warning, now I'll know for next year!" Her voice caught. "Will we still be together next year, Danny?"

Oh, shit! He went to her, took her in his arms. She stood stiffly.

"There's nothing I can say, is there. Except, I'm so very, very sorry. Shit, I don't know why you put up with me."

She sagged against him and buried her face in his chest. "Because I love you, that's why I stay. You just don't think about me. Show some respect for me—for my feelings."

He was reminded of his mother's words to a young boy years earlier, about respect. "I'm no good, Josie, but I love you so much." He felt her stiffen again. "I'm trying, Josie."

She turned her back to him, went to the kitchen.

"Try harder, Danny."

CHAPTER 21

▼

Our first Christmas…

DECEMBER, 1955

51 AC&W followed the Air Defense Command practice of changing the shift schedule and crew structures for the holiday season to allow for prolonged time-off for the shift workers. The Pinetree Line never shut down, so twelve-hour shifts were instituted to accommodate the change. Half the unit's Ops personnel would get six days off for Christmas and the other half six off for New Years. Danny and Russ drew the 2000 to 0800 shift through Christmas—eight P.M. to eight A.M. They would work with personnel from Able, Charlie and Dog crews. They would be off for New Years, from the 29th through January 3rd.

The Orderly Room closed down for the holidays, so Josie and Ollie were off for four days at Christmas and two more for New Years.

On the twenty-second, Josie was granted her wish for snow. Wet, heavy snow, typical for the coastal region, started falling at four in the afternoon and continued through the night. On the morning of the twenty-third she looked out upon five inches of snow and her spirits soared!

Danny left work that morning at eight-fifteen. He had to go slow driving in the wet snow, so never arrived home at Kye Bay till quarter to nine. He left his car with others at the top of the hill and walked down the slippery switchback.

Josie was in front of the cabin with five of the smaller children who lived at the beach year-round. She was balancing precariously on an unsteady kitchen chair to reach the top of a six-foot snowman she and the kids had built, trying to place Danny's Montreal Canadiens touque on its head. The kids were standing around watching as she stretched to reach the top of the head. When Danny came up behind her the children all yelled a warning, but he caught her before she knew what was happening and lifted her under the arms, high enough so she could crown the snowman.

At first startled, she screamed, "Danny!" The kids all yelled and giggled. Then she placed the touque at a jaunty angle and said, "There—just right! Thank you, my L.A.C." He lowered her to the ground. She said, "There, kids, it's all finished, and this is my Danny." She kissed his cheek. "My new friends and I made this guy, Danny."

"We just helped." said one of the kids.

"But you were all a big help!" said Josie.

A little girl, possibly a three-year-old, asked him, "Are you going to pank Josie?"

"Why would I pank her, sweetheart?" He tousled her hair.

A five-year-old said, "Because she put your hat on the snowman!" The rest of the kids all giggled.

"Do you think I should spank her?" He looked stern.

As a group, they chorused, "Yes! Spank her! Spank Josie! Giggle."

He grabbed Josie, sat on the chair, and put her over his knee. He raised his hand high. "Should I?"

Josie squealed, "Hey, you kids, I thought you were my friends."

Then the first little girl said, "But not hard, okay, Mister? Just pwetend pank her."

"Are you going to be a good little girl?" He asked Josie.

"I don't knooow…"

The kids drowned her out. "Yes, Josie! Be good! Or he'll spank! Giggle."

"Okay, Daddy, I'll be good. I promise." He set her on her feet and turned to the snowman. She stuck out her tongue at his back, bringing more gales of laughter.

He studied the snowman. "And who's this guy supposed to be?"

Josie turned to her helpers, "Shall I tell him?"

A chorus of "Yes!"

"But he might spank me."

To him they pleaded, "You won't, will you? Don't spank Josie—please?"

"Okay, how about if you guys tell me, then."

"No! You'll spank us!" Some of them backed quickly away from him.

The first little girl stepped forward. She apparently sensed some accord with him. Serious, she said, "It's you! Josie said it's a Snow Danny. So, it's you acause you're Danny." She stepped back, not totally trusting her position.

He pretended to appraise the snowman. He said, "Hmm." He walked around it twice. "Well, you kids…" He pretended to count and included Josie with a tap on her head. "You five little kids, and this big kid, did a fine job. I believe he looks just like me!"

That brought howls and, "She's not a kid! She's a lady!"

Danny said, "Y'know what, though? His nose is way too long." He pulled out the carrot nose, bit off half of it, and returned it to its place. "There, that's much better."

More howls of glee. Clearly these were crazy grownups!

Josie said, "Kids, I 'ave to go in now and make breakfast for my daddy—he spanks me hard if I don't." The kids laughed again. She added, "Don't forget, come around on Christmas Eve for some candy canes."

They all shouted, "We won't forget! Goodbye, Josie. Goodbye, Danny."

*   *   *   *

The next day, Danny, Ollie and Russ were in the Mess Hall for supper. Josie was at the barracks taking her turn on the laundry. Ollie made a sandwich to take to her.

"So, Tanner, did you get your shopping done?" asked Ollie.

Danny didn't look happy, "Well…most of it, Ol. I still have to get her a big…main gift. All I bought so far is gloves and a scarf and some sexy nighttime stuff."

"Shit, Danny, you've only got one more day, tomorrow's the twenty-fourth."

Russ piped-in, "You're in big trouble, Champ." A grin split his face.

"I just have no idea what to get her."

Ollie inquired, "How much do you want to spend?"

"Money's not a problem. I'll spend as much as I have to. I want to get something real special. It's our first Christmas, and…"

"Wait a sec—I have an idea. Can you get to town tonight? The stores are open late, till nine o'clock."

"Sure I can." He looked at the wall clock. "We don't go to work till about seven-thirty. It's only five-fifteen."

"Okay. I'll have to go with you. I'll handle Jo. I'll make up a good lie. Meet me at the car, I'll be about twenty minutes." She gathered her purse and Josie's sandwich and left.

In the car, headed for Courtenay, he said, "What's the scheme, Ol?"

"She totally fell in love with a coat downtown. She's been saving for it. It's pretty expensive, though, Dan..."

"The money's not a problem. A coat, though? Not very romantic is it. I wanted to get something special."

"Dan, it's perfect! You'll see—and she wants it so bad. She'll love you, Big Guy. It's at a place on one of those side streets off Fifth, England or Fitzgerald Street. I just hope they haven't sold it."

It was perfect. A dove gray, wool parka, with white fur around the hood and bottom hem and embroidered with stylized polar bears. It was hand made and the only one like it. Ollie said it was in Josie's petite size. The shop was small and exclusive—and expensive. He gave the clerk fifty dollars to hold it until he could get to the bank the next day, the twenty-fourth, for the balance of sixty-nine dollars.

On the drive home, Ollie asked, "Can you afford it, Dan? Even for her it's a lot of dough."

"Yeah, it's no sweat." He smiled at her. "I want to thank you, Ol. I owe you again." He put an arm around her and pulled her close. He kissed the top of her head. In his mind he said, *And thank you, too, Mom!*

"You owe me? Right!" she was remembering all she owed him. "You owe me nothing. Besides, I get to be there when she opens it!"

He grinned evilly. "You're right, you shit, it's not every day a guy gets conned into buying a friggin' platinum coat!"

"Don't give me that, Tanner, you're happy as hell and you know it! When you pick it up tomorrow get them to give you a box and take it to Russ. I'll wrap it and bring it when we come out tomorrow, so you can surprise her. If I know the little fart, she's already searched-out and found all the other stuff you got for her!"

"Great! By the way, what did you tell Jo we're doing? I should know so I don't screw up your story."

"I told her you and I were making out at a motel in Royston."

"Yeah, right...at least that wouldn't cost so much."

"Hey, I told you before—I might be easy but I ain't cheap."

"What did you really tell her?"

"I told her I had to get to town before six and you were taking me. Actually, when you think about it, it's not even a lie, is it."

"No, it's just what we did."

"Good. I'll see you tomorrow, for meat pie, of all frigging things."

"It's called tourtiere. She'll be quick to tell you it's not just meat pie, it's tour-tiere."

She laughed. "Yeah, sounds a lot like tort-*ure*, doesn't it? Russ is bringing some beer and I bought a bottle of rye. Should be fun, even though you guys have to go to work at eight."

It was traditional in French Canada to serve tourtiere on Christmas Eve after attending Mass. Ollie and Russ were going to stay over at the cabin till the 26th. They would be sleeping in the bedroom while Danny and Josie used the hide-a-bed. There would be no Mass for the Fearsomes, so they would eat before the boys left for work.

*   *   *   *

In the morning after their shift, Danny went with Russ to the Mess Hall where he drank two cups of coffee while Russ had breakfast. Afterward he drove into Courtenay, waited forty minutes for the bank to open, picked up the parka at the apparel shop, drove back to the base to deliver it to Russ, and arrived home at Kye bay at eleven-thirty. He noticed the ground was almost bare here. Josie's "snow-Danny" was sagging and tilted precariously.

After breakfast he went to bed, reminding Josie to get him up in time to pick up Russ at three o'clock.

He awoke to the sound of continuous Christmas music coming from the Baby Champ. He lay back and enjoyed the songs for fifteen minutes:

I'll Be Home For Christmas…It's Great To Be Home For The Holidays…I'm Dreaming Of A White Christmas…Chestnuts Roasting On An Open Fire…

He called out to Josie.

She came to the bedroom door wearing a housecoat. "Hello, Darling, did you sleep? Ollie just left with the car to get Russ."

"What's the time?"

"Ten to two"

"She's too early. He said three." He put his hands behind his head. "Love the music, Hon, you trying to get me in the Christmas mood?"

"I turned it loud to wake you up…" She came into the bedroom. "Ollie 'ad something else to do before picking Russ up." She went to the bed and kissed him passionately. "I hated to wake you…but, after Ollie left, I suddenly wanted you. Mean, selfish me, eh? I locked the door so we won't be disturbed." She

tossed the housecoat aside and got under the covers. He saw and felt her naked-
ness.

"Hmm," he murmured as he folded her into his arms, "yeah, you're real
mean."

"Now I'll show you 'Christmas mood,' my Danny. We 'ave one whole hour."
She ducked her head under the blankets, started to remove his boxer shorts.

She had his shorts down to his ankles. "A whole hour?" said he.

The blankets muffled her voice. "One entire hour." A hand appeared and she
threw his shorts to the floor.

Grinning, he said, "Maybe more, by the time she drives back here…"

"Shut up, you." She kissed his bare chest. She pushed her body against his.
"Danny, I love you so!"

As he moved over her, he said, "I love you, too. Merry Christmas, Honey…"

Their lovemaking and after-cuddling consumed most of the hour so they had
to rush to get showered, made-up, shaved and dressed for dinner. Josie was
flushed when she heard Russ's knock at three fifteen. Danny was still dressing in
the bedroom.

She called, "Come on in!"

"It's locked." Said Russ.

Oh, merde, I forgot the door. "Okay…coming." As she let them in she
explained weakly, "I must 'ave locked it when I went to the bathroom. Sorry.
Merry Christmas, Russ!" she kissed his cheek, then Ollie embraced her, awkwardly, because of the large parcel she was carrying.

Ollie whispered in her ear, "You little shit—you did it!" She had been fully
aware earlier that she was being rushed out the door.

Josie blushed and smiled secretly. "What could you mean?" She called to the
bedroom, "Danny, Ollie and Russ are 'ere."

Ollie added, "Yeah, get up Tanner, you horny devil!" She passed Josie the parcel. "Do not open this till tomorrow, passion puppy! It's from Danny."

"Aw, come *on*—no fair! It's Christmas Eve, isn't this close enough?" She
hefted the gift. "It's big, do you know what it is?"

"Not me, buddy. And if I did I wouldn't tell. Mine to you is one of those little
bitty packages." she indicated the shopping bag Russ carried. "I just came for
some of your torture pie."

"Where do I put all this stuff, Jo?" said Russ.

"Um, just on the table for now…under the tree, if it's presents."

He asked, "Where's all your snow? There's still a couple of inches up at the
base."

"Danny says it melts fast because we're right at the ocean." She stuck her lower lip out. "It barely lasted two days."

"Your snowman looks like he's drunk."

"Well, we did name him Danny."

"That explains it."

He put the bag on the table. He removed his topcoat, hung it on the back of a chair and said, "I'll let you sort this stuff out, Jo. But first, come here you gorgeous little thing—give ol' Russ a Christmas hug and kiss!"

She put the parcel on the table and they hugged, her feet swinging off the floor.

Russ asked quietly, "Everything okay, Jo?"

"Oh, yes, it's Christmas! And you?"

"Same, same…you know."

Danny caught them in the act. "Aha! A dupe in my own castle! Ollie darling, let us show them how it's done." They hugged.

Ollie murmured, "Happy Christmas, Tanner…happy whole year!" She sniffled and said aloud, "Dammit, I'm frigging crying. I love you guys." She pulled away from Danny, dabbed at her eyes, and added, "It's so good we can all be together. I'm actually glad now you two have this place! Shit, will somebody pour me a drink?"

"Beer or rye?" asked Danny. He looked at Josie whose eyes were also brimming, then at Russ, who shrugged, afraid to say anything. Danny prompted, "We have the whiskey sour mix you like, Ol."

Ollie said, "Strong, please."

"Me, too, Champ. Got Coke? A strong one with Coke," said Russ. Then he grinned, "Shit, fellow Fearsomes, we're all getting sentimental as hell. You'd think it was Christmas or something," which brought smiles all around.

Josie said, "For a change, me too, Honey. Not strong, though." He knew hers was whiskey sour diluted with ginger ale.

Danny mixed drinks while the others piled the few parcels under the tree. He handed each a glass.

"I guess we'd better not have too many of these, Russ," he said, "we don't know which Duty Controller we're gonna be working with tonight. The crews are all mixed up."

"You're right, if it's that dickhead, Kramer, the one used to be on Bravo, I could spend Christmas and New Years in the guardhouse—he'd just love to nail me. So we'll be careful. But we can surely have a couple."

"Sure can. If we're lucky it'll be one of the good guys. Anyhow, here's to friends and lovers! Honey, Ollie, Q, I love you all, I sincerely mean it. And here's to a merry Christmas!" They all raised glasses.

"I just wish you guys didn't have to go to work." said Josie, sadly.

"Blame Malenkov, Hon, he don't believe in Christmas, no more than Uncle Joe did."

She smiled. "I know, I'm sorry to sound sad. Let's all 'ave a good time." Looking at Ollie, she brightened and said, "Maybe we could open just one present tonight?"

Danny smiled inwardly at the way, in small matters, she still ceded leadership to Ollie.

Ollie grinned mischievously, "Sure. Here's the plan—we each get to open the smallest one with our name on it today. How does that sound, Jo?"

Danny and Russ nodded assent. "Sounds fair," said Danny.

"No! Not fair!" cried Josie. She was thinking about one of her gifts to him, a wristwatch, his most expensive gift and smallest in size. She conceded, "Okay, you bunch of rats—tomorrow, but early! As soon as the guys get home."

*   *   *   *

Just as they were ready to sit for dinner at six o'clock there was a small knock at the door. Ollie, who was nearest, opened the door, and in barged a gaggle of small children.

She said uncertainly as they swirled around her, "Why don't you all just…come on in!" She shrugged quizzically at Josie.

Danny noticed there were at least a couple more kids than were at the snowman.

Josie jumped up from the table. "Hello kids, you came! Merry Christmas!" She took a shopping bag from the cupboard. "Kids, this is our good friend, Ollie and this our other good friend, Russ." She started to hand out candy canes from the bag. Here, Ollie, you can help me." She gave a large handful to Ollie, who started tossing the canes to kids at the back of the group.

"You know what, I forgot all about it—it's Halloween tonight!" Ollie declared.

That brought howls from the kids, "It's not Halloween, silly! It's Christmas!" and, "She's crazy!"

Everyone got at least three candy canes, most of which went quickly into little mouths.

Russ growled, "Hey, you kids, those are my candy canes! Give them back, right now! Mine! Mine! Grrr." he stood up menacingly.

More howls. A couple of the kids, unsure, backed toward the door. "No they're not! They're Josie's! Aren't they, Josie! He's crazy!" Giggle, giggle.

Josie asked them, "Did everybody get some?"

"Yes! They're good!" There were even some "Thank you's."

"Okay, kids, we 'ave to eat our dinner now, so you will have to get going. Bye, bye, everyone. Merry Christmas!" she said, as she herded them toward the door.

Before she could close the door, the little girl that had first spoken to Danny at the snowman recited, "Thank you vewy much, Josie, and Mewwy Cwismus," followed by, "My mommy told me to tell you it." She beckoned Josie closer. "Can I whisper a secwet?" Josie bent down close to her. On tiptoes, she put her mouth to Josie's ear. "You're pwetty today, an' that old lady Dolly, she's is too…but you're pwettiest."

Josie answered aloud, "Thank you, sweety, you are pretty, too. Bye-bye." She kissed her on the forehead. She turned to the room and leaned back on the closed door. She smiled and shook her head.

"So cute," she said.

Danny asked, "What was her secret?"

"Oh, just how I'm pwettier than Ollie. But she said you're kind of pwetty, too, Ollie, for an older woman!"

"Horrid child!"

*   *   *   *

Christmas day dawned cool, but sunny and windless in the Comox Valley. When Danny and Russ arrived at the cabin, the girls were up and about. Josie had built a fire in the hearth.

With accompanying embraces, they said "Merry Christmas" all round. Josie and Ollie were both in housecoats. The guys shucked their tunics and ties. The odor of cooking bacon permeated the cabin.

Josie poured mugs of coffee for them. She stuck her lower lip out. "Ollie says we have to get us all fed before we can open our presents."

Ollie was slicing bread. "Christ, we'll never get to eat if she gets started on the stuff under the tree. Jo, you're a little baby."

"We all hope you never grow up, Jo," commented Russ. Aside to Danny, wiggling his eyebrows a la Groucho Marx and fingering an imaginary cigar, he said, "If she's a little baby, I've been chasing babies since I was fourteen!"

Danny suggested, "Why don't we open the presents after Russ and I get some sleep?" He cued Russ with an under-the-table poke.

Russ grinned. "Sounds like a plan to me..."

"No! No way, you guys! A deal is a deal! You can all go to 'ell" She giggled. "If you keep it up, they'll be *Easter* presents by the time we open them." She put plates of bacon and eggs before each of them. "There's toast, too. If Ollie ever figures out how to work the toaster."

"Yeah, yeah. Kindly note the mistletoe pinned to the back of my belt," said Ollie, "and Merry Christmas to you too, Jo."

They ate breakfast and then the opening of gifts commenced.

By agreement between them, Ollie and Russ didn't buy anything expensive. Lingerie, cosmetics and gloves for her; cologne, cuff links, and as a joke, pink boxer shorts with red hearts in size extra large for him; perfume and cologne for Josie and Danny. Russ offered to try the shorts on there and then, if Ollie would do the same with her lingerie. When she passed he pulled them on over his pants anyway.

When Danny opened the Bulova wristwatch, he strapped it on and shook his head.

"Way too nice, Hon. Thanks, I love ya." With a sheepish smile, he told them, "The only one I ever owned before was left in a pawn shop."

Russ said, "Oh yeah, Moncton. A truly memorable trip."

Josie had set the large parcel aside unopened and opened her smaller ones. She had noticed how anxious Ollie and Danny were for her to open it, so seizing the chance to get even, she managed a straight face and said, "Well, that was fun! Santa was good to us all." She started picking up empty packages and wrapping paper.

"Okay, okay, you little shit. The box, Jo—right now!" said Ollie.

She was all innocence. "Oh...this is for me?"

"Open it, or you die!"

When she pulled the parka out of its box, she was overwhelmed. "Oh. Oh, Danny! Look, Ollie—it's my parka!" She couldn't hold back tears. "Danny, you can't know how I wanted this! I 'ad given up. I thought they must 'ave sold it...it's so beautiful!" She wiped at her tears, hugged Danny. "It's so perfect, Danny! I love you, I love you, I love you. Ollie, you're a sneaky rat!"

Danny sent Ollie a look that summed up his feelings. Ollie beamed.

"You like it, Hon?" he asked stupidly. "Ollie took me..." He couldn't finish.

Russ said, "Put it on, Jo."

"Okay!" She draped it over her shoulders and walked the length of the room and back, smiling radiantly, imitating a fashion model on a runway. Ollie beamed and applauded.

"I'll wear it when we go to the dinner!" She referred to Christmas dinner in the Mess Hall.

Reminded, Danny asked, "What time do we have to be there? Does anyone know?"

Ollie said, "Four-thirty, and we don't want to be late."

"Okay. We have loads of time for some sleep; we still have to work tonight. Wake us up in time to get showered and dressed."

"Could you get in some wood before you go to bed?" asked Josie.

Danny went to the shed and brought back an armful of wood, then he and Russ went to bed.

Josie prevailed on Ollie to take a walk on the beach with her. They bundled up in warm clothing and set out along the strand. The tide was out so they could poke and pry at the seaweed, driftwood and refuse strewn along the tide lines. They stalked a heron standing still as a lawn ornament at the water's edge.

"He sees us."

"Shhh"

It flew off when they were still twenty yards away.

"Stupid bird."

"Shit!"

"We got closer than I can usually get. They know when you're close. They see you without even turning their head!"

Back in the cabin, Josie made hot chocolate. They sat in the easy chairs by the fire.

"This is the best part." Said Ollie. "Sometimes, Little Buddy, in spite of your weird activities, like eating meat pie for Christmas and trudging up and down beaches in the middle of winter, I miss those times in our room, drinking hot chocolate or tea from my illegal electric kettle and just talking."

"Me, too, Ollie."

"But I know how happy you are, being out here with Danny."

"Yes, but I still miss you and our talks."

"I hate the sight of your empty bed when you're not there."

"We'll just make sure we get together lots."

*   *   *   *

Christmas dinner in the Mess Hall—it was traditional in the Air Force that the single Airmen and Airwomen were served turkey dinner by the station's brass, from the Commanding Officer down to Senior NCOs. The youngest Airman on the base was declared "C.O. for the day." Within the bounds of propriety and military reality, he assumed all the powers of the real C.O. The honor this year went to a seventeen-year-old AC2 from Supply. Gerry Henderson of the Wild Dogs, the second youngest on the base, was declared Chief Administrative Officer. The two sat in a place of honor at the head table.

It was one of the rare times throughout the year when spirits, in the form of wine and beer, were served in the Mess Hall. While the Group Captain and other brass were hustling from table to table, targets of good-natured criticism for their poor serving skills, calls for a speech by the bogus C.O. rose from the rabble.

The young Airman was not sure he was up to the task, but with prompting from Gerry he made some proclamations. One was an order for all prisoners in the Guardhouse to be freed for the day, forthwith! From a table at the back of the room came a shout from four voices: "We're here, Sir!" That brought a look of mock surprise from the real C.O. and loud cheers from the assembly. Then he ordered the officers and NCOs to eat every ounce of leftover Brussels sprouts and squash, before leaving the building. When it was Gerry's turn to speak, he ordered the Officer's Mess closed for fumigation for an infestation of pests—it seems the place had been found to be crawling with officers! "We must be constantly vigilant," he declared, "if we let down our guard for even a moment, the entire station could be swarming with the creatures!" The real C.O. laughed tentatively.

By 5:45 the meal and festivities were over. The Foursome went for a couple of drinks at the crowded Wets, where the "C.O." and "C. Ad. O." were feted as heroes. They headed back to Kye Bay at six-thirty so the boys could get ready for work.

*   *   *   *

With the boys at work, Josie and Ollie built a fire and sat in the easy chairs sipping drinks and talking. They talked about childhood Christmases.

Josie remembered, "My mother, when she was alive, always made Christmas something special for me. She would buy and hide all those special Christmas things, things I never saw the rest of the year—huge shiny red apples, giant oranges, special Christmas-only candies and all that stuff. On Christmas Eve we would go to the Mass at night, then come home—and somehow, she would have all the special stuff out! Even my father would get involved, but Mama was the one in charge at Christmas. We always opened our gifts Christmas Eve after we ate, it was usually just a snack or small meal. They would make me the 'Pere Noel' to hand out the gifts, but when I was little I never lasted long because a big one with my name would come along and brat that I was, I would forget everybody else! The next morning, Christmas, my father usually took us out for a late breakfast at a restaurant a friend of his owned. After breakfast we would go visiting. The aunts were last, and then they always came home with us for dinner. Around them I would always 'ave to be so proper, ugh. But Mama always made sure I could 'ave some time in my room to play with my new stuff. She would ignore the company and stay there with me for an hour."

Ollie said, "With us it was my Dad. He went totally nuts every Christmas. I swear he'd spend half a year's pay. After we were in bed on Christmas Eve he'd get into the vino and ring bells outside the house, and I just *knew* it was Santa out there. Christmas morning was when it happened for us kids. We would get up as early as four-thirty! Mom would chase us back to bed three or four times, then Dad, all mellow from the wine, would convince her to let us up to stay. Old Joe, my dad, would buy every popular toy on the market. It was a riot. My six brothers, my sister and I, scrambling around through heaps of wrappers…we never unwrapped, we ripped and shredded and tore! Sometimes whole presents would get lost in the debris. Then we'd pig out on goodies all day and not be hungry for dinner later. For dinner, there would be food from every damn culture in The Soo—English, French, Italian and who knows what—mostly Italian of course. Lordy, I'm drooling now, thinking about the desserts!" She chuckled, remembering. "No midnight Mass or late meal on Christmas Eve. It was all Christmas Day for us.

Josie was captivated. "Sounds like it was fun. I was always the only kid at our place. Danny says his was like mine because his Mom made it special, too. He says his father was usually drunk at Christmas. He told me a sad story about how one of his brothers broke his new hockey game on purpose, and his Mom went out two days after Christmas and got him another one."

"I guess it was different for everyone," Ollie mused. "Russ says he often wished there were no Christmases when he was a kid. They heard about his mother dying just before Christmas so he always had bad memories at this time of the year. One year, when he was living with a family with kids of their own, they gave their kids toys and him a pair of boots and socks. What a sad thing, for a kid to wish there were no Christmas. He says he enjoys it more now than he did when he was a kid. Danny likely influenced him."

"That's so sad. How did he grow up to be such a great guy, I wonder."

"He's not bad is he?" said Ollie. "I suppose he must have his bad moments. Tough way to grow up. He puts on the crazy front, then when he and I are alone, just talking, I get to know the real guy. I believe he looks at us, the Fearsome Foursome, as his family." She looked pensive, then brightened. "By the way, he's really enjoying these past few days, being here at the cabin and all. Me, too, actually, it's the best Christmas since I moved from home."

"I'm glad you're enjoying it. Danny and I are, too. I thought you might be bored. It's mostly just been a lot of sitting around. And with the guys working it's been hard."

"No way, I love it. In fact, Jo, if I thought we could talk them into it, I'd be happy to do this again for New Years Eve. We could just sit around, getting smashed if we want, no hassle and no dressing up. If you'd have us…"

"Really? You feel the same way? Should we go for it? Do you think the guys would want to? Of course we would be happy to have you and you know it! We could invite some friends, the Wild Dogs…it would be fun!"

"I don't think Russ would be a hard sell. But Danny loves to dance."

"Well, we could…roll up the linoleum? You can bring your record player. I'll ask him, and you ask Russ. Let's try!"

"You're the one with the tough sale, Jo. Russ is not exactly fond of dances to start with. Hell, it's just the Rec Center. Same, same, same! No matter how much they decorate the place, it's still just an old hangar. If we were going to the Royal York or something it would be another story."

When Ollie broached the subject to Russ, he said, "Whatever the majority wants. I kinda like the idea. As long as we're not putting them out too much…I don't want Jo have to do a bunch of work."

When she asked him how Danny should be approached, he said, "How could Danny, the fearsomest of the Fearsomes, go against the majority? Tell Jo if she has a problem with the big dork, I'll talk to him."

Danny was out-voted—he didn't stand a chance. They would bring in the New Year at the cabin.

On December 29th the weather turned fair, with periods of sunshine and starlight, the temperature soared to a balmy daytime sixty-seven and an overnight sixty-two degrees. The unusually fine weather lasted for five days.

*   *   *   *

KYE BAY—DECEMBER 31ST–JANUARY 1ST

On New Year's Eve, the guys built a huge driftwood fire on the beach, just a few yards behind the cabins. Those Wild Dogs who were not working came bringing liquor and beer. Leo and Lorna, back from Christmas out of town, came. Three neighbors invited by Josie, and two others drawn by the bonfire, uninvited but welcome, came. Morrie and Anne MacKenzie came out to say hello, and stayed into the New Year. The Letourneaus, MacKenzies and one of the neighbors brought food to add to what Josie and Ollie prepared. Throughout the night the celebrants wandered in and out of the cabin. Ollie and Josie took turns keeping recorded music blaring from an open window.

At midnight, with all the required embracing, kissing and noise making, they welcomed the New Year of 1956.

At 12:30, Russ suggested to Gerry and Gil that they all jump into the water in their underwear, to see who could stay in longest. The temperature in the Strait of Georgia was a frigid forty-eight degrees Fahrenheit! They bet on it, the losers each to buy a case of beer for the winner.

At 12:35, the three stripped down. Bobby Gaines, always game, joined them, stripped to panties and brassiere. They charged at the water, but Russ stopped at the edge, laughing at their gullibility. They lasted all of fifteen seconds. Cheers and applause from the beach joined their terrible screams as they fled the water. Russ declared for all to hear, "Danny—I should have stayed on Bravo Crew! These people are just too stupid!" It was agreed by all (but Gerry and Gil) that Bobby won by one second—very likely only because she tripped before getting back to shore.

At 12:45, Gerry, Gil and Danny caught Russ unaware, stripped him and tossed him into the sea. He stayed in for half a minute, thereby replacing a protesting Bobby as the winner.

At one o'clock Anne and Morrie said good night and left for their cabin.

At two o'clock they let the bonfire die and all went inside to join Russ, who was sitting by a blazing fireplace with a bottle of rye. Those who couldn't get chairs sat on the floor and the party roared on till after four, with dancing, singing and lies.

At 6:30 A.M., Josie got out of bed to go to the bathroom. She had to climb over the inert forms of three Wild Dogs on the floor. One of the bodies mumbled, "Happy New Year, Mom."

On the second day of 1956 they would all be back to regular routines, trying to remember to write the correct date on their paperwork. There was no rest for the weary Wild Dogs, for D Crew would start a stretch of graveyard shifts on January fourth.

CHAPTER 22

▼

Came the storms of January…

COMOX—JANUARY, 1956

Danny learned Chrissy Manson had called him on the landline on December thirtieth and left a message for him to call her. The B Crew PBX operator wrote the message in a note and tacked it on the bulletin board. When Vera came on shift she put it in her tunic pocket and forgot about it. On January second she happened to be at supper with Josie and Ollie when she found the note in her pocket.

"Damn, I forgot all about this…Jo, can you give this message to Danny? It was a call for him a few days ago. I don't know if it's important. Tell him I'm sorry, I forgot all about it."

Josie looked at the note, it read:

> *30/12/55 0905 hrs.*
> *To: LAC D. Tanner (D-Crew)*
> *Call from LAW Christine Manson, 5 Air Div.*
> *Call her back ASAP. (R.M).*

She gave it to him that night.

When Danny reached Chrissy on the third, she said she had called him for three reasons. The first was to wish him "the happiest New Years ever!" The second was to say goodbye because she had taken her discharge after her three-year tour and would be going home to Alberta in two days.

Her third reason for calling was mysterious—she would only say, "Be really, really, careful Danny. I think somebody you used to know over here might try to do something to you." When he pressed her for details, she would only say, "It could hurt you, and Josie, too." She then asked, "How is Josie, are you treating her good? She's a wonderful and beautiful girl! You can be happy with her, Danny."

✳   ✳   ✳   ✳

On the fifth, he received the letter.

Danny was somewhat indifferent toward mail, so Josie always picked it up for both of them in her lunch hour. Before they took the cabin, he often let letters languish for weeks before bothering to check. She knew any mail he received would normally be from the Book of the Month Club, his correspondence course, or an occasional letter or postcard from friends at various bases across the country.

The letter arrived with some other mail. It came in a yellow envelope with a floral design and was postmarked Ladner, B.C. It was dated December twenty-third, but had been delayed because of the holiday mail rush.

He read it when they were at supper in the Mess Hall. When he finished reading he put the letter and its envelope in his shirt pocket under his tunic. Josie was curious but didn't want to pry.

"From Beth, my sister. She needs help with a problem and she wants me to go over there. She says hello to you."

"I'm sure you'll do what's best, Danny."

"Yeah." He was quick to change the subject. "So, how'd it go at work, Hon?"

"Just the usual. Oh, yes, Ollie wants me to go to town with her tomorrow; we want to go in the morning. There's a sale at a dress place. Can we get the car after you come from work?"

"Roger, it's all yours. I'll leave the key in the ashtray."

✳   ✳   ✳   ✳

He had lied about the letter being from his sister. It was from Evelyn Pollard. When he got to his barrack room, he stretched out on his bunk to read the letter again. It was written on paper matching the yellow envelope:

Dear Danny,

I hope this letter finds you well and happy and content with whatever girl-friend (or <u>girlfriends?</u>) you might have at your new base. I know you will have had <u>no problem</u> finding, shall I say, female companionship!? I just hope you are being more honest than you were in the past, about <u>whomever else</u> you are also seeing.

I am afraid, Danny, my news is not nice. It seems I have managed to get pregnant. I should say, WE have managed to get me pregnant. Because, of course, Danny, <u>you</u> <u>are</u> <u>the</u> <u>father</u>. (I have no doubt it will be a beautiful baby—for any child from your "loins" must be beautiful!!!)

My parents are aware of my condition (I am too far along to hide it any more), but they do not know who the father is.

I do not know what we (you and I) will <u>do</u> about this situation. What I mean is, it is <u>not</u> something I have had to deal with before. (It is the first time I have ever been in this "delicate condition"—ha, ha.) It is my hope that you will be willing to do the "right thing"—whatever that may be.

If I am to be your wife and raise this love-child with you, I would be a very happy girl. (I suppose I can say I'm a <u>woman</u> now!) Dad is pressing me <u>daily</u> to disclose the name of the father. You know Daddy—he will want to take strong action. I understand the R.C.A.F. frowns on this sort of thing and would likely agree with my father. You know there are people who can attest as to how close we were. The Morriseys, for instance—I often told Irene about our lovemaking.

This letter could have been rather "legalistic" and "long-winded" but I promise it is almost finished. All I ask at this time, is that you come to Ladner at the <u>earliest possible date</u>, so we can discuss this matter. Please come in person, instead of phoning me.

Always and forever,
Yours (Still) With <u>LOVE,</u>

Evelyn.

He told Josie, "My next days off, Tuesday, I'm going to see my sister to see what she wants. I doubt if I'll be more than two days over there." He chose those days off because they fell in the middle of a week, when Josie would be on duty.

*   *   *   *

JANUARY 8th—VANCOUVER

Danny managed to get a room in the barracks at Jericho. He phoned Moe Morrisey at the Liaison Office.

"Well, hello, Dan! Why don't you come to the office? We can have a coffee and talk about old times."

They had their coffee in the office. Danny's replacement in Liaison, Corporal "Red" Hodgkins, greeted him warmly. He, Danny and Russ had been crewmates and friends at Moisie.

After their coffee break, Red left the office for an errand. Moe shook his head at Danny. "Jesus, Dan, that deal of yours in the red alert last month—we still talk about it around here. It was a piece of work."

"We do what we have to do, Sir."

Moe got up and closed the office door. "Call me Moe, Dan. So how *have* you been? I suspect you're right in your element at a G.C.I. Still with that girl of yours? The one that stole you away from Evelyn?"

"Shit, yes. I'm closer than I ever thought I'd be to getting hitched. She's great, Moe."

"Have you asked her?"

"Let me put it this way—I'm almost ready."

Moe laughed. "Sounds like someone has finally nailed you! Speaking of girl-friends, it's too bad about Ev, or have you heard?"

He answered cautiously, "Heard what, Moe?" *Play this cool, Danny Boy.*

"Well, I hate to tell tales, but she turned out to be, ah, *loose,* I guess would be the word. She was fired from her job here over something pretty sordid. It's common knowledge around the base. Red would be able to tell you more. She has had no time for Irene and me since you left. We've only seen her once, and it was right after you were transferred out. Boy, we sure read her wrong!"

Danny thought, *Interesting. I have to talk to Red for sure!* To Moe he said, "How is Irene?"

"She's fine. Will you still be here tomorrow? Could you come for supper? She'll be pleased as punch to see you!"

"Tomorrow sounds great, Moe."

He made the call to Evelyn from the phone in the barracks.

"Hello?" He recognized her voice.

"Ev…it's Danny. I got your letter. How are you, Ev?"

"Well, I think you know how I am. I'm pregnant. You took your time about calling."

"Your letter just arrived a couple of days ago. I'm in town."

"We have to talk…can you meet me tomorrow night?" He had the date with Moe and Irene and in any case certainly did not wish to meet with her at night. He instead arranged to have lunch with her the next day at a place they used to go to in New Westminster. He agreed to pick her up at eleven-thirty at the Royal Columbian hospital where she had an eleven o'clock appointment with her doctor.

He found Red back at the Liaison Office after lunch.

"Hey, Red, are you busy? I need to talk to you—important."

"Sure, let's go grab a coffee."

When he told him about his problem, Red said, "Man, that broad never gives up! Tell you what, you should talk to a guy named Clayton something. You might know him. He's been here a long time. A Negro guy in M.E."

"Yeah, Clayton Carrington, I know him well. I helped him out in a beef once. Good ball player. We were on the same team for a couple of summers."

Clayton Carrington wasn't a person many people readily took to. He was one of the crudest, most irreverent men Danny had ever met, and a notorious womanizer even though married with four children. On the ball team they called him "Skin Dog." After a game one night, Danny rescued him from a certain beating at the hands of some punks in Steveston and he had been a grateful friend ever since.

At the Mobile Equipment garage, Danny was directed to a pair of boots sticking out from under a staff car. He kicked at a foot and Carrington rolled out. His coveralls and hands were greasy.

"Wrigley! You ugly sonofabitch, good to see you! I'd shake your hand, but I got grease all over me—you can't see it 'cause it's black." He laughed loudly at his joke as he wiped his hands on a rag.

"How've you been, Crayt? You black prick!"

"Let's go grab a coffee. Black prick is right! Are you talkin' about the *big* black prick?"

"You mean it's grown?"

"Fuckin' aye, Dan, you won't be wantin' to play drop-the-soap with this nigger no more! Jaysus son, we miss you on the team. I never saw anybody could kick a ground ball as far as old Wrigley!"

"Screw you, you one-fifty hitter."

As they drank coffees Danny touched briefly on his problem. They arranged to meet in the Wets after work.

"I'll buy you one, for old times," said Danny as he left the ME Section.

"I'll be there, Dan. Whatever it's about, if I can help…I owe ya, man."

In the Wets later, Ev's sordid story unwound. It turned out, after he left for Comox, Evelyn started haunting the Wets. She was there almost every night, at first questioning everyone she encountered about him. She became a familiar figure and was soon known as a lush. One night she and Chrissy Manson almost came to eye scratching when Chrissy told her to forget about Danny and leave him alone.

Ev then started dating men on the base. She slept around with numerous partners, soon earning a reputation as an "easy lay." There was even a rumor that one night, drunk, she had taken on multiple men in the Airmen's barracks. An S.P. patrol caught her with an Airman in broad daylight, having sex behind the Rec Center. The Airman was disciplined and she was fired from her job on the base and barred from the property. Carrington had had regular sex with her, starting in the late spring soon after Danny's departure, and continuing through the summer.

When she discovered her pregnancy, she wrote to the Commanding Officer, claiming a young ComTech was the father. Carrington and three other men testified on his behalf that they had all recently been with her. Their testimony, along with her recent conduct, cleared the boy.

"You marry that broad, Dan, five gets you ten you're gonna be raisin' a kinky-haired little nigger with a real big dong!" said Carrington.

When he heard the story, he reflected, *Ev, how could you sink so low! God help me if I had anything to do with it.*

*   *   *   *

JANUARY 9TH

The next day he met Evelyn as arranged and they went to a Chinese restaurant just off Marine Drive.

She looked tired, with dark circles under her eyes.

She said, "What will you have, Danny? You used to like the mushroom Chow Mein…"

"I won't be having anything, Ev, because I'm not staying."

"But, Danny, we have to talk…we have to figure out what we're going to…"

"Shut up, Ev."

"Well, pardon me! I…you can't talk like…"

"I said shut up!" He slapped the table between them. "Listen for a change. Shut up and listen to me."

"Now you just wait, don't you talk…"

"Ev, for God's sake—I know all of it. Don't make me say it. I know about all the guys you've been with. I know what happened at the base." He paused to take a deep breath.

"You bastard, Danny, if you think you can dodge your…"

He cut her off again, "Okay, you asked for this—I know there is a good chance this kid, *your* kid, will be black! Clayton Carrington and I talked and I know the whole story. Christ, Ev, didn't you think I had any friends around here?"

He watched all her pride leave her face. She looked at him wide eyed. Her features seemed to sag. She reached out for his hand but he pulled it away.

He stood up. He shook his head as he said, "Good luck, Ev."

She found her voice. She started speaking low, almost in a whisper, "This isn't over, you bastard. Do you hear me, you rotten bastard?" Her voice grew louder, "You will pay, Dan Tanner. My father will make sure you *pay!* I am going to tell him—I don't care what happens to me any more. Do you hear me? My father will drag you into court!" Now she was screeching, "I'll make you pay for the rest of your rotten life! Whatever *bitch* you think loves you? We'll see what she thinks of you now." She stood up, still screaming; a waitress came over to quiet her, tried to grab her arm. The last words Danny heard from her were, "Get *away* from me, chink *bitch!*" The proprietor joined the waitress, and they attempted to escort her toward the exit; she struggled and kicked at them.

Danny left the restaurant.

He left terrified, not knowing if she would go through with her threats. He couldn't know whether he would ever hear from her again.

CHAPTER 23

────────── ▼ ──────────

Then began the worst couple of months of my life...

JANUARY AND FEBRUARY, 1956

For the first time in his adult life, Danny was unable to act decisively. He was sure Evelyn would follow through with her threat. When he returned to Comox on the tenth he didn't know how—or *whether*—to tell Josie about her. He wasn't confident enough in their relationship to know how she would react, and so his very consciousness was paralyzed with the fear he could lose her. His thoughts ricocheted between telling her all about it, and keeping quiet and hoping she would never find out.

He was just as confused and afraid in the weeks that followed. Since his teen years, with imagination and panache, he had always managed to manipulate events in his favor. Now he felt everything was spinning wildly away from his control. As much as he loved Josie, he started avoiding one-on-one conversation with her and inventing reasons in his mind for staying away from the cabin. When the weight of the deceit became too much, he began drinking heavily. The drinking gave him more justification for being away and it soon became a cycle.

*   *   *   *

Two weeks after his return from Vancouver, Danny spotted Ollie when she came into the wets. She was there to meet Russ before going to town for a movie. He took his beer and joined her on the ladies' side.

He said, "Hi, Ol. Russ said to tell you he'll be here in about five minutes."

"I'm not happy with you, right now, Tanner," said Ollie.

"Oh oh, what did I do now?"

"For openers, what in hell are you doing here? Jo's out at the cabin, isn't she?"

He said, a little peevishly. "I'm on my way home, Ollie. Just stopped in for a beer after my shift."

She looked at her watch. "Yeah, but it's after six...did you call her?"

He became defensive. "Why is that bothering you? I think whatever time I get home is between Jo and me..."

"Bullshit, Tanner! You've been treating her like shit lately, leaving her out there while you party, who knows *with*. You know she gets scared and worried. And she's confused. Hell, you don't even call her. You just do your thing and to hell with her. It's not right. Luckily for you, she's convinced you're faithful—she can't believe you would screw around, otherwise she'd be long gone! I just hope she's right about that. You may think this is none of my business, Danny, but I love the kid. Either be with her or break it off and let her have a frigging life!"

To her surprise, he didn't disagree. "You're right, Ol, and of course it is your business. I *have* been treating her badly. There are some things going on I'm having trouble handling."

"What things?"

"Can't tell you right now." He looked down at his hands. "But it's serious, Ollie. I'm scared shitless—I'm scared I'll lose her over it..."

"Have you at least talked to her about it?"

"No. I don't know how to tell her...she wouldn't understand. I have to wait till I've got it all straightened out. And, please, don't you tell her."

"So, she just sits out there, wondering what the hell is going on? Wondering if you're screwing around or what! Have you looked at her lately? Really looked? She's not sleeping and she's tired all the time, worrying about you. Shit, she's even losing weight, while you run around, having a good time."

He stood up. "I don't need this crap from a so-called friend. You don't know me if you think I'm screwing around on her. I'm out of here." He headed for the exit thinking, *Losing weight! Oh, God, Honey.*

Ollie followed him. "Danny! Wait a minute..." She had to run to catch up. Out in the street, she grabbed his sleeve to stop him. "Hold it, Dan."

"Why, Ollie? Haven't you piled enough crap on me yet?" He twisted loose of her grip and started walking again.

She ran up beside him. "Dan, let me...let me tell her what you said about having to work out a problem. I won't tell her anything else. I don't want you guys to break up. Christ, Dan, I'm *your* friend, too. Let me tell her that much, so she'll understand at least some of what's going on!"

He kept walking. She stood still. "DAN!" she called.

He called back over his shoulder, "Tell her whatever the hell you want!" He kept walking.

He couldn't see that, eventually, it would be his very fear of losing Josie, and the way he was handling it—that would be the cause of her leaving him.

*   *   *   *

Two days after his conversation with Ollie, Danny walked into the Arbutus Lounge at five-thirty. His intention was to have one or two drinks and then to go home to the cabin and talk with Josie, to tell her essentially what he had told Ollie.

He didn't see anyone familiar, so he sat alone at an empty table and ordered a drink. He had decided after talking to Ollie that he must at least talk to Josie before things deteriorated any further. He was thinking about how to approach the problem, just how much to tell her and how much to withhold. If he had fathered a child with another woman, would she understand? Could he expect her to live with him with such a thing between them? What if Evelyn's father dragged him into court? All his fear of losing her flooded back and his determination dissolved. Maybe he would talk to her tomorrow, when he hadn't been drinking. Meanwhile, why not have another rye? *As long as I get home tonight...I can't leave her out there all night ever again. I have to get home at a decent hour. I'll watch the time. One or two more...*

At eight-thirty he was still in the bar and quite drunk when a noisy group of six people came through the door. There were four men and two girls, one of whom was Bobby Gaines. They sat at the large table in the center of the room.

Bobby spotted him a few minutes after her arrival, when he passed their table on his way to the washroom. She shouted, "Hey! Danny McTanner...my fav'rit guy! Wha's up, Dan?"

"Hey, Bobarino! Howya doing?" he said. He approached the group's table.

"Danny, come join us..." It was obvious she had had a lot to drink. Part of her hairdo had come undone and a curly auburn lock bobbed at one side of her face.

He waved a hand toward the men's room. "Okay, Bobby. First I gotta go see a man about a horse...be right back."

When he returned and sat with them, Bobby distractedly waved a hand by way of introduction. "I don' remember all these peoples' names. There's a Rick an' a George I think, an' a Louise, she's the female, and this guy's Ken or Glen...or something." She tried unsuccessfully to push the wayward lock into place.

Her slight dishevelment gave her an appealing, available, look. He noticed the guy beside her was acting especially possessive. He had an arm around her waist and held her close to him, awkwardly because of the chairs. She carefully ignored him when he started nibbling her ear. She gently took the arm from her waist and moved away, saying, "Look, Ken?...Glen? Danny's a good friend of mine, so be nice an' let us talk for a minute, okay?"

The guy, Ken or Glen, put the arm back around her and pulled her to him. He whispered something in her ear.

"Don't *whisper*, man, it's kinda' rude. An' the answer is no, I don't wanna to go anywhere else—we just friggin' got here!" She turned to Danny and laughed. "Shit, where do I find them, eh, Dan?"

The other girl and the three guys were in a conversation. Ken-Glen stared resentfully at Danny for a minute. Then he put his arm around Bobby again. He put his free hand on her thigh.

Smiling sweetly, she lifted the hand and put it on the table. Then she pulled free of the arm and turned to Danny, her back to Ken-Glen's attentions. But K-G was not giving up easily. He put the arm around her again, the hand back on her thigh, and murmured, "You want to be with me, or not?"

She murmured in reply, "No, Glen, I'm not *with* anybody! I'm here with everybody, okay? Now let me talk to my friend, just for a minute, will you?"

"Okay, okay...shit," said K-G.

She turned back to Danny. "So, Dan, what's up with you? Out on your own? Did you lose Josie somewhere? Or Russ?"

"Naw, just on my own—having a few...you know."

K-G lost control of his hands again. He draped one arm over her shoulder, so his hand rested on her breast. The other hand again found its way to her thigh.

She roughly pushed away the offending hands. "Cut that OUT! Okay? Shit, will you stop pawing me, f'Chrissake?" She gave the guy a malevolent look. "Danny, tell'm to keep his hands to hisself, willya...better yet, take him outside an' beat the shit outta him...he's friggin; rude an' I don' like him." She winked at Danny.

Danny found the guy's persistence amusing. He smiled as he suggested, "Yeah, Ken…Glen? Maybe you should kinda lay off, okay? The lady doesn't want you doing that."

K-G's posture became combative. He started to speak, "Who do…"

Bobby cut him off. "Glen, shut up. You don' know what you're messing with." She turned to Danny. "How 'bout we go an' find another table, Dan? We don't want no, um…fuss, do we? We'll have a couple more an' you can give me a ride back to the base."

Danny said, "I could just leave, if I'm…"

"Would you do that to me?" she asked. She turned back to Ken-Glen. "Hey…Ken, I'm kinda smashed an' I wanna go home. Danny'll give me a ride. Call me up sometime at the barracks, I'd love to see you again."

The man brightened. "Yeah, sure, I'll call you. It's Glen."

"Huh?"

"My name—it's not Ken, it's Glen."

She was on her feet to leave. "Great, you're sweet, Glen. Okay Dan, where to?"

Danny didn't want any trouble, so he suggested, "Back to the base. I should be getting back anyway." It was nine o'clock.

"Good plan, big guy."

In the car, she said, "Shit! I met those guys at the Lorne, earlier. The Ken guy, he maneuvers me into the back seat of the car an' was on me like a friggin' *rash*. He's not such a bad guy, I suppose. My fault; I guess I gave the impression I wanted some lovin.' Actually I was all ready for it…some loving."

"What changed your mind, Bobby?"

"I don't know…I think it was because he was so damned *eager*. Shit, can we find another drink somewhere? I don' wanna quit yet. But not the Wets, I do *not* wanna run into you-know-who."

"How about the Lorne or Elk? I could go for another drink, too." They were approaching the hill by St. Joseph's hospital in Comox.

"Great. You pick one."

"What time is it?"

She looked at her watch, but had a difficult time reading the dial. "I got…I got…nine fifteen."

Danny parked on Port Augusta Street, twenty yards past the front door of the Elk Hotel, where the street ran into the government dock. Inside, before they found a table, He said, "I have to find the john. Find us a table. Be right with you." He found a pay phone in a hallway and phoned Lorna, to say he had car trouble and would get home around ten or ten-thirty. Lorna said she would pass it on to Josie.

They sat at a table for two. The place wasn't busy, just four other customers.

"Well, not much choice, Bobby, it's a beer parlor." He waved to the waiter for two drafts.

"Beer's okay. Christ, Dan, am I ever fugging *smashed!* Oh, shit, you didn't hear that word...okay?"

"At's okay, it's only a word. I'm kinda pissed, too. The difference is, I know why I'm pissed—but why are you so out of it?"

"Long, sad story. Tell me yours an' I'll tell you mine."

"Not anything you should worry about, Bobby."

"Anything to do with Josie?"

He didn't answer.

She persisted, "Well?"

"In a way, yeah. Just...in a way. Now, what about you? Any of my business?"

"Get us another couple of these, will you?" She waved her empty glass. "About me, hmm? It's about I've finally given up on my man...I should say the guy I *hoped* would be my man. He showed up yesterday with his latest, a civvy babe from Campbell River. The sonofabish! He don' like Airwomen. Oh, we can be his friends an' party with him, but did y'ever see him date any of us?"

It took him several seconds to answer. He was having trouble concentrating. The beers, on top of all the drinks, had hit him hard. "D'you believe that about ol' Gil?"

"Oh, yeah. He's tol' me...thinks we all drink too much an' stuff. Drink too much? Shee-it, he should see me now!" she giggled.

"Anyway, you wasted too much time on him already, Bobby. You're a good lookin' girl, damn good-looking. You don' need him. Lot's of guys would be happy to get a beautiful girl like you."

"You are right, my fren'...and this is the day I quit wasting my time!"

"Atta girl." He touched his glass to hers.

Bobby wanted to talk. "Shit, I started out today promising myself I would forget the rat. To get over my friggin' *obsession!* I figured I'd find another guy and...aw, I'll admit it...I *wanted* to get laid. Get laid by some guy and forget all about Mister Gilbert Potter! Forever!" She giggled. "Trouble is, I got all smashed before I put the big plan into action. I sat with a couple of guys...came on to them big time. But one guy was married an' the other had pimples. As if I should be so damn choosy, eh? Anyhow...I said the next guy I meet today gets lucky. An' that was the guy you met, Ken or Glen or Ben."

"Glen. I think it was Glen, Bobby."

"Wha? Yeah, whatever. Anyhow…where was I? Oh, yeah, I *foisted* myself on those people, Ken and his friends, in the Lorne. I was hoping one of the guys would like me…you know, be attracted to a cute redhead. I kinda hinted I was, um, available. Glen made sure he was in the back seat with me in the car going to the Arbutus. But, he got so *tiresome* in the bar, just about *drooling* on me, doing that grope and grab stuff. I changed my mind about getting laid. I guess I smartened up."

"You did the right thing," said Danny.

"Yeah. I guess. Then, in walks ol' Danny Tanner, my crew-buddy. My dancing partner." she laid a hand on his. "But enough of my problems. Let's get 'nother beer!"

*   *   *   *

They left the Elk at ten o'clock. As he was unlocking the passenger door of the Ford for her she staggered and fell against him. He had to catch her so she wouldn't fall to the ground.

"Oops, sorry Dan. I am…rilly…fuggin' bombed. Oops." she said.

"S'okay, Jo, Danny's gotcha."

She leaned on the car, giggling and waving a hand weakly.

"Whasso funny?" he asked.

She put her hands to her cheeks. "You! You jus' called me Jo."

"Did I? 'Ats funny."

One of the other hotel patrons came across the road to where they were parked. Danny recognized him from the base but couldn't recall his name.

The man said, "Dan, you better not drive your car—the cops are set up all over the place. See, there's one parked right there. I know I ain't moving, I've had too much."

"Oh, yeah. Yeah, I see him. Don' wanna be doin' any driving. Thanks for the warning." An R.C.M.P. cruiser was parked halfway up the hill on Port Augusta. From where he was parked the only way out was the way they came in, right past the cruiser. They sat and watched in the rearview mirror as the officers checked three cars. It was plain to see they had set up there to nab hotel patrons.

Bobby said, "What are we gonna do? I don't wan' you to drive an' get a ticket or something."

"Sit here n' wait…I don' know what else." He glanced at his watch. "Yeah, we'll sit for a while, see if they go away."

"Whatever you say. You're the one that'll catch shit."

"I know. Already got enough shit 'n my life, don' need any more."

Neither of them even thought about calling a taxi.

Danny said, "We might as well get comfortable. There's a blanket in the back."

"I'm okay. Lots of antifreeze in me tonight." She snickered.

He reached for the blanket. "Here, I don' wanna start the motor to use the heater. They'll see the exhaust."

"Thanks." She put it around her shoulders.

Danny lay his head back on the seat. He closed his eyes, thinking about the scene with Josie when he got home. After a couple of minutes he sensed Bobby moving and then felt her nudge his leg.

She whispered, "Lookut I found—it's a mickey I had in my purse. I was gonna take it home. Think we should?"

"Yeah, but we'll have to keep it out of sight. Be ready to ditch it. What is it?"

"It's vodka, go ahead." She pressed the bottle against his leg.

"Thanks." He took a long pull, felt the warmth. "S'good…here, your turn."

They passed it back and forth. A half-hour later he opened his door just enough to roll the empty bottle away from the car. If they weren't drunk enough before the vodka, they certainly were after. He lay back again and closed his eyes.

Bobby said, "D'ya rilly think I'm priddy, Dan? You said I'm a good lookin' girl…does 'at mean the same as priddy?"

"I do. You are."

She whispered, "Thanks, Dan, you're nice. You called me Josie, though…" Her voice trailed off.

He could tell by her breathing when she fell asleep. He sat and looked at the stars, then felt his eyelids getting heavy. He checked the rear view mirror and saw the police cruiser was still in place. He dozed off.

Bobby changed position, causing her arm to flop over onto his lap, the back of her hand resting on his thigh. He saw the blanket had slipped off her. She woke up just as he was pulling it up around her. He was leaning over in such a way that their faces were inches apart. Her hand on his jeans turned palm down, fingers slowly grasping.

"Wanna kiss me, Danny?" she said.

He stared at her, laid his forehead on hers for a few seconds.

"Well, do you?" she asked again. She brushed back his forelock, letting her hand linger.

"Yeah." He took her into his arms. She pressed against him and they kissed.

Hearing tires on gravel, he glanced in the mirror. The police car was moving, turning onto Comox Road. He didn't tell her. She put a hand under his sweater, caressing his chest. They kissed again. He kneaded her breasts.

"I want you." She breathed the words.

"Not here. Jus' a minute." He started the car and pulled into a lane running beside the hotel.

She unbuttoned her coat and the blouse under it. She pulled his head down and pressed his face to her breast. She unzipped his fly.

"I don' wanna wait…" she had her hand inside his pants.

He said, "Back seat."

In the back, she squirmed out of her slacks and panties and then pulled his slacks down. He could make out her creamy thighs in the darkness.

He turned her so she was on top and said, "Put me in, Hon…"

He entered her and she moved frenetically on him.

When he came moments later with a shudder, he held her tightly and whispered in her ear, "I love you, Honey."

She lay silent and still for a half minute before saying, "You love…who?" She knew he didn't mean her.

"You, Jo…" Addled by the liquor and passion, he confused her for Josie. The only times in over eight months he had been with a girl in his car had been with her. Realization lit his face. "Oh, shit! I'm sorry, Bobby, it's always her and…I'm drunk. Sorry, I…"

"Jesus, Dan, what the hell are we *doing?* Jesus! She's my friend!" She was frantically dressing, as if she feared Josie would peer in the car window any second.

As he zipped up, he mumbled, "Oh, God…if she ever finds out…I love her so mush, Bobby…"

"Of course you do." She was somewhat sobered by the enormity of what just happened. "Danny—this better always be our secret!" She pounded the back of the seat in front of her. "Our *dirty little secret*. Christ, what were we thinking?"

"We weren't thinking."

"I suppose. Just get me back to the base. Right now!"

Ten minutes later he let her out at the women's barracks and then drove home to Kye Bay.

*   *   *   *

Nicole St. Pierre happened to be passing a window on the stair landing when she heard a car stop outside. She saw one of those FighterCOps, Bobby Gaines, get out of the car and go around to the rear door of the barrack. She couldn't see who the driver was. She went back to her room and saw the time. She spoke aloud, "This is something for my diary." She took a scribbler from a drawer and wrote in it:

11:08 PM, January 12, 1956. License number CJF-043. Green car. B. Gaines.
She didn't think much more about her latest sighting.

When Danny arrived home Josie was asleep. There was a note on the kitchen table:

Darling—

Sandwich and pie in fridge.
Thank you for calling
I'm tired, it is 10 o'clock and

I'm off to bed. Love you—J.

He ate the sandwich, cleaned himself up in the bathroom, undressed, and got into the bed beside her. He looked at her outline in the dim room and wondered once again at her beauty. Reflecting on what he had done that night, he resolved to straighten up. She didn't deserve what he was doing to her. He brushed his lips to the side of her neck before laying his head down to sleep.

In the morning Josie tried to get out of the bedroom as quietly as she could, but Danny awoke as she was getting dressed.

He said sleepily, "Hi, Hon."

"Hi, I'm sorry, I didn't want to wake you up yet." She bent and kissed his forehead. "You got home."

"Yeah, about ten-thirty, I guess. Got time to lie down for a minute?"

She smiled. "To lie down, maybe. But not to do what you 'ave in mind."

"I just...there's something I have to say to you." He sat up, smiling. "And it's all I have on my mind. See? I'm sitting up."

She sat on the bed, knees drawn up under her. "Okay."

"Okay. First, I'm sorry I was late getting home…again. Next, I…this is hard for me…I've been-been more than unfair to you lately, staying out, leaving you here alone. Please believe I love you…"

She interjected, serious now, "I know you do, Danny. It's why I'm still here." He detected some frustration in her tone.

"Let me finish saying this, Jo. I…I have some things going on. I'll tell you all of it when I know it's all over, I promise. I'm asking you to wait. Anyway, It's something I haven't been able to handle yet." He considered telling her about him and Bobby the night before, but fear won a battle with guilt in his mind. He rationalized it would just hurt her unnecessarily and further strain their relationship. Best if she never knew. His decision not to tell her was an error in judgement they would both come to regret.

"I know there's *something* going on. Ollie told me. Couldn't I help you, Darling…to handle it?"

"You can help by just being here. That's all I can give you now. Please trust me. But what's important now, what I want to say, is…I won't be treating you badly any more, starting right now. I'll be here with you—*everywhere* with you. We'll do things together. I know you don't like to drink much. And I know you don't like it when I drink too much. It all stops now! I don't need it, I need you, Jo! I know my promises haven't been worth anything. But I…with your help, Hon, I want to try. You're too precious for me to lose." He shook his head. "Jesus, I hope I said that right. Do you understand me?"

There were tears glistening in her eyes. "I do. I will help. When you need me, tell me how. You know I love you." She paused momentarily. "But—you just made a promise. It's not the first time. I want you to know, Danny, I 'ave not been happy these past weeks. So now, I'll make a promise to you. If it starts…happens again, I promise you I will not stay out here anymore. I hope you understand. That's *my* promise and I *will* keep it."

"Fair enough," he replied, "I do understand." He jumped out of the bed. "Okay! We better get moving, I have to get you to work."

"Wait! One more thing…I ordered a phone. I'll pay for it but I must 'ave it here, Danny."

"Okay, Jo. *We* will pay for it." He knew why she wanted it. He didn't have her complete trust. He didn't resent it.

"And," she said, "can you take some books back to the library today? They're three days overdue. They were due on the ninth."

*   *   *   *

For the rest of January and into February, things were as they had been when they first moved into the cabin.

They began spending time regularly with friends again, Ollie and Russ and the Letourneaus, a thing they hadn't done much since the holidays. The Fearsome Foursome took in movies in Courtenay once a week, often going to the Arbutus for one or two drinks, then to a restaurant. The card games in the cabins resumed, with them hosting or visiting Lorna and Leo.

And they had their walks on the beach—Josie's second-favorite times with him.

One late-February afternoon, they spotted the heron about fifty yards away, at its usual spot near the water's edge.

Josie put a hand on his arm to stop him and whispered, "Danny, look! Ollie and I got right up close to it one day. Let's see how close we can..." Before she could finish speaking, the bird flew away, wings flapping lazily. "Hey, stupid bird!" she cried.

Danny was laughing, "I guess this is as close, right here! It must have read your mind."

Giggling, she sat down on the sand. "Oh, merde! That was so funny—'let's see how close we can get' and the stupid thing flies away that second. Stupid bird!"

They sat and laughed together on the damp beach.

She hugged him. "Oh, Danny, I just thought about the time when we almost missed the train!"

"Oh, shit yeah. That was scary."

"Do you remember what you said, what you said to me, when we were running?"

"Hmm. No, I don't..."

"You said..." She giggled. "You said, 'Josie, you run like a girl!' I remember thinking, 'Of course I do, you wouldn't want me any other way, stupid L.A.C.'"

"You're right, I wouldn't. Who would?"

She sobered. "Danny, it's so good when we're together—when we can laugh. We 'ave to always remember, about how good it is."

"You got it, Babe." He stood up and she followed. "Let's go back. It's getting cold. I'll light the fireplace."

"That won't be the first thing...not if I have any say! Come on, we'll race, but you 'ave to run like a girl, too!" They were about seventy-five yards from the cabin. She took off running down the beach.

Halfway home, puzzled that he hadn't flown past her, she looked back. He was running in a comical knock-kneed fashion. She collapsed in the sand, laughing helplessly. Now he sprinted for the cabin and passed her, winning the race.

"Not...not fair! You big shit. You always 'ave to cheat. Big shit!"

When she got to the cabin door, she called, "You 'ad better be undressed when I get in there!"

He was.

There were three weeks of such peace before the next storm struck.

CHAPTER 24

▼

All my sins, all my lies—came back on me...

After lunch on a day in mid-February, Josie was walking from the Mess Hall to the barracks with Nicole St. Pierre. They heard a horn beep behind them. It was Danny in the Ford.

He stopped beside them and said, "Hi, Honey." He didn't recognize her companion.

"Hello my Darling! Danny, this is Nicole, call her Nicky." To Nicole she said, "You go ahead, Nicky, I'll be here for a minute." She jumped into the car. "I was going to the room. I spilled soup on my sleeve so I 'ave to change my blouse. I'm surprised you're not still in bed."

"Couldn't sleep. I had to get some gas and some air in a low tire. I'm out of Brylcreem, too." He pulled the car over to the curb. "I was going to catch you in the Mess after lunch, but it looks like I'm too late."

She stuck out her lower lip. "Poor little Josie has to be all alone till midnight, because her mean old L.A.C. is working the stupid evening shift."

He grinned. "You're trying to make me cry, but I have to work to support you and your huge appetite."

"Shut up, you."

"I have to get going. See you after work. Love you." He squeezed her hand gently.

"Ollie has the Dog Pound for tonight. We're going into town for some shopping after work. I love you, too." She pecked his cheek and got out. "Bye, Honey."

Nicky had stopped outside the barrack block, waiting. She stared at the Ford. She was sure she recognized the car from last month. She would check the license number she had written in her diary.

When Josie caught up, she said, "Is that Danny's car, Josie?"

"Yes."

"I guess he's your boyfriend, or you wouldn't be calling him your darling."

Josie smiled. "He is my Darling."

"Didn't he used to go with Bobby Gaines, the FighterCOp?"

"No, only me. We've been going together since last May, when he was still stationed at Vancouver."

Later, Nicky found Josie in the laundry room.

She said, "Josie, I know something I should tell you…"

"Okay…shoot!"

"It's not, uh…the best news. Can you come down to my room? There's something I have to show you."

"Sounds scary, Nicky, I hope you're not passing gossip again." They started toward the stairs.

"It might mean nothing…but as your friend I think you should know. One night last month I saw that same car drop off Bobby Gaines. It was around eleven at night."

"Well, he probably gave her a ride from town, or maybe from work. They're on the same crew at 51."

"Yes, that probably explains it. I wrote it down. I write stuff I observe in my diary. It's stupid, I know, but this way I won't gossip. I just tell it to myself."

In her room she shuffled through several True Romance magazines till she found the scribbler. She opened to the page she wanted and pointed to the entry for Josie.

The date leapt off the page! Josie remembered it because of the overdue library books.

"I-I 'ave to go…" she said stiffly. She turned quickly and left the room.

*   *   *   *

When Danny got to the cabin at midnight, there was a note on the table:

I am at the barracks.

I will be living there from now on.

Please do NOT try to contact me.

You broke your promise again—

now I am <u>keeping</u> mine!

I will pick up the rest of my things later—

I hope you won't be there because

I DO NOT want to see you.

Danny figured she would come for her things after four thirty the next day, thinking he was on duty. He called Russ from Letourneaus' in the morning and asked him to tell Ellen Schmidt he would be late getting to work.

"Okay, Champ, I'll tell her you're stranded in town with car trouble. She won't mind anyway."

He parked the Ford away from the cabin so she wouldn't see it when she arrived.

He was at the table when a taxi pulled up outside and she got out. He saw her talk to the driver, who turned off the engine and sat back to wait for her. She seemed surprised to find the cabin door unlocked, and stopped in her tracks when she came in and saw him at the table.

After glancing at him for just a second, she tried to walk past him to the bed-room. He could see her eyes were red-rimmed and puffy.

He stood up. "Whoa, hold it, Jo." He held up the note. "What's this all about?"

She kept walking.

He followed her toward the bedroom. "Hon, please! What's happened? I just want to know…"

She wheeled on him, "You screwed her!"

"What? Who…"

"You slept with Bobby Gaines! You lied about car trouble to be with her, then you sat 'ere and lied to me the next morning—didn't you!"

"Hon, I…"

"How many times, Danny? Where did you do it? Did you sleep with her in any of our places? And you lied to me about going to see your sister, too. You went over to Vancouver to do it with that Chrissy! How many others, Danny? Couldn't you at least pick someone I don't know? Did it 'ave to be Bobby? And I was 'ere alone, night after night, feeling so sorry for you and your *problems*. Your only damn problem was too many 'babes' wasn't it! You're a bastard, Danny Tanner!"

"Chrissy? No! About Bobby, I was going to…"

"You were going to what? Tell me? Just when were you planning to do that? You're a liar!"

She turned around and left the cabin. He stood in the bedroom. There was a cold knot in his gut. He went to the door in time to see her taxi turn up the hill.

*   *   *   *

Danny's first reaction was to get away from the cabin. When he arose the next day he took a few of his clothes, locked the door and went to the barracks. Russ, ever the suffering friend and sounding board, was sleeping. Danny paced the floor muttering and now and then pounding the locker door till he woke him up.

With sleep in his voice, Russ asked, "What in hell are you doing, Champ?"

"Oh, you're awake—good. I need someone to talk to…" He looked sheepish. "Hope I didn't wake you up."

"Yeah, yeah, well, I had to wake up to talk to you, anyway, didn't I. What's up?" He sat up in the bunk.

"Aw, shit, I've screwed up…with Jo."

Russ grinned, "Let me guess. All her fault, right?"

"Go to hell. You know better."

"So, you know what to do. Go and apologize. And whatever you did, don't do it again."

Danny flipped the note onto the bunk. "It's not gonna be so simple this time."

Russ read it and sighed. "Jesus apeshit Christ, what promise did you break this time? You're either gonna have to keep your promises or quit making them. Have you tried to call her? She's a good kid, Dan, and she loves you a lot and it's time to crawl a little. Give her a call and get down on your knees. She deserves it."

"She won't talk. She came to Kye Bay after four thirty to avoid me. It's why I went to work late, because I wanted to talk—she found out about something…"

"About what?"

"I…got pissed-up and ended up getting laid…last month."

"God *damn* you, Dan! Couldn't you do without, for Chrissake? Hell, can you blame her for getting out? Who was it?"

"You know I won't tell you that."

"Okay. Someone I know?" Danny nodded. "Then it's someone she knows, too. What in hell is the matter with you? To do that to her...aw, just fuck off! She's better off without you." He lay down and turned his back.

"I intended to tell her, Russ...it was just some drunken, uh, fumbling. Hell, the babe told me I called her Josie."

Russ turned and looked up, disgusted. "But you didn't tell her, did you? Then she finds out somehow, as if you couldn't see *that* coming. You *stupid* prick, Dan! I'm starting to find it hard to be on your side." He sighed again. "But, I'll try talking to Ollie. If she doesn't decide to hunt you down and shoot you, maybe she'll talk to Jo...to see how bad it is. Now, can we get to bed? We have to work at four-thirty."

"Yeah, thanks for the support...friend." He said it sarcastically.

"Wrong is wrong, Dan...and Josie's my friend, too. Don't forget that."

Danny didn't try to call Josie. He waited to hear from Ollie.

*   *   *   *

Two nights later at work Vera handed him a sealed envelope.

"What's this, Vera?"

She just shrugged and walked away without answering. He looked at the envelope. He knew the handwriting well. It was from Josie:

Danny,

First, I wish to say I appreciate that you have done as I asked and not tried to contact me. It would be a waste of your time and an unnecessary nuisance to my friends and me.

I am writing you so you will have absolutely no doubt in your mind— whatever you and I had is over. Forever.

I once loved you—more than you ever deserved to be loved. But you ruined that with lies and broken promises. You find it easy to make promises, Danny, and just as easy to break them! I will be a long time getting over you but I must try or you will destroy me, as you have destroyed what was once our wonderful love. For, when you were being the real

Danny (or is the liar and cheat the real you?) at least the Danny I first met and fell so deeply in love with—it was wonderful to be with you and I was the happiest girl in the universe! But what you have become now has just made me more and more miserable. Your cruelty—yes, cruelty—in hanging on and making me hang on (and hope) is the worst part. Every time you came back with the promises my heart filled with joy. Then you would crush me! As you have just done again. I cannot let it happen to me ever again! I hope you will understand. You said it to me long ago—no one else will look after me, so I must do it myself. Perhaps you truly loved me, in your way, but your way is no good anymore. If you do love me, as you always say you do, you will wish me to have a happy life, and leave me alone.

It is bad enough I am to be known as "the broad who shacked up with Danny Tanner." Have you ever even considered that? How I sacrificed my reputation to be with you? Now I will also be the one who couldn't keep Danny Tanner. If only they knew—keeping you is now the last thing I want to do.

Another thing—in your selfishness you have ruined our beautiful friendship with Ollie and Russ. What a sad thing! That alone makes me want to cry. But I have done enough crying, thanks to you. Now I will get on with my life.

As I said in my note, I do not want to even see you. I am sure we will encounter each other around the base. I will not acknowledge you. As you know, I still have some of my things at the cabin. How I hate that place now! Could you let me know a day or time when you will not be there, through Russ or one of the girls on your crew? (Bobby Gaines perhaps?)

I wish you the very best in your future.

Sincerely, Josie Connor

When he read her letter Danny's insides again went cold. *Christ—forever! She wishes me the best in the future? What future?* He scrunched the paper into a ball and looked for a place to throw it away, but changed his mind, straightened it as best he could, and put it into his tunic pocket. Later he put it in the leather case he used for his study materials.

In the weeks following her letter, he reverted to his same unfortunate behavior of mid-January, when he had been preoccupied with Evelyn's pregnancy. The rent at the cabin was paid up to the end of March, so he began spending most of his off-duty time there. He found it useful as a refuge, to hide his drinking and his shame. Sometimes the drinking caused him to forget about duty. Russ had to cover for him on three occasions when he was late or missed work.

His guilt also caused him to be less than comfortable around Ollie and other friends. He knew how fond of Josie they were and began to resent that they tended to take her side. He fully realized he was the one at fault, but grew weary of evading questions and answering criticism, expressed or imagined. He sought out the company of people who didn't know her, not always making good choices.

*   *   *   *

The tone and words of her letter belied the heartache Josie was suffering. Contained in it were some untruths whether she knew so or not. She did not "once" love him—she still did, desperately, and "keeping him" was what in her heart she most wanted to do. And of course she did not "hate the place now," but in fact cherished every familiar square inch of the cabin and longed to be back there with him the way things were. If he were to smile at her and speak to her, she would quite possibly leap into his arms!

She had hesitated for some time before penning the word forever in the second paragraph, horrified at its finality, and second-guessed her own meaning in ending the letter by wishing him a good future. Was she wishing for, "a good future someday with me?" She agonized over even sending the letter, and had torn up several versions. When she handed it over and Vera left the room with it, she physically started after her to retrieve it, before stopping herself.

There were truths there, too, however. She was crushed—terribly hurt and humiliated by his perfidy and manifest lack of respect for her. She was determined to preserve her sense of self by putting him behind her and trying to get on with her life.

After leaving him, she was lost. Her world was upside down. She would see or read something and form sentences in her mind, ready to tell him about it before realizing it couldn't be. Favorite things, once shared, would have her looking around for him. Only Ollie's presence made living in the barracks bearable. Ollie, and their room, had always been her safe harbor, a place to run to in a storm. Now, somehow, the room and the whole building became foreign and even the people she knew so well were strangers. The cabin was the only place where she could feel comfortable, but she couldn't go there. She hoped time would help her adjust to her new situation. She ventured from the barracks only occasionally, certainly never to the Wets for fear of encountering him. There were forays to the snack bar; checking first at the top of the stairs to see if he was there. She learned from Lorna he was still living at the cabin, so decided to forgo retrieving the rest of her things. She spent many of her off-duty hours in the barracks, reading, listening to the radio or Ollie's records and doing almost daily laundry. (Necessary because most of her clothes were at the cabin.) She was having difficulty concentrating on anything for more than half an hour. It took days to get through three chapters of a book she was reading and then she retained little of it. Ollie left her alone with her misery at first, but then after two weeks passed, she decided the time had come to get involved.

She sat on Josie's bed, "Do you want to tell me about it?"

"Ollie, I don't want to bother you…"

"Bullshit! We've been bothering each other for a year. Why stop now? I remember something you once reminded me of, about best friends…hmm?"

Josie had to smile.

"Shit-all-to-hell! Is this a smile? I haven't seen one on you for a couple of weeks." She changed course, "What did he do?"

"Oh, Ollie, he's a-a bastard!"

"But what bastardly thing did he do?"

"Well, you know how he was out at night a lot…and he told you he had some kind of problem? It was all lies! He was seeing…sleeping with other girls."

"Not Dan, I don't believe it. What makes you think that happened?"

"I don't think it, I know it…"

"When? When was he supposed to have done it?"

"Remember that Chrissy in Vancouver when we went there? He must 'ave been talking to her on the landlines all the time he was with me. Remember he stopped at her table when we were in Vancouver? I saw him talking to her there. I got one of her messages by mistake…asking Danny to call her back. His next days off he went to Vancouver. He said it was to see his sister but I'm sure he lied about it. There is at least one other girl, too." She could no longer hold back her tears. "It's someone we *know*, Ollie…someone right here!"

"Do you know who it is?"

"It's Bobby Gaines."

"No way, Jo…you're imagining things."

She pulled away from Ollie, dabbed at her eyes. She composed herself before saying, "I 'ave proof."

"What proof?"

"Somebody saw them. It was the twelfth of last month. I know the date. Danny sat with me the next morning and lied about that night!"

"Who? Who saw them?"

"It doesn't matter who, Ollie, I believe it. He didn't deny it and he hasn't tried to defend himself. It's true."

"That bastard. That *bitch!* But Jo, you have to be sure. Don't let…"

"I *am* sure." She looked forlornly at her friend. "I 'ave to forget Him. I have to never see him again…I can't let him hurt me this way again!"

Ollie looked thoughtful. "So now I know why Gaines hasn't been coming around…she was like a fixture in this room before."

"And she was my friend."

*   *   *   *

Ten minutes later, Ollie stormed into Bobby's room. She closed the door. "Gaines! I just found out you've been sleeping with Danny Tanner."

Bobby blanched. She didn't answer right away.

"Well?" Ollie pressed.

"Oh, shit. Oh, shit. I don't know what to do Ollie…"

"You could try dying, just for starters! What in hell were you thinking? And all the time you were doing that, you were supposed to be Jo's friend? Jesus, you bitch!"

"Wait…wait, you said…*all the time?* It wasn't like that. It was one stupid damn…*minute*…just once." There were tears in Bobby's eyes as she went on. "Can I tell you what happened?"

"Yeah. I'm sure I'll be interested—I'm sure Jo will be interested, too—in how you jumped in the sack with her guy!"

"Okay. If you calm down, I'll tell you…and then you can tell Jo if you want."

"Oh, no, dearie—*you* are gonna tell Jo!"

"Fair enough, but I'll tell you first." She told Ollie exactly what she remembered about the night at the Elk Hotel. "I will never again be as ashamed as I am about this…"

When she was finished, Ollie said, "Will you come with me, right now, to talk to Josie?"

"Yes, I want to. This has been weighing on me, Ollie."

Josie was dozing, fully dressed, her book on the floor, when they came in the room. Bobby stayed behind Ollie.

Ollie said, "Jo, I've got Bobby Gaines with me. She has something to say to you."

Josie sat up, startled. "What?" She glared at Ollie.

"Bobby has something to say to you..."

"No, that bitch has nothing to say to me! How dare you bring her here."

"Jo! Be fair. Give her a minute..."

"Why, so she can lie? No thank you."

Bobby pushed past Ollie. She went to her knees in front of Josie, tears streaming down her face. She tried to take Josie's hands in hers but they were jerked away.

"Jo...please listen. Listen for just a minute. It's important to me...and to you!" Josie just sat and looked past her.

Bobby continued. "Jo, if I could take that night back, I'd give anything..." Sparing neither detail nor herself, she related the story. "Jo, please believe...it was one *stupid, stupid, drunken* minute. He called me by *your name*, Jo...he called me *Josie!* I know you can never forgive me or ever call me your friend again, but Danny loves you. He loves *you*, Jo!"

Icily calm, Josie said, "Get out, Bobby."

After she left, sobbing, Ollie said, "So, Jo, it wasn't as bad as you thought..."

"She's lying. He screwed her, Ollie, and she screwed him. And she wasn't the only one." She picked up her book.

✳   ✳   ✳   ✳

After trying for a month, Ollie finally persuaded Josie to get out of the barracks. She and Russ took her out to a movie in Courtenay, then to the Arbutus and a restaurant. Josie dryly commented that they could now be called the "Fearsome Threesome." In the next week, they talked her into first another movie and then a couple of hours at the Wets. (Russ "scouted" Danny's plans for the evening, ensuring he wouldn't show up there.)

Josie was determined to hang on to her friendship of Ollie and Russ, so the threesome's routine became what had been the foursome's; one or two movies a week and an occasional evening in the Wets. She received news from them about Danny of course. She pretended the reports were of no interest to her, but was discouraged by what she heard. It filled her with anguish to hear how he was behaving.

She would think, *He must be hurting so!* Then she would harden; *Not my problem anymore.*

CHAPTER 25

▼

We both made choices we would come to regret terribly…

COMOX—FEBRUARY AND MARCH, 1956

Josie was in the Wets with Ollie and Russ. She had just told them she was going back to the barracks when she heard a familiar voice behind her.

"Hello, little stranger! Do you still jive good as ever? I just fed some nickels into the box and I'm ready, all I need now is a good partner." It was Gord Schaefer. He leaned over the back of her chair, his hands resting lightly on her shoulders.

She looked up. "Hello, Gordon. How are you?"

"Can we talk on the floor? My nickels are a-wastin…"

She thought for a second. "Okay, why not? I haven't danced for a long time."

"I haven't seen you around, Gord," said Josie as they danced.

"They sent some of us up to Cold Lake…for four long, cold months. Man, they named that place right."

They danced the three jive numbers and she invited him to sit with them. She introduced him to Russ. When they got up to dance again, Russ asked, "So, who's the big guy, Ollie?"

"An old flame. She went out with him when she first came here. He's a pretty good guy…I guess."

Russ grunted, "He better be."

*   *   *   *

Gord called Josie two days later to ask if she wanted to go out. She wasn't sure. She suggested he call her again the next night. When she hung up the phone, she thought, *Why not? He's good looking, he's clean, a good dancer…and he likes me.* When he didn't call the next day she was mildly disappointed, but didn't let it bother her. When he called on the second day, she agreed to go out.

They went out together three times in the next five nights. At the end of the third date, he parked the car by the shore, just off the Lazo Road. He pulled her close and they kissed.

She said, "I love the seashore, don't you? Look at the moon on the water. It's so pretty."

"So are you pretty." He said. He kissed her again, passionately. He forced his tongue past her lips. Her desire heightened with the heat of it and she felt her body responding. He put an exploring hand under her sweater, then onto her thigh and then to her pubis, where he stroked.

I can't do this, said her mind. But her body had other ideas.

He said, "I want you, Josie. Right now."

She whispered, "Gord…I can't…"

He took his hands from her and sat straight. "Josie…I told you once how I was…am, falling for you. You said we had to know each other longer. If I have my way, we're going to be man and wife some day. Some day soon."

"Gord…I'm not ready for talk of marriage. I…"

"Okay," he said, "I won't rush it…but you are beautiful and I believe I'm not exactly, uh, unattractive…am I?"

She smiled. "No. You're quite 'andsome in fact…"

He kissed her, this time starting gently. He explored with his hands again. She knew she should stop him, but did not. When he stroked her again, she couldn't keep from moving her hips with him. She was thinking, *This is wrong! Tell him to stop. Tell him!* Another part of her mind was saying, *Why not? Nobody cares about me, or what I do.*

He whispered, "I want you so bad, Darling. And you want me."

God help me, I do! "Gord…I can't do this. I can't…"

But she did.

The sex wasn't natural or spontaneous. Her mind was screaming, *This is wrong. It's wrong! Forgive me.* Her guilt took all but the physical pleasure from the act.

When he came, he rolled off, zippered his pants and sat up behind the wheel.

Before she knew what she was saying, she blurted, "Are you…are we, um, all done?" Her only other partner had always prolonged the sex and then lay with her afterward, holding her as they whispered of their love.

She sat up. She leaned close and kissed his cheek. "Wasn't it good, Gord?"

"Oh, yeah, it was great! Was it good for you?" He started the car.

"Yes…fine," she replied.

Her mind wouldn't be stilled on the way back to the base. *Would I love to jump on you and do it again,* she thought. *Maybe come more than once—and then lay with you and snuggle up. Laugh with you about our love. Maybe even do it again! We could make up a funny name for your thing. Peter is taken, though. Maybe 'Speedy?' Josie Connor, stop thinking this way! It is mean and wrong!*

With Danny, sex had always been an act of love. She was quite sure this was not. *But perhaps one day…*

She sighed and made herself move closer to him. She pulled her feet up under her and leaned on his shoulder.

When he parked at the base, he asked, "Are we going to do this some more, Josie?"

The directness of the question made her anxious and uneasy about what was coming next.

"I…I don't know. I can't answer that now, Gordon."

He looked straight ahead out the windshield. He had sensed her disquiet, but still pressed the issue. "Are you gonna go back to that guy?"

What is he saying? He's talking about Danny! She said, "What guy do you mean?"

He turned to look at her. "Listen, don't take this wrong, but you know I don't believe in beating around the bush. I heard you were shacked up with a guy. I can't help but wonder why you've been playing so hard to get…when it figures you must really love the screwing. How come we had to go out three times before you came across? You said it was good. You said you liked it."

She was numb. The words hammered at her mind. *Came across? Screwing?* She couldn't answer him right away. *Tanner's horny broad! Tanner's shack-up!*

"Well?" he insisted.

She moved away from him. She was angry. She didn't know if she was angry at Gord, at Danny—or at herself.

She recovered her composure and said. "If I 'ave been with or stayed with someone is no concern of yours. But yes, I did go with a guy steady, a guy I was once close to. That is over now and has nothing to do with you and me. I will appreciate it if you never mention it again. As for my 'loving to screw' as you say it, you are the first since Da...since the other guy. I 'ave to like someone a lot before I'll ever do that with him!" Her mind said, *Is that true, really? Or is he right, and I just "love the screwing?"*

He looked out the windshield again, "Well, aren't you touchy. But I guess you like *me* a lot then!"

She opened the door. *Right now, Gordon Schaefer, I am not so sure. Oh, Josie, Josie!* "Now I have to get in. Good night." She got out of the car.

"Wait! I'm sorry if I hurt your feelings. Get back in for a sec, will you? I want to talk to you about something...something else."

"I do have to go..."

"Two seconds, Josie. Honest." He smiled.

"Okay. Two seconds."

He told her he wanted her to go to Vancouver with him for a weekend at the beginning of April, after payday.

"I'll 'ave to think about it, Gordon...I'll let you know. There's lots of time." She knew he wanted a weekend of "lovemaking." She wasn't sure if she wanted the same.

When she got to her room she was glad Ollie was asleep. Her face burned with anger, embarrassment and frustration. At one moment she regretted having sex with him; at another, she looked forward to doing it again. *Damn you, Danny!* She lay awake for hours, and went down the hall at three A.M to take a warm shower before she was able to sleep.

*   *   *   *

A difference between Gord Schaefer and Danny Tanner, a difference Josie didn't see, was that he was insecure about his sexual image and his insecurity caused him to exaggerate his prowess and success, to himself and to others. He never allowed the truth to hinder a good story and he never worried about a girl's reputation. His mates at the 409 Squadron maintenance hangar were getting a running commentary on his affair with her, in which he claimed he and Josie had had sex just about every night since they met.

Danny and Russ were in the Wets after a day shift, sitting on the men's side. They were still there at six-thirty when Gord and some friends came in and sat at the next table.

Quietly, Russ told Danny who he was.

Danny shrugged, "It's her right to go out with guys, Russ, and it's her life. I don't like it and I wish it were me, but it's not—so best of luck to her. But I don't think I'll hang around here. I'm going somewhere else to drink."

Then they overheard Schaefer.

"I'm telling you, man, she just loves it. She's not happy unless I got my dick in her! She was shacked up with some guy for a few months—the poor guy's likely screwed right out. She's just a little broad but she screws like an amazon."

One of his friends asked, "Is it the broad from the Orderly Room you used to date last year?"

"Yeah, Josie Connor...still wild as hell..."

Before he could say another word, Danny had him off his seat, gripping the front of his tunic. He backhanded him across the face.

Danny snarled, "Are you talking about Josie Connor, you puke?" He drew back his right fist and drove it into Schaefer's face. Two of the friends jumped on him, tried to pull him off. Danny shook them off and drove another right into Gord's face, starting his nose bleeding. Now five or six people helped to subdue him, holding him away.

"Not in here, man!" said one. "Take it outside, you guys."

Danny shouted, "YEAH, COME ON, YOU SON OF A BITCH! COME ON OUTSIDE SO I CAN KILL YOU..."

Gord sat down in his chair, dabbing at his nose and trying to compose himself. "I'm not going outside, creep. What the hell's eating you, anyway?"

Danny lunged at him, but Russ got between them. He had seen the bartender pick up the phone. "It's okay, Champ—he'll get his. He's a coward."

Danny pushed him aside and made another lunge. Schaefer jumped up and put his chair between them. Russ got hold of Danny's collar and managed to hold him back. A couple of bystanders joined Russ and they were able to restrain him.

As he was pulled back, Danny pointed at Gord. "If I...even HEAR of you talking like that about her, you wormy bastard, you're DEAD!"

Gord wouldn't look at him.

Russ said, "Gordo—you do not know how lucky you just were. Josie's a good friend of ours, you prick! If Danny doesn't kill you, I will. That's a promise!" He turned to Danny. "Come on, Champ, let's go find somewhere else to drink, it stinks in here."

They left and went to the barracks where they changed into civvies before heading into Courtenay. Russ knew he had to stick with Danny or he would find Schaefer and put a real beating on him. In town, Danny put away one rye after another, more than Russ had ever seen him drink. They closed the Arbutus lounge, then headed back to the base, with Russ driving the Ford. Back in their room Russ heard Danny quietly sobbing in his bed before he mercifully fell asleep.

*   *   *   *

Josie and Ollie heard about the incident in the Wets the day after it happened, but not what prompted it. It was the talk of the barracks. They heard no mention of what had been said about her.

Ollie said, "The guy loves you, Jo. I know it's not right to go after Gord, but he's not himself…"

Josie's eyes blazed. "Why do you always defend 'im? He's *exactly* himself—it's always his first reaction—to beat somebody up!" She sighed. "Oh, Dieu, poor Gordon—he doesn't deserve this."

"You really like this guy, don't you! Or should I say love him?" said Ollie.

"I don't think I love him. He's nice, and good-looking, and I like him. He says he likes me a lot. He treats me…pretty good. We 'ave made love…well, at least had sex." She looked at the ceiling, then at Ollie. "I just realized something…I suppose I'll have to ask for a posting away from here! I have to get away from this. Do you think they'll give it to me?"

"Jesus, Jo…why? Is it so bad? Could you leave Gord behind just like that?"

"Oh, yes. I think I could leave him." Her next words surprised Ollie. "But can I leave Danny behind? But of course I have to, or he'll destroy me, Ollie!"

She decided she would go to the cabin after work to pick up her belongings.

*   *   *   *

"Son of a *bitch!*" Schaefer looked once again at his image in the mirror. The face looking back at him sported a vivid shiner and a swollen, split lip.

He had been ribbed about it all day at work: "Hey, Schaefer, what does the other guy look like?" or "Did you run into a door?" or "Gord, you been talking when you shoulda been listening again?"

He couldn't even lie about it because some of the guys were with him when that Tanner bastard hit him and challenged him to go outside. He claimed to all he was "sucker punched"—a claim not far from the truth. His face burned with humiliation as he recalled his frozen fear, how he had been afraid to even look at the guy. *Did anyone see how scared I was?* He learned after Danny left the club he was the one Josie Connor had been with before him. He was also told about Danny's reputation as a fighter. A guy named Tuck told him at work that this guy Danny—Danny Tanner was his name—was as tough as they come.

Why did the little...why did she have to have an ex-boyfriend like this guy? Shit! Look at my fucking eye! I'll have to stay in for a week. As well as a braggart and coward, Gord Schaefer was vain. Now he had lost face with his peers and it sat heavy in his gut. *There has to be some way I can get even with the prick.*

*   *   *   *

KYE BAY

It was five o'clock. Danny had been drinking for the better part of the afternoon in the Riverside. He was drunk and had to concentrate to stay on the road as he negotiated the hill down to Kye Bay. The crew was starting a round of graveyard shifts and he came to the cabin to pick up a uniform.

The Dog Pound was parked in the driveway when he arrived so he parked his car on the side of the road. He staggered a little when he got out.

He saw Jake dozing in the driver's seat of the station wagon. He rapped on the roof. Jake jumped and rolled the window down. "Hey, Danny," he said, blinking.

"Hey, Jake, how's it hangin'—you looking for me?"

"No, I gave Josie a lift. She's inside picking up some stuff." He patted the dashboard. "You know me and the Dog Pound, errand boy for all the ladies. She said she wouldn't be in there long. Jeez, you're in fine shape, Dan. I hope you're going to get some sleep before tonight."

"You can take off, Jake, I'll drive her back—I have to go to the base anyway before work."

"You sure? I don't mind waiting..."

"Yeah, I wanted to talk to her anyway...you don't have to wait. See you at midnight."

He watched Jake leave before he went into the cabin. A cardboard carton and her suitcase were on the floor just inside the door. He found Josie in the bedroom. She was still in uniform but had taken off her tunic and tie. She held an armload of clothes she was packing into a carton. She looked up briefly at him, then back to her task, startled at his presence.

"Hello, Jo," he said.

She didn't answer. She concentrated on folding and packing the clothes.

"Not talking?"

She looked up at him again. "Hello, Danny. I didn't expect to see you…" She bent again to her packing. "I won't be 'ere much longer. Jake is waiting for me outside."

He went to the refrigerator and found a beer, said over his shoulder, "Jake's gone. I told him I'll drive you back." He fished in a drawer for a bottle opener.

"Why did you do that, Danny?" She looked exasperated—trapped.

He returned to the bedroom. "I have to go the barracks anyway. Am I allowed to give you a ride, or tell you how great you look—how beautiful?" he tried for The Smile, pried the cap off the bottle and took a swallow.

She said only, "Danny." She closed the flaps on the carton. She started to lift it then changed her mind and picked up her tie.

"Here, I'll get this." He picked up the box.

She protested, "You don't 'ave to…"

"Hey, no problem." He carried it to the front door. He put it on top of the other one. When he returned to the bedroom, she was sitting on the bed, staring straight ahead. "You didn't answer my question, am I allowed or not?" he said.

"Danny, let's not talk now, okay?"

He started to show his hurt. "Bullshit! I just want an answer. Is it *allowed* to tell her frigging highness how good she looks? How she's still the best looking girl I ever knew?" he finished the beer and put the bottle on the dresser. "Well?"

She was still sitting. Her eyes flashed anger. "Do you tell that to Chrissy when you go to Vancouver? How about Bobby, did you tell 'er too, Danny?" She looked away at the wall.

"I should have known you'd bring up the Bobby shit again—I'll never regret it enough, will I? And Chrissy was before I ever knew you. You know that!"

"Oh, yes, because you told me so—a liar told me so."

"And then there's your Gord, now there's a real prize! Get rid of him, Jo. You can do better, he has no respect for you…"

"Don't *you* talk about respect for me! Because of you I'm lucky if *anybody* 'as any respect for me. And don't talk about Gord, after trying to beat him up! But I should have been ready for that, shouldn't I!"

"Josie, he's no good…"

She cut him off. "Oh, *shut up* Danny!" She got up from the bed. She shook her head. "Will you just take me back to the base, please." She went to get past him at the door.

He blocked her way. "Jo, Honey…this is your Danny. We shouldn't fight in here. This is where we make love!"

"Where we *used to* make love, you mean. Please let me by..."

He grasped her arm. "Can't we talk?"

"About what? It 'as all been said. Let me go." She pulled free from him.

Still blocking the door, he took her by both arms, not roughly, and asked, "Not even a kiss, Jo? A goodbye kiss? We never did do that, you know." He placed a hand on the back of her head, pulled her to him, and put his lips to hers.

For just a second she wanted to press her body against him and melt into his arms. Then, suddenly aware of what was happening, she twisted her face away from him. She tried to push past him but he tightened his grip and forced her face around and kissed her again. She tried to pull free but this time he was too strong. She submitted to the kiss passively, mouth closed and eyes open, determined not to encourage him.

He realized she wasn't participating and broke off the kiss. "Jesus, you can be a bitch, Josie."

She twisted from him and, ducking under an outstretched arm, got past. She was frightened and confused. At the front door, she remembered she no longer had a ride. He was still standing at the bedroom door.

She turned back to him. "Danny, we can talk another time—when you haven't been drinking. I promise we will. It's no good like this You get...you know, when you drink...I promise I will talk to you later. Now, could you please drive me to the station?" She picked up one of the cartons.

He stepped toward her. "Jo...Honey...we used to make love, right here! Jesus, we were *in love* here! Do you hate me so much now? No way! We love each other—you know it! What we had just can't end like this." He felt a burning in his eyes.

She walked toward him, still holding the carton. "No! Danny! I don't 'ate you. But you must face the fact—what we *had* is all over. You ruined it...*it's over.*"

Something snapped in Danny when he heard those words. A roaring started in his head. He slapped the carton from her hands to the floor. He grasped the top of her blouse and jerked it open. Buttons popped and the bodice gave way. Her brassiere was exposed and one strap snapped. The force of it caused her to stumble forward against him. He grabbed her arms and shook her like a rag doll, in his passion forgetting his strength. His grip on her arms was like a vise.

He shouted, "LISTEN TO ME, JOSIE...THIS IS DANNY! YOUR DANNY! YOU LOVE ME AND I LOVE YOU! CAN'T YOU UNDERSTAND? WE BELONG TOGETHER...JO, I LOVE YOU..."

His voice wavered. The roaring stopped. Quietly, he said, "Shit, Jo, I love you…" He let go of her. He had to turn away from the terrible hurt and fear in her eyes.

She stepped back, clutching at her blouse. In a dead voice he had never heard, she said, "You hurt me…you hurt my arms." He had never before touched her in anger. She rubbed her arms where he had grabbed her. "How can you say you *love* me?" She backed quickly away from him. She could not believe what just happened.

He fell to his knees before her. "I'm sorry. Forgive me Josie!" he sobbed. "Oh Jesus, Jo…I never, never want to hurt you. You…you make me crazy!"

She lifted her suitcase to the table, took out another blouse, took the torn one off and threw it to the floor. As she buttoned the new blouse, leaving the ruined brassiere on, she said. "How can a boy who loved his mother like you did…who helps people…jumps in frozen lakes to save kids…'ow can you do *this* and call me Honey! How can you say you love me?" When she closed the case, she sighed, lifted her arms and let them drop to her sides. "Oh, just go to 'ell! I pity you, Danny." She went to the door, leaving her boxes and suitcase behind. Before shutting the door, she looked back at him through her tears and sobbed, "See you."

She swiped at her eyes as she ran to Lorna and Leo's cabin. She would get Leo to drive her.

After she left, Danny stood up. He didn't move from the spot. He spoke in a whisper to the empty space where she had last stood before closing the door, "Forgive me, Josie, please forgive me." Then once again, "Forgive me."

When there was a knock a few minutes later, he didn't hear it. He still stood in the same place. Leo opened the door, glanced his way, and bent to pick up the suitcase and a carton by the door. He said, "She wanted me to get her stuff, Dan…"

"Yeah, okay, Leo." He indicated the carton at his feet. "There's another one here." He didn't move.

After Leo left, he stood for over half an hour, staring at the door and then went to the refrigerator, took out a Pepsi, got a part-full bottle of rye and a glass from the cupboard and poured a strong drink. He poured the balance of the rye down the drain. He took the three remaining bottles of Lucky Lager and poured them after the rye.

Carrying the drink, he went to the bedroom door and looked in. He shuddered, as a man finding himself in a morgue. There were tears streaming down his face. He wandered through the cabin, touching objects as he went. He completed two full circuits of the place, then sat in her favorite easy chair, absently fingering the material of the arm. He remembered how she looked there, small and childlike, seeming to take up just a corner of the chair. He took a long swallow of the drink. He finished it in two more swallows and stood. He saw the blouse on the floor, picked it up and went back to the bedroom. There was a palpable ache in his belly. He lay on the bed, curled in the fetal position, clutched her blouse to his breast, and sobbed.

It was the lowest day in his life.

*   *   *   *

Ollie wasn't in the room when Josie returned to the barracks.

She started to unpack a carton from the cabin. When she opened the closet she spotted the parka Danny gave her for Christmas. She took it from its hanger. She went down the stairs to Nicole St. Pierre's room.

When Nicky came to the door, she said, "Nicky—you were admiring this." She threw the parka on a bed. "Here, you can 'ave it...it's yours."

Nicky was stunned. "Oh, Josie, do you mean it?"

"I do. I don't want it and it might as well get some use."

"Thank you, I..."

"It's okay, Nicky, enjoy it." She turned and walked out.

*   *   *   *

Danny was still on the bed when Leo pounded on the cabin door and stuck his head inside.

He called, "You in here, Dan?" receiving no reply, he came in. He looked in the bedroom, went in and poked Danny's shoulder. "Hey, are you awake?"

Danny stirred. He sat up on the bed, swung his feet over the side. Tears were still wet on his face.

"Leo, what's up?" he managed.

"Russ called our place from work. You're supposed to be there."

"What time is it?"

"It's about one-thirty."

He repeated, "One-thirty." He appeared bewildered. "I'm on graveyards, right?" He was sluggish. He got up, moving aimlessly. "I...I don't have my uniform here, do I?" He looked around, perplexed.

"Damned if I know. You'd better sit down again. Will you be in trouble?"

He sat. "Um, no…yeah…maybe…can I use your phone?" He was feeling around under the bed. He mumbled "My shoes…"

"Your shoes are on your feet. Stand up—are you drunk?"

He shook his head.

Leo looked skeptical. "Oh yeah, I'm not so sure. Come on, you can use the phone."

The walk across the yard cleared his head. It also made him recall what he had done. He phoned 51 and asked for Ellen. He told her he was feeling sick and had overslept.

Ellen said, "No sweat, Danny. I'll cover—I'll grease it with Donahue—hell, you can do no wrong in his eyes, anyway. It's our last shift, so relax and get to bed. I hope it doesn't screw up your days off."

If you only knew.

"Thanks a million, Ellen, I owe you."

"No you don't—get back to bed. Get better!"

He stared out a window after he hung up the phone, then joined Leo at the kitchen table.

"I don't have to work…"

Leo said, "You need a drink, pal. Name your poison. It's rye, isn't it?"

"Yeah…thanks." He took the offered glass but didn't drink. "Is all this gonna wake Lorna up?"

"No, she's okay. I delivered Jo-jo and her stuff to the barracks. Do you want to talk about what's going on with you two? If it's none of my business, just say so. But if I can help…"

"That's okay, Leo." He took a sip of the drink, then looked at it in alarm. He pushed it at Leo. "No! Oh, shit, no more booze…I'm sorry, I shouldn't have taken it…"

Leo took the glass from him. "Don't worry about it, it's only liquor. If you've had enough, you've had enough." He put the glass on the kitchen counter.

"Leo—I've screwed up—I've lost her. I've lost it all. It was so good. She's so good."

*   *   *   *

Gord called Josie and told her his version of his confrontation with Danny. He said he loved her, then he didn't call for three days. She was tempted to call him but decided to wait for him to make a move. She told herself she had already once in her life pushed herself into a relationship that turned out to be a disaster. She would let this one take its course.

*   *   *   *

On the day after Josie gave away her parka, Ollie and Russ were talking in the snack bar.

"Damn that Tanner," said Ollie.

Russ asked, "Okay, okay, so tell me what my chum did this time..."

"Shit-all-to-hell, Russ, you don't go beating someone up, just because he's dating your ex-girlfriend! It's as if he's gone totally out of control."

"What're you talking about?" He was afraid Danny had tracked down Schaefer.

"You know what I mean, him smacking Gord Schaefer in the Wets because he's seeing Jo. Didn't you hear about it?"

"Wait a goddam minute, Babe. I'm not happy with Dan myself right now, but that is *not* the way it happened! I was there and I know what went on."

"You were there? What went on, then?"

He told her what happened.

"Gord talked like that? About Jo? Are you sure?"

"I told you I was there, didn't I? Just because we're not happy with Danny is no reason to forget he's our friend. And a damn good friend. You and I—Josie, too for that matter—all three of us have had reason to be damn glad he's our friend. I hope the hell you're not forgetting it. The guy's having a tough time and he might have screwed up, but he's our friend and he truly loves Josie. What he did is what any good man would do."

"I see. We heard an altogether different version. By we, I mean Jo and I."

"Well, I can see how you'd believe it. He's not an easy guy to like right now. And the drinking isn't helping." He shook his head. "I was so damn happy for him before all this—for both of them. Shit!"

"Should I tell Josie the real story?"

"Won't hurt, might help," said Russ.

"You know, you're right about his friendship. I hadn't thought about it, I guess because *she's* been such a friend. Thanks for showing me that." She put her hands on his and said with a smile, "You're not so dumb, Knight."

"Dan doesn't know what way to turn—what way's up," Russ said. "He knows damn well the drinking is making it worse but he can't face himself when he's sober. He loves her too much to just forget her and go find some other woman.

He's convinced he can get her back, yet does all the wrong things. He doesn't believe what they had is gone. It's tough on him. And something else, Ollie—there's no way Danny Tanner *ever* had a bad thing to say about Josie. Like about them sleeping together—you and I were the only people he ever admitted that to, and it was Jo who first told us, not him. He would deny it till hell freezes to protect her name, even after they moved into the cabin and it was common knowledge! He sure as hell ain't gonna let some low-life like Schaefer get away with it."

"He's not so bad, Russ...you disliked him from the first time you met him."

"Yeah, and I was right—talking like he did about Josie proves he's no good. You didn't hear it. If it weren't for Jo, I'd lay a beating on him myself. Danny still might do that, if I can't stop him."

"Yeah, but it sure won't help him with Josie. She says he's always too ready to beat someone up."

Russ was thoughtful. "I'm going to tell him that. It may save Schaefer's life. It could even score some points with Jo." He sighed. "Do you think there's any way she would ever want him back?"

"I don't think so. I hope I'm wrong, but I'm afraid it's kaput. She's been hurt too much, Russ. But it doesn't mean she'll ever stop loving him."

"Shit!" said Russ.

Ollie said, "There's something else. If I tell you about it will you promise to keep it under your hat?"

"Sure...what is it?"

"You won't say a word? To Dan or anyone else."

"Ollie, you know I won't. I just said so."

"Okay. She has applied for a transfer. Our Sergeant showed me the memo and asked me if I knew what was going on. I convinced her to sit on it for a while...it's in her desk drawer, and isn't going anywhere unless Jo presses the matter. Sergeant Wilson has her neck out a mile."

"Shit!"

*   *   *   *

When Ollie told Josie what had occurred between Danny and Gord, she said, "Are you sure that's right, Ollie? Gord told me it was just because he's seeing me."

"Jo, come with me."

"Where?"

"Just to the phone, come on."

"Why, Ollie?"

Ollie was already in the hall. "You'll see, trust me. Come *on*!" She phoned Russ at 51. "Russ, I'm going to put Josie on. She wants the truth about the other night in the Wets." She passed the receiver to Josie.

When Josie hung up, she looked vacantly at Ollie. She said, "It's not true. You and Russ are lying for the bastard."

Ollie had a revelation. "You don't *want* to hear the truth! You don't want to give yourself any damn reason to go back to him, do you! That is just stupid, and it's unfair. It's unfair to yourself, Jo." She shook her head. "And Josie—please don't ever call Dan Tanner a bastard in my company again. I've come to realize he's a damn good friend and I won't have it. Not even from you. He's having a bad time, but he's still Danny. As for you, kid, you'd better start figuring out who *your* friends are."

"I once thought *you* were my friend, said Josie coldly. "Fine, Ollie, you go ahead and lie for him. There are things he has done to me you don't know about." She walked out of the room.

The next morning she informed Ollie she was moving to another room. After work she moved her belongings into Nicky St. Pierre's room.

CHAPTER 26

▼

I knew I must change—I prayed it wasn't too late...

MARCH, 1956

When Danny pushed that glass of whiskey back at Leo, he began a transformation. He made a solemn promise to himself—and silently to Josie—to make himself worthy of her. He knew what she wanted of him was no more than she deserved; for if ever there was a person on this earth without fault, it was his Josie.

Determined to be patient, he first had to fight down the real fear she would find love with another man. (A thing he had read by Emerson came to mind: *'What torments of grief you endured, from evils that ne'er arrived.'* Evils he hoped would never arrive!)

With that fear subdued—but not vanquished—he set about to change. He did so with no illusions. He had no idea how long she would abide but he instinctively refused to believe she had given up on them altogether. He trusted Russ and Ollie to point out to her the worthlessness of Gord Schaefer and prayed she would heed them before it was too late. He told himself if it was not in the cards for him to have her, he could be happy for her if she found a good man. Schaefer was not that man.

As he fought his way out of his private wilderness he asked no one for help. He knew going it alone would make his task tougher, but that would be his sackcloth, and the result would be tempered by his effort. He eventually did get support and advice from Russ, Ollie and Leo, not sought but gratefully received. Of their friends only Lorna Letourneau didn't support him, believing what he had done to Josie was unforgivable. He began to get together with Ollie and Russ more frequently, and those two made it their mission to keep him up to date on Josie.

He decided to keep the cabin till the end of April. It had been a symbol of them as a couple and now it would be his refuge. He spent much of his off-duty time there, knocking off his Grade 12 mathematics and reading Book of the Month Club issues that had been piling up. The telephone Josie ordered arrived and he decided to keep it, reflecting, *She'd like that if she ever comes back. Small thing, I suppose, for the cows have long gone, but she will like it—if. And with it here I won't have to face Lorna's scorn when I need to make calls.*

Certainly there were moments when he came close to chucking it all and straying; heading to the Wets or into town, but he acknowledged, without reservation, that their problems were a result of his drinking and what went with it, and that brought him back on course. Whenever things seemed to be too much, the weight unbearable, he walked the beach at Kye Bay.

Now and then he did meet with friends, usually declining offers to drink or at most having one beer. He kept some cold beers at the cabin for Russ and Leo when they visited. He was surprised and inwardly proud when he discovered a dozen could last him three weeks!

Without telling anyone, he bought a diamond engagement ring. He carried it with him everywhere in its little maroon velvet box.

With this new attitude, he realized now that he had handled the problem of Evelyn's pregnancy poorly, and all his agonizing over the paternity had been because of uncertainty. He must know for sure whether or not he was the father, before he—or Josie, if she were ever inclined to do so—could deal with it. It was time to face the music!

He would have to go to Vancouver and confront Evelyn again.

He went to the Pollard's house as soon as he arrived in Ladner. After ringing the doorbell, he had second thoughts and almost fled from the porch. Before he could run, however, Evelyn's mother opened the door.

"Why, Danny, what a nice surprise! What brings you to Vancouver? Won't you come in..." She called to the interior of the house, "Jake, look who's here. Come in, come in, Danny."

"Thanks, Mrs. Pollard. I-I hope I'm not intruding..."

"Nonsense," said Jake Pollard as he strode across the living room, "we're happy to see you Dan!" Indicating the sofa, he said, "Grab a seat, Dan. I don't know about you, but I'm ready for a beer—must be five o'clock somewhere, eh. How about it?"

Danny sat. He didn't want to drink a beer in the middle of the day, but said, "A beer sounds good, Mr. Pollard."

"Call me Jake, Dan."

Mrs. Pollard said, "I'm afraid if you're here to see Evelyn, she's not here. You didn't know she moved out?

"No I didn't know. Moved?"

"Afraid so. You see, our Evelyn got herself in trouble..."

Arriving from the kitchen with two beers, Pollard said, "She means pregnant, Dan. Women always find it hard to say that word, so they say stuff like 'trouble' or 'in-the-family-way' and such." He chuckled. "She refused to tell us who the father is, so of course we had a bloody great family row."

"Now she says she's going to go away to have the baby," said Mrs. Pollard. "She talks about going to Calgary. I hope she means to give it up for adoption."

Her husband declared, "Hell, she can accomplish all that right here in Vancouver. I think I was a bit too hard on her when I found out...fathers forget their little girls grow up. She's twenty-four, after all, and everyone's entitled to make a mistake. I've been trying to tell her it's okay, but she's scared, and her feelings are hurt."

"Has she left? For Calgary, I mean."

Mrs. Pollard shook her head. "Not yet."

"Do you have a phone number for her?" Danny asked.

Mrs. Pollard looked guiltily at her husband, "Yes. I'll get it. It's in my purse."

"We do?" said Pollard, "First I heard about it."

With some irritation, she said, "She didn't want you to know, Jake. Can you blame her? I begged her to give it to me, in case there's an emergency. I'll get it for you, Danny."

*   *   *   *

"Hello."

"Evelyn...it's Danny."

"Oh. Hello Danny. How are you?"

"I'm okay, Ev, how about you?"

"You know how I am, Danny. How did you get this number?"

"I saw your Mom. Any, um, complications?"

"Complications? Oh, you mean the pregnancy. Actually, no, it's been a good pregnancy, if being pregnant and single can be good, that is." She chuckled and he could hear the irony. "Still two and a half months to go, but so far so good." Her voice sounded harder than he remembered it.

He didn't know what to say. This was very uncertain ground. She said, "I am glad you called, because there's some things I must say to you. I don't want to see you, though, and don't want you to see me; for one thing I'm fat as a pig. But mostly I'm embarrassed—more like ashamed. I tried to do a terrible thing to you, Danny. I'll tell you right now; and this is the truth...after our last time together I had periods, menstrual periods. Do you understand what that means?"

It took him a moment to answer. "Yes."

"It means you couldn't have been the father of this baby."

"I know."

Bitterly, she said, "Well, I'm glad you know something. *I* don't even know who the fucking father of the baby is! As you've heard, I had a hell of a lot of fun after you left, I think I was trying to screw every man at Jericho, even slept with a married negro. Anyway, I've been trying to work up the courage to phone you to tell you this. Courage hasn't been my strongest suit lately, so it's good that you called me. You're safe, Danny—the timing's all wrong and you were long gone, my friend. And by the way, I did not tell Daddy that it was you...he still thinks you're a saint and who am I to disillusion him. The truth is you and I would never have worked anyway. I swear one of us would have killed the other before another year went by. The weirdest thing is, when I wrote to you and tried to trap you it wasn't because I wanted you; in fact I hated your guts. At that time I wanted nothing more than to ruin your life."

"Aw, Ev, I was pretty rotten to you..."

She cut him off, "Like I said, we wouldn't have worked. Beyond the not bad sex, there really wasn't anything else, was there? But, all in all, you're a decent enough guy, and I hope I haven't already ruined things for you."

"Know what? You have just proved you're pretty decent yourself, Ev."

"Yeah, yeah. Have a good life, Danny. Good bye."

She broke the connection.

*   *   *   *

Back at Comox, he decided to tell Ollie about what had transpired. He started with the letter from Evelyn and ended with his latest trip to Ladner.

"Can I tell Jo about it? It'll explain a lot for her. I think it's what had you so screwed up in the first place, isn't it?"

"Yes, tell her. Like I should have done months ago."

"You need the points, Big Guy."

"Christ, don't I know it."

*   *   *   *

Ollie next suggested to Danny that he answer Josie's letter, even though many weeks had gone by. He hesitated to do so, believing she would take whatever he said as just more promises.

Ollie pressed. "No, make it clear you *don't* promise anything. Apologize for what you did wrong and explain the rest! Show her she has some wrong info. Shit, she's probably secretly hoping to hear from you—she actually felt bad for you when I told her what happened with that Evelyn. I'll help you write it if you want."

Russ joined her. "I think it's a good idea, Champ. At the very least, you can give her your version of things—like why you smacked Schaefer in the Wets. She may not believe everything, but at least she'll have to wonder. It might just make her stop and think before making any, uh, other commitments. But you'll have to be totally straight with her." Then he gibed, "And it'll show her you've actually learned how to write, too."

Ollie ticked off the things Josie was concerned about as she knew them—Bobby Gaines, Chrissy, his attack on Gord, staying out all night, and whatever had happened between them at the cabin. She said with an ironic smile, "It's a long list, Tanner. You have a lot to answer for—I'm not so sure you *deserve* her forgiveness."

He wrote the letter.

Ollie read the finished product when he handed it over to her to deliver. He thought it too long but she said it was just right. She put it in an office envelope and typed Josie's name on it, then dropped it on her desk when she was out delivering files.

Josie found it when she returned. Ollie watched from her desk as she slid the letter partly out and recognized Danny's writing. Ollie was dismayed when she threw into a wastebasket—but a minute later she saw her take it out and put it into her purse.

When Josie's coffee break came she went outside and around to the rear of the HQ building to be alone. It was a cool day, one of the last of winter. Fine drizzle was falling, barely wetting her shoulders. She opened the envelope and leaned on the building as she read. When she finished she stared off into space, barely noticing when the letter fell from her fingers. After a few seconds she bent to pick it up and had a moment of panic when she didn't see it at once. She found it where it had blown against a chain link fence ten feet away, picked it up and read it again. It was written on two sides of a sheet of loose-leaf paper.

He opened by stating he was writing because she wouldn't take his phone calls and he wanted to clarify some truths, adding: *I do not expect you to come running back to me because of anything I write here. I make no promises Josie—you have good reason to believe any promise from me is empty. I can only say I am trying. There is just not enough ink to tell you how sorry I am for every time I ever hurt you, in all the big and small ways.*

He spared himself not at all when he wrote about him and Bobby: *There is no excuse. The fact we were both drunk does not make it right. Bobby and I were both ashamed when we realized what we had done, she demanded I drive her to the station right away. Don't hate her—I am the one at fault—I betrayed our love and that is unforgivable.*

About Chrissy: *Chistine Manson had left Vancouver before I went there. She and I were over when I started seeing you.*

About Evelyn: *Josie, you are the girl I want to be with for the rest of my life and I could lose you because I might have made someone else pregnant. It was not mine, but I didn't know that then. She threatened to tell you. She threatened to take legal action. I thought I could have been forced to marry her. I was so afraid I couldn't function. How could I tell you? Would you ever understand?*

About Gord Schaefer he wrote, *I will never be ashamed, nor will I apologize for hitting him to stop the filthy things he said about you. He is no good, Jo. If this letter accomplishes just one thing, I wish it to be that you have nothing more to do with him!*

And about hurting her at the cabin: *I shall always carry the shame of putting my hands on you in anger—shaking and hurting my Josie like I did. When I saw the hurt and fear in your eyes I wanted to die!*

He knew Ollie and Russ had told her about his efforts to improve. *I had to change, Josie, for us to ever have a chance. The way I was behaving wrecked what we had, and what we had was so good! You may not be interested, but I have finished my Grade 12 math at last. (Even the cursed geometry!) I am determined to be worthy of you—it's slow going, but I hope you can just find it in your heart to wait.*

He concluded: *I do love you. I love you as much as any man can love a woman. I believe you love me, too. If you do not, then phone or write to me and tell me so—just say Danny, I do not love you! Then I will believe it and never bother you again. I want only for you to be happy. If it is to be without me, so be it and I will love your memory forever.*

I hope, pray, you will read this. For us. It is the truth.

*   *.   *   *

Josie stood holding the damp page. She looked up at the leaden sky. *Oh, Danny—is it? Is it the truth?* She folded the letter and put it back in her purse.

The letter succeeded in doing just what Ollie hoped; it planted the seeds of doubt.

After supper Josie took the letter and went to Bobby's room, where she found Bobby alone.

She said stiffly, "Bobby, I 'ave a question…"

"Sure, Jo. Anything."

She handed Bobby the letter. "Is this part about Danny and you the truth? Right here…"

Bobby scanned the letter. "Yes, Jo. It is the truth. My part wasn't as innocent as this, though. But that's so typical of him, isn't it?" She handed the letter back. With teary eyes she said, "Jo…I-I'm so ashamed…"

Josie placed a hand on her arm. "Don't be, Bobby it happened. You are sure this is true?"

"Every word," she said emphatically.

"There were no other times?"

"No!" cried Bobby. "God Jo, no!"

"Thank you, Bobby." She smiled and said, "I want…I would like us to be friends again. Could we?"

Bobby nodded. She couldn't speak.

Next, Josie phoned 5 Air Div and asked for Chrissy Manson. She was told there was no longer an L.A.W. Christine Manson at Jericho. She hung up quickly and stared at the phone for several seconds.

Too many stories matched; his and Bobby's, Chrissy not even at Jericho any more, and what Russ and now Danny had to say about the fight with Gord. He just might have told the truth about all of it!

She anguished. *Can I trust this, Danny? I want to so much. I just don't want to be hurt any more.*

She phoned Gord Schaefer and told him she must talk to him and wanted to meet him later. She wanted to confront him about what he said about her. He told her he would see her in the Mess Hall for supper. When she went for supper at four-thirty he wasn't there. She waited around till the mess closed at six o'clock. Assuming he was stuck at work or forgot about meeting her, she phoned his barracks but was told he wasn't in. She never saw him at the Mess Hall or the

Wets in the next two days. She phoned several times but never reached him and he didn't return the calls.

*   *   *   *

When Ollie decided to do some investigating of her own, she had no way of knowing Josie had already been checking on Danny's letter. She had been understandably hurt when Josie moved from their room, but it hadn't lessened her affection for her Little Buddy. She had started to suspect that Josie might just be looking for a reason to at least see Danny again. She understood Josie's hurt over the Bobby Gaines thing, but she accepted both Bobby and Danny's assertions of the circumstances and that it had been just the one time. She decided she would try to get confirmation of what she believed. She would talk to Bobby again, and she would somehow get the facts about Chrissy and Danny's trip to Vancouver.

She was pleased when Bobby told her about Josie's recent visit. When Bobby told her about the renewal of their friendship, she declared, "That puts you one ahead of me, Gaines." She saw the significance of the visit—Josie was having doubts. *So, Kiddo, you're checking, too!*

She phoned an acquaintance in the Orderly Room at Jericho to confirm Chrissy's departure date. She was given Chrissy's civilian address. When Ollie asked about a civilian employee named Evelyn Pollard, the story was recounted for her.

"Thanks, Janet, I owe you a beer. It was good talking to you."

"It's nothing, Olivia, I knew Dan when he was here. I liked him."

Next she wrote to Chrissy in Medicine Hat, Alberta:

13/3/5

Dear Christine,

My name is Olivia Conti. I met you last June with my friends, Josie Connor and Danny Tanner, when we were in Vancouver for Danny's fastball tournament. I introduced myself to you after a game when the team got together at the Wets in Jericho. I hope you will remember us—we got lost when I drove us in Danny's car to the wrong side of the airport when we were looking for the ball field. I remember how badly you felt about it.

Josie and Danny are the best friends I have—or ever could have. They do not know I am writing to you. They are breaking-up (and breaking their hearts) over something I believe you can straighten out.

Something happened in January and caused Danny to travel over to Vancouver. I think you know something about this. If you do, please write to me at:

> L.A.W. Olivia Conti,
>
> R.C.A.F. Station Comox,
>
> Comox, B.C.

Any help you can give me to get to the bottom of this may rescue J and D's wonderful relationship. I am afraid something truly awful will happen if we don't do something quickly. Could you also tell me what date you left Vancouver to move to Medicine Hat?

Chrissy, please write to me as soon as possible.

Your hopeful friend,

Olivia Conti

Chrissy's reply arrived promptly on the eighteenth:

Dear Olivia,

I received your letter yesterday on the 16 of March. It was nice to here from you. Of coarse I remember you and Josie really good. You wear both very pretty girls and nice too. Please pardon my awfull writting and spelling I'm not very good for writting letters as a mater of fact I am terrible. So Please phone me so I can tell it to you instead. You can make a colect call if you want or you can pay for it. please phone me quick becouse I want to help those people too Olivia. It was on January 5 when I left Jericho.

Signed
Christine Manson

Ps (I must be stupit) my phone number is—Evergreen 6442 it is in medicine hat were you wrote to me. Im usally home between 3 and 5 o'clock.

Ollie phoned her right after work.

"Hello."

"Is this Christine?"

"Yes…who is this?"

"Christine, it's Olivia. I wrote to you about…"

"About Danny and Josie. Thanks for calling me. I'm sorry about my writing…can you believe I was great in Math and Science but I still can't spell good enough to write a letter? Please call me Chrissy, Olivia. What do you need to know?"

"Call me Ollie, it's the name Danny stuck me with. Would you be willing to tell Josie, about those dates? She thinks you and Danny still had something going while he was going with her. She thinks he went to see you over there a week after New Years. But you weren't even still there, were you?"

"No, I wasn't. I checked on the date, after I got your letter. I got away one day early because of our days off. I left there on the fifth. I didn't know Danny was coming over—I would have loved to see him before I left." She paused for a second. "Oh! Oh, gosh! Not *that way*…I mean just as a *friend!*"

Ollie laughed. "Yeah, Chrissy, don't make things even more complicated! So, you're sure you left on the fifth."

"I'm positive. I looked on my ticket from the train."

"Why did you phone him in December?"

"I had to warn him about somebody who was trying to make trouble for him."

"Okay, Danny told me about that. Was it about a girl named Evelyn?"

"Yes. She's a civilian. She was claiming Danny made her pregnant, but he didn't. It was somebody else…I'm pretty sure I know who it was."

After a pause, Ollie said, "Chrissy, I thank you so much for this."

"It's okay, I like Danny, he's a great guy…the best! You should make sure Josie knows it. We went out on dates a lot when he was here but I, you know…*like* him, too."

"I understand. Would you be willing to tell all this to Josie?"

"I sure would! Put her on."

"She's not here right now…but we might call you. Thank you again, Chrissy."

"You don't have to thank me, Ollie," said Chrissy. "Look, I have to leave for work soon, so if we're finished I better go."

"Okay, Good bye, Chrissy."

*   *   *   *

When Ollie knocked on Josie's door Nicole answered. "Hello, Ollie…"

"Nicky, Is Josie here? I need to talk to her."

"Come in."

Josie was at the dresser, writing. Ollie saw she had lost more weight.

When she saw her, Josie said, "Ollie. It's good to see you." She turned the paper she was writing on face down.

"Hi, Buddy. Can we talk…alone?"

Nicky said, "I'll leave, if you…"

Josie said, "No Nicky, it's okay. We'll go out in the hall."

In the hall, she said, "Let's go to our…I mean your room."

Ollie looked at her as they walked. "Jesus, Jo…you're damn skinny!"

"I 'aven't been sleeping so good, or eating…" She looked down. "Does it show so bad?"

In the room, she asked, "No roommate yet, Ollie?"

"I'm waiting for my old one to come back."

"Oh."

"You're welcome back anytime, you know."

Again, she said only, "Oh."

"I mean it—whenever you're ready."

Josie didn't comment. "What did you want to talk about?" she asked.

Ollie said, "Here, let's sit. I hope you can stay for a few minutes…"

"I can." They sat on the unused bed. Josie smiled and said. "Okay, *shoot!*"

"First, did you read Danny's letter?"

"Yes. I did read it. He explained some things. I don't know what to think…"

"He told the truth, Jo. All of it's true!"

"About Bobby I know. I talked to her. It's still not right, what they did, but I do believe her when she says it was only once. She feels so bad about it…" Her voice trailed.

Ollie began, "I have proof you're wrong about Chrissy. I talked to her on the phone today—she's in Alberta. She left Vancouver on January *fifth*—even earlier than Danny said. She would have already been home in Alberta by the time he got to Van. I have her phone number. You should phone her…"

"It won't be necessary. I-I don't need to, if you spoke to her I believe you. So…she wasn't even in Vancouver?"

"She wasn't. Thank you for believing me, it means a lot to me." She paused, "Then, that pregnant bitch who wasn't pregnant. How about her?"

"If he had just *told* me. I would 'ave taken any baby that was his and been happy to be its mother! Doesn't he *know* that about me? He should know that.

And that could 'ave happened to me, you know…one little slip is all it would take."

"Apparently he was just too damn scared of losing you to think straight. Next, do you believe Danny about Gord Schaefer?"

"I don't know…" She put her face in her hands, shook her head back and forth. "I don't know. I don't want to believe that about Gord. I just don't know!"

"Jo, you *do* know. If I accomplish nothing else this day, I want to get you away from Schaefer!"

"I just don't know, Ollie." She looked up forlornly. "If 'e *did* say something bad about me, is it so terrible? I'm not an angel, you know. I'm not so good I can't be talked about. I just don't *know*." Ollie saw tears on her face and it was just natural for her to put an arm around her.

"Okay, forget him for now. About Danny, you told me there was something else he did to you. Want to tell me?"

"He hurt me." She sat up straight, wiped her tears.

"I know…he broke your heart, and it was wrong of him. He knows it was…"

"No. Not that way. I mean, um, physically."

"Are you saying he's *hit* you?"

"No, he hurt my arms. I went to get my stuff at the cabin, to bring it here. It was right after he hit Gord…I think the next day or two days after. He showed up there and he was drunk, and bitter. I told him we were through and he went kind of crazy. He didn't hit me but he grabbed my arms…hard! And he shook me." She didn't mention the torn blouse. "Danny never hurt me before, Ollie. See, I'm still bruised." She pulled up her sleeves.

Ollie couldn't help but smile. "Shook you. The bastard!"

Josie said, "It's not *funny*, Ollie—it hurt!" Then she had to smile. She wiped at the tears. "Well, it did!"

"Of course it did, kid. What hurt most, your arms, or him *doing* that to you?"

Josie bowed her head. "You know."

"Can you forgive him for it?"

"Of course. But there's other things…out all night, leaving me all alone…"

"He *is* trying to change. He blames himself for everything, and rightfully I suppose. Shit-all-to-hell, he doesn't even drink! Jo, he's trying hard and he's doing it for you."

Josie looked straight at her. "Is he really trying? I 'ave heard it all before, you know. Many times, and so many promises. It's why I left. What happens if I go back to him, Ollie? I *have* a guy now. It doesn't matter if I don't love him as much as Danny. I have a guy and I think he likes me…maybe *more* than likes.

Anyway, the truth is I don't need *any* guy, do I? If Gord doesn't work out, it won't be the end of the world. I applied for a transfer. Sergeant Wilson said nothing will 'appen till the summer."

Ollie chose not to pursue the subject. "Well, kid—you'll have to make the choice to leave. Nobody else can make it for you, can they? And I won't say any more about Gord. If you think can be happy with *him*, fine." She smiled. "Let's not talk about it anymore today, okay? How about a game of Rummy?"

Josie shook her head.

"C'mon, chickenshit, one game! You don't want anyone else to see those red eyes, so stay here for a little while."

"One game."

When Josie returned to her own room, she was up five games to two.

*   *   *   *

Danny learned on the twenty-third of March he was being sent on T.D. to Victoria for a week, starting Monday the thirtieth. Moe Morrisey had requested through the Sector Commander to have Danny on loan for the project. He would be working with Moe and Red Hodgkins, briefing Air Force Reserve units from across B.C. They would bring the Reserves up to scratch on equipment and procedures currently used at AC&W Stations, so they could update their training. Moe wanted him to meet them at a motel in Victoria on Sunday afternoon, the twenty-ninth, to "put our heads together" and be prepared for Monday. They would meet there at two-thirty.

*   *   *   *

On Friday, the twenty-seventh, Josie took her morning coffee break with Ollie. They sat at what had always been their favorite corner table, out of earshot of the rest of the room.

Ollie said, "Hey, this is like old times, Jo. By the way, your color's better today."

Josie smiled. "We've 'ad some good talks right here, haven't we? And that's what I want to do now. There are two questions I want to ask you." She was trying to be business-like.

Ollie looked at her expectantly. She sensed that Josie had come to a turning point.

When she didn't answer, Josie grinned, "You're supposed to say 'Shoot, kid!' aren't you?"

Ollie smiled. "Oh, yeah, I forgot. Okay—*shoot, kid!* You have my full and undivided attention."

"I know you will be honest and say if you're not sure about these things." Josie took a deep breath before continuing. "First, are you convinced—without any doubts—that everything Danny is saying is the truth? I 'ave to be sure, Ollie. And do you honestly believe he wants to change? I don't want to change him—I loved him for what he is. But, Ollie, I do want him to, oh, merde, what's the word...I want him to *respect* me, to think about me before he goes off and does things. I don't want him to *not* 'ave any fun...I loved him because he was fun. Oh, it's hard to say it right..."

Ollie had waited as Josie struggled with the words. "Would you be asking this if you weren't at least *thinking* about going back to him?"

Josie smiled. "Could you just answer...please?" She whispered, "Shit-all-to-hell!"

"Okay, am I sure. *Yes*, Jo, I am totally, absolutely, one hundred percent *certain* what he said about Bobby, about Chrissy, about your Gord Schaefer—and about being sorry for all he's done—is all true. As for him changing, you asked if he wants to. I not only believe he wants to, but he will! Hell—he already has! He's not drinking. He isn't interested in going out much. He's studying like crazy—he says it would go faster if you were there, but he's getting it done. He wants to be just what you want him to be—*whatever* you want him to be."

"How can I be sure? I can't imagine him not drinking. How can I be sure!"

Ollie suspected Josie needed to justify a decision already made. She delivered her coup de grace: "Don't you be forgetting who this is. This is Dan Tanner! I don't know of anything he sets out to do that won't get done. Besides, you can't have everything perfect. There are no perfect people. But—God damn it—there is a perfect couple, Jo!" She paused before asking, "How many questions was that? What's your other question?"

Josie looked down at the tabletop. "I'm...I'm thinking about writing to him. To suggest...to see if he would be interested in us starting to see each other...not to go back to living together, not right away. Just go out, like on dates...maybe with you and Russ like we used to. I'm thinking maybe we weren't, um, ready...maybe not *mature* enough to do what we were doing. I'm quite sure *I* wasn't."

"Why a letter? Why not just phone? Or meet with him and tell him..."

"No, I want my feelings to be clear. I want to have a-a test period. Just dating—no sex and no cabin at first. I want to protect myself. I want him to understand he 'as to respect me...prove he really has changed. If I try to talk to him it might all come out wrong. It has to be a letter."

"Want to show me the letter?"

"I didn't write it yet. I try and I can't get it right. There are some things I 'ave...done, too. I want to-to make sure Danny knows and understands, before I...before I will be with him again. Anyway, first I 'ave to meet Gord and break off with him. I've been trying to see him all week. I want to do that first...face to face...not by phone."

"Okay. Sounds fair. Don't wait too long, Jo."

"About the letter...do you think I should?"

"Oh, yes. It's a great idea—do it! Don't wait. Write it and send it. Or I'll deliver it to him—what the hell, I'm starting to feel like the friggin' post office lately anyway."

Josie looked satisfied. "If you speak to him please tell him I'm not seeing anyone now. You know he was worried about Gord and me."

If I speak to him? You can bet your little ass I'll speak to him!

*   *   *   *

Josie tried several times that day and the next to reach Gord. When she got hold of him on the third day, he said he couldn't talk right then but he would call her on Monday. She decided she couldn't wait. She wrote a note telling him she wouldn't be seeing him any more. *Dieu! My life is all notes and letters these days.* She gave it to Bob Allen, one of his 409 friends, to pass on.

She didn't complete the letter to Danny. Just as before, she threw away several copies.

*   *   *   *

At nine-fifty on Sunday morning, Ollie came to her room in a panic.

"Did you send the letter, Jo?"

"No, not yet. I didn't write it. I can't get it right. And I haven't heard from Gord. I have to get that done first. I sent him a note but I don't know if he got it..."

Ollie cut her off. "Shit, Jo! Dan's leaving today—on T.D. He might already be gone! I just found out from Russ. They've been on the damn four to twelve shift so I haven't seen him."

"Leaving now? Are you sure?"

"Yes!" She neglected to say it was only to Victoria and only for a week.

Josie ran from the room, up the stairs to the hall phone. Ollie ran after her. Another girl was using the phone. Josie paced. She signaled frantically at the girl.

Ollie said loudly, "This girl needs the phone, right now! It's an emergency! Can you call your party back or something?" The girl hung up and Josie dived for the phone.

Ollie told her the number for the Cabin. Josie dialed. There were ten rings with no answer.

"Are you sure it's the right number?"

Ollie recited the number again. Still no answer. Josie banged the handset on the wall and looked pleadingly at her.

"Try the barracks." Said Ollie.

Danny was carrying his flight bag down the hall, car keys in his hand, when he heard, "Phone for Tanner!" He hesitated, deciding whether he should go back. The guy yelled again, "Is Tanner here? It's a girl—says it's important."

He stopped, put his bag down and went to the phone. He picked up the dangling receiver.

"Tanner here." The line was silent. He repeated, "Hello! Tanner here."

"Danny?"

"Josie." His stomach flipped. "What can I do for you, Jo?" *Jesus, idiot, don't sound so damned formal!* He tried again, "How are you, Jo? It's good to hear your voice." *Not much better, idiot!*

"It's-it's good to 'ear you, too. I'm fine, Danny…well, not so good…"

He said, with concern, "Is something wrong, Honey?" *You called her Honey— stupid.*

He called me Honey! "No. I'm fine really. And you?" She was getting her composure back.

"I've been better. So, Josie…?" He left it hanging.

"Danny, I got your letter." When he didn't say anything, she went on, "I was going to write a letter to you, but Ollie just told me you are going on T.D. She told me just now. And I wanted to talk to you before you go away. I believe what you said in your letter—all of it. I 'ave told Gord Schaefer we're through." She paused before declaring, "Danny, it's good to hear you! Don't talk…I 'ave to finish. Are you leaving soon? How long are you going to be gone?" She knew she was babbling but couldn't stop.

"I was halfway out the door...I'm supposed to be down in Victoria by two-thirty. It's a week."

"Oh. Okay, I'm going to say this fast, before you go. I was thinking...wondering if...if you would be interested in...you and me, um, seeing each other? Not to live together...just maybe go out, you know, maybe with Ollie and Russ. To see if we want—if we want to be together again. I was going to put that in the letter." She took a deep breath. He didn't say anything. "Are you there, Danny?"

"I'm here."

Ollie grinned when she saw Josie sit on the floor, twisting the cord in her fingers.

"Oh, Danny, I want to be with you again!" Any idea of a test period or a letter went out the window. "I believe your letter! I remember every word. And I-I will *never* say 'I do not love you.' I *do* love you! Always!" She waited expectantly. She couldn't know he was having trouble speaking. "Say something, please Danny?"

"You know I love you, Jo."

Hearing those words, she choked up. After a moment she was able to say, "Okay, go on your T.D. Can you call me from there?"

"Yes—tomorrow. Be in the barracks at noon. I'll call you there."

"I will! You 'ave made me so happy! Go now, to your damn T.D. Good bye. I love you." She hung up.

Still sitting on the floor, she said, "Oh, merde! Ollie, I said it all wrong, didn't I."

Ollie swallowed hard before she could answer. "Kid, you said it perfect! Kinda fast, but perfect."

He phoned her at noon the next day. Then he phoned after supper the next three evenings. They spoke of their love and the future.

CHAPTER 27

▼

We were about to realize the terrible consequence of my actions…

COMOX—THURSDAY, APRIL 2ND

Gord called Josie in the Orderly Room on Thursday afternoon. "Hi, Sweets—sorry I never got back to you. How's things?"

"Didn't you get my note? I gave it to Bob. Did he give it to you?"

He lied. "No, I never got a note. What's it about—the Vancouver trip?"

"No…Gordon, I 'ave to talk to you. Today. Can you *please* meet me somewhere?"

"Sounds urgent or something. How about in the Mess Hall at supper time. I'll be there about five, okay?"

She went to supper at four-thirty with Ollie. She told Ollie she was meeting Gord.

"I just hope he doesn't 'ave his friends with him…I want to tell him and get it over with…he's not easy to talk to when his friends are around."

"You're too damn worried about his feelings, Jo. He obviously doesn't give a damn about yours, or he wouldn't keep standing you up. I'll wait with you. If he doesn't show up this time, just tell him on the phone!"

They waited till five-forty. She was ready to take Ollie's advice and to go back to her room, when he came in with four of his friends. She could see as she sat beside him he had been drinking. His black eye had faded to a yellowish hue, but was still noticeable. Ollie stood behind her and listened.

He asked, "Hi, sweet thing, what's up?" He leaned back, tilting the chair. "Have you been avoiding me?" He grinned and winked at his friends.

"Gordon…I have to talk to you. Would you be free after supper, so we could talk?"

"I guess so, what's it about? How about right here, right now?"

"It's, um, private…" She looked apologetically at his friends. "And it's important."

"Okay. Meet me at the parking lot in an hour."

She looked at her watch. "At twenty to seven?"

"I guess. See you at my car at twenty to seven."

As she walked away, he gave a thumbs-up sign and leered at his friends, he murmured, "Nice piece—I'm tellin' you." They all grinned as they watched her walk out.

∗   ∗   ∗   ∗

She waited by his car in the cold drizzle. She had changed into civilian clothes, a light jacket, sweater and slacks. She wasn't dressed for the weather but she didn't expect to be outside for long. At seven o'clock he still hadn't shown up, so she moved to the rear door of her barracks and stood just inside, where she could see him approach. When he arrived at seven fifteen, she walked quickly across the lot to meet him at the car. He pulled her close and tried to kiss her but she turned her head and pulled away. His breath smelled of beer.

She was anxious to get it over with. "Gordon, we have to talk…"

He said, "Get in. We'll talk in the car, out of the rain." When she got in he asked, "Where to?" He started the car.

"We don't 'ave to go anywhere, Gord, we can talk here. It won't take long."

He engaged the clutch and they started moving. "I gotta go into town for some gas anyway. We'll talk on the way."

"Okay…"

"I have to see a guy, too…" He was vague. He drove through the gate and turned right onto Little River Road. It was not the way to town.

"Where are we going?"

"Just down here a little ways. There's a place we can talk."

"Oh…okay…I 'ave to get back. We won't be long?"

He passed the corner of Kilmorley road, turned to the right onto a gravel road and then left onto a narrow, rutted track, where he stopped the car. In the almost total darkness, she could just make out thick underbrush and small evergreens on both sides of the road. Colors were changing from green and brown and yellow, to gray and black.

"How's this?"

"It's okay, I guess."

"So, what's up?"

She took a breath. "Okay. This is nothing against you, Gord...but I don't want to go with you any more. I hope you understand..."

"No. I don't understand. Hell, Josie, we were just really starting to get to know each other. I realize I was kind of mean the last time we went out, I was scared you'd go back to that Tanner guy, so I was a little pushy...but I do really like you."

"Well, the truth is, I 'aven't got over Danny. We are going to be...back together." Another deep breath. "Also, you 'ave been saying things about us..."

"Saying what things? I told you what the creep did! Who are you going to believe, Josie, him or me?"

"It's not important any more who I believe. I want to be with him. I don't know how these things happen...or why...but he's the only one I want to be with. I'm trying to be honest with you." She put a hand on his before she continued, "We can't see each other anymore. I'm sorry for this, but..."

He shook her hand away. "Just what I thought." He was staring straight ahead.

"What?"

"I said it's just what I fuckin' thought!"

"Please don't swear. What did you think?"

"You're Tanner's slut! Just a damn pig.

She could hardly breathe. "Who...who do you think you are? You can't talk like that to me!"

"Bullshit. You're a slut and you likely always were and always will be."

She felt the tears start. "You take me back...right now!"

"Fuck you." He pulled her to him, not gently. "Come on, sweets, you know you like it. Quit playing around." He put one hand on her breast and tried to push the other inside her slacks at the waist. She pulled his hand away from her slacks and turned so he couldn't touch her breasts.

He turned her roughly, yanked her sweater up to her chin and forced both hands inside her brassiere.

She pulled at his hands but he was too strong. "Gordon! Don't."

"Shut up and come to Gordy." He pulled one hand out of her sweater and tried to unzip her slacks.

Now she was angry. "Gord—I said NO!" she moved as far right as she could on the seat, reached for the door handle. He grabbed her jacket and used it to jerk her back to his side.

"Gord, stop it! Right now!"

He didn't stop, so she slapped his face.

His return slap was immediate and violent!

In all her life she had never been struck—by anyone. Her ears rang. Her eyes watered. "D-don't you *dare* 'it me!" She went to slap him again but he grabbed her wrists. She cried, "You *'urt* me...take me back to the barracks, *right now!*"

"You don't want to go back to the base." He took her face in both hands and kissed her, mashing her lips painfully against her teeth. She twisted her face and moved away. She scrabbled to the right and reached for the door handle. He took a handful of her hair this time and used it to haul her back to him and mashed his mouth to hers again.

"Mmm—mmm." She swung weakly at him with her little fists. He released her from the kiss. "GORDON! I said *stop*—and I *mean it!* You 'ad better take me back now. I don't like this."

"Gee, that's too bad, because I like it a lot." He jerked her slacks with a hand under each side of the waistband, causing her to fall hard onto her back on the seat. He ripped the side zipper open and started to pull the slacks down, he managed to get them halfway off when she kicked out with both feet, making him pause. The look on his face turned her cold with fear. She reached behind her and opened the door but she couldn't pull free from him.

"STOP! STOP THIS!" She screamed out the open door. "HELP! HELP ME! EEEE!" *Oh God, somebody please hear me.* She screamed again. "HELP! HELP!"

"Shut up!" He slapped her hard, dazing her for a moment. He managed to get her slacks down to her ankles. Pulling herself up by gripping his jacket, she half sat up and clawed at his face, scratching him enough to draw blood. He frantically grabbed for her hands but caught only one. With her free hand she clawed him some more. He drew back a fist and drove it into her face, breaking her nose and splitting her lip. Blood ran down her lips and chin.

"Jesus!" He yelled. "Fucking little *bitch!*" He punched again, this time the blow glanced off her forehead. "BITCH!"

She was dazed, felt herself losing consciousness. The will to fight was leaving her. *Oh, Danny...Mama...He's going to do it! I can't fight him.* She whimpered, "Please d-don't hit me anymore."

He pulled her slacks past her feet and off. Then he jerked at her panties but they wouldn't come off. With two hands he ripped the crotch and one side seam apart and threw slacks and panties aside. He unzipped his fly, pulled his pants down and forced his knees between her thighs. He was over her, penis in hand.

At the sight of it her will returned. She thrashed her lower body right and left, trying to prevent his entry. She didn't scream again. It became a silent struggle. She clawed at his face, drew more blood

You might kill me, but I will never stop fighting…you pig!

He drove a fist into her face, hitting her mouth and jaw and dazing her again. He punched her again. She went limp. He planted his forearm across her throat and held it there, keeping his face against her shoulder to prevent her scratching it. Her fists beat weakly at his head and back. She made choking sounds as he lay on her and entered. Because of her frantic struggles, the penetration was awkward and painful. He leaned his full weight on his arm, jamming it into her throat, choking her. His breath came in snorts as he thrust violently into her.

She tried to scream again, but the only sound she could make was "Gghh, Gghh…" She ceased her struggle. She could get no air. "Gghh…" Her eyes bulged and her face was purple. She saw flashing, varicolored lights. "Gghh, gghh." Her arms waved feebly. *I can't breathe! I'm going to die. Oh, God. Oh, God. Help me please. He wants to kill me…Danny? Danny help me?* "Gghh."

Then it was over.

He lifted his arm off her throat as he climaxed. He rolled off her and rose to his knees, still between her legs. He was panting. She felt his semen drip onto her belly. She heard her own breath—hoarse, ragged gasps. She realized her head was hanging outside the open door. She closed her eyes and lay still, terrified he would hurt her again. She waited.

He sat up. She heard him say, "Here, Josie my love—here, you stuck-up pig!" He threw her panties at her. They landed on her face. She didn't move.

"So, you don't want to see me anymore? So get outta here!" He grabbed the panties and threw them out the open door. He pushed at her with a foot. "There! Go get your panties. Go and see your precious Danny, stupid *bitch*. Get out and walk!" He gave her a last vicious kick, catching her in the ribs.

She half fell half crawled out onto the road. The car sped away, showering her with mud and gravel. She knelt in the mud, picked up the panties and held them to her breast. She remained there on her knees in the darkness for fifteen minutes, rocking slowly back and forth.

Her scream, when it came, was feral, the scream of a mortally wounded animal. "AUGHHH! DANNEE, DANNEEEE, DANNEEEAUGHHH!" She retched and vomited down the already bloody front of her jacket.

After another fifteen minutes, her little body started to feel the pain. Her head throbbed from the blows. Her nose felt as if it had been ripped from her face. Her jaw hung slackly. There was not a part of her that didn't screech with the pain. She trembled uncontrollably. When she tried to stand, her head spun and her vision blurred and she staggered drunkenly. She had to sit down. She lost track of the passage of time before she struggled to her feet and started limping along the dark road, wearing only her sweater and light jacket, naked from the waist down. After twenty steps, she stopped and tried to pull her ruined panties on. They were too tattered to stay up so she let them fall to the ground. Her flimsy indoor shoes were soaked. She staggered back to where he had parked, searching in vain for her slacks but they were still in the car. She turned back and started out again, still trembling violently.

When she reached a paved road, she stopped and looked around dazedly, unsure of the direction back to the station. She staggered on. Two cars passed, both coming toward her. At first sight of the approaching headlights she lurched off the road and hid—the first time in wet shrubs, the second in a muddy road-side ditch. She feared the lights meant he was coming back to hurt her some more.

She didn't see the next lights when they approached.

CHAPTER 28

▼

LITTLE RIVER ROAD—THURSDAY, APRIL 2ND

The couple was driving from Comox to their home at Little River.

The woman shouted, "Steve! Stop! Stop the car!"

"What for?"

"There's someone on the road! Just back there, it's a child, I think. I saw it in the headlights—on the left."

"Are you sure?" The man backed the car slowly. "How far?"

"Go slow, and be careful, we don't want to run it…run him over! There! See?" The woman was out of the car running to Josie. "It's a girl, Steve! My God, she's hurt badly!"

Josie had managed to limp and crawl as far as the blacktop of Little River Road and then half way to the corner of Kilmorley Road. It had taken her over an hour to get that far—a distance less than a quarter of a mile. When the couple bent over her with a flashlight, she screamed and cringed away from them, eyes wide in horror.

"It's okay, dear," said the woman, "you're hurt badly, but it's going to be okay. I'm a nurse and I'll look after you. You're going to be fine." At the sound of the kindly voice, Josie clutched the woman's arms. "Steve, get her into the car and wrap her with our coats. We have to get her to the hospital fast! I'll get in the back seat with her. Hurry!" He lifted her with ease and got her into the back seat.

On the way to the hospital in Comox, Josie trembled violently. Every minute or so she screamed pitifully and tried to get up. The woman gently pushed her down and stroked her forehead.

In an almost inaudible voice, she said, "Danny…help me?…Olivia?…Mama, are you here?" Blood bubbled from her nose and mouth with every breath. She grasped the woman's hand in a death-like grip.

*   *   *   *

The base hospital received a call from St. Joseph's Hospital in Comox: "We have a young lady of yours, named Josée Connor. She's critical after a beating—multiple trauma." The Duty Medical Officer was called. He called the Senior Medical Officer and the Chief Admin Officer.

The Service Police received a call from the R.C.M.P.: "We have a young woman who's been assaulted—Air Force I.D. tags say she's AW1 Connor, Josée. She's at St. Joseph's Hospital. Badly beaten, possible rape, might not make it. She's asking for a Danny and an Olivia, no last names."

Service Police Corporal Howard McCallum, who knew the girls, called Ollie at the barracks. "Josie Connor is hurt bad. Get ready, we'll give you a ride. You had better hurry Ollie, they said she's real bad!"

Ollie threw on some clothes. She stopped as she passed Bobby Gaines' room.

"Bobby, phone Russ! Josie—bad accident! Tell him to stick by the phone and I'll call him."

*   *   *   *

At nine thirty, she phoned Russ from the hospital. She was crying as she told him, "Russ, they think she might *die!* Jesus, Russ, he hurt her so bad. It was Gord Schaefer. She went somewhere with him in his car. I told the cops she was with him. Russ, the poor little thing…she's hurt so bad! He tried to kill her!"

A minute later Russ barged into Gil and Gerry's room. Jake MacDonald and Gerry were there playing cards.

"Where's Gil?"

"He's in the washroom. What's up, Russ?" Gerry answered.

"Jake, come with me. I need your help. Gerry—get Gil and meet us at the front door." He explained to Jake what had happened as they went down the stairs. When they were all gathered at the door, Russ said "Jake, do you know Schaefer's car?"

"Sure do."

"Go make sure he can't drive it anywhere—get the tires, Jake."

"You got it." Jake took off running toward the parking lot.

"Follow me, guys. That bastard hurt Josie."

They took half a minute to get to Schaefer's barrack block. They checked to see where his room was and went up the stairs.

Outside his room Russ whispered, "You guys keep an eye out here in the hall. Someone get the window at the stairs." He knocked on the door and walked in. Schaefer was packing a suitcase. His roommate lay on a bunk.

Russ looked around as if lost. "Shit, I guess I got the wrong room. Howya been, Gordo?"

"I'm okay. You?" said Schaefer. He wasn't happy to see Russ.

"I'm good…Jesus, Gord, what happened to your face? You must have found a real live one. Who was she? Anyone I know?"

"Naw, a broad from town…"

"What broad? I want to know, in case I ever run into her."

"Just a broad from town…"

"No name? What's her name?"

"I told you. I don't know…"

"Well, okay then, I'll be going. See ya…" He turned as if to leave the room, then suddenly wheeled back. He grabbed Schaefer by the front of his jacket and brought a knee up viciously to his groin. What started as a scream turned into a choking sound, "G-g-ghu, g-g-ghu." Schaefer tried to double over to relieve the pain, but Russ straightened him up and sent another knee into his groin for good measure. He puked explosively. Russ twisted to one side so only a little of the vomit hit his pant leg and shoe.

Russ turned to the roommate. "You! Get outta here! You didn't see anything, got it?"

"Okay, man…" He quickly left.

Russ raged, "Now, you goddamned piece of crap!" He spun Schaefer around and, grabbing a handful of curly hair, slammed his face into the locker door— one, two, three, four times. With each slam Russ screamed, "JOSIE!" Slam! "JOSIE!" Slam! "JOSIE!" Slam! "HER NAME IS JOSIE CONNOR, YOU ROTTEN *BASTARD!*" Slam! "I'M GONNA *KILL* YOU!" He picked up an alarm clock from the dresser, turned his man around, and hammered it into his face, the force of it driving him back against the locker.

Gil stuck his head through the door.

"Russ! Cops! They're outside." He looked at Schaefer. "Jesus!"

Russ pulled the ruined face close. "You're lucky, prick. When the Mounties are finished with you, I hope Danny Tanner gets to have a go." He let go and Schaefer collapsed to the floor, sobbing and retching and clutching his groin. Russ kicked him in the gut before hurrying out.

Outside the building, they passed two Mounties and Corporal McCallum heading in. The Corporal called, "Hold it, Knight!" Turning to the Mounties, he said, "You go on ahead, it's room twenty-six." When they were out of earshot, he spoke to Russ, "I hope you guys did a good job on him. Josie's in a bad way. The cop says he's never seen a worse beating!" Looking Russ squarely in the eye, he added, "I didn't see you here tonight—and you never saw me—okay?" he trotted after the policemen.

"Right. Okay Corp," said Russ.

*   *   *   *

ST. JOSEPH'S HOSPITAL, COMOX—THURSDAY, APRIL 2ND

Doctor Adam McKay thanked the nurses for their work. Josie had just been brought back to Emergency from X-ray. He glanced at his watch. 10:40 P.M.

"Pull the curtain closed, would you, Harrison? I'm going to stay here for a bit…just want to go over this case in my mind. I believe we've done all we can for now but I want to be sure. Is the Air Force doctor still in the building?"

Nurse Harrison answered, "No. The Air Force people all left."

"Hmm, okay. She'll be staying here with us. Close the curtain and let's go over this case."

He stared down at Josie, absently stroking his steel-gray mustache and then his bald pate, as if to magically transfer hairs from one to the other. When he first saw her diminutive body two hours earlier, he had thought he was dealing with a child of eleven or twelve years. He remembered thinking, *What in hell was this kid doing out on a night like this?* He had been surprised when he saw her developed breasts and pubes.

He picked up her chart now to double check. *September, 1936…makes her nineteen.* Reading from the chart, he reviewed her injuries, remarking aloud to the nurse as he read the entries:

> *Cranium—probable concussion, also contusion and cut on forehead just below hairline—four sutures in place.*

"That's a ring cut," he muttered.

> *Patient was semi-conscious when found, shows no combativeness.*

"Good, likely no brain damage."

Face & lips abraded, contused, puffy. Indication of 2 broken teeth.

"Damn!"

Mandible dislocated. Reset. Some swelling.

"This guy wasn't holding anything back, was he?"

Neck and throat grossly contused.

"He tried to strangle you, didn't he? Better check for laryngeal or pharyngeal damage." He scrawled a note on the chart.

Thorax left lateral, contused. X-ray shows two cracked ribs.

"We have them taped up, she'll be uncomfortable, but there's nothing sticking out."

Knees abraded and contused.

"She got that from crawling along the road, according to the officer."

Vaginal examination is incomplete—evidence of forced penetration.

"We'll get a Gyno man in tomorrow to have a looksee." He wrote on the chart again.

X-rays completed @ 2120 hrs. No further trauma indicated.

"Small mercy, I suppose."

Urinary catheter, oxygen tube and IV drip—all in place.

"She won't need the oxygen any more, but we'll leave the catheter in."

Patient has been in and out of consciousness. Sod. Seconal, IM, q4H, for pain if she wakes up.

He wrote more orders on the chart and then placed a palm gently on her forehead. He muttered, "My, my, kid, you took on one mean bastard, didn't you! You're a brave little girl. Maybe you shouldn't have fought as hard as you so obviously did. If you have no hidden damage—which would surprise me—we can make your body better. But your mind? Well, we'll see."

Just then Josie stirred. The doctor heard her small, hoarse voice say, "Mama? Ollie? My Danny, come back…please, Danny?"

He mistakenly concluded, "So—the bastard has a name!"

"There're some new orders on her chart, Harrison. Watch her vitals for an hour or so, then, if there's no change, you can move her to the ward. Do we have a private for her? She doesn't need a lot of stuff going on around her. Her X-rays look good except for the ribs. She should come around soon now. She's really a hell of a lot better than she looks, physically anyway." Glancing at the patient, he said, "Looks like she might be a pretty little thing, hard to tell though. Is the other young lady here? The one who was with her in Emergency?"

"Oh, yes. She's down the hall." The nurse chuckled. "I don't think she'd leave if we *ordered* her out."

"Good. She's the 'Olivia'—one of the names she keeps asking for. She identified the man who did this, to the police." He waved a hand toward Josie. "When we move this one to the ward it won't hurt to have a friend there when she comes around. She has no family nearby, they're back east—Quebec. I want to talk with Olivia again. I'll ask her to let the ward staff know if and when this one starts recognizing and talking."

"I'll get her for you."

"After I speak with her, I'm going to find some food." He patted his ample midsection. "Tell the wards they can find me in the cafeteria if they need me."

*   *   *   *

Russ didn't reach Danny in Victoria till almost eleven.

Danny was in the room he and Red were sharing. They had been out with Moe for a late snack. He was in the washroom preparing for bed when he heard the phone.

He called, "Red, can you get the phone?" He looked into the bedroom and saw Red was already asleep. *Dozy Bastard!* He crossed the room and picked up the receiver.

"Hello…?"

"Dan? It's Russ."

"Hey, Q! What's…"

Russ cut him off. "Dan, Josie's been hurt. She's hurt real bad. Ollie says she might *die!* She's asking for you. They've got her at the civilian hospital in Comox." He heard the receiver at the other end thump against something. "Dan? Dan! Dan, are you there? Shit!"

Danny dropped the receiver without hanging it up. He sprinted to Morissey's room and pounded on the door.

Moe opened his door. "Dan, what's wrong? You're white as a…"

"Moe, it's Josie—my girl! She's been hurt. It's bad. I have to get up there, Moe…"

"Yes, you do!" Morrisey thought for a moment. "Look, tomorrow's briefing is just a recap, Red and I can handle it. Get going, Dan. And Dan, don't drive crazy—it won't help her if you kill yourself. Give me a call at Div when you get a chance. Good luck—get going."

"Thanks, Sir…I'll call you. Thanks."

He was in the car by ten after eleven. It was raining, light but steady, as he drove from Gorge Road onto the Island Highway, forgetting about the new route from Douglas Street. He talked to himself as he negotiated Four-Mile Hill and drove through Colwood. "I'm coming, Honey. Danny's coming!"

The rain was heavier as he started the climb past Goldstream Park onto the winding highway over the Malahat Mountain. "I'm coming, Babe—please be okay. God *damn* this rain!" Near the summit the rain turned to wet snow, rapidly accumulating on the road. He got behind a slow-moving truck pulling a bull-dozer on a flatbed trailer and couldn't get around it. He cursed and yelled and pounded the dashboard until, almost to Mill Bay, he was able to get past. That truck may have saved his life by forcing him to slow down on a dangerous stretch of highway. After Mill Bay the road started to level and straighten and the rain let up and he calmed down somewhat. By the time he was through Duncan the rain stopped and the road was drying.

*   *   *   *

At 11:30, Ollie called Russ again.

"She's going to make it! The doctor talked to me. He says the injuries aren't as bad as they look. She's been to X-ray. They let me see her but I don't think she knew me." Ollie's voice broke. "She-she's…oh, shit, Russ…both her eyes are black…there was blood all over her clothes. I only recognized her because they told me it's her! He even broke her *teeth!* She keeps saying 'Danny,' and 'Olivia,' and 'Mama' in a little tiny voice. I-I had to bend close to hear her." Ollie spoke through her sobs, "Her mother's dead…s-since she was a kid, but she's calling for her! Russ—find that bastard! Kill him! KILL HIM, RUSS!"

"I came close, Ol. The cops have him now. I phoned Dan in Victoria. I think he's on his way. I'll come and join you there. You okay, Babe?"

"Of course I'm not okay."

*   *   *   *

At Cassidy, near the Nanaimo airport, Danny noticed he was low on gas. It was after one A.M. and he had to drive blocks out of his way in Nanaimo to find a gas station open. Then he lost his way and took a couple of wrong turns before finding his way back to the highway. He sped out of town. Now he was just seventy miles from her, on a level and fairly straight road.

As he raced through the tunnel of his headlights, he muttered, "Jo, Honey, hang on…hour and a half. Oh, Jesus, what's happened to you?"

*   *   *   *

Russ got a ride to the hospital with Jake. He found Ollie in a small anteroom near the second floor elevator. He sat beside her. "Any news, Babe?" He asked.

"I don't know. Shit, she's in a coma or something, I'm scared for her, Russ. The Doctor's not so sure now she's gonna be okay. Did you find him?"

"Yeah—I found him. But right now I'm worried about Jo…"

The elevator door opened and a nurse and orderly appeared, pushing Josie on a Gurney. Russ and Ollie went to her. This was a nurse Ollie hadn't met.

"We're her friends…"

The nurse said, "Sorry, Miss, only relatives."

Ollie blew. The anxiety of the night boiled to the top. "Don't be so damn stupid, you bitch! Her only relatives are in frigging *Quebec*!" She had pushed her face close to the nurse's. "The doctor *told* me we could see her—I'm one of the people she's been *asking for*, for Chrissake…"

Russ pulled her away and spoke to the nurse. "You'll have to excuse her…she doesn't mean it. She's right, though, Doctor whats-is-name says we can see her. Honest!" He of course didn't know if that was true any more than he knew the doctor's name.

Ollie, contrite, said, "Oh lord…I am sorry. I know you're just doing your job. Let us in with her, just for awhile? The doctor, Doctor McKay, says…"

Before the woman could answer, another nurse arrived from down the hall. It was Harrison from the ICU. She took the ward nurse aside and spoke quietly to her.

"Okay, kids, you can stay." Said the ward nurse. "Whatever you do, don't disturb her. If you want to get all hysterical, get out of there and do it somewhere else." Looking at Ollie, she added, "And try to watch the language around here." She smiled at them. "She won't know you're here."

Ollie said, "We understand. Thank you."

"Now, you can make yourself useful. Help me move her."

They followed the Gurney into a small ward and Ollie helped move her onto the only bed. The hospital gown fell away and she saw the ugly bruises on the side of her chest. Russ stood back helplessly. He couldn't take his eyes from her. There were tears running down his face. When the nurse left the room he looked at her injured face and whispered, "Jesus, Jo…Jesus." He choked off a sob. Ollie put an arm around him.

They heard her hoarse whimper, "Danny…Are you here? Mama?"

"Jesus, Ollie, is she gonna be okay?" said Russ.

✳   ✳   ✳   ✳

COMOX—FRIDAY, APRIL 3RD

Danny encountered little traffic after he was through Parksville. He drove through Courtenay at 2:30 A.M. and pulled into the hospital grounds five minutes later. He left the car by the Emergency entrance, its door open, and ran into the building.

A receptionist was half-awake at her counter. He rapped on the glass partition. "Josie Connor!" he shouted, "Where do I find Josie Connor?"

"Sir, it's almost three in the morning! Visiting hours are…"

"Listen, my-my sister is in here…she came in tonight sometime. She's Josie Connor. It was an accident or something. Come on, I just drove up from Victoria, I have to see her!"

"Oh, I see. I believe they've taken her to a ward, Mr. Connor." She pointed to a hallway. "Take the elevator to the second…"

He ran down the hall. At the elevator he asked a man in hospital whites, "My sister is here. She's been injured. I just got to town. Where do I find her?" The man shrugged and shook his head.

A voice behind him said, "Was she brought in last night?"

Danny spun around to see a short, stout man. He said, "No, tonight…" he looked at his watch. "uh, yeah, last night. Do you know where she would be?" He saw the rubber tubing of a stethoscope sticking out from a pocket of the man's tweed jacket. "Are you a doctor?"

"Yes. You say you're her brother? Is it the young Air Force girl? Miss Connor?" He spoke with an accent that could have come from Australia or New Zealand.

"Yes! Josie Connor." The elevator door opened for them.

The doctor took Danny by the elbow as he stepped in. "She's on the ward. Come with me. I'm on my way to check on her. I'm Doctor McKay." He pronounced it McKie. "I was on call when they brought her in to Emergency. Is your name Danny, Mister…Connor?"

The elevator stopped at the second floor and the doctor led him along a hallway.

"Yes, I'm Danny. Is she gonna be okay, Doc?"

McKay evaded the question. "Her injuries are serious. I believe she's been asking for you."

"I was down in Victoria. I just arrived now. What happened to her?"

"That can wait. You say you just arrived now?"

"Yeah, I did. Why is it so important?" Danny was impatient with the questions.

"I wanted to be certain you're not the…person…who assaulted her. Here we are." The doctor stopped at the nurses' station. He asked the ward nurse, "Where have we put Miss Connor?"

"Two oh six, Doctor," she said. She pointed down the hall. "She's still the same."

"Thank you. I'll just check her chart for now. Then I'll be going home." He turned to Danny. "Before you go in there, Danny, we had better have a talk."

"What about? She is okay, isn't she?"

"At this point I can't be sure…we're still assessing her injuries. She suffered a severe beating, and was probably raped, but hopefully she will heal. Now, a young lady named…Conti? Do you know her?" Danny nodded. "Well, she told us a Danny was coming up from Victoria. But he is supposed to be *engaged* to Miss Connor. He would be her fiancée, not her brother."

"Okay, you caught me. I said I was her brother in case it's family members only, to make sure I could get in to see her. I'm sorry." *Thanks, Ollie!*

"Well, Danny, she won't know you're here—but go to her. Her friends were here. I don't know if they're still..." Danny was half way to 206. McKay smiled and shook his head.

*   *   *   *

When he went into the room, Russ was sitting beside Josie's bed on the only chair. Ollie was standing behind him. Danny walked fearfully toward the bed and stopped five feet away. When he saw her battered face he almost threw up.

He swallowed hard. His mind aroar, he whispered, "Oh God, Jo!"

Russ stood up, "Hey Champ," he said quietly, "here, sit down."

"Thanks, Q."

Ollie came over to Danny. All she could say was, "Tanner..." then she lost her composure, clung to him and buried her face in his chest.

He put his arms around her, felt her tears wetting his shirtfront. He looked at Russ, "Who?"

"Schaefer."

He nodded.

Ollie said, "They arrested him, Dan. The cops."

"Okay." He looked again at Josie. "Jesus, look at her. My poor little Jo!" He asked himself, *What have I done?*

Ollie stepped back from him, dabbed at tears, and turned to the bed. Danny could see how drawn with worry her face was.

"She hasn't moved, hasn't woke up once." Staring fixedly at Josie, she added, "Shit, I keep wanting to check and see if...if she's breathing." Her tears flowed again. "When I first saw her down in emergency she was moving and calling out. She was calling for you and me. Now she just lies there...nothing."

Russ said, "She's gonna be okay. She's gonna be fine!" He spoke with certainty.

"Go to her, Dan," said Ollie. She gave him a little push and followed him to the bed.

He stood over her, saw the injuries again. His hands involuntarily went to his face, covering his mouth. *Oh Christ!* He started to place a hand on her brow but jerked it back, as if afraid he would do more damage. He sat in the chair, took her hand gently; it was dry and warm and limp.

He whispered close to her ear, "Danny's here, Hon."

She lay unmoving, eyes closed. Her skin, where there were no bruises or bandages, was pale and waxy, like a porcelain doll.

A nurse came to the door. She quietly asked, "Did one of you leave a green car outside by the Emergency door? They want it moved."

"I'll get it, Dan. Got the key?" said Ollie.

He fumbled in his pockets. "I must have left it in the car…"

She patted his back. "Okay, big guy, I'll go and move it." She thought for a second, "You know what? Russ, you have to work tomorrow. You're gonna have to get some sleep, and I know I have to—right now my butt's dragging about four feet behind me."

Reluctantly, Russ said, "Yeah, I guess so."

"Tell you what, Tanner, how about we take the car out to the station. I'll get it back to you tomorrow after work. Shit, it's today *now*, isn't it! I'll bring it back. I'm coming back anyway." She smiled, "Knight'll even put some gas in it."

Ollie was taking charge.

*   *   *   *

They left him alone with her. He still held her limp hand.

He took the ring from his pocket. He had no idea where it should go, so he put it on the middle finger of her right hand. *It's good enough, Honey, you and I know what it's for and that's what counts.* He leaned over her and softly kissed her mouth; it was awkward because of the side rails on the bed. He brushed a tendril of damp hair from her brow.

At five-thirty there was a first hint of light coming through the window when a young night nurse came in with a paper cup of coffee. She whispered, "I thought you could use this. It's just regular—one and one. Here's some extra cream and sugar." She put three sugar cubes, a small cream container, and a plastic spoon on the bedside table with the coffee.

It was hard for him to take his eyes off Josie. "You're very kind, thanks a million." He looked at his watch—the one she gave him for Christmas. "Jeez, I had no idea it was so late!" He tasted the coffee and then added two cubes of sugar.

The nurse said, "Doctor McKay says you are to stay as long as you want. You can help us while you're here, watch her closely and tell us right away if she wakes up—or even moves." She paused before adding, "I'm sure she'll be okay…we're all rooting for her. She's about the same age as me, you know."

*   *   *   *

Josie lay unresponsive for three days. This was not due to the physical injuries. It was as if her journey from that dark track to where she was discovered on the roadside was a final, monumental, physical effort—and now, having made the effort, her injured body was content to rest while her mind hid from the world. She could be described as sleeping, rather than unconscious. Her only movements, startling to Danny at first, were occasional twitches of her body or limbs, accompanied by frowns and grunts, as a person having nightmares.

Danny never left the hospital for those three days. He was out of her room only for brief forays to the cafeteria and to answer calls of nature in the public washroom down the hall. Russ spoke to the Crew Chief, Ellen Schmidt, and, with Paddy Donahue's approval, he was allowed extra days off. Late at night he would sometimes doze off, then wake with a start and reproach himself for sleeping. What if something should happen, what if she should die while he slept? He hated himself for the thought, but couldn't stop it from getting into his mind.

D Crew was working the dayshift so Russ and Ollie joined the vigil in the evenings after work. On Saturday and Sunday they dropped by once or twice during the day, to see if there was any change in Josie's condition, and to bring snacks and drinks for Danny.

"We have to keep your strength up, Tanner, Jo's gonna need you big time when she gets out of here. Drink your milk, you big shit!"

When Russ came to the hospital he always stopped at the door to ask of her, before stepping in. Then he would walk with obvious trepidation to stand beside Danny and stare down at her for minutes. He told Danny, "Champ, I have to *make* myself come here. It's hard seeing her like this. I keep asking, 'Is this really Josie lying here?' Yet I know I have to come…for her and for you."

Early Monday morning, before sunup, Danny had been in the basement cafeteria. The night nurse had made a practice of being in the room if possible whenever he was out. He found her there when he returned.

"I brought you some apple juice." She pointed to a glass on the table. "Guess what? Josie opened her eyes and tried to turn over…about ten minutes ago!"

"Did-did she say anything?"

The nurse laughed, "No. She actually growled at me when I straightened her pillow. She got right feisty."

"Oh, man. That's good news, isn't it?"

"I would think so. Maybe it won't be long now before she comes around. Let's hope so. She's lucky to have you, Danny."

Yeah? If you only knew.

Later, as the early morning sun turned the windows from black to gray, he saw Josie move her head slowly from side to side. Her eyes fluttered, then opened to swollen slits. She began to cry softly, tears welling and coursing down her cheeks. He dabbed at the tears with a tissue, and took her hand.

Her hand closed weakly on his, and in a small voice, hoarse because of her injured throat, she said, "Danny?" Her lips were cracked and dry.

He couldn't speak. His eyes stung and he felt the tears stream down his own face. *Oh, Honey—at last!*

"You're here." she croaked.

So are you! "Yeah, Honey...Danny's here. It's gonna be okay."

She turned to his voice. "I knew you're here. I knew it all the time." She frowned, "I got your letter."

He was puzzled. "My letter? I know you did..."

"He 'urt me, Danny."

"I know he did, he'll get...it's gonna be okay. You get better, Jo. Can you do that for me?"

She nodded and smiled faintly. "I will try, for you. I'm so tired...thank you for coming...I'm sorry...I'm..." her voice trailed off and she dozed, snoring quietly through her broken nose.

He sat there, staring hopefully at her, still holding her hand.

A little later the night nurse spoke from the doorway, "Want more coffee? My shift is almost over..."

Without turning from Josie, he said, "She woke up. Just now! We talked...she's tired, though, went back to sleep."

"Good! Oh, good. I'll put it on her chart—and that she spoke to you. Did she recognize you?"

"She did. My name was the first thing she said."

"Good. Just come to the desk if you want more coffee. She's fine now—I'm sure she's a lot better than she looks." She smiled and made conversation. "So, you two are engaged! Have you set a date?"

His face reddened. "Uh...no, not yet."

*   *   *   *

When Josie woke up again at eight o'clock, Danny was down the hall in the public washroom.

She asked for him. "Danny? Danny...are you 'ere? Danny?" When she heard no answer, she became agitated. She snapped her head from side to side, trying to see around the room. "Danny...please? I can't see you."

She tried to shout. "Danny? Help me! Danneee!"

A passing nurse heard the hoarse croak and ran into the room. Josie was twisting around on the bed, her neck straining to lift her head off the pillow.

"There, there...he's just out for a minute, dear. He's coming right back."

She lay her head back on the pillows. She cried, "Is he gone? Did he leave me here?" Her eyes were open as wide as the swelling would allow.

He heard her cry from the hall and came into the room at a trot.

The nurse said, "Here he is now, Josie..."

"Danny?"

"Right here, Jo! I'm not going anywhere."

"You didn't leave me."

"Never gonna happen, Jo. Danny's right here." He leaned close and whispered, "I just needed to go for a leak." She smiled and relaxed.

He took her hand between his two.

"What 'appened to me? Where am I, Danny?"

He gently squeezed her hand. "You...you got hurt, Hon. You're in the hospital. They're looking after you here. It's all gonna be okay..."

"Why did he hurt me? I don't know why he did it..."

"Only he knows why. He's no good, Jo..."

"You don't *understand*, Danny...I-I can't *remember*...I just remember him hurting me! *Why* did he hurt me? I don't know where we were...just the car in the dark." A tear escaped from the corner of her eye.

"Hon, don't worry about remembering. Don't try now. We can talk about it later. You just get well. Everybody wants you to get better. Okay?"

Her hand gripped his tightly. Her voice was shrill as she croaked, "He kicked me, too...an' choked me. Danny, I thought I was going to die!" She was becoming agitated again.

"Don't try to talk."

She swallowed. He could see it was painful.

"I am hurting so much. I want to sleep again…but it hurts too much. Will you stay 'ere if I go to sleep? I'll be afraid if you're not 'ere."

"I'm not going anywhere." He looked at the nurse, who had stayed in the room. "Can't you give her something…?"

She said, "You bet I can. The doctor ordered a painkiller for when she wakes up. I'll be right back."

He nodded. He stroked Josie's forehead. The pain showed in her face. She was biting at her lower lip. Every so often her little body twitched, her eyes flew open and she quietly gasped. He said to himself, *Honey, send all your pain to me. I'm bigger and uglier, and God knows I deserve it!*

The nurse returned with a tray. She whispered, "Josie, I have a needle for you."

Josie nodded. "Good…thank you."

When she went to sleep, the nurse said, "Sir, you should get up and move around a bit. This would be a good time; she'll be asleep for at least an hour…"

"Are you sure?" He stood up and stretched. "Do you have any more coffee? And call me Danny, would you? How's chances of getting another chair in here, for when our friends come?" He flashed The Smile.

"Okay, Danny. I'll get one and be right back. By the way, you can use this washroom when you need to…" She indicated a door on the other side of the bed.

She was back in two minutes with a straight-back chair.

"I grabbed an extra from the desk. It's never used…not as comfortable, but…"

"It'll do fine. Thanks a million," said Danny.

*   *   *   *

At ten-thirty he was asleep, his head resting on his arms, crossed on the metal side rails of her bed. Josie awoke when she turned in her sleep and caused a stab of pain in her ribs. She looked at him and saw he was sleeping.

It was then she discovered the ring.

She tried but couldn't remember how and when she had got it.

She pulled at it, watching him closely to make sure he didn't wake up. She grew panicky when it wouldn't budge, but she wet her finger with saliva, and managed to work it off. She put it inside her pillowcase. When a day shift nurse came by to take her vital signs Josie made sure Danny was still sleeping, then gave the ring to her.

"Could you put this somewhere safe for me, please?"

Placing it on her medication tray, she said, "I sure could. I'll put it at the desk in an envelope with your name on it. We keep patients' valuables there." As she attached the blood pressure cuff, she asked. "How are we feeling this morning?"

"I am 'urting...a lot."

"Well, you've been through a lot, haven't you. You're going to be sore for some time. We can give you a shot in about two hours." She entered the vital signs on a chart she took from the foot of the bed. "Has your friend been here all night? I see the doctor is allowing all-night visitors."

"Yes, poor Danny. He was up all day, too." She indicated the ring. "Please don't tell him about that."

Danny slept till eleven-fifteen. When he woke up, he leaned close and gently kissed her. Her eyes fluttered open.

"Hello, sleepy 'ead," she said, trying to smile.

He smiled back, "Sorry about dozing off—haven't been getting much sleep lately." He could see she was in pain. He took her hands in his. "You're hurting."

"Yes. My nose, my chin...I mean my jaw. And my side." Tears appeared at the corners of her eyes. "It's all *over* me. Danny, I-I can't stand the hurting! I'm sorry I'm so...so weak about it!" Her face was drawn.

"You are not weak, Jo. I'm gonna see if they can give you something. I'll be right back." He got up and went to the door. "Be right back, I promise."

He returned in a couple of minutes with a nurse.

"Josie," said the nurse, "We can't give you another needle till twelve o'clock." When she saw Josie nod and try to smile, she relented. "Oh, what the hell. I'll give it a little early. And then I'll speak to McKay and see if we can do better for you."

*   *   *   *

When Ollie came at five, Josie was resting, eyes closed, and Danny was reading a dog-eared copy of *Look* magazine.

Ollie announced, "Here I am, fans, in Technicolor, 3D, and stereophonic sound. Ta-da!" She stood beside Danny and he told her the good news about Josie's awakening.

"She's going to be okay; Dan, I just know it."

Josie opened her eyes and turned her head. "Ollie? Is that you...in Technicolor and-and all that?" she said in her hoarse voice.

"D'ya hear something, Tanner? Must be a chipmunk in here. Should I have brought some peanuts?"

"It's just me, Ollie." Croaked Josie, "Hi. Thank you for coming."

Ollie grinned, "Yeah, well y'see, there isn't a decent movie at the E.W., and I have to do something with my time." She bent and kissed Josie's brow.

"You haven't changed," croaked the patient.

"You think you want me to change?"

Josie smiled. "One can only hope. No, I didn't mean it, don't you *ever* change!"

At that point Danny excused himself and went into the washroom.

"Ollie," said Josie, "can you stay? I mean for the evening? Danny should go home and get some sleep. I don't think he's been out of 'ere."

"I agree—we'll kick his butt out of here. I'm good for the evening anyway, so you'll have company."

When he returned, Ollie said, "Tanner, you're tired and you're starting to smell bad. Go home, take a shower, and get some sleep. I'll stay here with Jo. Last thing we need is for you to get sick or something. You need a decent sleep."

"I'm okay. I'm staying…" he said stubbornly.

Josie's voice was raspy as she said, "Ollie's right, Danny. Go home to the cabin where it's quiet…get some rest. Can you stay with me till he comes back, Ollie?"

"Sure can. Move it Tanner, we'll see you later." She flipped him the car keys.

He yielded. "Okay, okay! Shit, I never could win against you two. I'll go." He leaned over the rail and kissed her cheek. "See you later, Babe."

"Please come back later?" she whispered.

"Oh, yeah, no fear. Ol, if anything…if there's any change…"

Ollie smiled warmly. "I'll call you. Get outta here."

*   *   *   *

When he returned at nine-thirty, Josie was sleeping. Ollie was reading the same copy of *Look*.

"Well," she said, "You look less like a corpse, Tanner." Glancing at Josie, she added. "She's just had a needle. Probably sleep for another hour."

"She needs it…sleep, I mean."

"Shit Dan, she hurts so bad. It's hard to sit here and watch. I want to hurt for her. I love that little kid…" She dabbed at a tear. "I have to go—I guess it's your shift, Dan."

He tossed her the car keys, "Yeah, my shift. I'll let you know if anything...you know..."

"I know," she said.

*   *   *   *

When Ollie came on Tuesday, Danny was sleeping, sprawled back in the chair. Ollie kicked his foot. He awoke with a start, looking guilty.

She said, "The patient's doing well, but the boyfriend's in a coma!"

Josie said, "Is it you, Ollie?" Her voice had lost some of the hoarseness.

Ollie leaned over the bed. "Jo...can you hear me? It's Ollie."

She opened her eyes. "I can hear you. I just can't see you well because my eyes are still swollen. Is Danny 'ere?"

"Oh yeah, he's right here."

"I'm here, Jo."

"Good. Does anyone want to give me a hug?"

"We both do. Shit-all-to-hell, everybody does! Me first, then she's all yours, Tanner."

They hugged her, each in turn. It was awkward because of the side rails and IV tubing.

"Can you stay long, Ollie?" asked Josie.

"I got the day off. Old Wilson isn't so bad, after all. I can stay as long as you want me to. I brought some things I figured you'd want—your purse, a night-gown, hairbrush and makeup kit. Nicole says hi."

"Oh...good. Thank you...and thank you for coming."

Ollie looked at Danny and shrugged as if to say, "Where else would I be?"

"What day is this? I 'ave lost track."

"It's Tuesday. You've been here for four...no...five days."

"Danny, did you stay 'ere all night?"

"Yeah, I did."

"You should go. You should get some sleep. But come back, okay?"

"No, I'll stay..." His relief at the change in her this morning was almost as overwhelming as his anxiety of the past four days.

Ollie said, "She's right, Tanner. Take the car, get some sleep and come back later."

He admitted to himself he was dog-tired. He kissed her before he left. "See you later, Hon."

When they were alone. Ollie said, "Well, Little Buddy, you're back in the world of the living!"

"Yes. Well...not...I can't remember some things. Could you hold my juice for me? It's hard to drink because I can't sit up."

Ollie held the cup and straw so she could drink. She took two long sips. The bruising made it difficult for her to swallow.

"How do you mean, you can't remember?" asked Ollie. She still held the cup. "Had enough juice?"

"One more sip...mmm, it's good. Cool. I was thirsty." She pulled away from the straw. "Well...I can't remember *going* with Gord...I just remember we were in the car. It was, um, in the woods. I slapped 'im...and he slapped me hard..." Her lower lip quivered as she recalled the assault. "And then I told him to stop. I got the door open and tried to get out. I yelled at him to stop...and I screamed for help. I kicked and scratched him...he slapped me again and then he punched me. He was trying to get my slacks off...he wanted, you know..."

"Jo, you don't have to talk about it now..."

"Yes I do! I 'ave to tell you about not remembering. Then he punched some more and started to choke me. I thought 'e was going to kill me. I was so scared!" She looked away. "Anyway, he did...sex to me. Then he kicked me, and he pushed me out in the mud!" she stopped and swallowed.

Ollie's eyes were filled with tears. "The bastard! Jo, he..."

"Let me finish! I was on the ground. He drove away so I started walking...when I saw cars coming I thought he was coming back to kill me so I hid in the ditch. He wanted to kill me, Ollie!" She looked puzzled. "After that I don't know what 'appened. I was in a ditch, then I woke up here. Ollie...what I'm worried about is, the last thing I remember before—is sitting in the lunchroom with you! It was the day I asked you if I should send a letter to Danny. There is nothing in between! I 'ave tried, but there is nothing. Did I send Danny a letter? After the first one?"

Ollie said, "No, you told me you didn't get it written. You told me the day he was leaving."

"Leaving?"

"Yeah, he went to Victoria on T.D. last Saturday. Don't you remember?"

Josie shook her head.

"You talked to him on the phone, just before he left. He came back early when you...when you got hurt."

"I-I can't remember. The last thing was us...you and me...in the lunch room."

"Jesus, you're missing more than a week. Damn, Jo...I should have been with you when you went to meet him!"

"You couldn't know this was going to happen, Ollie. I don't want to tell Danny about my memory until I figure out what happened. There might be something...something that might hurt him. I don't want him hurt, Ollie."

She didn't mention the ring.

*   *   *   *

Ollie figured out she had no memory from the morning of March twenty-third to the moment in Schaefer's car when the assault started, a period of ten days. She decided she would tell Doctor McKay when she saw him.

A nurse came in later in the morning with some clear, lukewarm soup and more juice. Josie managed both fairly well with a straw and Ollie's help.

"Shit-all-to-hell! Look at you eat! There's other patients, Jo!"

"Shut up, you! Don't make me laugh. It 'urts."

"Oh, shit, I'm sorry!"

The nurse unhooked her from the IV drip and took it away. Then she got her out of bed and made her go with Ollie into the washroom to pee. Josie saw her face in the mirror.

She croaked, "Oh...oh, Dieu! Look at me—I look like a prune! I'm a prune with bandages, Ollie! Oh, merde!"

"Not a pretty sight, for sure." Said Ollie. She added, "You'll heal, Jo."

"I'll 'ave to hide out for weeks!"

"Best place to hide would be in my room—our room. At least now I'm used to that ugly prune puss!" Ollie looked at her intently.

"You mean to move back?"

"I sure do."

"Yes! Oh, yes!"

They decided Ollie would move her things from Nicole's room for her.

The nurse came back at noon with a needle.

Danny came in at one-thirty. The head of the bed was raised and she was sitting up. Ollie had washed and brushed her hair for her and she was wearing her nightgown. The bandage on her head had been replaced with a smaller plaster.

She held her arms out to him. "Hello, Danny—come and hug me. Don't say a word about how ugly I am." He reached over the side rail and took her awkwardly in his arms.

"Feeling better?"

"Yes, much better today. Wait…where's the button for the nurse?" She found the call button pinned to the pillow. She pressed it five times. When there was no response, she pressed it a few more times. "This is the only time I 'ave buzzed them, so…"

A nursing aide came in on the run.

Josie said, "Would you take down these…damn…bars, please? I'm not a baby. I want to hug my friends and it's in the way."

"Okay. But they have to go up when you're sleeping." She dropped the rails down.

"Thank you. Now, Danny…"

He held her close for a full fifteen seconds. He whispered, "I love you."

"Thank you for coming. Did you get a good sleep?"

*   *   *   *

That evening Ollie went to Josie's room in the barracks to get her things for her. She saw the parka on Nicole's bed and added it to her pile.

"That's mine," said Nicole.

"What do you mean, it's yours?"

"It is. Josie gave it to me…"

"Yeah? Well guess what, you just fucking gave it back to her, Nicky."

"You don't understand, she gave it to me!" She blocked the door.

"And I just told you, you're giving it back! Can *you* understand? And, I believe that's her radio, too." The Baby Champ was on Nicky's dresser. "Put it on top of this pile and get out of my way." She stepped past Nicole holding the Baby Champ in place with her chin. "Shit, look at this parka…I'll have to take it to the frigging cleaners."

*   *   *   *

Josie's injuries healed steadily. A Gynecologist examined her and found no permanent damage. Dr. McKay changed her over from the I.M. Seconal to 292s and sleeping pills. On Monday morning they set her broken nose. The pain in her jaw eased enough for her to eat solid food. Also on Monday, Danny applied and received approval to take two weeks of his annual leave, to begin in four days, after D Crew's days off.

He received a message to call Doctor McKay. When he reached him, the doctor told him he was pleased with Josie's physical healing enough that he would soon be discharging her. He warned Danny that in spite of her present good spirits there was a real danger she might go into depression when the ramifications of the rape sunk in. He ticked off the signs of depression he should be on the lookout for. He added that Ollie would be watching Josie for the signs, too.

He said, "Are you aware she has lost some memory of events leading to the assault?"

"I know she was kind of, uh, confused about what happened in the car before it happened."

"I've recommended to the Medical Officer at the base that she be seen by a psychiatrist to help with her memory and perhaps forestall other ah, problems. I suggested the name of an excellent person here in Courtenay."

"Should I tell Jo...Josie...what happened, about the stuff she forgets? Would it help her if I did?"

"No, it might do more harm than good. I'm not a psychologist or psychiatrist but I have treated cases like hers. Dan, you should check with Doctor Sturtridge, the psychiatrist. Josie might be blocking out something too terrible for her to handle, although I can't imagine what could be worse than the attack. Miss Conti tells me Josie is not overly religious, and that's probably good. Sometimes strong, ah, beliefs...can bring on feelings of guilt after a rape."

Danny winced at the word. "No, she isn't very religious."

The doctor went on, "Now—without asking whether you and she have, ah—sexual relations, I must warn you not to be insistent. She'll likely need some time before she'll feel comfortable with it."

"I won't. Thanks again, Doc, for everything."

"I felt we should have this talk. Good-bye and good luck to you, Dan."

*   *   *   *

After work on Tuesday he arrived at the room carrying her suitcase and found her sitting on the edge of the bed. There was a fresh white bandage on her nose.

She exclaimed. "Danny, I was up walking! Want to walk with me?" Her voice had improved but was still hoarse.

"Sure. Did the Doc say it's okay?" He put the suitcase on the chair. "Ollie sent this..."

"Oh, good. Tell her thanks for me." She hopped off the bed. "They want me to walk around. They fixed my nose."

"Great, Hon." He took her hand.

"It's sore now, though. The guy was teasing me. He said my nose is so small he could 'ardly find it to fix it."

They strolled hand in hand through the hallways. After twenty minutes she told him she was tired and her ribs hurt so they headed back to her room. He helped her onto the bed and cranked the head up. He noticed she wasn't wearing the ring.

He asked, "Where's the ring?"

"Ring?"

"Yeah…it was on your finger."

"Oh, um…they wouldn't let me wear it. It's against the rules. It's with my stuff."

Her answer puzzled him. *That's all you have to say? Well, Honey, I have lots of time.*

He said, "I see. Just wondered. By the way, today was my last shift. I'm on days off, then I took leave, starting right after."

"Are you going somewhere?"

"No. Just want to be around for you, Hon."

"Oh."

✳   ✳   ✳   ✳

When he walked into her room on Friday at eleven, she was fully dressed, sitting in a wheel chair ready to leave. Her bruises had faded more and the swelling around her eyes was almost gone.

"Surprise! I'm going home!"

He smiled. "They're kicking you out, you mean. They're afraid you're gonna start some serious eating and bankrupt the place."

"Shut *up*, you." she squealed. "They won't let me walk out. I told them you would push me."

As he wheeled her toward the elevator, with her suitcase and purse on her lap, the day shift nurses were lined up at their station. She was greeted with:

"Good-bye, Josie."

"Good luck."

"Get well soon!"

"Look after her, Danny!"

She smiled for them. "Thank you. You are all so kind. Get me out of 'ere, quick, Danny, before I decide to stay!"

He said, "Hell, they're glad to be rid of you." He waved to them. "Thanks, ladies…for everything. You've been great."

In the elevator, she said, "I have to report to the Base Hospital tomorrow morning."

"How long are they gonna keep you there?"

"It's not to stay, just to report in. There's a doctor coming, to help me with my memory. I still can't remember…some things."

As he helped her into the car he noticed she still wasn't wearing the ring. *There are no rules to keep you from wearing it here, Honey!* He didn't comment.

She moved close to him on the seat and curled her feet under her. She patted the dashboard and said, "Good old J.H. My favorite car."

He drove through Comox village, turned left on Port Augusta Street and then onto Balmoral Avenue, heading for the road to Cape Lazo. As they passed the golf course she looked around and was suddenly agitated.

"Where are we going?" She sat up straight and put her feet down.

"Kye Bay. I figured you'd like to stop at the cabin. How long has it been since you saw it? I thought I'd take the road around Cape Lazo…"

Her words were rushed, ran together, "I-I would, b-but I 'ave to stay on the base tonight 'cause all my things are there, and I should check at work and I 'ave to go to the 'ospital in the morn…" She was trembling.

He realized, *She's scared as hell!*

A fleeting, terrifying memory had come to her—as an object at the very periphery of her vision, it was there, but she couldn't identify it.

"We don't have to go if you don't want…I should have asked you first" He slowed the car. "But, what's really wrong, Hon? You were scared. Really scared."

She shook her head. "I don't know what was wrong. When you didn't go the right way, I became so afraid." She calmed down, smiled. "I *would* like to see our cabin. And this road is fine, keep going." She pulled her feet up again and leaned on him, crisis over.

There was a cool onshore breeze blowing when they got out at the cabin.

Josie shivered. "It's cold today. Windy. But sometimes I like it when it's windy. I walk on the beach and don't worry about my hair blowing and I imagine the wind is bringing all the beach stuff into my hair and my mind. The sights and smells, the sounds of the seagulls and other birds…so I can keep them all with me until my next walk. Silly, eh?"

"Not silly at all. Just Josie Connor. It is cold though, want to go inside?"

"Yes!" She headed for the porch.

Inside, she walked around the place, touching familiar things. "Oh, Danny…I love this place so! It's just an old cabin but…"

"We've had good times here, Hon. I rented it for the summer. I'm hoping you're going to want to come and stay…" He was uncertain of his ground. He was thinking of the missing ring, but still didn't know how to ask her what it meant.

"Danny! All summer? How much will it cost…?"

"It cost a ton. But I have the money Mom left me…she'd be happy I'm spending it on us. I'm hoping after the doctors are done with you, you'll stay here with me. They'll probably give you some sick leave…"

"Oh, Yes I would! But I don't know if I'll be able to…to make…" She sighed. "Yes, I do want to stay 'ere. But be patient with me." She moved to him and he held her.

"Hey, Baby, I just want us to be together…it's all I ever wanted." He kissed her brow.

"Thank you for still wanting me here."

"I love you, Jo. Do you believe I love you?"

"I know you do." She stepped back, became animated. "Okay, we'll see what the M.O. says tomorrow then look out, 'ere I come!" Her giggle was still raspy but he loved it. "Could we light the fire and sit?"

They sat on the sofa before the fireplace. He put an arm around her and she sat against him with her feet pulled up. The cabin warmed. At two-thirty he woke her up.

"You and my arm were both asleep. It's time to get you to the base. Ollie has all your stuff back in the old room for you."

"Mmm…I guess you're right. But if I could, I would just stay right here"

At her barracks, she said, "Thank you, Danny. Will you call me later?"

*   *   *   *

Danny was somewhat perplexed and troubled by her reaction to him. Remembering her phone call the day he left for the T.D. and the conversations when he called her from Victoria just confused him more. He knew she had been genuinely happy to see him when she woke up in the hospital, and she had been calling for him the night she was hurt. When he left her side for a few minutes she had panicked and made him promise to stay close by. Before their problems, she had never been reticent about expressing her love, yet thinking back he realized she had not once said the words "I love you" since his return. She was as affectionate with him as ever, but behaving almost as if she considered him just a close friend. Coincidental with her silence about the ring, it served to increase his apprehension about getting her back. A friend was not what he wanted to be to her.

Quit beefing, he told himself, *be thankful she at least wants to spend her leave at the cabin—for whatever reason.*

CHAPTER 29

▼

The M.I.R.—Medical Inspection Room—was known by all but the fastidious as the Base Hospital. (It was, after all, not a room but a building with wards and all.) Each morning at eight o'clock "Sick Parade" was held, when base personnel with complaints ranging from hangnails to fractures, from hangovers to heart attacks, were seen and treated. Josie had not had to go to the M.I.R. since she signed-in to Comox so the place wasn't familiar to her. She went to the counter where a Corporal Medical Assistant was receiving the sick. It took a minute before he understood she had been told to report.

She was ushered in to see the Senior Medical Officer. He was a lanky and sympathetic Squadron Leader, whose unruly red hair was thinning on top, showing a freckled pate. He asked her in a British accent how she was feeling and explained he had left her in St. Joseph's after consulting with Dr. Mckay. They had agreed she would receive better care there considering the ah...specific nature of the assault and her injuries. The reason he had ordered her to see him was to tell her she was going to be treated by a psychiatrist in Courtenay, to see if she could "untangle that memory problem." Her first appointment was set for the next morning at ten. He told her to see the dental clinic in the same building to get something done about "those bashed-up fangs."

"And...let me see...Oh, yes! I'm putting you on sick leave, effective today. I've notified your section head. We'll start you off with forty-five days...then we'll see how you're coming along. I'll extend it if needed. You must hang about here for a bit, then if the psychiatrist and dentist are done with you, you can travel to your home if you wish, or just take a nice trip somewhere." He gave her a conspiratorial wink. "I'll make sure you have ample time to do whatever you wish. If you do need more time just ring me up and—Bob's-your-uncle—it shall be done!" He winked again. "The R.C.A.F. can do without one Airwoman for a month or two, I rather think, don't you?" He wrote something on a pad. "This is something for your pain, the Pharmacist will fill it." She had seen the Pharmacy sign at one end of the waiting room.

"So then, AW Connor, off you go for now! Come in if you have any complications…and good luck. You've had more than a bit of bother haven't you?"

She said, "Yes. Thank you, Sir…um, my side still hurts…the ribs."

"Actually, it will be sore for a bit. You must rest. All we can do for ribs is tape them up and give you the pills. If they're still achy after a week, come see us. Will you need transport into Courtenay for your appointments?"

"Um, no…I 'ave a friend…no. Thank you." She couldn't tell him where she would be staying.

He smiled. "Fine!" He passed her a slip of paper. "Here's Doctor Sturtridge's address in town. Off with you, then. Dental Clinic's down the hall."

As she left the building after seeing the Pharmacist and getting a dental appointment, she thought, *Forty-five days! I can go to the cabin! And Danny's off for two weeks, too.*

She saw the Ford in its parking space so she phoned him at the barracks.

"Danny, they gave me a month and a half—maybe longer if I want!"

"Great, Jo. So, what are you gonna do with yourself?"

"Be with you. At the cabin…if you still want me there."

If I still want her? "You know I do, Josie."

"Then let's do it! I don't want to be on the base with all the people. Everybody will ask questions. I 'ave to go to Courtenay for the other doctor at ten tomorrow. Can you drive me there? Then we'll come back here for my stuff."

"Sure can. I'll pick up some groceries while you're in there."

"No! Don't! I want to do it with you…please?"

He knew how she loved grocery shopping. "Okay, I'll twiddle my thumbs and wait for you."

*   *   *   *

Josie was relieved to find that Dr. Allison Sturtridge, Doctor of Psychiatry, was a woman. She appeared to be in her mid-forties. Large-boned, with somewhat severely cut clothes and auburn hair worn in a braided bun. She was quiet-spoken, genuine, and solicitous of Josie's well being. Josie was comfortable confiding to her from the start. They chatted for most of the first visit about Josie's childhood, her family and her life in the Air Force. She arranged for Josie to come in twice a week for three weeks so they could work together to regain her lost memory. After three weeks, they would see how she was responding before setting more appointments.

*   *   *   *

After her appointment they did the shopping and went to the base to pick up some clothes for Josie. Back at the cabin just before noon, he noticed she was favoring her side. She told him her ribs were "a little bit sore." After lunch and some argument he convinced her to take a 292 and rest in bed for an hour, and she slept soundly till four fifteen. It wasn't going to be easy to convince her she wasn't fully recovered.

Ollie and Russ came by after work and stayed for supper, which Danny and Ollie cooked.

When she came in the door, Ollie produced the parka. It was in a dry cleaner's bag. "Look what I found, Jo."

"Oh, but I…"

Ollie shook her head and frowned at her. "Just put it away, okay?" Danny was looking the other way.

"Yes…okay. Thank you." She took it to the bedroom.

After supper, while Danny and Russ had at each other in their always-cut-throat games of cribbage, Josie convinced Ollie to go for a walk. She took something from her purse before they left the cabin.

When they were gone, Russ commented. "Jesus, I hated to see her so hurt, Champ…I should have killed the sonofabitch!"

"Gil tells me you tried to do just that."

"Yeah. Maybe it's best the cops arrived when they did. I just hope she's gonna be okay. Be gentle with her, Dan—and for Chrissake behave yourself." Then pointing at the board he said, "Your hand was eight."

"What're you talking about?"

"Your hand was eight. You pegged ten."

"Bull. My hand was ten."

"You're screwing me."

"Beating you maybe."

"Screwing me."

*   *   *   *

On the beach, Ollie said, "Listen, stupid, your good friend Nicole was happy to give the parka back."

"Oh. I shouldn't 'ave given it to her…I was so angry and hurt that day. Thank you."

"It was nothing. So, I guess you're glad to be back at the cabin? You're looking happy enough."

"I am trying to be…"

"Trying? Jo, remember what Dr. Sturtridge told you, get on with your life. You and I both know your life is with Dan."

"I said I'm trying. He 'as been so wonderful…I don't want to disappoint him, or hurt him."

"I don't think I like the sound of that. How could you disappoint him, Jo? The guy friggin' worships you." When she didn't get an answer after they walked a hundred yards, she pressed, "There's a problem, isn't there. Better tell me all about it, Little Buddy."

Josie turned back toward the cabin, walked a few paces and then stopped. Ollie caught up and saw she was crying.

"Jo…Let's talk, dammit." She sat down on a rock. Josie joined her.

Josie looked forlorn. "Oh, Ollie, what if that…damn pig has made me pregnant?"

"Oh, Christ. Do you have any reason to think he did? Morning sickness?"

"Yes. One time…well, three times in one day. It wasn't in the morning."

"How about your period?"

"I don't know! I can't remember if I had it. I was due the week when I can't remember anything. But you know mine are never regular. I-I know he…came in me that night." She pounded her thigh with a fist. "And we slept together one other time…had sex once, when we were going out. It was before Danny hit him in the Wets. I didn't use anything. So stupid!"

"Would Nicole know if you had your period?"

"No. I never told her anything personal. If only I didn't screw him! I didn't even love him. Just gave in like a damn horny…tramp!"

"Oh, no! No more of that talk. You are not a tramp! Don't get feeling guilty. You're not the villain in this, Schaefer is! You have to get tested…go to a doctor in town, not an Air Force M.O. I'll help if you need money."

Josie took something out of her pocket. "Look at this. It was on my finger when I woke up at the hospital."

"It's a diamond." She took it from Josie's hand. "I don't recall seeing it before…"

"I took it off in the hospital, it's been in my purse. How can I give it back? I don't ever again want to see the pig!"

"It's from Schaefer?"

"Who else, Ollie? He *said* he wanted me to marry him!"

"Josie, you were trying to break up with him. It's why you went in his car with him. How could you have accepted a diamond? It doesn't make sense!"

"I know it doesn't…not now, at least. But did I make up with him? Was I too stupid to say no? Maybe it was what we fought about. Maybe it made him angry. I don't know what I said to him! If I could just remember."

Ollie handed her the ring. "Look, put it away. Just till we figure all this out. Your period might be screwed up because of your injuries or the drugs. Don't worry about giving the turd back his ring. From him it's probably a fake, anyway. Dan's your guy, Jo."

"Okay. But you can't tell Danny. I don't want to 'urt him…he doesn't know I…"

"The only way you can hurt him now, is if you don't stay with him."

As they headed back to the cabin, Ollie saw her wince and bend to favor her left side.

"Are you okay, Jo? You look like you're hurting."

"A bit…the doctors said it will hurt for another week. I'll be fine."

"Hell, Kid, you've been so upbeat I forget you were beat up! You look tired, too. Have you got painkillers? If you don't, then get some. If you do, use them, for Chrissake."

"I will. They gave me 292s. I forget about them. I'm so worried about my period I can't concentrate. I'll take one when we get inside."

Three of them hounded her into bed an hour later. Ollie gave Danny hell for not seeing her fatigue. She made them promise to get her up in an hour, but they left her alone and she slept through the night.

The next day after lunch she came out of the bathroom with a huge smile. She hugged Danny mightily.

He said, "To what do I owe this? Don't get me wrong, I love it!"

"Oh…nothing special. I just like to be close, and hugging is close, isn't it?"

"It sure is. We could've got closer but our buttons were in the way."

"Funny guy."

Later, when he went out to give Morrie a hand with a blown-down clothes-line, she called Ollie.

"It started! I'm so relieved."

"Great news," said Ollie. "I told you, you worry too much."

*   *   *   *

She and Danny spent the two weeks of his leave almost exclusively at Kye Bay. There were excursions into town for her appointments and to do some shopping, each time followed by quick dashes back to the cabin. She made it clear by her actions she wanted nothing more than to be close to him. He would hold her for hours as they lay together at bedtime or in the middle of the day. Sometimes he could feel her trembling. She didn't volunteer to make love and he didn't ask her to.

Walking on the beach, preparing a meal or just when passing him inside the cabin, she would stop, come close, and cling to him.

One morning Danny had been awake, quietly watching her when she woke up, she turned to him sleepily and said, "Thank you for being here with me. Thank you for keeping our cabin. I love you, my Danny."

With those few words, he felt the tightness that had been inside him for weeks leave him. Josie was with him—and she said she loved him!

At the start of her third week with Dr. Sturtridge, there was still no recall of events leading to the assault. The curtain across those ten days remained drawn. The doctor was perplexed, especially when it appeared there had been no traumatic event she was subconsciously blocking. The terrible event was the beating and rape—and she remembered those in detail.

During the sessions Josie discussed, freely and honestly, her past and present relationships. They talked about Danny; about Schaefer; about family and about friends.

"You have to honestly decide, Josie, which of your relationships are healthy; which are beneficial to you. At this time, I would think it obvious you and Danny love each other, but ask yourself, is this okay as it is, or is change needed. I believe the two of you are able, and ready now to make it work. Hang onto your friend-ship with Olivia and Russ...they're valuable to you; I notice when you talk about either of them you always smile and even laugh. It's largely because of them, and Danny of course, that you have not had any problem with depression and proba-bly won't. As to your father, you are carrying around far too much guilt there. Don't. You might wish to drop him a line, just the 'hello I'm fine' kind of thing.

See then what happens. But don't dwell on it. Considering what you've been through, you are surprisingly well adjusted, Josie. Just remember to believe in yourself. Have faith in your ability to make good choices."

Dr. Sturtridge's conclusions regarding the memory loss could not be described as daring: The missing time would or would not come back, tomorrow, next week, or next year, and if it did it could be a sudden recall or a gradual one. She saw no reason for the time being to continue their sessions but told Josie to call her if she had any problems she would want to discuss.

*   *   *   *

APRIL 14TH

Twelve days after the attack and rape, Ollie phoned from work. Josie answered the phone.

"Jo, it's Ollie. Guess which two lowly L.A.W.s are gonna have to start taking orders, effective tomorrow!"

"What are you talking about?"

"Think, Jo. I'll give you a hint—the green sheets are out…"

She caught on. "The guys got their hooks?"

"Yep."

"Both of them! Danny will be so 'appy…can I tell him?"

"Yeah, but nobody else better find out till tomorrow when it's announced—deal?"

"Oh, yes. Tell Russ congratulations for me. Isn't this great? They both deserve it so much."

Twice a year, in April and October, a Promotion Board at Air Force Headquarters awarded all permanent promotions for enlisted ranks from a list of eligible personnel. The twice-a-year format meant there were always dozens of promotions on any base the size of Comox. That triggered the traditional "promotion day" celebration. After work, all the newly promoted NCOs celebrated in their old messes and clubs before being welcomed into the new. The parties went on till the (often postponed) bar closings.

When he and Russ dropped in to the Wets at four-thirty, Danny was there for the first time in a month. By way of celebration, they were subjected to unmerciful ribbing from the rest of the Wild Dogs. Danny didn't want to leave Josie home alone too long, so they didn't stay. The Dogs understood—Josie was, after all, one of their members. And, as Gerry pointed out, "The subjects of our celebration ain't necessarily necessary for a celebration, anyway!"

Danny was surprised when Craig Tucker, whom he had once beaten and thrown into the sea, approached him. There were new hooks pinned to his uniform sleeves.

Tucker said, "Hey, Tanner...Dan, can I shake your hand? You're a good man and you deserve the hooks. How is your girl friend? What happened to her...that was real bad, man, she's a sweet kid."

"Thanks uh, Tuck, I appreciate that. Congratulations yourself...I'll tell Josie you asked about her." He thought, *I'll be damned!* "We're just leaving for the Corporals'...want to join us?" On their way up the road Russ's body language said he wasn't pleased with the company, but he went along with the situation. Tucker joined some people from his own section when they arrived at the Corporals' Club.

The first person to greet Danny and Russ was Ellen Schmidt, "Welcome to your new club." They could see she was well into the celebration as she put an arm around each of them. "The two best FighterCOps at 51!" she exclaimed.

Russ said, "You're prejudiced, El...but thanks!"

"Bullshit! You guys deserve it, big time. The only bad thing is, we're likely gonna lose one of you off the crew. How's Josie, Dan? Are you two enjoying your leave? You slackard."

"She's getting there, El...it's been hard for her."

"I bet it is! I can't imagine how I would handle something like that. I hope they lock the bastard up with a chocolate key. Life's hard enough, but a guy like him right on the base, we don't need that."

They had a couple of drinks and at five-thirty returned to the Wets to pick up Ollie. They went to Kye Bay for supper and a quiet Fearsome Foursome celebration at the cabin. During supper Ollie and Russ embarrassed Josie by checking her nose to see if it had straightened perfectly. Her bruises were all but faded to nothing. She had a small scar on her brow just below the hairline.

When she inspected the nose, Ollie said, "Shit! I was hoping yours would be crooked like mine."

Russ said, "You're as gorgeous as ever, Jo."

She beamed.

Leo came by after supper to have a drink and congratulate the boys. Lorna, still angry with Danny, did not come with him. Leo's contribution to the celebration was an old joke: "Well, fellas, you don't have to worry about catching the clap any more, it's a disease of the privates, and you're Corporals now!"

＊　　　＊　　　＊　　　＊

When his leave ended Danny went back to work with the Wild Dogs. The crew was working the 1600 to midnight shift. Donahue called him aside on his first day back.

"I wanted to congratulate you, Dan. You've done a terrific job and you deserved the promotion. You and Russ both." He shook hands. "The C Ops O wants you to see him when you come in tomorrow. And Moe Morrisey would like to hear from you." Danny felt guilty. He had forgotten his promise to call Moe.

"Thanks, Sir. I think you had a lot to do with my hooks and I appreciate it. Any idea what the C Ops O wants?"

"I do. But I'll let him tell you."

"Ellen figures either Russ or I'll be sent to another crew. It makes sense…"

"That could be what it's about. Tell your girl we're all pulling for her, Dan."

"Thanks, I will. Now I'd better get to work, I guess."

He went to work fifteen minutes early the next day and reported to the NCO i/c Ops and was ushered into the C Ops O's office.

F/L Hewitson greeted him with, "Tanner…Corporal Tanner. I wanted to tell you how happy I am about your promotion. I tried to get it for you back in October. I'm sure you'll justify our confidence in you." He inquired about Josie, expressing his wish for her full recovery, "How is she doing so far?"

"She's getting better every day, Sir. Thank you for asking. And thanks for…your faith in me."

Hewitson told him he was to be the new Crew Chief on E Crew, beginning on the first of July. The present Crew Chief had been promoted to Sergeant and was to be transferred out.

"Everyone tells me I'm pulling you off a hell of a good party outfit in that D-Crew." He smiled and joked, "Surprised we didn't wake up one morning to find the whole bunch of you in the lock-up—Wild Dogs indeed. Hate to break up a good thing, but we all have to move on, don't we."

C H A P T E R 30

▼

We had an early and glorious summer…

COMOX—MAY, 1956

When May arrived and the weather warmed, Danny and Josie went back to their old routine, staying in the barracks when he was on the graveyard shift and at the cabin the rest of the time. For a time, Josie was uncomfortable about being around anyone but intimate friends so they didn't go out much.

At work one day, Russ said, "Ollie wants me to feel you out about getting Jo out of the cabin. She figures we can all go to a movie in town like we used to. Maybe go to a restaurant after. What do you think?"

"I'll give her a try. She may be ready by now."

Josie was hesitant, still fearful of meeting people. After some thought, however, she said, "Yes, okay…I'll phone Ollie."

The next night they went to the early show at the E.W. It was a cool evening, giving Josie an excuse to wear her parka. Her bandages had long since been removed and her bruises were just a memory. Danny felt the familiar constriction in his throat when she emerged from the bedroom all dressed, for she was as lovely as ever.

In the theatre, Danny put his arm around Josie and she leaned close to him. The picture was *Some Came Running*, with Frank Sinatra, Dean Martin and a new actress, Shirley McLean.

Part way through the picture, Danny felt Josie's shoulders become rigid. She straightened in the seat, and moved slightly away from him. She picked up her purse, placed it on her lap and fidgeted with it.

He was attuned to her moods. He whispered, "What's wrong, Hon?"

She shook her head. "Nothing," she said.

But it was obvious she was agitated.

"You sure?"

She didn't answer. She sat back in the seat, but a minute later he felt her shoulders begin to shake.

He pulled her closer and whispered to her again, "Honey, you're crying...what is it?"

"I 'ave to get out. Take me out of here!" She stood and took her parka from the seat back.

Ollie and Russ stood up to allow them to squeeze by.

Ollie said, "What's up, Jo?"

Josie didn't answer. Danny shrugged and said, "We're going out for awhile...we'll be right back." He hurried to catch her. At the door to the lobby he told an usherette Josie felt sick but they would be coming back in.

He followed her as she walked a few yards along the sidewalk. When he caught up, she turned and clung desperately to him. She sobbed into his jacket. He held her, cradling her head with one hand while she cried for five minutes. He felt helpless. When he tried to talk to her she shook her head back and forth without taking it from his chest. She continued to sob.

Ollie and Russ came out and found them. He signaled to them to say nothing, so they stood a few feet away and watched.

Her crying stopped and without lifting her head, she said. "Take me home."

He told Ollie and Russ, "She wants to go home...sorry." He shrugged again, helplessly. They all went to the car.

No one spoke for the entire drive to the base. Josie sat close to him, but not touching. When he drove through the gate she sat up and looked around.

"Where are we? Where are you going?"

He took her hand. "We're at the base, Hon...taking Ollie and Russ home."

"Oh."

He stopped by the Airwomen's barracks. Ollie opened the rear door. Then she leaned over the seat.

"Jo, are you okay?"

She nodded her head once.

"Do you want to come in...stay in our room tonight?"

"No. I 'ave to go home."

"I didn't think so." Ollie turned to Danny. "I just wanted to give her the choice, Dan." she explained.

"I understand. I'll call you in the morning," he said.

"You'll call me tonight. I mean it, Tanner."

Russ leaned in the driver's window. He murmured, "You sure she's okay, Dan?"

"No, I'm not. I'll let you guys know. We'll get home now...sorry about the movie."

Josie surprised them, "Good night, Russ...and Ollie. I just need to be home. I'm sorry."

He had just turned onto Knight road when she started crying again. He put his right arm around her and pulled her close. She resisted for a moment and then relaxed against him and her crying subsided. His own tears of helplessness almost caused him go off the road at the top of the Kye Bay switchback.

"Sonofabitch!" he muttered as he braked the car.

She looked up. "Language, language." She said with a little smile. "You 'ad better use both hands, Danny...we're almost home now, anyway."

"Yeah. I'd better." He continued cautiously down the hill.

Inside the cabin, he pleaded, "Can you tell me what's wrong, Hon?"

Her response was to turn and cling to him. They were standing just inside the door.

He said, "Josie—Honey—you're scaring me! What is it?"

She just shook her head and went to the bedroom. He hung up their coats and followed her. She sat on the edge of the bed and he sat beside her.

"Honey," he said, "want to talk to me?"

She reached for his hand, "Yes. I do. First, I need some fresh air...and some time to think; to sort out my mind. I want to walk on the beach. Would you come?"

"Sure. Right now?"

"Yes. I'll be out in a minute. I 'ave to...to fix my hair. Could you wait in the kitchen?"

Alone in the room, she went to the wardrobe, opened a suitcase and took out the ring. She stared long and hard at it, then returned ring and suitcase to the wardrobe. She quickly brushed her hair and came out wearing her parka. She gave him a wan smile, went to the door and waited. He threw on a jacket and joined her on the stoop.

"All set?" he said as cheerfully as he could. She didn't reply but started across the grass of the yard. When he caught up, she linked an arm through his. They walked farther than they usually did. When they reached the point just before 51

Beach, where they could see the outline of the radomes at 51, she stopped. She turned, clung to him again. After two minutes, she stepped back from him.

"Danny, I remember."

He didn't understand. "Remember?"

"It came back...those days I forgot. I'm remembering things...not every-thing..." She made a decision. "Let's go back now and I'll tell you about it. It's kind of cold. I shouldn't 'ave dragged you out 'ere."

"Sure, let's go back in."

At the cabin she hugged him. She pulled his face close and they kissed. She took his hand and led him to the bedroom. They sat down as before.

She wiped her tears and looked at him. She sniffled and said, "Danny...I remember. When Dean Martin said that word, about the girl...when he said she's just a pig. It-it's what he was calling me before he hit me...Schaefer. He called me a pig and a slut." She looked up at him. Her eyes were forlorn. "He said I was your pig! He called me that, so I slapped 'im...."

"Jo, I..." He tried to speak but she shook her head.

"Let me finish. I wanted to tell him about you and me. Tell him I was coming back to you. It's why I was in his car with him. I shouldn't 'ave trusted him when he drove the wrong way but I didn't know. He went to a dark little road and I told him about us. He called me those names and started to try to...to do sex to me. I tried to fight...and he started hurting me. He punched and punched, till-till I was almost, um, unconscious. I fought as 'ard as I could, Danny, but he is too strong. He choked me till I couldn't breathe. He wouldn't stop. I thought he wanted to kill me...I thought I was going to die!" Her lips trembled as she fought not to cry.

She pulled away from him slightly. "Danny—my memory is all mixed up. I remember I was going to write you a letter, but then I think I remember *talking* to you. I wanted to tell him I couldn't see him anymore because I was going to always be with you. It was why I *went* there with 'im." A puzzled look took over her face. "Did I send you a letter? Did we talk..." Then realization. "We did! We talked on the phone! Yes. You were in Victoria?"

Danny nodded, afraid to speak and interfere with her thought process.

"There is another thing I 'ave to tell you," she continued, "It's about him and me..." She hung her head. "Danny, I...I..." She couldn't look at him. Her tears started again. "I...we..." She looked at the dark window and then back to him. "I did it with him, had sex with him. We did it one time. I mean before that night. Do you understand what I am saying? I was so confused, I thought I 'ad lost you. I didn't care about myself any more. Danny, I know there is no excuse...I just did it. I'm so ashamed!" It was as if she couldn't believe her own words. "I loved *you*—but I still did that with him. Can you ever forgive me? Oh, Honey, I don't deserve to 'ave you, but I love you so much!"

She took a breath. "I am telling you this because I remember now...when we talked on the phone you said you wanted to marry me." She looked at him beseechingly. "Please, Danny, forgive me? I'm not a pig and a slut, am I? Am I, Danny?" She blinked and swiped at the tears now flowing down her face.

He spoke intensely, "No you're not. *You are not, Jo!*" He pulled her close. "Oh, Jesus, Honey, what have I done to you? You're the sweetest...the purest person I'll ever know! You have to believe that or that bastard Schaefer wins! Don't let him win, Josie."

As if she hadn't heard him, she said, "You don't 'ave to marry me, now. It's what I want the most, but I'll understand if..."

He smiled and raised his voice above hers, interrupting her. "Josie Connor, this is the biggest pile of *bullshit* I ever heard."

She sat in stunned silence. Did he think she was lying? "No, Danny, it's...I'm telling the..."

He cut her off, "It's bullshit, because you have done nothing to forgive—repeat, nothing! You must believe that. Christ, Honey, I'm the one here who needs forgiving. I'm the one who drove you away to meet a guy like Schaefer. *I* did that, not you! All you ever did was try to keep us together; you stayed until I made it impossible for you to stay. I'll go down on my knees every damn day to beg your forgiveness—and to thank you for coming back to me. To thank you for ever being with me in the first place!"

He took a deep breath before going on. "It was that bastard Schaefer who took you to that road in the bush. It was Schaefer beat you senseless and raped you! You couldn't know he was going to do it. Don't you ever again talk of being in the wrong. If you do, Honey, he wins! You have to beat him, Honey—for us! Do you understand?"

She stared at him for a long moment. In a small voice, she said, "Yes, I do. Thank you..."

He wasn't finished. "I did ask you to be my wife. I still want it. I want it more than I want anything in this world. Why in hell do you think I put that ring on your finger in the hospital?"

She gasped. Wide-eyed, she whispered, "You? It was from you?"

"Of course it was. I put it on you the first night. I bought it months ago."

"Oh!" She was still wide-eyed.

"Where else would it..." Then it dawned. "Oh Christ, I see."

"Yes, you see? I couldn't remember anything…so I thought it could be from *him,* and I just forgot. I was afraid to let you see it. If it was from him, you wouldn't understand, maybe you would think I *wanted* it, wanted to marry him, and maybe I would lose you. I didn't know what to do with it. I took it off and gave it to the nurse when you were sleeping. Danny, I almost threw it away! Why didn't you say something about it?"

"Hon…this is going to sound so very stupid. When I saw you weren't wearing it, I…I thought it meant you weren't sure about us, or maybe didn't want it. Didn't want *me.* When I asked about it you evaded the questions. I guess I was afraid I'd hear something I didn't want to hear." He smiled ruefully. "I did tell you once I'm a coward."

She shook her head in disbelief. "Oh, Danny, we 'ave been so stupid."

"Well…I have, anyway. Where is it? The ring."

"It's here. Wait." She hopped off the bed. She went to the wardrobe and got the ring from the suitcase. She shyly held it out to him. "I want to be your wife, my Danny. I want to be with you forever."

He took it and reached for her right hand. She pulled it back and held out the left. She pointed to the correct finger. "It's this one. You put it on the wrong finger before."

In a voice husky with emotion, he said, "What the hell do I know about that stuff." He slipped the ring onto the proffered finger. "Come here, you." He pulled her close and they kissed tenderly. He kissed the tears from her eyes.

Then, suddenly, he groaned and flopped back on the bed, hands covering his face, feet kicking in the air.

"Oh, shit," he moaned, "I'm engaged! Dan Tanner is friggin' engaged! Won't somebody out there *save* me? I could end up *married!*" He sat up, looked to the window and screamed, "HELP! SOMEBODY HELP!" He covered his face again.

Any tension remaining between them evaporated at that moment. She giggled her wonderful giggle. She pried his hands apart and squealed into his face, "SHUT *UP,* YOU! What about poor me? And you didn't phone Ollie and she'll kill you and then I'll be a widow! Big, stupid *Corporal!*"

She jumped on him and pressed her body to his. She whispered into his ear, "I want to make love with you now. I missed it so much! Can we?"

He grinned. "Did you ever see me turn *that* down?"

She made a show of peering down the front of his pants. "Are you 'ome, Peter?" She giggled again.

Said he, "I think ol' Pete's gonna be happy having you around again, Babe."

They made tender, glorious love.

*   *   *   *

Afterward as they lay together, clothes in a heap on the floor, she said, "Danny, we said and did such terrible things to each other. It was as if we looked for ways to hurt. I...we...didn't trust our love enough."

He thought about what she said before he responded. "I couldn't say it better."

"We must never do it again. No more hurting."

"I hope not. The day when you came for your things at the cabin...that's when I knew it had to stop. What I saw in your eyes made me want to crawl in a hole. I never want to see it again. Then, the first night in the hospital...seeing what I had done..."

She hugged him. "Shh. I want us to heal now. No more blaming, okay? I want us to be happy. Always."

He said, "You got it. Starting right now."

He had been absently stroking her thigh as they talked. She was aroused again. She pulled his head down to her breast. She arched her body to meet his. "Can I be a slut and a pig for you? Just for tonight?"

With a wide grin, he repeated, "You got it—starting right now!"

CHAPTER 31

▼

COMOX—JUNE, 1956

Ollie and Russ were in the Snack Bar. Ollie had read a message at work from Air Defense Command, ordering Cpl. Russell Knight transferred to 31 AC&W Squadron, R.C.A.F. Station Edgar, Ontario, to be effective July first. The message had arrived at Comox two days earlier. It also stated that Cpl. Knight was granted fifteen days Compassionate Leave, commencing June fifteenth.

Ollie asked, "When were you planning to tell me about it, the day before you leave, on the frigging fourteenth? Or *were* you planning to tell me?"

Russ looked uncomfortable. "I *was* going to tell you when it came in…just couldn't figure out *how.*"

"I don't get it. You've barely been here a year. Since when do they transfer you after one year?"

"You know us FighterCOps get moved around a lot. It's not like I'm some 407 Airframe Tech…"

"Bullshit. I know there's more to this. I just don't understand the big secret."

He looked down at his hands. "I've never bullshitted you, Ollie, so I won't start. I requested a transfer."

She put a hand over her mouth and stared at him.

When it became obvious she wasn't going to speak, he went on, "I…I have to get away. I have to get the hell away from this place."

"Why, for Chissake?…Why?"

"It doesn't matter why. I just have to go…"

"What's with the compassionate leave?"

He looked past her, at a picture on the wall behind her. "I told them I heard from my sister in Ontario…you know we were separated as kids. I told them I wanted to go there and find her. That's the reason it's to Edgar, it's close to Toronto." His grin was forced. "I guess I've learned a few things from the Champ...about how to work the system."

She shook her head. "But you didn't really hear from a sister, did you?" He just nodded. With an ironic grin, she said, "Shit-all-to-hell, Russ, I've had guys dump me...but they didn't want to run three thousand miles to get away!"

"It's not about you, Babe."

Tears were glistening in her dark eyes. "I'd like to know what the hell it *is* about. Don't you *owe* me that?" She pushed her mug to him. "Get me another one, will you? I don't have any money with me."

He went to the counter. She wiped at her eyes with the back of her hand. He returned with two mugs.

Ollie spoke as she stirred her coffee. "Knight—I know why you can't stay here."

He looked trapped. "Yeah?"

"You're in love with Josie."

He looked down at his coffee mug. She stared, waiting for him to speak but he didn't.

In a flat voice, she said, "You are, aren't you, Russ."

A full minute passed before he replied, "I'm sorry, Ollie..."

"Shit, so am I sorry! But I can't blame you. She's certainly easy to love."

"Ollie...Dan must never know this. I'm his best friend."

"He never will. I promise you."

"Josie either...never!"

"Never, Russ. Don't worry." She looked away. Then she bowed her head. "So, you and I...we were just...what?"

"Ollie, it's not the same kind of...aw shit, couldn't I love both of you? I loved being with you, we had a lot of fun. You'll be okay, you're smart, and tough—and you *know* you're beautiful...you'll..."

She hissed, "Oh no, Knight. Don't start bullshitting me, now. Don't even try it!"

"It's not bullshit. I...I...you're the greatest thing that ever happened to me. That's the truth. It's one reason this is so tough. One reason I have to get away."

"Yeah, right. Will you at least write to me? I know how you hate to write letters, but this is me, Russ." She reached for his hands. "When you...*if* you ever get over her...I'll be around. I'm *not* in love with anyone else and I never will be. Will you do that for me, Knight? Keep in touch at least?"

He tried hard to smile. "Yeah, Ol, I will. You know you're my Babe."

Ollie stood up. "I have to go…I'm going back to the barracks." She wheeled and walked quickly to the stairs. The world around her was a blur through her tears. She could barely make her way to the barracks. For once, she was glad Josie wasn't in their room.

After she left, Russ sat for half an hour with his head buried in his arms.

*   *   *   *

Josie heard from the Crown Prosecutor who was trying the case against Schaefer. She was required at a meeting in his office at the courthouse in Courtenay to run through her testimony.

She was asked to describe the attack and the time shortly before and after.

The Prosecutor told her Schaefer's lawyer, a high-profile criminal attorney from Vancouver, would use the common defense of the time—he would attack the victim's character. In fact, they had already made certain allegations regarding her morals in an attempt to have the charges dismissed before trial.

She would be asked if she had had voluntary sex with Schaefer on the night of the attack.

She answered the prosecutor, "No. Of course not! Can anyone believe I volunteered to get raped?"

"Why were you in his car?"

"I didn't want to go in the car, but he insisted. I went with him to tell him we were through. He had been saying things—lies about me, so I didn't want to see him any more. He got angry when I told him that, and he hit me and tried to…to do sex. I fought him."

Had she had sex with Schaefer on previous occasions?

Her reply disclosed nothing. "What has Gordon Schaefer been saying? Would anyone believe anything he says?" The prosecutor seemed satisfied with the reply.

What came next was the question that had filled her with dread. She was asked if she had ever lived with a man.

She spoke carefully, "Well! Mr. Schaefer is truly desperate! I think he will say anything. What man could he be speaking of?"

The phrasing of the next question told her that at least this prosecutor knew nothing about her and Danny: "No apartment in town? In Courtenay or maybe Comox? Perhaps with a man from the air station?"

She again managed to reply without quite lying, "The Air Force doesn't allow us to live in town. We 'ave to live in the Airwomens barracks…for the single Airwomen. No men are allowed in there."

The Crown was satisfied with her testimony. He told her there would be a Preliminary Hearing before a judge in one week.

She left the office thinking, *Danny—how can I protect you?* What would the Air Force do to him if the truth of their relationship and the cabin came out?

Back at Kye Bay, when Danny came home from work, he could see she was troubled.

"What's up, Hon?" he asked, as they embraced in the kitchen. "How'd it go with the prosecutor?"

She took his hand and led him to the table. "Danny...I want you to trust me about something. We have to stay at the base for a while, we have to stay away from the cabin. I don't know how long...maybe a few weeks."

"Shit, Jo, why..."

She interrupted, "Please, Danny...trust me. I love you; you know I do. But I 'ave a good reason for doing this. We can see each other there on the base, but...I can't tell you anything right now. You must believe it is terribly important for both of us."

He was disappointed but went along. He knew and trusted her wisdom.

They moved that night into the barracks. She wondered if her decision would be too late.

The decision came easily to Josie. Whatever happened to her—even what happened to Schaefer—was no longer important. In her mind it was paramount now to protect Danny at any cost. She would lie under oath if necessary. She didn't tell Danny about the upcoming hearing. He had demonstrated in the past he would never stand by and allow her to sully her reputation on his behalf.

*   *   *   *

On the day of the Preliminary Hearing an R.C.M.P. officer drove Josie and Ollie to the courthouse.

During the proceedings Josie's intelligence, wit and courage were apparent as never before. The judge was a tall, friendly-looking man with patrician features capped by wavy white hair. She was surprised to see he presided from one end of a conference table in what looked like a meeting room. A female court reporter sat beside the judge. The other participants sat at the long sides of the table. Schaefer was present, sitting between two attorneys. His features, which she had once thought handsomely chiseled, now just looked hawkish, and his smile a malevolent sneer. After she was seated across from him she made a show of rising to move as far away down the table from him as possible. She gazed steadily at him for a moment and then didn't look at him for the balance of the proceedings. Ollie moved to sit beside her. Dr. McKay leaned close, touched her arm and winked encouragement.

They heard evidence first from two R.C.M.P. Constables, followed by written statements from Mr. and Mrs. Stevens, the couple that found her on the road, and Dr. Sturtridge, who was out of town. Dr. McKay then described her injuries in detail. Ollie gave evidence—lied convincingly—saying she had seen Josie enter Schaefer's car, having waited with her at the rear door of the barracks.

Then Josie was questioned.

First, the prosecutor questioned her about events before the attack. She was then asked to describe the attack and the events following, which she did in a straightforward manner, never wavering, and never looking at Schaefer.

When it was the defense lawyers's turn, he made a show of reading from a yellow legal pad and began, "Miss Connor…"

"L.A.W." said Josie.

"I beg your pardon? L.A.W.? What is that…L.A.W.?" He looked at the judge, who shrugged.

"It's my rank. Leading Airwoman. It's what you should call me—not Miss." She nodded toward Schaefer. "Don't you know who he raped?"

The attorney protested. "Your Honor, the witness is…"

The judge smiled. "I suggest you use correct titles, Counsel. Let's get on with it."

"Yes. Well now, Miss, er, is it *L.A.W.*? Isn't it a fact that…"

She interrupted again. "Yes."

"Yes?"

"Yes, it's L.A.W. You asked if it's L.A.W." She smiled sweetly. "It is."

The court reporter stared down at her machine to hide a beginning grin.

"Thank you I'm sure. Now, to my question…" He paused, expecting another interruption but she just smiled and raised her brows in anticipation. He continued, "Isn't it a fact, *L.A.W.* Connor, that you and the defendant had *consensual* sex on the night of the alleged attack? That you *wanted* to have sex with him and did so, willingly? That you were not raped at all?"

Without any sign of nervousness, she replied, "Would you mean after he beat me and broke my nose and my teeth? I suppose after that I may have consented. Or could you mean when he was choking me…and I thought I was going to die?" She saw he was about to protest and raised her voice, "And I'm so lucky he cracked my ribs and was strong enough to force my legs apart…I might 'ave missed out!" She smiled. "I enjoyed it so much I tried to crawl 'ome after to tell my friends what a nice time I 'ad! I was naked from the waist down when they found me. You see my panties were ripped apart and my slacks were in his car. The police found them there." She pointed to his legal pad. "Doesn't it say that on your papers? I'm sure it does, if you look."

The reporter's grin widened, the judge fought to keep from smiling, and the prosecutor chuckled.

Anxious to get quickly off that subject, the defense went on hurriedly. "Is it not also true you and the defendant, ah, regularly had consensual sex, before the night in question? In fact, didn't you do so almost nightly for several months? Answer yes or no, please!"

Regularly? Nightly? You bastard, Gordon!

She would have none of his answer-yes-or-no business. "Is that what he told you? I thought that story was just for his friends. The answer to your question is no!"

"Are you saying…"

"I am saying no."

"Mr. Schaefer may have a far different story in that regard…"

"I'm sure he may. But it would still be just a story, wouldn't it."

It had become another area the defense was anxious to vacate.

After consulting his notes again he asked, "Do you, or did you ever, live with a man…out of wedlock?"

She had awaited the question nervously, but she kept her composure. "'Ow many?" she said with a smile.

"Pardon me? Did you say how many? How many…what?"

"How many men? How many men do you want me to be living with? It's your story—do you want me with two…three…maybe four? It's your story." *No lie so far.*

Even His Honor chuckled.

Exasperated, the defense lawyer said sarcastically, "Just one will do, Miss…er, excuse me, *L.A.W.* Just one will do."

"That doesn't sound like much fun." Everyone but Schaefer and his lawyers smiled with her.

The experienced attorney was realizing what a formidable witness this pretty little girl would be before a jury. "Your Honor…please!" he pleaded.

The judge took a moment to compose himself. "Yes. L.A.W. Connor…please answer the question."

Outwardly calm, she lied.

"No. Never." *There, it's done.*

Her stomach churned. She reminded herself it was for Danny.

The lawyer tried an old courtroom device. He looked carefully at his notes, then looked at some other papers. He selected a page and nodded knowingly. He leaned forward and in an ominously quiet voice asked, "Are you sure?"

She fought to keep her voice level. "I am."

In a louder voice, "Are you sure that is the answer you wish to give?"

"Yes."

Then he made a rare mistake. "Is it your testimony then—under oath—that you don't share, or never have shared an apartment, or...or whatever...with a man?"

Or whatever? He knows nothing! Or is he trapping me? She looked him square in the eye. "That is my testimony, Sir!"

"Are you quite sure, ma'am?"

Before she could answer, the prosecutor spoke up. "The question has been answered at least three times by my count. Stop badgering her. If you have more questions, get on with it!"

His Honor concurred.

CHAPTER 32

▼

SUMMER, 1956

Events around them moved swiftly for Danny and Josie that summer of 1956.

A week after the Preliminary Hearing, the judge ordered Gordon Schaefer held over for trial by jury on charges of rape, involuntary confinement and assault with battery. Later, on the advice of his lawyers, he pleaded guilty to the single charge of assault and battery, thus avoiding a trial. On the last day of June he was sentenced to eighteen months at the Okalla Prison Farm. He would serve ten months and would be discharged dishonorably from the R.C.A.F. He eventually returned to Calgary to live with his family.

When Josie was told, her only thought was, *You're safe now, my Danny. It's over.*

She called him that night, to move back to Kye Bay.

*　　　*　　　*　　　*

Danny and Josie got married.

Once the thing was decided it was he, the once reluctant groom, who now wanted to move quickly. They decided to be married by a judge in Courtenay on a Saturday, June twelfth—just three days before Russ would leave for his new posting.

Danny's sister, Beth, arrived by bus the night before.

Moe Morrisey gave the bride away. Moe and Irene had car trouble in Nanaimo and were delayed getting up the Island Highway; they therefore met Josie for the first time just a half-hour before the wedding.

Ollie, of course, was the bridesmaid and Russ stood with Danny—more correctly he leaned on Danny, having imbibed all night with the Wild Dogs.

After the short civil ceremony, Danny and Josie waited for Moe and Irene while they found a hotel room. The reception, held at the cabin, served also as Russ's farewell party. It turned out to be the last great party for the Wild Dogs. In addition to the D Crew members and the out-of-towners, there were members of Danny's new crew, staff from the Orderly Room, and some Kye Bay neighbors—including Lorna Letourneau, who planted a kiss on Danny when she arrived.

*　　　*　　　*　　　*

At ten-thirty, Ollie found Josie outside, sitting on a lawn chair looking out at the sea. Ollie stood beside her and put a hand on her shoulder.

"Everything okay, Little Buddy? You look down…you're supposed to be happy."

"Everything is fine, Ollie. I *am* happy! I was just thinking…some things are so 'ard to believe."

"What things?"

Josie leaned her head on Ollie. "It's just…it's hard for me to believe I was lucky enough to find the one man in this whole world who loves me. Loves *me*, Ollie!"

"Yeah. It's a surprising world sometimes, isn't it? Now listen—you should get your new husband and get the hell out of here. Sneak away, get a room and be alone somewhere. These drunks aren't gonna miss you."

Josie giggled just as Danny came out. "Why do you think I'm waiting out here? We booked a cabin at the Ocean View." She took his hand and they started for the Ford.

"Good!" said Ollie, laughing. "I'm told it's a nice place. I'm sure you'll enjoy your stay, you sneaky little shit."

Danny called back as he opened the car for her; "Don't you be squealing on us, Ol. We don't need those clowns showing up. And don't let them burn the cabin down!"

"I know nothing, I see nothing, Tanner." *One man indeed, Little Buddy!*

Just when the party began to lose momentum in the early morning hours, Russ woke up and got things rolling again. "What a bunch of jeez'zly party poopers! C'mon, let's have a little life around here…an' some frigging music! Are you people all stupid?" The few diehard Wild Dogs and friends partied on till noon.

Monday morning found Mrs. Danny Tanner back at work in the O.R., and her husband working the first of five four-to-twelve shifts. The couple couldn't get any annual leave on short notice but were able to get the second two weeks of August for a honeymoon. The rent for the cabin was paid up for the summer, so they decided there was no better place to live.

*   *   *   *

The summer also brought the inevitable breakup of the Wild Dogs, through transfers, releases, and promotions.

Russ left for Ontario on the fifteenth. Josie stayed in the barracks with Ollie for two nights to keep her company.

Danny moved on to his new crew.

In short order, Gil Potter, Gerry Henderson and Mitch Kobiashi were transferred out, Ellen Schmidt left for officer training and Vera Cornwell took her release after serving her three years. By August, D Crew had taken on a different look from what Danny first encountered.

Two weeks after Russ's departure, Ollie was at the cabin for supper.

Josie said, "We got a letter from Russ. He seems kind of...lost. I suppose it's the new station and everything. Did he write to you, Ollie?"

"Oh, yeah. Shit-all-to-hell, I never would have believed it, but he's written three times already. It's downright spooky—certainly not like Knight. He doesn't say a hell of a lot, but it's good to hear from him."

"How many times did you answer him?"

Ollie blushed. "Four, so far. Number five is just about ready to mail." Josie and Danny were grinning. "Hey, I love the guy. Don't know why, but I do." said she with a shrug.

*   *   *   *

For a honeymoon the newlyweds traveled on the C.P.R. *Canadian* to Calgary, with a week's stopover in Banff. Danny paid twelve dollars extra for a roomette on the train—and got his money's worth. (Josie called it her lower berth.) In Banff, Josie dragged him out every afternoon, to walk the town or take a bus tour. The rest of the time they made love, slept late, and lazed around their room.

Josie phoned Ollie as soon as they arrived back on August thirty-first.

Ollie said, "How did it go, horny one...ready for the divorce yet?"

"Never! I think I love him even more, if that's possible. I took lots of pictures this time. When they're developed, you can come and let me bore you. How is Russ? Is he still sending lots of letters?"

"I think he's tapering-off. It's been a week since his last one. Have you guys checked your mail? There's probably a dozen letters from him."

The next day Danny and Josie drove to Courtenay to shop and then to the base to pick up the mail. There was one letter from Russ, addressed to Mr. and Mrs. D. Tanner. It was postmarked August eleventh. It was the usual chatty stuff, not saying much—*missing you wish you were here excuse my lousy writing how's everybody out there say hi to the old crew...*

*   *   *   *

A week later, there was a letter to Danny from a FighterCOp he had known at Moisie.

When he read the return address, he said, "I'll be damned, Art Haywood. We used to call him 'Haywire' at Moisie. Great guy."

He opened the envelope and read. Josie saw a lost look come onto his face. The page fell from his hand and fluttered to the floor.

He muttered, "Russ...No! No! God *damn* it, Russ." His head dropped to his hands on the table.

She picked up the letter and read:

Dan,

I know you and Russ Knight were close friends, so I thought I had better write to you.

Russ and two other guys from the GCI were killed near Barrie, on the 3rd of September. The car he was in was hit by a train at a level crossing on Hwy 93. I'm sorry to be the one to tell you, Dan, but I know you would want to know. I was told they all died instantly.

Russ told me you're married. Congratulations, I bet your new wife is quite the girl. It doesn't seem like the best time to say so, but I wish you both much happiness.

All of us at Edgar are sad and in shock over Russ and the other guys. The RCAF gave him a funeral. It seems Russ had no family on record.

Yours truly, Art Haywood.

She rushed to him. "Danny…is it true? Would this guy…" She dropped to her knees in front of him, laid her head on his lap and sobbed, "Oh, poor Russ!"

They stayed like that for fully ten minutes, she with her face buried in his lap and he staring blankly at the wall, tears streaming down his stricken face.

He pounded the table with a fist. "Jesus, Hon, he's…they already buried him! I should have been there with him when they buried him. I'm…*we* are his family, Ollie and you and I! We're his *only* family." His fist kept pounding, over and over. "Russ, Russ. Hell, Q, why? Why you?"

Josie stood and put an arm around him, grabbed at his wrist, afraid he would injure his hand. "I know how you love him…we all do, Danny." He stopped the pounding and looked at her, lost. She wrapped her arms around his head, pulled him to her breast and rocked him gently. She murmured, "Poor Russ…my poor Danny…"

Then she thought of her friend. She looked pleadingly at him. "Danny…how can I tell her? Ollie! Something like this…"

"Yes! Someone has to be with her…"

"I'll go to her. I must. But, Danny…'ow can I tell her? I don't know how to do that!"

"We'll do it together. Let's get up to the Station."

"I'll bring the letter."

They told Ollie and showed her the letter in the parked car. Josie was in the back seat with her.

She looked at them each in turn and then out the car window at nothing. "Oh, Baby…" she whispered. She looked at each of them again, then said, "I'm going in." She opened the car door. She had shed not a tear.

Josie said, "I'm going with you."

"You don't have to come with me."

Josie said, "I know, Ollie, but I *am* going with you." Then to Danny, "I'll call you, Honey…will you be okay?"

He nodded. "I'll go to the barracks…tell the guys."

Ollie hadn't left the car; she closed the door. "I changed my mind. I don't want to be around anyone. You two are the only people I want to see right now. Could we go to the cabin?"

Danny said, "Good idea." He started the car. "I'm getting a bottle, Jo—we'll need a drink. I can get it at the club."

He stopped at the Corporals Club. "I won't be long."

He was back in five minutes with two bottles of rye. They headed for Kye Bay.

In the back seat with Josie, Ollie sat and stared out the window. Then she began to softly cry. She turned finally, and clung desperately to Josie and wept aloud. Josie held her friend, helplessly stroking her shoulder.

When they stopped at the cabin, Ollie dried her tears with the back of her hand. She said, "Shit-all-to-hell, I can't get those two stupid bottles of champagne out of my mind!" With a sad little smile, she added, "Y'know guys, we're all better for knowing the little fart. Dan, you lost the best friend anyone could have. I hope it was fast…I can't stand thinking he suffered."

"Amen." said Danny.

With Josie acting as nursemaid, Danny and Ollie got monumentally smashed.

At six the next morning the three were sitting on the beach, loudly singing *Rags To Riches* as they watched the sun rise over the mainland and turn the sky and sea bloody red. When a neighbor glared at them from an open door, Josie sent her a middle finger and the concert continued. When the sun was getting high in the sky, they decided their rendition couldn't hold a candle to Russ's, so they ended the concert and went inside. Danny fell asleep on the sofa at ten. At eleven-thirty Ollie staggered into the bedroom where she slept all day and most of the night.

CHAPTER 33

▼

Too quickly, Honey, our years together passed…

In May of 1957, Ollie left Comox, on transfer to Air Force Headquarters in Ottawa.

In September of the same year, Danny was transferred to 32 AC&W Squadron at Foymont, Ontario. Josie left the Air Force so she could be with him. Soon after the Tanners' arrival at Foymont they traveled with Ollie to Orillia, to see Russ Knight's grave. With Ottawa just two hours down Highway 17 from Foymont, they regularly visited back and forth with Ollie.

*　　　*　　　*　　　*

In 1958, 51 AC&W Squadron at Comox ceased to be—victim of poor siting and governmental austerity. The radar at the site continued to operate in an air traffic control function. Two years after that the ADCC at Jericho was closed and the remaining 5 Air Division units were incorporated into the 25th NORAD Division, headquartered in Washington State.

Danny was promoted to Acting Sergeant in '59 and a year later to full Sergeant. Also in '59, Ollie made Corporal and was transferred to Lahr, Germany.

In 1962, when Danny was the NCO i/c Operations at Moisie, Olivia Jeanne Elizabeth Tanner began life as an Air Force brat.

The next year when they were stationed at Alsask, Saskatchewan, a second child arrived, a boy they named Russell, whose middle name was Quentin. (They chose Quentin when Danny adamantly vetoed Quimby!)

*   *   *   *

Ollie returned from Europe in 1963 and in the following years was posted to Trenton; then in turn, Namao, Ottawa, and in '75 to North Bay. She kept in touch with the Tanners for the rest of her life. Young Olivia and Russell grew to love visits from their irreverent "Aunt Ollie."

The Tanners, too, moved around the continent on transfers. They even lived for two years in North Dakota, when Danny did a tour there. The FighterCOps were now called Air Defense Technicians—AD Techs. Wherever they were stationed, Josie was a good Armed Forces wife and hostess. Above all, however, she was always the loving mate to him and mother to their children. Like many other service wives, she worked at a variety of jobs over the years to augment the family's income. Now and again, especially after a letter or visit from Ollie, she felt the tiniest longing to be in uniform and part of it all again. Then she would look at her family and be content.

For their entire life together, each of them teased the other with pet names from that long ago train ride. She would playfully refer to him as "My L.A.C." and he would call her "Babe," or "AW2 Connor."

In the early sixties, Danny developed an interest in writing. He collected volumes on the subject, took after-hours courses whenever he could at colleges and universities near his various bases, and invested in a word processor. With Josie's help and encouragement, he submitted short stories to several publishers. (He told Ollie at one point he felt he must be a professional writer because he had dozens of rejection slips to prove it!) He was surprised—though Josie wasn't—when, after fifty or more submissions, two of his works were accepted and published in national magazines. Then, again with her urging, he started a novel. He soon found that the larger project would be much slower coming to fruition. Josie was his proofreader, copy editor, critic and faithful supporter during the long process as he worked on the story and endless revisions and rewrites. While working on the novel, he wrote and published two more short stories, gaining him some small recognition in literary circles and something positive to include in his query letters to publishers.

For a number of years after Russell's birth, Josie experienced some unexplained symptoms. After her twenty-eighth year her figure had naturally become fuller (by age thirty she had resigned herself to size eight petite), but in the late 1960s, inexplicably she started to lose weight. She still had the voracious appetite of her youth, but the weight loss continued; it was gradual, however, and only noticed by Josie herself. For some years she had tired rather easily, but now she would become fatigued for no discernable reason, and often was ready for her bed by early in the evening. As time passed, worry over the symptoms would keep her awake in the night. Not wishing to disturb Danny, she would eventually get up and putter around the house or sit and read in the living room, where he would find her sleeping in the morning.

CHAPTER 34

▼

In 1970, when Olivia was eight and Russell seven, it was discovered Josie had a cancer called Hodgkins disease.

Her illness did not greatly affect the family for three years after the diagnosis—because she wouldn't allow that. The children were almost unaware of the disease through the early years of its existence.

Soon after she was diagnosed Josie began corresponding with her father, but did not tell him about the cancer. Paul Connor had retired some years earlier and was living alone in an apartment in Sherbrooke. His three sisters had all passed away before he received the first letter from Josie. She told him of her life, sent him photographs of her family, and he replied promptly to every one of her monthly letters.

Danny took his release from the service in 1972—the three services together were now called the Canadian Armed Forces. He left as a Master Warrant Officer with a twenty year pension. He took a position with a Vancouver-based firm that did security consulting for the Canadian government. The job paid him substantially more than his recent Armed Forces salary. When his pension was added in, the family found itself financially comfortable. His position required him to travel to government installations across the country. (He visited Ollie at North Bay whenever in Ontario on business.) They bought a house in the Vancouver suburb of Burnaby, the first they had ever owned.

The next summer, 1973, they rented the old cabin at Kye Bay so Josie could once more be at the place she loved so much and the children could see where their parents had fallen in love. They traveled to the island on weekends and holidays. By the beginning of 1974, with his Air Force pension and the income from his writing, Danny was able to quit his job and be with the family every day. They had a home built in Courtenay and sold the Vancouver house. When Mrs. MacKenzie, now widowed and in her mid-eighties, decided to sell, they bought the Kye Bay cabin. Josie and the kids spent summers and most weekends there. He added two bedrooms to the cabin and had a studio built in the basement of the Courtenay house. He was now writing full time and worked either in the studio or at Kye Bay.

*   *   *   *

By late 1974 the disease had progressed; Josie was going through the terrible cycles of sickness and remission, and the ordeal of her therapies. Now, too, the symptoms were apparent to the children.

It was eleven-year-old Russell who asked the question that Danny had been dreading. He and his father were repairing the fence at the front of the cabin, and had stopped for sodas. Josie was at the hospital undergoing chemotherapy.

Russell tried to sound detached, but there was a slight tremor as he said to Danny, "So…I guess Mom might die, hey Dad?"

Danny heard the torment in the boy's voice and was silent for a long moment. He stared at the front door of the cabin.

Finally, he replied, "Good question, Tiger." He stood. "Come inside. It's time for you kids and I to talk about it." He led off toward the door.

Inside, he called to Olivia, who came out from her room.

Danny indicated the kitchen table. "Sit down, kids."

He told them about the diagnosis, describing what he knew of Hodgkins. "It's a kind of cancer…do you understand that?" He spoke of the symptoms, the treatments, and the possible prognoses. "Yeah, Tiger, your Mom could die. But she could also live…it could go either way. If anyone can beat this, it's your mother; because she is a fighter—she's one of the most courageous people I've ever met." He spoke of the things Josie had done. He described her courage during and after the assault by Schaefer; and how she had stood up to the Prosecutor and protected him at the preliminary hearing. He told them about her chasing off the intruders right here at the cabin. ("Wow," said Russell, "our Mom's like Annie Oakley!")

When Danny told Josie about the conversation, she said, "I must talk to them, Danny. I must prepare them."

She told the kids that whatever happened, they must not be sad. "Okay to miss me…I know I will miss you. But try always to remember the good me—

your healthy mother—and all the wonderful times we have had together. Instead of mourning my death, how about celebrating my life." She added with a smile, "If I am to die, I want my last times to be happy…so don't be moping around making me feel sad, you!"

✳   ✳   ✳   ✳

A bad time for Josie was when the chemotherapy caused her hair to fall out. She had been warned that it would happen, but was dismayed when she found the first clumps of hair on her pillow. She had always been proud of her appearance—since she was a little girl she had repeatedly been told she was beautiful—and through the years she only rarely left her bedroom without spending time carefully applying cosmetics and fixing her hair. Her one hundred brush strokes had been a bedtime ritual that she rarely neglected.

She found a gray kerchief she had had since the fifties and wore it to hide the "shame" of her baldness. When Olivia, now fourteen, commented on the kerchief's drab color, saying she looked like the old Greek women in *Zorba the Greek,* Josie answered, "Maybe so, but it's for sure better than walking around with my bald head showing!"

On a bright summer afternoon she was at the cabin, curled in her chair reading. Danny and the kids had gone into Courtenay earlier in his pickup, to buy supplies for some ongoing renovation project. She heard the truck pull into the driveway, and Olivia came in with an armload of bags.

"Hi Mommy. They didn't have those Spanish onions at Safeway, so we had to go to the Supervalue store in Comox."

"Okay, Darling…need help to put stuff away?"

"No, you stay put. It's only three bags anyway." She put a last tin into the cabinet. "There. All done."

She came into the living room with her hands behind her back.

"You have to shut your eyes, Mom."

"Why?"

"Because I have a surprise for you."

"You better not 'ave a frog, like when you were eight!"

Olivia made a face. "That was awful…you should have spanked me!" She giggled. "But it was so funny. You jumped two feet!"

"You mean funny for you." She had to smile, remembering.

"Okay…shut your eyes. It is *not* a frog…or anything alive. Shut your eyes."

"They're shut, they're shut!"

Olivia removed the kerchief, and pulled a most ghastly hat from a bag. It was a cheap, narrow-brimmed, straw thing, with a bright green ribbon and garish plastic flowers covering the crown—daisies, carnations and petunias—there were even grapes and cherries in the mix! Olivia set it just so on her mother's head.

"What *is* that?" asked Josie, eyes still closed. "Is that a hat?"

"Don't look, I'll be right back." She skipped off to her bedroom and returned with a hand mirror. Holding the mirror in front of Josie, she said, "See?"

"Can I open my eyes…won't be able to see if not."

"Shut up, you. Look!"

Josie looked aghast at the mirror. "Oh, honey, it's…it's very bright, isn't it." She was trying to not hurt Olivia's feelings.

Olivia giggled again. "It's supposed to be funny, Mom…like a joke."

A joke. Thank God!

Josie turned the joke back on the girl: "Oh, no, Darling! It's just lovely. I just 'ope you didn't spend all your allowance…at some expensive boutique. I like it so much, I'm going to wear it on the beach. Come, we'll go for a walk right now!" She held the mirror as she fussed with the hat, tilting and turning it. She giggled. "I'm not sure which is the front, are you? Dieux, Olivia—it's so ugly it's beautiful!" She hugged her daughter.

They were both giggling helplessly as they went out the front door, headed for the beach.

They encountered Danny and Russell, stacking bundles of shingles in the yard.

"Look, Dad!" screamed Olivia.

"What in hell is that on your head?" asked Danny. "You look like Carmen Miranda!"

"It's my new 'at. Olivia bought it for me! We're going to the beach…want to come with us?"

"Jesus apey Chr…I'll go…but only if you walk way out ahead of me, so I can pretend I don't know you."

A week later Olivia arrived home with another atrocious creation. Josie wore one or the other of them around the Courtenay house and at Kye Bay. She drew the line, however, at wearing them in town.

And then Danny and Russell got into the act, bringing home hats of all kinds for her. Soon there was a pile of headwear for her to choose from in a corner of their bedroom. The other residents of Kye Bay got used to seeing the pretty, crazy lady with the wild hats walking their beach.

*   *   *   *

By late fall any hope of surviving the cancer was lost, and Josie was almost totally bedridden—getting up for short periods only, at her own insistence, to sit in the living room. It became too much for her even to travel to the cabin. By Thanksgiving Day she was in the hospital more than at home.

Christmas that year was a solemn affair for the Tanners. Josie was terribly ill and hospitalized, but insisted they go to the cabin without her. They didn't go, but told her they did.

*   *   *   *

In March of the next year, 1976, Josie lost her battle and ended her pain when she died quietly at St. Joseph's Hospital in Comox. Danny had always thought his life would end with hers, but now took strength from her courageous and cheerful acceptance of the inevitable. Olivia and Russell, who had promised their Mom they would get on with their lives when she was gone, gave him strength, too. "She's gone now, Dad, but we still have her...we always will." said young Olivia. Standing beside her coffin, unseeing through his tears, he silently thanked her for the wonderful job she had done with the kids.

Josie's last wise act—her last kindness—had been to prepare her family for her death; she had always remembered her pain when she had not been prepared for her own mother's passing.

She lived long enough to see his novel accepted by a small publishing house. When he showed her the letter and advance check, she smiled tiredly and said, "Of course. Took them long enough, though."

She died five months before her fortieth birthday—twenty-one years, almost to the day, after she and Danny met in that Montreal railway station.

*   *   *   *

Paul Connor came from Quebec for the funeral. Danny had phoned to tell him of her death. M. Connor said Josie had expressed in her letters her wish to be buried in the Comox Valley and he felt it would be the right thing. She had told him how much she loved the area and how she felt she belonged there. He was pleased when Danny told him she would have a Catholic funeral. He flew from Montreal the next day.

Danny and the kids met him at Vancouver Airport and they took the ferry from Horseshoe Bay. They saw a partly bald, white-haired man, who appeared older than his actual years. He was polite to them, but stiff and somewhat formal. The first meeting had been difficult for both him and Danny, but during the ferry ride Olivia and Russell captured their grandfather's heart and he soon loosened up. Olivia couldn't believe her Grandfather had never seen the ocean, she and Russell pointed out islands and boats and ships—even a pod of porpoises. When Russell accidentally knocked his hat off and it flew away behind the ferry, they were much relieved when he laughed uproariously and said the hat was old-fashioned anyway. Perhaps a porpoise would find and make good use of it, he suggested with a smile. They told him of the treasures of Kye Bay and how their mother loved to walk the shore. Olivia promised to take him for a walk on the beach and he said it sounded wonderful.

When he and Danny were alone at the house after supper, with Russell in the basement recreation room and Olivia in her bedroom, he talked of Josie.

"I think, Danny, my daughter was not 'appy at home after her mother passed. I know now, from 'er letters she was a special girl…a special woman," His mouth turned up in a small grin. "it is 'ard for me to think of 'er as a woman. You must be so very sad. She wrote well of you. And you 'ave two beautiful children—good children. I know you made her 'appy, Danny. She sent me pictures every year, since she…got sick. Your little Olivia…she looks so much like Josée when she was the same age, I cannot look at 'er without feeling amazed. I see her in Russell, too, don't you? When the first pictures came, I was so 'appy to 'ave grandchildren. I thank you for that. I wish…I wish I 'ad kept better in touch…" He bowed his head, his natural stoicism preventing him from displaying emotion. "Is there a place where I could take a rest? I am fatigued…and I wish to be alone for…" A tear on his cheek betrayed him before he could turn away.

"Yes, certainly," said Danny. He called, "Olivia, come and show your grandfather…your grand-*papa*…where his room is, would you?"

Olivia bounced from her room. She took his hand. "Come on, Grandpa…there's a bathroom here and one upstairs where your room is. I'm so happy you're here…Russ is, too. We put your bag up in the room already. I hope you'll stay after the funeral. For a-a few days?" Olivia was starting to take on Josie's role in the home.

*   *   *   *

Some of the old Wild Dogs came; Gerry Henderson, Jake MacDonald and the former Bobby Gaines. Gerry, now a Captain, was stationed at Holberg at the north end of the island. Jake was out of the service and living in nearby Campbell River. Bobby had married a chiropractor and lived in Victoria. She had kept in touch with Josie and Ollie over the years.

There were floral wreaths from Mr. and Mrs. Ian and Irene Morrisey of Belleville, Ontario; Mr. Gilbert Potter of Regina, Saskatchewan; and Leo and Lorna Letourneau of St. Petersburg, Florida.

Danny's sister Beth came from Vancouver. She had remarried and her new husband accompanied her.

And Ollie came. She was at first angry with Danny, saying he should have told her much sooner how close to dying Josie was, so she could be with her. (Josie forbade him to tell her.)

Ollie soon relented, however, "Aw, hell, Dan...I knew in my heart she didn't have long. I'd be stupid not to." Her lips trembled. She fell against his chest, put her arms around him. In a small, hurt voice, she asked, "God damn cancer! Did she suffer a lot, Danny? I didn't want her to suffer...not again. I bet she was brave. Was she?"

"She was, Ol."

"You gonna be okay? You and the kids?"

"It won't be easy, but we'll be okay. Life goes on, Ollie. Unlike you, the kids and I were prepared for it. As prepared as we could be, at least." With a catch in his voice, he continued, "But, Jesus, I loved her. Nobody can know how much."

"*She* did, Dan. Jo knew how much."

"I hope so. I remember how bad we started—the pain I caused her. She was so patient with me. I learned from her...how to love."

At the house after the service, Ollie said, "At least we were around for this one." She was remembering Russ.

Ollie stayed for three days after the funeral. She slept in Olivia's room, and at bedtime they talked together. For Ollie it was as if the years fell away and she was with another roommate.

Paul Connor stayed for a week. After Ollie left the kids insisted he go with them to Kye Bay for a couple of days. He made Olivia and Russell promise to bring Danny to see him in Quebec. They, in turn, made him promise to come to the coast again.

"That would be up to your father."
Olivia said, "Don't you worry about him."
Russell added, "Yeah—we'll handle him, Grandpa!"

*   *   *   *

For a year after Josie's death, Danny lived with an emptiness inside him that he thought would always be there. Eventually, he was able to partly fill the void with family, friends, and his writing—but the place that had been Josie would always remain empty.

EPILOGUE

▼

COMOX—DECEMBER, 1978

Ollie Conti is tired. She has been sitting in airplanes and terminals for nine and a half long, wearying hours. Her day started at five in the morning with a drive from North Bay to Toronto. The Air Canada flight had taken off at nine thirty Toronto time, with stops at Winnipeg and Calgary. Now her blue-gray suit and even her woolen coat are wrinkled, and she feels the need for a bath and change of clothes. She has no idea what the time is here. Her numbed brain tries but fails to remember how many time zones she traveled through; she has never been clear on how it works. *Shit, eight hours difference? Can't be that much, can it.*

She had arranged for Danny to pick her up here at the Comox airport, but there is no sign of him yet. There were only four other passengers with her on the Twin Otter from Vancouver but she watches fifteen or twenty people board for the return flight. *Well, that never changes; 'It's Friday, gang, let's get the hell out of Comox!'*

She takes in the once familiar surroundings, standing in the doorway of the small civilian terminal under an overhanging roof. Light drizzle is falling out of a low overcast. She steps out a few feet from the building to get a better view of the base. There, to her right is the hangar line, dominated by a large cantilevered hangar. *There's 409 Squadron, or at least used to be.* Turning to her left, she walks to the corner of the building. *Aha! The Snack Bar would have been...there, in the Rec Center...if that is the Rec Center. Mess Hall over there...can't see it, must be wrong. The HQ Building...damn! why isn't it all more familiar to me? HQ must be hidden behind the Rec Center. Of course there would have been some changes after this many years.* She steps back to be under the roof again. *And of course, it's raining, but at least there's no snow and it's December, gotta love it.* She hears but can't see a jet taking off. Her nose twitches slightly as the breeze brings the familiar, acrid smell of exhausted jet fuel.

A car drives up and parks beside the one remaining taxi. Someone leaps from the front passenger seat almost before it stops. She sees Josie skipping towards her. She is dressed in a floppy gray sweater and faded blue jeans. There is a wide grin on her face as she approaches Ollie.

Omigod! It can't be… Ollie looks for somewhere she can sit down.

Josie!

She feels the blood rush from her head, puts a hand out to the wall of the building for support. *Shit-all-to-hell!*

Josie speaks to her, "Aunt Ollie? It's…"

Another voice, male and urgent, "Ollie, are you okay?"

Danny!

Her head clears and she feels some of her weariness melt away. She holds her arms wide for the girl, who steps into her embrace.

Hugging the girl, she exclaims, "Shit-all-to-hell! Tanner—she's Josie! I thought she was Josie. Let me see you, Kid." She pushes the girl to arms' length. "Olivia Tanner, I thought you were your mother. Danny, she's beautiful!" Smiling, she turns to him, "Well, come on you big shit, give me a hug…get that over with." She and Danny embrace affectionately. "And I guess I'd better watch my language around you-know-who." She nods toward Olivia, who is still holding her hand. "Don't want to corrupt her like I did to her look-alike."

As they walk to the car, Ollie and Olivia hand in hand, Ollie asks, "Where's Russell? I hope he didn't leave home or something. I want to see the little fart; he still owes me a game of rummy.

Olivia answers, "He's at his hockey practice. It's just outside the base. We're picking him up and then we're going to Kye Bay. We're staying out there at the cabin for Christmas!"

"Sounds Great," She pulls the girl close with an arm around her shoulder. "Olivia, honey…you are gorgeous! I can't get over it. How does the old song go, Dan…seventeen and a beauty queen? You're a bit taller than your Mom was."

"I'm sixteen, not seventeen, and I'm only five four. Russ calls me the midget because he's already five eleven. Wait till you see him, by the way. We're talking ug-lee! He's really big and ugly now, Aunt Ollie."

"No way he's ugly. Coming from your Mom and this guy—no way."

Danny has picked up her bags and is stowing them in the trunk. He goes along with Olivia's gag, "Hey, kid, your brother can't help how he looks."

Olivia giggles. The sound of it is so familiar it stops Ollie in her tracks.

"You'll see. Ug-lee!" More giggles. Ollie and Olivia get in the back seat.

When they drive onto the road that runs along the west boundary of the base, Danny turns back toward the main gate.

"I thought it would be fun to take a run around the base. An old friend got me a pass. It's just for the unrestricted areas. There's some new stuff but a lot of the old buildings are still here. The Wets is in a new building and there's a new HQ."

He pulls up at the gate to show his pass, then turns right, and drives slowly along the road.

Olivia says, "This is the first time for me inside the base. We go past here a lot, but I've never been in."

"Well, your Dad and I'll give you the two-bit tour." Ollie points out a building on their right, "That *used to be* the Airmen and Airwomen's club. We all called it the Wets. I was introduced to your Dad right there, by your Mom." Danny has stopped the car. "One day, Kiddo, I'll tell you about the times we had in that place. I'll tell you all about the Scope Dopes, the Wild Dogs, the Fearsome Foursome...but later." She looks wistfully at the old building.

Danny comments, "It's used for something else now; storage I think."

The car rolls on another half block. Danny indicates a row of two-story H-blocks on the left. "There's the men's barracks. I lived in...that one. Our room was upstairs at the back."

"And there's the Airwomen's just ahead," says Ollie, "where your Mom and I shared a room."

Danny stops across from the building.

"Did you have, like dorms?" Olivia asks.

Ollie chuckles, "Just two beds, two small dressers and two closets. Your Mom, and I had some wonderful times there. See the third window from the left, on the second floor? That was our room. There was a rule against electric kettles and other appliances, but we had a kettle. We had many a long talk or a game of cards over mugs of tea. Mugs we pinched from the Mess Hall. Jo...Josie...had a little radio. I believe we heard Elvis for the first time on her radio."

The car rolls on.

Danny points right, "The Airmen's and Corporals' clubs are both in this building now—the Mess Hall, too."

"What's the *Mess* Hall?" asks Olivia.

"It's where you eat your meals. All the single people eat there."

Olivia giggles, "Was it a mess?"

Ollie chuckles, "What's in a name, eh? Actually, the food wasn't bad at all when we were here. We used to make sandwiches to smuggle out to each other, and take desserts to the barracks in our purses for late-night snacks. Your Mom had one hell of an appetite, Kid. Don't know how she stayed so petite."

"And here's the new HQ building, right where the old one was," says Danny.

"Your Mom and I worked there, in the Orderly Room."

The car continues around the loop. "Here's the old Rec Center," says Danny. "There was a canteen upstairs. We called it the Snack Bar. You could get burgers and cokes and stuff, and it was where we bought our soap, tooth paste, shampoo, and things like that."

"We used to dance to a jukebox there, too. It only cost a nickel, didn't it Dan?"

"Yeah, maybe a dime. I think we got five for a quarter—whenever we *had* a quarter."

"But don't forget, a quarter's all we paid for a beer in the Wets."

"Yeah, I think you're right. Ollie."

They move farther around the loop and past a row of hangars and parked aircraft.

"And this is the hangar line where the peons toiled and got greasy. The real Air Force, I guess." A hundred yards farther they drive through an intersection. "Up that road was the base hospital."

They complete the loop and arrive back at the main gate. Danny turns left, drives past the married quarters, and pulls up at the base's ice arena.

Looking back the way they came, Ollie says, "If you go that way from the gate, it takes you to 51 beach, as we called it, and the radar squadron where your Dad worked."

"I never knew that," Olivia says, "Do you mean the Air Force beach? I've been there."

"Josie loved it there."

"So do I!"

Danny pulls into the arena parking lot. He toots the horn and a handsome boy leaves a group of kids and trots to the car. He is carrying a large hockey equipment bag.

"And here," says Danny, "is Russell Q. Tanner. Ta da!"

Ollie exclaims, "Olivia, you little shit, he's gorgeous!"

It takes Russell a minute to jam his bag into the trunk. He comes to the side of the car. Ollie rolls down her window. He leans in and they hug.

"Hi, Aunt Ollie."

"Squeeze in the back here with us, you hunk. You can help me beat your sister all the way to the cabin." When he gets in, she kisses his cheek and brushes at the shock of blond hair on his brow. She puts an arm around each of them and they ride that way to Kye Bay.

*   *   *   *

At the cabin Danny issues his orders: "Olivia, you and Ollie go ahead in, here's the key. Take a couple of these grocery bags in with you. Hold on, Russ—take Ollie's bags and I'll get the rest of the groceries."

Inside, he asks, "Are you hungry, Ol?"

"Famished. But could I get cleaned up first? I feel like I just flew three thousand miles in these clothes. Come to think of it, that's just what I did, isn't it? I'd like to change, then I could use a drink, if we have time." She looks around the cabin, "You've made some changes. I like it. The bigger window makes it brighter, and gives a better view of the beach, too."

"Yeah. Don't forget, the old shack has been here since the forties. It was overdue for some renovation. It was either fix it up or get rid of it, and you know I could never do that. Needed a lot of work on the plumbing and electrical, both were pretty archaic. We added a couple of bedrooms, too. The kids and I did most of the work."

Continuing her appraisal, Ollie strolls toward the fireplace, runs a hand along the back of an old, faded easy chair. She doesn't mention she recognizes the chair—she's picturing Josie sitting there with her feet up, reading.

"Jesus, Dan…she haunts this place."

He nods. "She does. I feel her every time I walk through the door." The heaviness in his heart shows on his face.

"Don't ever lose it." She says.

"Bet on it. As long as I'm alive." His mood brightens and he says, "We're just having a cold supper, so take your time, Ollie. You'll be sleeping with Olivia in one of the new bedrooms. There's two beds."

"Sounds great."

"I already put your stuff in the bedroom for you, Aunt Ollie." Says Russell.

*   *   *   *

Ollie, now wearing gray slacks and a beige sweater, sits between Olivia and Russell at the supper table.

She announces, "Well, Dan, I finally pulled the pin. I'm out!"

"Good for you! It's about time."

"Yeah, twenty-six years, almost twenty-seven. Long enough for me. Shit-all-to-hell, I was starting to act like old Willie. I'm on my rehab leave as we speak."

"Any idea what you want to do?"

"Oh yeah, I want to sit on my duff. Maybe do some traveling after a while. I'd like to start by staying here with you and the kids. I mean for longer than the couple of weeks I mentioned. I could help out…cook and clean, or whatever…"

Russell cries, "Yeah, neato!"

Olivia says, "Cool…I mean, we'll love that. We will love it a lot!"

"Done deal," says Danny.

They are quiet while they eat. When they finish the cold cuts, salads, and cheese, Danny says, "How about some ice cream, guys? I know it's December, but why not."

"I'll get it, Dad," says Olivia.

Ollie asks, "So, Russell, what position do you play?"

"Defense. Sometimes up on wing."

"Do you play ball in the summer?"

"Yeah. Mostly at shortstop…I've been pitching some too, since last season."

"Any coaching from the old man?"

"Oh, yeah—and he's tough."

"It figures. He was no slouch himself, you know, until he met a certain lady. Then she was all he thought about."

"You should hear him." Russell imitates his Dad: "Keep your shoulder in! Get your *ass* to the *grass* on those ground balls!"

Olivia is placing bowls of ice cream on the table and grinning at her brother's impersonation. She glances sidelong at Ollie, who winks and grins back at her.

"Come now, I'm not *that* bad," says Danny.

Both kids say, "Oh, yes you are!"

Olivia adds, "I know. I play in a girls' league."

After the ice cream, Ollie turns to Olivia, "You know, kid, this won't be the first time I've roomed with a beautiful girl."

Olivia blushes, "I'm not *beautiful*, Aunt Ollie."

"Dan, she's just like her mother, doesn't even *know* she's beautiful. Look at you. You must have every guy in the Comox Valley after your little bod."

The girl's blush deepens. She looks down at her hands; "I do not! Shut up, you."

At the sound of the so familiar phrase, tears come to Ollie's eyes. She leaves the table without a word and almost runs to her bedroom.

Olivia looks at her father, devastated.

He says, "Just an old memory, Sweetheart." His smile and nod tell her to go to Ollie. She goes to the bedroom door and enters timidly. She sits on the bed beside Ollie.

In a small voice, she says, "Aunt Ollie that was rude of me. I-I am so sorry. I would never want to make you sad."

Ollie hugs the girl.

"It's okay, Little Buddy. Really, it's okay."

CANADIAN AIR FORCE TERMS & ABBREVIATIONS

R.C.A.F.—Royal Canadian Air Force

A.D.C.—Air Defense Command. The branch of the R.C.A.F. charged with air defense of the continent.

The Pinetree Line—Name for the string of interconnected radar bases across Canada.

Sector (Air Defense Sector)—a designated geographical area in Canada containing radar units and fighter bases, under command of a Sector Commander, and charged with defense of a part of North America.

A.D.C.C. (Air Defense Command Center)—A Sector's Headquarters.

C.O.C. (Combat Operations Center)—5 Air Division's Operations Room.

AC&W Squadrons (Air Control and Warning)—ground radar units that carried out surveillance, control, identification and interception of air traffic.

AW Squadrons (Air Warning)—units that carried out surveillance and intercepts only.

Ops—operations (as in Ops Room or Ops Building.)

G.C.I. (Ground Controlled Intercept)—a fighter intercept controlled by ground radar; also the name often used for AC&W Units.

G.C.A. (Ground Controlled Approach)—approach and landing controlled by ground radar.

Search Radar—long-range surveillance radar used at AC&W and AW units.

Height-Finder—radar used to determine an aircraft's altitude.

Radar Scope—the display screen on which an operator sees detected flying objects.

Track (also 'Target.')—a detected and tracked aircraft, which was assigned a Track Number.

Blip—the actual small image on the radar scope indicating an aircraft. From it a scope operator estimated a track's strength, position, course, and speed. Altitude is read from the height-finder's blips.

Radome—large dome protecting the radar's antennae.

Plotting Table/Plotting Board—The table or vertical board on which tracks were displayed (by "Plotters")

Tote Board—The board where data other than tracks (weather, fighter status, etc.) was displayed.

FCO (also FtrCOp or FighterCOp)—Fighter Control Operator.

AD Controller—Air Defense Controller. A Commissioned Officer trained to control interceptors.

Duty Controller—the AD Controller in charge of a crew and shift Ops.

C. Ops. O.—Chief Operations Officer. (Earlier called Senior Controller.) A senior AD Controller, the officer in charge of all Ops at a unit.

C.O.—Commanding Officer (usually of a station.)

O.C.—Officer Commanding (usually of a squadron or unit)

C.Ad.O.—Chief Administrative Officer

C. Tech. O.—Chief Technical Officer

S. Tel. O.—Station (or Unit) Telecom Officer

i/c—"In charge" as in NCO i/c Ops, or NCO i/c Ident, or "Who in hell is i/c this bloody mess?"

Ident—the function of identifying detected aircraft (as 'Friendly,' 'Unknown,' or 'Hostile.')

Control—Ground control of aircraft by radar. Also called 'Fighter Control' or 'Intercept Control.'

Intercept—interception of a hostile or unknown target by fighter aircraft—for identification or destruction—under control of an AC&W or AW Unit.

Scramble—order for fighter-interceptors to take off for an interception.

IFF (Identification Friend or Foe)—a method of identifying an aircraft by electronically altering its radar echo.

CAP (Combat Air Patrol)—Interceptors flying a patrol pattern.

Air Defense Alert—Condition Yellow, Orange or Red—1950s version of alert conditions indicating expected attacks against North America. (Later called Defense Condition—DEFCON)

Exercise (or Operation)—a practice Air Defense operation simulating actual conditions.

QR (Air)—Queen's Regulations (Air)—R.C.A.F. Law

S.O.P.—Standard Operating Procedure.

D.R.O.s—Daily Routine Orders. Daily orders from a C.O. to a Station; includes orders, announcements, personnel changes, etc.

U/S or U.S.—unserviceable (as in, "If it ain't U/S don't fix it.")

A.F.U. and N.F.G.—(All F——ed Up, and No F——ing Good)

SNAFU—(Situation Normal, All F——ed up!)

U.S.A.F.—United States Air Force

Callsign—Name used to identify units over radio and landlines. (E.g. 51 AC&W was "Waterfall")

Roger—radio jargon for, "Message received and understood."

Wilco—radio jargon for, "Message received, will comply."

5 by 5 (or "5 square")·—refers to the strength (1 to 5) and clarity (1 to 5) of a radio transmission.

S.A.C.—Strategic Air Command (U.S.A.F.)

NORAD—North American Air Defense.

Landlines—the land telecommunication system operated by A.D.C.

PBX—a manual telephone switchboard machine.

Teletype—early method of transmitting printed information such as flight plans and weather reports.

MUFAX—a method of transmitting weather maps.

Flight Plan—a plan filed by all flights before take-off, detailing route, check points, schedule, and planned altitudes.

Check Points—points along a flight's route where it must report to A.D.C. on an assigned radio frequency.

"Air Filed" Flight Plan—an illegal and unreliable flight plan filed after take-off.

Dress Blues—(#5s) dress uniform of the R.C.A.F. for parades, ceremonies, travel, etc.

Battle Dress—(#5As) daily winter uniform of the R.C.A.F.

Summer Khakis—(#6s) R.C.A.F. summer uniform

ClerkAdmin—Administration Clerk

T.D.—Temporary duty. (Also "Tactical Decision.")

NCO—Non-commissioned officer (Cpl, Sgt, Flight Sgt, WO)

O.R.—Orderly Room; Also Other Ranks or Ordinary Ranks (non-commissioned personnel.)

SP—Service Police (later AFP—Air Force Police.)

CANADIAN AIR FORCE RANKS
(In use from the beginning of the R.C.A.F., up to the 1967 formation of the "unified" C.A.F.)

Enlisted Personnel Ranks:

AC2/AW2 (Aircraftman/Airwoman 2nd Class) Lowest rank—new recruits. "Acey Deucy"

AC1/AW1 (Aircraftman/Airwoman 1st Class) After six months service,

L.A.C./L.A.W. (Leading Aircraftman/Airwoman) After eighteen months service,

Cpl. (Corporal), Sgt. (Sergeant), F.Sgt. (Flight Sergeant), WO2 and WO1 (Warrant Officers 2nd and 1st Class).

Commissioned Officers Ranks:

O.C. (Officer Cadet), P.O. (Pilot Officer), F.O. (Flying Officer), F.L. (Flight Lieutenant "Flight Louey"), S.L. (Squadron Leader "Skew-ell"), W.C. (Wing Commander "Wingco"), G.C. (Group Captain "Groupy"), A.C. (Air Commodore), A.V.M. (Air Vice Marshal), A.M. (Air Marshal), A.C.M. (Air Chief Marshal).

(Canadian Armed Forces ranks after 1967 unification:) Private, Corporal, Master Corporal, Sergeant, Warrant Officer, Master Warrant Officer, Chief Warrant Officer, Officer Cadet, 2nd Lieutenant, Lieutenant, Captain, Major, Lieutenant-Colonel, Colonel, Brigadier-General, Major-Gen., Lieutenant-Gen., General.)

978-0-595-35909-7
0-595-35909-4

Printed in the United States
47654LVS00003B/78